AF235253

temporoparietal

temporoparietal

(modern young man in search of Being)

Kris Ellis

Copyright © 2018 Kris Ellis

The moral right of the author has been asserted.

Apart from any fair dealing for the purposes of research or private study,
or criticism or review, as permitted under the Copyright, Designs and Patents
Act 1988, this publication may only be reproduced, stored or transmitted, in
any form or by any means, with the prior permission in writing of the
publishers, or in the case of reprographic reproduction in accordance with
the terms of licences issued by the Copyright Licensing Agency. Enquiries
concerning reproduction outside those terms should be sent to the publishers.

Matador
9 Priory Business Park,
Wistow Road, Kibworth Beauchamp,
Leicestershire. LE8 0RX
Tel: (+44) 116 279 2299
Fax: (+44) 116 279 2277
Email: books@troubador.co.uk
Web: www.troubador.co.uk/matador

ISBN 978 1788038 904

British Library Cataloguing in Publication Data.
A catalogue record for this book is available from the British Library.

Printed and bound in Great Britain by 4edge Limited
Typeset in 11pt Adobe Garamond Pro by Troubador Publishing Ltd, Leicester, UK

Matador is an imprint of Troubador Publishing Ltd

To M.H

(O brave new world that has such beings and time in it)

In the world into which we are entering, in a time of mass accumulation and mass domination, of universal utilitarianism, crushing misery and banal happiness, it will again be the task of the individual to seek his own philosophical truth. No objectivity will teach him.

(Karl Jaspers, *Man in the Modern Age*)

I'm a high-tech lowlife.
A cutting-edge state-of-the-art bicoastal
multitasker,
And I can give you a gigabyte in a nanosecond.
I'm new wave but I'm old school,
And my inner child is outward bound.
I'm a hot-wired heat-seeking warm-hearted
cool customer,
Voice-activated and biodegradable.
I interface from a database,
And my database is in cyberspace.
So I'm interactive,
I'm hyperactive,
And from time to time,
I'm radioactive.
(From *I'm a Modern Man*, George Carlin, November 5th
2005, Beacon Theatre, NYC)

To whom, from where, does one write a letter to the world?
(Stanley Cavell, *The World Viewed*)

Chapter One

The Appalachians

Whatever doesn't kill you can still fuck you up
for the rest of your life.

I read this book by Bill Bryson about the Appalachians. I forget the title but it was really cool. Apparently hiking the Appalachian Trail is like walking to Scotland and back seven times. Two thousand four hundred miles of mountain ranges, rapid rivers and dense hardwood forests full of bears. Not just bears of course. Mosquitoes that paralyse your central nervous system with one bite. Rats' crap full of viruses that suffocate you when you lie on the ground. Mooses running around crazy with rabies. Lightning bolts that vaporise you in a millisecond. Copperheads that nestle in your nuts while you're fast asleep in your tent and whose poison kills in ten minutes, so in the unlikely event of there being help around, no one would be able to get to you in time. And then of course there are the bears. They chew you up if they catch the faintest whiff of chocolate. Man, getting murdered is almost a holiday! I must stop saying 'man'.

The thing about a bear is, if it attacks you, one book will tell you to stand still and another will tell you to run away, even though, as they also tell you, a bear can move much quicker than you. And they can climb trees. So basically you're fucked whatever evasive action you take. And yet I'd feel cheated if there was no bear trying to munch on me.

Of course my biggest problem would be the cleanliness issue. In fact that would be the only reason for putting myself through all this pain. Extreme problems demand extreme solutions. Even if they don't work, at least life stays interesting, and you get to wipe from your mind a lot of the stupid things people worry about in day-to-day living. If you get hungry, you just pick something off a tree and eat it wild, without worrying whether a squirrel's shat on it. And cos you're out walking fourteen hours a day, every day, hot or cold, sometimes you don't get to wash yourself for a week. Apparently it's not so bad. On the first day you feel like, nah, I'm alright, a little bit sweaty, but that's OK. Second day you're thinking, my hands are dirty, I'm getting very sweaty, I must stink. Third day, you think, God, I'm a mess, I don't wanna eat anything with these hands, I don't even wanna, like, smell myself. Fourth day you're feeling a little bit better, getting used to it. Fifth day you can't even remember what it was like to be clean. And by the sixth day it's, you know, normal.

"And the seventh day?"

You have a wash and the process starts all over again.

"Why do you feel this need to go to extremes?"

I don't know. I suppose because in extreme situations you haven't got time to choose, because you haven't got time to think. All my problems come from thinking too much. But you know that already.

"Are you aware that the Appalachians are the most popular location for Vietnam vets with post-traumatic stress disorders?"

Rambos? No kidding. I'm definitely going.

"All this is, of course, a fantasy. You like fantasy, understandably. You are a creative teenager. Fantasy is safe and fun. At the moment you are fantasizing about being on some TV survival show."

Not at all. This is real. This is my life.

"No, it is a coping mechanism. A way to avoid dealing with things as they really are."

But I don't like things as they really are.

"Good. We are making progress."

2

Chapter Two

Two Photos

But to be young was very heaven
(William Wordsworth, *The Prelude*)

I've got two pictures of me. One when I'm five years old; probably about four and a half, actually. It was taken before we had the extension, before my dad's accident, before I started to think too much. When I look at it I can see in my eyes the one thing that I've lost by the time the other one was taken, when I'm about ten or eleven, when, according to Mum, something in me 'soured'.

In the first picture, I'm happy. Very. But totally happy without even thinking about being happy. You can tell. Look at my eyes. You know this is a big day. I'm going to school for the first time. I should be shit-scared in that picture. But I'm not. Then I look at this other picture, when I'm older and having my passport picture taken. My eyes just ain't the same eyes. These eyes have seen things. You know, this boy (older photo) has been through some rough times in the playground. This boy (younger photo) hasn't seen those hard times yet.

This boy is small; he's got a cool haircut. What I mean is, there aren't a lot of people, even small boys, that could pull off that haircut. But I feel this small boy pulls off that haircut in a major way. Basically he looks like the sort of guy that in World War II would have got into some kind of Spitfire, gone up and shot down a few Jerries, come back down and gone 'Hawhawhaw!', like that, but

3

real, like, suave, cool, but at the same time, you know, never taking anything too seriously, knowing he'll always get the job done.

Secondly, I'll tell you why I'm impressed with this kid. Not only is he pulling the haircut off; look at the purse! There ain't no way around it, that's a handbag-stroke-purse. But at the same time, he doesn't look homosexual or gay in any way. Not only that, he looks good. I mean very good. I mean, like, this kid is just impressive. He's pulling that bag off. What I mean is, he's not self-conscious about it, he's not anything. He's almost proud. Other people looking at this kid are gonna say, that kid's got style, he's got, like, streetsmarts. He's just a cool kid. He's fly. Why? Look at him, man! Look at the tie; that tie's a kickass tie! Look at the collar on that shirt!

Girls? What are they gonna make of him? Older girls, they're gonna think he's cute. Younger girls? I dunno – I think they'd like him. For the simple fact that he's pulling off an outfit that could make someone look incredibly stupid, yet he's making it look good. He's making it look amazingly good. Look, plimsolls. Not many people can pull those off. Knee-high socks! I don't know anybody but this kid that could do that. The gap there between the knee and trousers – impressive. Cool shorts. And the jumper. He just looks – very nice. You know, he looks like he's put a lot of preparation in.

What is this kid gonna do in life? He doesn't know yet, but he ain't concerned. He just knows that he's gonna go to school, have a good time. But that's it – he doesn't think too much. You can tell he's just had a life of playing with Lego, micro-machines and He-Man figures. He ain't seen none of the harsh realities yet. And he doesn't know of harsh realities. He just believes that, like, you know, good things happen to good people and bad things happen to bad people. And as long as your mum and dad are there, no one's going to break into the house. You know what I mean? He's naïve, but at the same time he likes it that way.

And what about the other kid? The older one. This kid looks worried, paranoid and neurotic. One: he ain't pulling off the hair

4

where the other one was pulling off the hair. The shirt: it's gone downhill. That shirt's travelled with him. The younger kid looks, like, fresh, new, ready for the world. The older one looks ready for bed. He basically wants to get back to this younger kid; but he knows he never can. And that's it.

This one's trusting; this one isn't. This one has faith in certain things; this one doesn't. This one looks forward to Saturdays; this one just wants, like, school to end. Forever. But this kid wants to go back on a Monday; he loves school. He's ready for the women; he's ready for those, like, small milks they give you at break time; he likes the teachers, he likes the company. This boy doesn't. This one wants to make everyone proud, whereas this one thinks he's already failed. And that's the difference. This kid's ready to fight; and this kid's all fought out. This one believes in something; this one's forgotten what he was believing in. This kid doesn't need to believe in anything, cos he doesn't care to believe in anything, because he doesn't need to. Whereas this boy can't find anything to believe in; or what he did believe in's just failed on him.

And that's the difference. This kid's cool. And I'll never be that cool again. That's why I keep the pictures; to remind me of what I'll never be like again.

Chapter Three

America America

America is the most unknown country of all
(Werner Herzog)

My heroes are guys who go right to the edge, then step over and plummet. Guys like Dennis Hopper and William Friedkin. They don't fall to their doom (though not through want of trying). A cuff from a threadbare denim jacket snags on an overhang and leaves them swinging over the abyss until a rope feeds down from heaven and plucks them to safety. A miraculous blip of good fortune interrupting the normal run of catastrophe. Is there any other way to live?

Everyone has to start with extremities. You're born and you're one extreme. And if you're nothing, you're gonna stay nothing. For the whole of your life. Take my Uncle Phil. He doesn't worry about too much. Just lives day to day. How he is now is perfect. He's levelled. But he's, like, forty-two. It's taken him that long to get levelled. This is what I mean: everyone has to start with extremities.

When Phil was born, he was a bit wild. I don't know the ins and outs of everything, but I remember he often had to be fetched out of 'troublement with the police'. And he got into fights a lot. You know, he just lived. But he was a crazy mother. If you were to say to someone, 'Jump off that pier into the water', a normal, sane person would reply, 'That's too dangerous.' But Phil would have jumped.

As I see it, Phil's got a different BIOS setting. It's like when we first get our motherboard, our BIOS settings are on 'safety virus scan', so that everything that comes towards us we check a thousand times. We're like, 'mmm, could do that, probability of survival ninety-nine per cent; OK, go with it.' With Phil's BIOS, he's like an old-school motherboard that was brought out in the early nineties. It didn't have that virus protection and it didn't have dual BIOS. It didn't have the option to save itself. His BIOS was like, 'Everything's fine right now; I'm happy.' Next day, same message. Whereas a new BIOS is like, 'Right, got to check for viruses tomorrow. Remember that. We might seem OK now, but, phew, trouble round the corner.' That's more like my BIOS.

Phil's got the ability to live life in the here and now. But there are certain drawbacks to that. You don't look to the wider picture. You don't question things. But then you could argue, what's the point? Because there are certain 'why' questions you're never going to know the answer to. There have probably been times when Phil's been less than honourable. I don't know of any, but I'm sure there will have been, because of the way his BIOS works. That sort of person is going to do some things that end up upsetting people connected to him. But he's got great self-belief, because he never questions himself. It's like, 'I'm gonna put this glasshouse up,' (Phil's into gardening these days; that's what I mean by being levelled) 'and I'm gonna do it this way.' And the reason he believes so fully in his assembly method is that he's never thought of any other way of doing it. That's just *the* way. Whereas I would be going, 'Could be put up like this. Could be put up like that. Glass needs ultra protection. Oh man, I don't know what to do!' So I take my hat off to Phil.

With me some kind of laziness always sets in, which I don't entirely understand. I don't have the drive to keep at anything. And I won't go and find that drive even though I know full well in the back of my mind that I'd be a better and a healthier person for it. But in the end I can't be bothered to drive to the drive. I'm scared, that's what it is. Fear. If I drive to find something to

7

be driven by, I'm scared that it'll all be a waste of time, and yet I will have given myself fully to it. It's like why people get afraid of going into relationships again. They get into a relationship, give themselves fully, get rejected, or it doesn't work out, and then they fear ever getting into a relationship again. That's exactly part of the problem with me.

It's the extremity thing again. I could get up off my ass and go and do something; but my mind says to me, 'Why bother, when it ain't gonna be enough?' So I would rather put myself through boredom, and all that stuff, just so I can say, 'I've decided to be bored and I've decided to have nothing. I'll give that nothing a hundred per cent, because I know that if I try my hardest to do something, it ain't ever gonna be enough.' I know that if I try to get a job, a bit like the one I used to have watching CCTV in a hut, a bit like the one in the ice factory, a bit like the one in some office, a bit like the one everywhere, I'm not gonna become a millionaire, I'm not gonna be this and I'm not gonna be that. And yet I'm gonna be stressed, and I'm gonna be working hard. Whatever I'm doing, I'm still gonna be pushed down by the man. Or the woman.

So I'd rather be able to say, 'Screw you, I may have nothing, but at least I'm bored not working for *you.*' I mean, why be bored earning twelve grand a year? Or twenty grand? Twenty grand a year's gonna buy you nothing. It's not gonna buy you happiness; it's gonna buy you worry. It's gonna put you into situations where you think, 'I'll take this little bit of money, and it'll get me this.' But because you're only earning that, you're gonna lose that job eventually; they'll flush you down the toilet because they can find another one of you in Estonia or wherever, who'll work for even less just like that. So you end up with shitloads of debt, then die. It's a downward spiral. Don't jump into the system unless you're gonna rise to the top. All or nothing.

I guess it's different when you're actually needed. When you can control who's pushing the buttons. But to get there you gotta be someone who hustles twenty-four-seven. And I won't do that;

8

not because I haven't got the energy (as I said, when I do decide to do something, I give it everything, even when that something is nothing), but because I'm too scared of failure. Because if I give my all to something, and that all isn't good enough, then I'll have given everything for nothing.

I wanna be like the guys in the CKMY4 video. You know, doing stupid things and getting paid for it. Like getting in a barrel and rolling off a roof. Or pissing on an electric fence and getting electrocuted. Or taking a crap out of a window at eighty miles an hour. Most people would say those guys are just wasting their time. But personally I don't see it as a waste of time at all. I see it as having fun. I know some people would say it's just sick. And I'm not saying it's for everybody. Some people would say those guys are immature, irresponsible and lost. But I like their kind of lost. It seems happier than mine. Those guys aren't thinking; they're just doing. Like Phil.

It was probably thinking about what Phil would do in my situation that made me decide to take off to America. That and a copy of *On the Road* which J-J, my video tutor, had lent me. And of course my tendency to go to extremes. Mum was cool about it. But then she always is.

"Mum, I'm leaving. I don't care where I go, but I'm going."

"All right, Matt. But you've got to come up with where you want to go."

"I just need to go, Mum. This place is doin' my head in."

"OK. I think you should go away for a little while. But I don't think you should go just because you need to run away. If you genuinely want to go somewhere, I think you should. But you need to come up with a plan."

So I came up with a plan. Pretty quick, seeing as how I'm generally lazy and uninspired. I got my eleven-year-old brother to go down to town and buy a map (at the time I couldn't go into town without having panic attacks). I gave him plenty of money. He came back with a forty-eight by twenty-four foldout which I put up on my bedroom wall. Then I got a pin and asked

9

myself where I would like to go. I definitely wanted to go to New York, so I stuck the pin there. I definitely didn't want to go to Boston. But I wanted to see JK's grave and his house and home town in Lowell, and I realised that was closer to Boston than New York, so I stuck another pin in Boston and joined the pins with a green and red shoelace I'd previously got from Asda on one of my nocturnal supermarket drop-bys in happier days with S. Then I stuck another pin in Chicago, because of blues and music my granddad loves. Kansas City, because Kansas is meant to be beautiful. Denver because it broke up the trip from Chicago to Las Vegas. Vegas because it's Vegas, and my family likes to gamble. All these places I wanted to see, and all of them would take me far away and supply me with enough to worry about, enough to think about and enough to do, so that I wouldn't have to worry, think or do anything about the shit that had happened back here.

Granny gave me a budget backpack guidebook from ninety-six and I looked on the Internet for loads of stuff about where to stay and eat. I blew a couple of hundred on a pocket PC because I saw it, was bored and thought I needed some kind of excitement for at least five seconds of my life, not realising that it would turn out to be one of the handiest things in the history of the world, especially when you're on a cross-America trip.

I don't go in for clothes much, so my whole wardrobe fitted easily into a large black bag with an extendible handle, so you could pull as well as carry it, which I thought was pretty neat. Three black shirts, two pairs of jeans, three pairs of black socks, a spare pair of shoes and a lot of pairs of pants, because you can wear a pair of jeans for two weeks running, but you can't do that with pants. I never normally wear a vest but the money belt, inside which I had neatly arranged five hundred dollars in cash and two thousand five hundred dollars in traveller's cheques, itched like crazy (I've got sensitive skin).

What else did I get into that kickass bag? A big book of American maps; the charger for my pocket PC; batteries; toothpaste, several multi-packs of toothbrushes (so I could bin the used ones yet maintain reserves), deodorant, soap, shaving equipment, stuff like that, and a copy of my film script, *born2run*, which was too big to squeeze into the string backpack I also took with me. This backpack contained the budget guide to America, *On the Road* and *Catcher in the Rye* (another lend from J-J), a CD player, CD case holding several CDs (Junior Senior, Röyksopp's *Melody A.M.*, Massive Attack, U2's *The Joshua Tree* (only U2 worth listening to), Fischerspooner, *NBK* soundtrack, *Mutations* by Beck, Garbage's *V2.0*, The Smashing Pumpkins' 'Bullets With Butterfly Wings' and 'Zero', 'Time Out' by the Dave Brubeck Quartet, Jeff Buckley's *Grace*, Pearl Jam's *Vitalogy*, Evanescence's *Fallen*, Deftones, 'mOBSCENE' by Marilyn Manson, Satie's *Gymnopédies and Other Piano Works* and a recording of Kerouac reading extracts from his books), a thirty-five-mil camera on long-term loan from college, and a torch. And that was it. Not a lot really; but I was in a hurry.

I left Heathrow at 9.34am in a triple-seven two-hundred-and-fifty-seater that could travel up to a maximum speed of seven hundred miles an hour. I remember reading that. I went by American Airlines because they have bigger legroom and I didn't want any in-flight deep-vein thrombosis. A woman with tanned skin sat next to me. I tried to make myself talk to her, but couldn't.

There was a choice of three movies: *Chicago*, *Maid in Manhattan* with J-Lo and something with Steven Seagal and a rapper. I wasn't gonna go with the first two crappers. A musical? It ain't gonna happen. I went with Steven. It was awful. There were these prisoners in Alcatraz and one of them, who's about to be executed, knows where a load of gold is hidden. It's the first execution in California for a certain number of years, and the woman judge who made the call has to be there to witness it (not too logical; never mind). But some other criminals, who are superb in ninja and all that shit, get into Alcatraz and take it over to get to the prisoner who's about to die and make him tell them where his gold is. But Steven Seagal happens to be in the prison at the time as an undercover cop (what else?) and he

11

buddies up with a friendly inmate, the rapper (who else?), who's some *crazy* mother and handy with guns. Together they kick ass, spray bullets, bring down helicopter gunships, wipe out shitloads of heavily armed bad guys and save the woman judge. Then they all go home, untraumatised by the ambient carnage. It was the kind of high-concept action thing that makes a few global millions before winging its way through the stratosphere on a triple-seven (look out, passing martian UFOs!). But I wasn't complaining. I had six or seven hours to kill.

When I had finally had enough of Mr Seagal kicking ass in Alcatraz, I returned to my seat, and the tanned woman said 'hello' and offered me a Rolo. She was Mexican and pretty; not beautiful or sexy, just nice to look at. Then I noticed that this was true of only one side of her face; the other was pretty messed up, all compacted and sunken in. It crossed my mind that she might have the Ebola virus. I had to accept the Rolo, however, causing a thousand germ issues instantly to shoot through my brain.

I had to queue up at JFK and fill out some form about how long I was going to be there, whether I was intending to work, where I was staying, you know, so they can find you; all that sort of stuff. I'm not much good at filling out forms, especially when I don't know half the answers, so that took me a long time. And when I finally got to the front, some Hitler-type woman who was ordering the queue ('You, now; you, now; that one to there; that one to there') told me I needed to get another form ('right over there'). So I was instantly screwed over and had to go and find this other form and start again, with the queue now massive. The whole thing took me an hour and forty-five minutes, and I ended up being one of the last people to go through the passport control booths.

"Whataya here for, kid?" The passport man was a proper New Yorker; he's got the badge on and everything.

"Just a holiday."

"How long for?"

12

"Yeah, just here to have a good time."

He nodded. Non sequiturs obviously didn't faze him.

"Still in school?"

"No, finished."

"All-right." He's, like, talking in this proper Brooklyn accent. "You got ninety days, kid." And he gets this big stamp and he goes CLONK and he looks at me and smiles and hands me back my passport with this yellow you're-allowed-into-the-United-States ticket thing stapled to it. "You got ninety days to have a good time." And he held and rounded 'time' like a bluesman smoothing out an endnote. I just knew I'd arrived.

So I'm finally in and walk through to get my luggage, but now I can't find my bag anywhere and I start to get into a tizzy (my bag ain't here! where is it? where is it?), until a handler points over to where it is. Turns out I'd forgotten the colour. Or color, in the American version. I look like a right idiot. Anyway, I pick up the bag and walk out into the departure lounge area where they've got boards and signs with bus connections and all that, but it's too much information for me to take in at this particular moment in my life.

"You! I give you a ride into New York!"

"Alright, then."

I mean, I'm knackered and I just wanna go, just wanna get somewhere.

"You come with me!"

He was Puerto Rican, and it suddenly crossed my mind he was going to take me to the car park and shoot me. I could see it now: 'English Boy Shot at Airport'. I was going to falter at the first fucking hurdle. He opened up the boot of this huge black Lincoln, which was plenty big enough to stick a body in.

"No, I pick it up for you. I pick it up for you." And he puts all my stuff in the boot and then opens the passenger door and sits me in the front.

"Nice car," I say, "really like your car," thinking I need to suck up to him at this point. But what I was really saying was, 'Please don't shoot me.'

As we drove through the city I fretted about what kind of conversation I should initiate to maintain our blossoming friendship, but I was saved by his speaking first.

"You on your own?"

Not being streetsmart yet, I thought I'd play the happy English guy on his first trip to the US plus first time in New York, amazed at how everything seems bigger over here etc., etc. At which point the Puerto Rican cabbie turned to me and said, "Man, I'm worried about you." And he looked so concerned that I started to worry, too.

"Here, take this. And this. This is for you." It was a tourist map and a guide booklet. "This normally cost money." On the back was written 'not to be resold', so the bastard was lying. But he was a nice bastard. Slim, not fat, you know, normal, late thirties, just going into forties possibly, tanned skin, clean shaven, no moustache or anything, quite well dressed in short-sleeved white shirt, cos of the heat, and black trousers (or 'pants' as the Americans say). I also noticed his arms were quite hairy. He was a family man. He got a call on his mobile (or cell phone) and it was his daughter. "Yeah? You gonna be at McDonald's? I pick you up from there." She had a boyfriend and he started winding her up about it. She was about thirteen/fourteen – the kind of age where you can wind 'em up about boyfriends. He then turned to me again with that look of concern. "Be careful, now. Be safe. Don't go around Central Park at night."

Family man drops me off at a hostel on the eastside of Manhattan, 102nd or 106th Street, telling me the price is seventy dollars. I don't really understand American money yet. Can't really register in my head how much everything is worth. So I give him ninety-five dollars. That's about sixty-five pounds for a ride from JFK to Manhattan, which is fifteen miles as the crow flies, or twenty point three miles if you drive it, and takes thirty-four minutes when there's no traffic, or up to one hour ten minutes if the streets are busier. No wonder he said, "Ah yes, OK," and looked chuffed when I handed him the money. Then he pointed the way towards Riverside which I am supposed never to take,

14

shaking his finger and no-noing with his head, before his sleek limousine glided off into the hot New York afternoon. I found out later that a yellow cab would've only cost thirty-five dollars, which pissed me off.

The hostel had a pretty unsociable atmosphere. The advert said 'friendly staff', you know, 'run by lively people'. But I walk in and they ain't friendly, they ain't lively. They're all out of liveliness.

"How long d'you wanna stay?"

"Two days."

The guy was in his twenties – twenty-six or twenty-seven. You could tell he didn't want to work there and I was holding up his time. He wasn't a deadbeat or anything. Just a kid trying to do his job, but, you know, it weren't that interesting, and he weren't that lively. I kinda sympathised and paid the money. I mean, I've done plenty of shit jobs in my time.

He doesn't show me the room but just tells me where it is, and I'm struggling to visualise and starting to panic a little. People are walking past me talking different languages, and I'm thinking, shit, man, I should never have come, I'm hot and sweaty and I'm in this place. I mean, it wasn't an awful place or anything, more like a dorm or hall of residence; but not a nice hall of residence. The walls were like hospital walls which you can wipe clean. There was a linoleum floor with some tiles coming off but really well polished. It was like a communal space but with really tight corridors and small rooms. And there were pictures of jazz musicians all the way along the wall; hence Jazz on the Park. You know, the greats: Louis Armstrong, Dizzy Gillespie, Fats Domino, and that woman singer that got her permit-to-perform pass taken away in the fifties; Simone, Nina Simone, that's the one. I'd come across her in a JK *Letters From* book, when Joyce Johnson writes saying she saw Nina Simone stand up and sing and play in a restaurant somewhere, and it was a piece of history. Don't know why she had her cabaret pass taken away; my granddad would be the one to ask. Then some crazy people you could never imagine, guys with massive hair going WHOOOWHOOOWHOOO! with staring eyes and looking like nutters that I didn't recognise at all, and I don't think Granddad wouldof either.

Eventually I find the room on the second floor and put my card in the lock which goes NNEEENNNNN and the door opens like in a prison. Inside there are all these iron cot-style bunks, just like a prison again. There's no one in there, but I can see other people's stuff all around, including these ginormous backpacks leaning against the walls. I'm getting a bit paranoid with my bags and I see these big lockers, but they won't work without tokens. So I leave my stuff and go all the way back downstairs, get some tokens and come all the way back up. Get there. Put a token in. Put my bag in. Shut it. Forgot the big bag. Shit. How am I ever going to get that into this locker? Put another token in. Open it up. Get the key. CCKSSHHHH, CCKSSHHHH, KERCCKCK, KERCCKCK. Getting it in. Getting it in. Get it in eventually. Then I think to myself, God knows how I'm ever gonna get that out again, but never mind for the moment. Shut it. Lock it. Shit, need to take out my other bag. Go to unlock it THINKING, like a NORMAL person, that when I unturn the lock the token will fall back down for me to collect, like most lockers, right? And I would have another go, by just putting the token in. Like at the swimming baths. They do that at the swimming baths, don't they? You put the token in, or fifty pence, and it's like a deposit. You know what I mean? CLINK. Pause. Where the fuck's the token? You don't get it back! It's like you have to pay twenty-five cents for those tokens a time. So it's a money-making thing. That token allows you to lock something in there until you open it up again; but then you need to put in another token that costs twenty-five cents.

All the way back downstairs. Get some more. Now I'm like, fucking give me ten dollars' worth. Slam it into the machine that's going KERKERKERKERKERKERKERKERKERKERKERK-ERKER as the tokens crash down with everyone looking at me. You can imagine: at twenty-five cents each, ten dollars buys a fair amount of tokens. But I just thought, I ain't going back downstairs again. I've still got some of those tokens at home.

I'm now lying in bed, sweating, and all I can hear is the outside New York. No air-conditioning. I'm lying there thinking, what have I done? What have I done? And I can hear proper New York sounds, no bullshit: sirens going WHUUUP WHUUUP (even the sirens sound cooler and scarier). 'Hey Jimmy! pass me the ladder!' Normal street sounds, but American accents and American noises and American heat, and, just like New York buildings, when I open the curtains, three feet away a brick wall. Because it's just so packed in. Wherever you stay in New York, unless it's Trump Tower or somewhere like that, you're gonna be looking at a brick wall. Of course if you twist your neck a hundred and twenty degrees and look up, you might eventually see a patch of sky.

Chapter Four

Proper Proper

America is the original version of modernity.
We are the dubbed or subtitled version.
(Jean Baudrillard, *América*)

I decide to go out for a bit, you know, I'm bored. It's only four in the afternoon but I've been up for hours if you think about it. So I'm walking around the streets thinking, holy shit, this is not like a touristy place, this is proper America, proper New York like you see in the movies. There's like all these rappers walking around everywhere. Proper people doing proper things, going about their daily lives. People sitting on steps outside brownstone buildings and talking. Italians talking to each other like they're in some gangster movie. I went into a little store, like a corner shop, to buy a Coke (only one dollar, amazing!) and it was just like that store in *Taxi Driver* where, you know, he shoots the robber, and I'm almost waiting for something like that to happen, thinking omigod. The store was owned by an Asian guy who was very polite, 'Ah, nice to meetchoo, son, nice to meetchoo.' These places are always owned by Asians or Puerto Ricans or Mexicans or Hispanics. Best places to buy a bottle of Coke – everywhere else is a dollar fifty. And there's the kids playing outside with the ball. And you walk down the street and there's the penned-in school and all the little New York kids playing within this cityscape, but just like you see in the movies. The occasional tree. Old men sitting on benches. You know, America like you would genuinely see in a movie, but it was *there* happening, before my very eyes. The odd weird homeless guy walking around going HUHUHU-HAHAHAAH and a person begging and stuff; it was like proper proper.

Anyway, I walk down the street and I see this lady and I think, she looks alright. She's like middle-aged, not especially attractive, but not ugly. She looks a bit stressed like she's trying to get home from work. I choose her because she looks friendly; she doesn't look like she's going to shoot me. In actual fact, and this sounds harsh, she looked like if she tried anything, I thought I could probably knock her over. You know? I was thinking like I could run away from this woman, or this woman doesn't look like she could overpower me. I feel safe speaking to this woman. So I go up to her and say, "Excuse me, I'm looking for a subway."

She looks at me and says, "Yeah, there's one down there. Over there. Where do you want to go?"

"I don't know, really, I've just arrived."

"Oh yeah? I thought I heard an accent. Where are you from? Ireland?"

They always think you're either Irish or Australian or from New Zealand or Scotland or Wales.

"No, I'm from England."

"Oh yeah? Where from?"

So we have a brief conversation about my geographical origins and then I say, oh right, so it's down there, thank you very much. And I carry on walking. Only thing is she's walking that way, too, so I end up following her. I say reassuringly, "I'm not following you," and she says OK, and I cross the road, you know, to keep things on the level.

But she crosses the road, too, and says, "I've got to go down this way." And then all of a sudden she says, "Hang on a second."

And then totally out of the blue this woman says she's got tickets for some Shakespeare thing this evening. I'm thinking it's a play. She says, why don't I go with her? And I'm thinking oohuhohuhoh what's happening here? And I kinda half say,

"Yeah", not really clearly, because I'm unsure about what I should say at this moment.

And she digs around in this large handbag and gives me her phone number and says, "Give me a call at seven."

"Alright then. Thank you."

We go our separate ways.

I eventually wind up at the Lincoln Centre, take a look around and find a Borders. Borders was the saviour of my American trip. Whenever I needed some place to just sit down, chill out and take everything in, I always knew that on the top floor of Borders would be a café that would be reasonably priced and comfortable. So I go up there and order this amazing drink which is a kind of coffee Slush Puppy. It's like an iced coffee but whirred around in this machine so the ice is really tiny fragments crushed up just like the slush puppies you used to have as a kid. When you drink it, it's like drinking flavoured ice, like a snow cone. I enjoyed it so much I had another one and watched as they tipped all the coffee in and then the cream, and then the ice, and then the machine went BRRRRRRRRRRRR and mixed it all up. Only I drank this one too quickly, and one, I got a rush off it because of the caffeine, and two, I got a headrush because of the cold. I thought for a minute, man, I'm gonna puke, but I was OK again soon after.

So I'm watching New York go by, and now, as JK would have put it, I'm quietly digging it. All those thoughts of 'I shouldn't have done this' have gone; now I'm thinking, this is fucking amazing. Sitting up there on this bench and looking down I'm seeing all these yellow cabs going up and down the street, all these American people with fit women everywhere. Ah, I'm thinking to myself, ah, man, I'm glad I came. And then I've got this number of this woman.

I decide to celebrate by going down to the corner and having a proper, from-the-stand, New York hot dog. It was just a cart that a seller had parked up at the street corner, and businessmen and everybody were going up and buying from him. The seller was, again, Puerto Rican, or maybe Brazilian. I could be being harsh. I mean, I couldn't exactly say what his genealogy was, but to me he looked from that area of the world. Anyway, I go up to the guy.

"Can I have a hot dog please?"

"Whaddya want on it? Sauerkraut?"

What the fuck's that? I'm thinking. "No, no that's fine."

"How many d'ya want?"

"One."

"Mustard?"

"Yeah, OK." With more enthusiasm than that.

And I was well chuffed that I'd got this proper New York hot dog. Heeyyyyy! I mean, I was starving, but this was something special. And it was only a dollar fifty, which is about seventy-five pence, and a lot bigger than what you'd get over here. And not only that, but I ate it, gulp, gulp, gulp, gulp, and I didn't wash my hands. I was like, fucking brilliant! I went back up and asked if I could have another one, which I ate more slowly this time, waiting around a little while, just taking everything in, getting into it all, and then, as it was now seven o'clock, I went over to a phone and called the lady up.

I told her where I was and she told me to cross the street where there was an art gallery, so I went over and there were all these black guys arguing about money and betting on basketball. And I'm like standing around there trying my best not to look nervous, but I'm thinking, shit, man, this is gonna kick off. I couldn't really make out any conversation; I just heard phrases like, and this is not bullshit, 'Yo, dog!' and 'I'll fuck your bitch.' Now I know this sounds harsh, and politically unacceptable today, but on my American travels I met every stereotype, and saw every stereotype, ever. And if you imagine proper rappers in black gangster movies, these boys were talking like it. I'm not being horrible, but they were. They were living up to the stereotype. They were joking around of course; just talking to each other this harsh, arguing and playfighting, while cop cars WHUUP-WHUUPED by, and I'm thinking, shit, this must be normal. So I just stood there; and to be honest with you I was kinda pleased with myself, because they seemed to respect me enough not to cause anything, even though I was standing out from the crowd. So I obviously didn't look totally weak or out of place because they didn't try anything. In fact they completely ignored me. It was just as if I wasn't there. And that surprised me; I expected something to kick off. Then I thought, this kinda stuff must happen all the time, and we're in a big open place.

And also, and this is harsh, but I haven't had a lot of experience with black people, so being in a surrounding where all of a sudden there's a lot of black people, I've got to admit to you I was thinking I didn't know how to take them. That makes me sound kinda racist. But it was just that I was thinking, I don't know how to talk to these people; they talk different. I don't know whether they're going to respect me or not cos, you know, they've got issues. And they think I've probably got issues. So there's a little bit of watch out, suspicion on all sides. But it was weird because everybody just got on. Obviously there were times when people didn't get on, but everybody was just left to themselves. Quite a few black people, I'd sit next to them, and they'd talk to me like normal. For some reason I didn't think that was going to happen. It was like when I was in the back of a taxi in Chicago speaking to the big black guy in front who couldof been some kind of blues musician, like Big Bill Broonzy.

"Man, I'mma never gonna go to Wrigley Field."

Wrigley Field in Chicago is named after the guy that came up with the spearmint gum. That was his baseball field and in the fifties he banned black people from going there.

"Why ain'tcha never gonna go to Wrigley Field?"

"Man, they would never let me go there. That Wrigley that owned that field, he said no black man could go in, and I said, nope, I'm never goin'."

"What, aren't you allowed in now?"

"I'm allowed in there now. But if they didn't want me in there then, I ain't goin' in there now."

Again, proper stereotype. But he was genuinely pissed off about it all, and told me why.

"See this boat down here? I used to be a porter there. I had to go through the trademan's entrance evraday!"

"Man, that's a bit harsh. Do you hate white people?"

"I don't hate white people. Some of the older generation, possibly, but not you."

"Why not me?"

"Cos it ain't got nuthin' ta fuckin' do with ya!"

"Oh, right."

He had a way of saying 'fuck' that didn't sound harsh at all. 'Hey, fuck, man!', 'Yeaahh, fuckit!' It was like he was saying but not saying the f-word.

Anyway I'm back standing at the art gallery with 'yodog!' and 'immagonnafuckyabitch' whizzing round my ears, and the woman drives by – with her husband. I'm now thinking uhh-huhh, like what's going down here? Am I about to be kidnapped or something? Is some kind of sex orgy being planned? They park up round the corner and come back to meet me, and we shake hands. He was from Eastern Europe (instantly the kidnapping theory comes to the fore and I'm calculating the street value of my internal organs), Hungary or somewhere; not that that is necessarily Eastern Europe really, but you could tell straightaway he was proper European from that part of the world cos he looked, like, big, hairy, big nose: a happy fellow, but serious at the same time. He used to work for the government back home, but the jobs all went. Turns out the lady had met him when he came to America. She was studying theatre, he had worked in the theatre as well; she wasn't an actress but backstage, hence the tickets for the theatre – except that it's not the theatre, but I don't know that yet. She was also some kind of teacher at the university, so she was pretty open-minded and well educated. They had actually lived in Europe for a little while and I think that's why she had warmed to me originally and why she wanted to meet me. So I walk with them round the corner and make some lame sort of conversation, like can't believe how big the cars are here in America, which became a bit embarrassing when, after I've been going on and on, he says, "Actually my car

23

ain't that big." Turns out he drives a Ford Escort Estate. I mean, I was not expecting the first personal vehicle I climb into in New York to be so unspectacular you wouldn't see it on the streets of Freetown, unless it'd been dropped-down and customed-up, or used for ramming.

We drive around, nearly getting into several crashes, cos that is what it is when you drive in New York; people are beeping each other, shouting at each other, we get stuck in traffic and she starts moaning that we're going to be late, and all of a sudden domestics start happening right in front of me. But we eventually get to this place which turns out to be an arts centre, but for select members only. Me and the lady get out and the husband drives off, because he doesn't want to go in and would prefer to watch some show on TV, which is why she had the spare ticket in the first place. Obviously he trusts his wife with me, so we walk in, and I tell ya, I've never been in a place like it. Marble-floored and looking like the Garrick Club or something. There were lots of old guys sipping Pimm's or something and going, 'ra-ther'. Tom Wolfe had been there the week before in his white suit talking about his new book. This was the sort of place I could imagine Woody Allen going to now and again to see some previously unseen Bergman silent movie.

As we go up the stairs there's posh wooden panelwork perfectly maintained that looks almost Victorian, though I don't know if you would call it that being in America, and more antiques than you can cram into an aircraft hangar. And it was all top-notch and the genuine article. Huge well-polished, well-waxed sideboards with big, ornate mirrors built in and gold clocks on top. I mean, I'm no expert, but this was not new, flash gear. It wasn't like they'd gone, oh, let's get a designer in, go out to Christie's or wherever and get a job lot of antiquarian artefacts. You got a sense that these things had been around here for a while; this was old money, not new. Proper old-fashioned antiques. It weren't like leather seats in the hallway, you know; it was a six-piece set of all-wood chairs, a posh coat stand, a grandfather clock and portraits on the wall, handpainted not prints, of important people that were obviously connected with this place from years ago, all with 'tashes and looking like Victorians. This was not a place ashamed to be old-world wealthy.

And upstairs they're showing this weird fucked-up film. We walk across the squeaky, highly polished parquet floor and sit down on these seats they've just unfolded, because it's not a proper theatre and they're just projecting onto this small screen. It's the weirdest thing; there we were in this posh building watching a weird movie. It was, like, made on no budget and looked like a student film. This guy was God. And this other man was a normal person. Right? And he was having issues with his woman. And God was fucking things up for him. Or was he the Devil? I can't remember. But weird things were just happening all the time. I'm sitting there going, take it all in, man, take it in, this is New York, this is normal. And there's a guy in front of me, old guy, there are a lotta old people, and the weird film is really freaking him out. Lose the first row. Lose the second row. Pretty soon it's just me and the lady.

I'm thinking, this is fucking boring, but I don't wanna say anything. Then she turns to me and says, "Let's go, this is boring." I try to make out I can see something of value in it, being a film student and all, so I say, "It's up to you, I'm fine," because I don't want to upset her, and maybe she was just being polite in case I was bored. But luckily she's had enough.

"No, to be honest with you, this is really boring me. Let's go."

So we walk and talk and she apologises to me, saying she must've got the wrong date because this is not what she thought we would be seeing. I think what she thought we were gonna see was some kind of speech or a talk about Shakespeare or something, and not this movie we ended up seeing. I say I don't mind, I'm up for anything and honestly this was enjoyment enough, which was true, because it was an interesting experience, if a bit weird. Then she kept asking me, where are you staying? Where are you staying?

"I'm staying at this hostel."

"What one?"

"Jazz on the Park."

"Where is it?"

"I don't really know. Can't remember." That was concerning me a little. "I'll have to find it."

"Oh man, I'm worried. You haven't really got anywhere to stay, have you?"

"I have got somewhere to stay."

"You haven't really, have you?"

"I have. I have."

"Alright."

So we're now walking down the street and she says, let's catch a cab. She flags one down. As soon as we get in the back she says, "I'll take you somewhere to eat." So she buys me dinner at some diner Italian restaurant, not swanky, just nice and middle of the road. We both had pasta and sauce. I just had what was there on the menu but she wanted a certain type of pasta with a certain type of sauce, and she had to ask the waiter nicely, who was proper-type Italian; you know, the other type of Italian, the bald-headed, skinny guy type. We talk about stuff while we eat and I try not to act like an idiot. Then we tip the waiter and leave and I say that I'm gonna be fine from here. She says again that I haven't got anywhere to stay, and I say again that I have. Then she says I could stay at her place, but there's no room cos they only live in a small apartment. I say, honestly I'm gonna be fine, I know where I've gotta go.

And the truth is I'm like a homing pigeon. I can never remember the names of streets, but if you put me somewhere I recognise, say, that building there and that building there, somehow I know that if I walk down there to there, turn right, walk down there to there, I'll be where I want to be. Don't know why I'm like that, I just am. So I knew where I was going; I just couldn't explain to her where I was going. So that's why she thought I was bullshitting.

"Well, if you've got any trouble you just give me a call."

"Honestly, I'll be fine. Thank you very much for a fantastic evening. It was really interesting." Shook her hand. She disappeared.

26

I disappeared. Never saw each other again. You gotta realise, this is my first day in New York, and already a lot of shit's happened to me.

I get back to the hostel around eleven thirty, twelve o'clock, and I'm in a good mood now. New York's cool. I've met this strange person who invited me to this weird film. Americans must be really friendly. I go in, wave to the guy, cos he obviously doesn't want to talk, and I go up the stairs to my room. JZZZJZZZ NNEEENNNNN. Go in. My happiness instantly disappears.

There's this guy and he goes, "Ellooo." He's like this Russian, he's from Belgrade or somewhere like that, telling me, "I hudto leave my countree and I've beeen wanndering round Amerrrica for seex munths. I'm not meant to bee heere, but I'm an archeetect in my home-a countree. I studeed at thee Insteetute of, " whatever, whatever, "eeen Bellgrrade."

And I'm like, "Alright?"

But he's got this weird 'mmmm mmmm' intenseness as he talks, and he's also got this scary laugh BRUUAHAHAHA! when he gets into something. I'm thinking omigod, and I'm just trying to take it all in my stride, and then he lies down on his bed and starts telling me all about his experiences, and then he goes, "I have shower now. I have shower." Takes his towel and goes off.

Then two guys walk in. English. I think, fucking English guys, typical. They look around my age, maybe a bit older, twenty-four-twenty-five. These boys have been travelling big time; those huge packs leaning against the wall were theirs, though I thought at first they belonged to the Belgradian. They've been in Australia for months. Come up to San Francisco, travelled across by car to New York. Flying home the next day. I'm looking and thinking, fuck it, lucky rich bastards muttermuttermutter under my breath. They think I'm foreign and aggressive, but I say, no, I'm English. Then one of the guys, as soon as he gets in, lies down on the bed the other guy was lying on before. Straight down. Not like me, checking the sheets, making sure there are no stains. Normal people just get in fucking bed.

27

I didn't think anything, and I don't wanna start any trouble, so I'm lying down on my bed fully clothed, trying to look normal about it and wearing my money belt, while these guys are all walking around in boxers and stuff. It was hot but I ain't taking my clothes off. However, I did undo my shirt and put my vest on. My vest-wearing habits are all down to this American trip and the money belt chafing my sensitive skin. A lotta people thought it was strange and figured it was just an English thing. And I suppose I became a bit self-conscious about wearing one, cos I don't know of anyone else that wears a vest other than old men. But it wasn't like a Rab C. Nesbitt string vest, or anything like that. And even though a lotta people take the piss, cos it's not the sort of thing people wear nowadays, I've become a fan of vests. And where my body's become used to vest-wearing, if for instance I go to work without wearing one, I get really sore nipples. It's like that area has become habituated to a high level of softness, so that if I wear anything else, cos even designer shirt material is rougher, especially around the seams, it kills it. I suppose I've just become accustomed to feeling that softness, and the nipple area's become weaker over time. Anyway, I'm talking to the English guy when the Belgradian comes back in and goes, "Who's tutched my pillow?"

And the English guy says, "Sorry, sorry I didn't realise this was your bed."

"No, eet's OK. That eez my bed." In that intense kind of way of his, like, 'Eet's alright, I couuld fuck you uupp.'

"It's OK, it's OK, I'll swap."

"No, you stay there, you stay there." Then he goes over to this other bed and says, "Theeze beds are meant for certain people. But YOU stay there." Then he gets in and says, "Goodnight!" Just like that.

But then he gets back up and he's talking again and I'm thinking what the fuck was that about? Cos he's talking to me, sitting there on the edge of the bed, talking, talking, talking about his experiences in America, places he's been, that sort of stuff.

"Weeeth your accent az an Eengleesh genntlemann, you couuld bee eneetheeng. BRUUAHAHAHA!" Getting really excited. Just a crazy guy, you know. He couldof been a computer hacker, he was that kind of intelligent, but not normal. "An archeetect, yeess. I'm staying weeth frriennds. They goinng to gett mee Greeen Caard. Sooon I weel have a job. BRUUAHAHAHA. Mmmmm mmmmm." You know, cool guy, I don't mean to be mocking him. He was a cool guy. He didn't stab me; I liked him.

Finally we all get ready to go to sleep, then, "Helll-llooo," and this big fat German walks in. "Helll-llooo. I'm in New York." Like that. Another dispute follows over the beds.

"You are in my bed."

"No, thees eez MY bed."

And I'm thinking, clash of the titans now, Belgrade versus Germany.

"No, it is my bed."

"No, MY bed."

"No, the number. My token is a six."

"No, thaat wuz last night."

I didn't get involved but I'm thinking, why don't they give you the same fucking bed if they know you're gonna stay two nights? Not go, hmmm, tonight I'll give 'em a five, tomorrow a six, ha ha?

"No, zis is my bed."

And then the Belgradian goes, "I like thee bottom bunnk," in his intense way.

"Oh. I like ze bottom bunk."

"I WANT thee bottom bunnk."

"I will have ze top bunk. Hmmm."

Me and the English guys are just lying there, silently going hum-hum to ourselves.

The poor Belgradian I think was beginning to regret the decision to let the big, fat German guy have the top bunk. HH-HMMMMMEEEEKKKKZZZZCCKKK. This guy is in his underwear. He's like flabby and everything. EEEEECCCK-KKKZZTTCHH. He's got his, like, vest on. EEKKRRRPPPP-

29

POOOOOLLLLLLSSHHHHHHHCCKKKKKK. The whole thing's creaking under the weight.

The Belgradian guy's like proper Eastern European. 'I bee STRROOONG. Eeef hee crruush my boddee, I stay on bottom buunnk.' You know, he's like, 'I weeel nevvvver suurrennder.' So he's lying there, and you could see he's, like, I fuucckeeng haate theesss German mann. You take my buunk, you take my FREEDOMMM! So he keeps still, just lying there.

"Turn out ze light pleeze?"

I'm pretending to be asleep. The English guy's pretending to be asleep. The other English guy's pretending to be asleep. The Belgradian guy, he ain't gonna be getting up to turn no lights out for this German guy. So I'm listening to all this.

"Pleeze turn out ze light." In that kind of musical German voice.

Nothing.

"Hell-ooo."

"Hell-oooooo."

"Hell-oooooooooo."

Five minutes go past.

"Someone pleeze turn out ze light!"

Nothing.

EEEEECCCKKKKKZZTTCHH. HHHMMMMMEEEEK-KKZZZZCCKKK. NNNNSSHHHHHHHCCCKK. RRRR-RCKCKCKCKCZZZZZCCHHH.

And I just looked out the corner of my eye and caught the eye of the Belgradian or Ukrainian, or wherever he was from; he was from one of those fucked-up countries, anyway. We didn't comment at all between each other. It was like, yup, we know we've seen each other, and we know we could both turn the light off. But neither of us is going to comment on it at all. OK? That kind of look passed between us.

EEEEYYYYNNNNN, NYYYYYYERRR, NYYYYERRRR, NYYYYERRRRR. Back down. Naked feet on linoleum floor. CLLUUCCCK   CLLUUCCKK   CLLLUUCCKKKRRR.

30

"Aaahrrr, Aaahrr, Aahrrrrr," just like that. Upset jolly, fat German guy. CLCK. Trip. "Ohhhhrrrrr."

HHHMMMMMEEEEKKKKZZZZCCKKK.
EEEEECCCKKKKZZTTCHH.
EEKKRRRPPPPPOOOOOLLLLLSSHHHHHHCCK-KKKKK.
Plastic fucking sheets on all these beds. NNNNRRRR-RNNNNNNRRRNNN.

Him trying to get comfy.

I look over at the English guy who I realise is also awake. So we've all been awake when the German guy wanted the light turned off, but no one would turn it off.

Eventually, peace at last. I look around and feel relief. Then all of a sudden.

"Snnckkghh. Snnckkghh. SZNNNNNNNCKKKKGGGG-HHHHHHHHHHHHHH."

Fucking snored all night. All night. It was like that scene in *Full Metal Jacket*, like one of us was gonna get up and hold a pillow over his head while another beat him with the soap. But we didn't. And in the morning he got up at five o'clock.

HHHHHMMEEEEKKKKZZZZCCKKK.   CCKKKRRRR. EEEEECCKKK.

"Sorree I woke you up. Iz eet OK if I leave door open?"

"Uhhhhh whaaa? Yeeahh, wha'ever."

I left the hostel and New York the next day.

Chapter Five
Mona Part Two

Girl power

One of my reasons for travelling across the US was the fact that I'd been head-done by girls back home, especially Mona, Alice and S., all girl-powered granddaughters of baby boomers: beautiful and intelligent teenagers, but age-incorrect in terms of drink, drugs and sex; in your face, to your face, callous, attitudinal and scary. Toxic yet intoxicating. I don't mean to sound bitter, but I definitely needed to get the hell out. Doing a JK and running away to JFK to escape the emotional heat looked like my best option at the time.

I'll begin with the shortest and therefore probably least harmful of my relationships, though of course the one doesn't necessarily follow the other, time and intensity being inversely proportional to each other. So while it was over almost as soon as it started, I was completely smitten with Mona, and so maybe she did more damage to my mental health than I realised at the time. But I would never hold that against her. I mean, you don't hold things like that against beautiful girls.

Obviously, you're gonna think Mona's parents must have been big-time Leonardo fans. However, that was actually not the case, and she could get quite annoyed with anyone who thought they'd made this 'clever' link, looking at you like you were some sort of idiot and making a point of saying, 'It's got nothing to do with the painting,' as though this was the millionth time she'd had to say it. Her parents were actually deeply into Celtic stuff as I recall, especially her dad, and I remember finding out on the Internet that Mona is related to Epona which is some sort of horse goddess, and I knew she was well into horses, like ridiculously into horses, as well as, you know, into her earth. Not that the horse link is any cleverer, since her parents couldn't have known anything about any future equestrian inclinations when they named her, obviously. In Arabic it means 'unreachable wish', which I discovered later. But I guess that's always the way.

Mona's dad was also a Satanist-Buddhist, which was a strange combo, and a real Aleister Crowley fan. He even went to live down in Hastings in his youth just to be near Crowley's death place. He was a secondary school teacher of, I don't know, some bullcrap, but managed to keep the Satanism to himself. You know, he didn't wear red eye-lenses and a black coat or anything like that. He looked like a normal person, though he did wear an upside-down pentagram (seems you can wear them one way or the other way, and the other way's the wrong way). But as I say, to look at him you wouldn't think anything of it. Apparently he used to believe a lot in the teachings of Satanism, like it's better to think of yourself than others; you know, pretty weird stuff, but outwardly you wouldn't be thinking, holy crap, this guy's a Satanist. He got out of this, I won't call it a phase, since it went on too long for it to be a phase and he was obviously well into it, but he changed a bit once he met Mona's mother; but at the same time he still had these Satanic leanings. But Mona would always say he wasn't an evil person or anything, just a normal person who was well into the teachings of Satanism and Aleister Crowley. And his wife didn't seem to mind. She was also a teacher, but a Buddhist, which he then ended up being as well, like you do. I don't know how the Satanism combined with the Buddhism, but they seemed to make it work out OK. And they had the equipment. In the house there were those kneeling things and a big bowl and tied to it a little whacky thing that goes BONG and you whacked it and that's supposed to help with prayers and meditation. I don't know enough about the practices, and by the sounds of it the mum was more into it than the dad, but they both, you know, practised some sort of Buddhist activity; they weren't just going around saying, 'I'm a Buddhist' or anything.

They were a pretty weird family but middle class and lived in this posh housing estate behind the badlands of Lower Street, you know, one of those new developments that are called something suitably countrified like Orchard Glade (even though there's no orchard in sight for twenty miles and no glade for three hundred years), with spanking new houses on it which seem on the face of things to be really nice to live in, especially if you don't know any of the prehistory of the area, which people from outside who move in generally don't. So it's a great place to live until you go for a Sunday stroll and take a wrong turn and end up being stabbed.

As I say, their house was a kind of shrine to alternative deities. I have certain issues with all that and to me it's just posing and being a weekend eco-warrior. You talk the dropout talk but then you take your money from the man. How is that possible? But I don't want to get started on one of my rants. Mona was the most beautiful girl I've ever seen. Long brown hair with little ringlets at the end, extraordinary blue eyes with amazing eyebrows, lovely complexion, amazing figure, very slim, nice waist, healthily proportionate breasts, not huge nor small; the perfect size. Celestial orbs. I've no idea where that phrase comes from. Probably some Shakespeare which I soaked up without knowing. Whatever. For some reason 'celestial orbs' always came to me when I saw Mona's firm and creamy-white breasts. I was besotted with her. I thought she was absolutely stunning. She was fit and fabulous and she was the first girl that broke my heart. And she didn't do it by surgically severing each string with a scalpel, like you expect a woman to do; she used a meat cleaver. Rick in *Casablanca* stands alone on a train platform in Paris with a comical grin on his face and looking like a guy with his insides kicked out. Well, I ended up sitting on some grass outside a drum 'n' bass night club in Newquay, looking like one of those Japs who's just been disembowelled with a 'Ha!' and

34

a lightning-quick nukitsuke by a *Kill Bill* female shogun with a wakizashi.

Again, hindsight; now I know. She'd just broken up with her boyfriend and I was quite literally, just, what do you call it?, her transitional guy, and I wasn't quite aware of that situation, whereas nowadays I would know that. But I was young and full of hope and thought, this can work out, you know, and didn't just accept it for what it was, which would have been the better thing to do.

Anyway, Mona was going down to Cornwall and I was due a holiday. I was still working on the lorry and she said she was going down to Newquay. It was just the sort of place I'd hate to go, let alone follow a girl down to. Surfers; fuck surfers. You know, hippies, basically; just the sort of people that piss me off. They really irritate me, you know? Save this and save that. They don't lead normal lives. I haven't got anything against real hippies. Real hippies I respect. But it's these weekend hippies, these, like, weekend eco-warriors, you know; I mean, how the hell am I meant to respect you, when you're only doing this on a part-time basis? Half of the things you're fighting for, and half of the things you say I should give up, you make use of every bloody day. You know what I mean? I mean, how did you get to your protest? You probably went in a car. And yet you're demonstrating about pollution. Don't get me started. I'm like Kerouac in that; he didn't like hippies either, and that's where he and Neal Cassady fell out. Just don't get me started. But there are just certain people that irritate me. Like anarchists. It's a feeble joke, I know, but how *can* you be in an organised group of anarchists? Half of the things they're talking about, they're just doing it to be trendy. It's a posture. I mean, just be honest: you're doing it because you wanna meet women. You know these anarchy meetings are not because you wanna be anarchic, but because you wanna sleep with that other anarchist. Anar-*chic*. Do you know what I mean?

So, anyway, I don't wanna go down there to Newquay, but I wanna go just for Mona. However, I don't wanna go on my own. Mona's going with seven girls. Who've I got to go with? Keith. The worst person to go with ever. The man hates leaving Freetown. He's balding, he's slightly overweight. These girls are never going to be interested in him. If there was ever a wingman not to be taking with you on a mission to Newquay to see seven nubile women, it was Keith. But unfortunately Keith was the only co-pilot I had.

So off we went in my banger of a vehicle, a Fiesta that could barely get to Ramsgate, let alone Newquay. It cost like two hundred quid. We fill it up with petrol. Neither of us has got a good job. Keith is working part time at a go-cart track. I've got hardly any money – I've got ninety quid to my name. He hates camping. I hate camping. But we're goin' camping.

Off we set. As I said, neither of us likes camping, especially in the sort of campsite we went to, which is the worst sort of campsite: a field. And everyone's crammed in. You don't get any of that woodland outdoor feel. Anyway, we get down to Newquay. Epic drive. We decide to leave at midnight. No fucking bullshit. We drive for about forty minutes; can't work out the way there! We're already lost. Right? So we turn round and drive forty minutes back home. Decide, let's go on the Internet and try and get a map. So it's about half past one and all we've done is driven forty minutes there and forty minutes back, never getting nowhere except back to the beginning. I know, I know, I know, this is not like me. It's Keith who's just like this. He's, 'let's just go'. Keith's very much like that.

Anyway, we get some kind of plan. Keith's my map reader. Got a torch which he sits there with, pointed at the map on his lap which he's poring over. Off we go again. I don't know what route we took, or how we did it, but eventually we get there; but about four o'clock in the morning the car is acting very strangely. If I rev it, it revs really high, but there's very little forward momentum. Right? And there is a slight smell of smoke. But I'm thinking, dah, it'll be alright.

We get there about half seven and the campsite doesn't open till eight. I'm knackered and feeling uhhhhhhh – it has not been the easy six-hour journey that we thought it would be, even with there being no traffic, because of the car suddenly being limited to around thirty because of this problem, which was obviously a clutch problem, that I didn't yet know the cause of. So we get down there, park up and think, the car, fuck it, let's just enjoy our time here, we'll worry about getting home when we have to worry about getting home, right? Keith has brought along some old family tent thing and we start putting it up, knackered, both of us miserable. Grass is all dewy and wet. We finally get the tent up and go straight to sleep.

Get up around twelve o'clock, feeling like, can't sleep anymore, what the hell are we doing here?, let's go into Newquay. I'm, like, shall we drive? Keith's like, yeah, let's drive, let's drive, it'll be fine. Yeah but we wanna go for a drink, how we gonna get back? I won't drink, I won't drink, I'll drive us back. I'm like, no, you will drink. He goes, OK, let's drive it there, we'll catch a taxi back and we'll walk back in the morning and get it. OK, sounds fair and reasonable.

We find a parking space but we have to search for quite a while cos we wanna find one that's OK to leave the car in overnight. Eventually we find one and park up. The car's still acting very weird; again we try and just ignore that.

We get to Newquay. Already me and Keith are in a place that is not our place. Instantly we're like, this fucking place is dreadful. Everyone's all like, hey, man; you know, it's all just that whole fake bullcrap surf culture. Rich kids. I hate that. I really hate that. It's like, man, I've dropped out of the system. Only because your daddy pays for your house and you're driving a brand new Mini. That ain't dropping out of the system! That's what I mean by fake hippies. They're the sort of hippies I can't stand. Rich hippies! They make no sacrifice because they've got everything they need anyway. You know, they'll say, I don't go to work, because I don't believe in it. Well, I don't believe in it either, but I have to go to work, because I need the money. 'Yeah, but I don't go.' ONLY BECAUSE YOUR DAD GIVES YOU ALL YOUR MONEY! You see what I mean? It just reeked of that. It's

37

all that hippy culture, but you go into a surf shop and there's this surf suit for two hundred and fifty quid for these down-and-out trendy hippies. You know what I mean? It doesn't add up. You got major consumerism mixed with hippy culture; how the hell is this compatible?

Anyhow, you can see how me and Keith were taking all this; it's eking out of us. We're both getting the rage. Keith loves Elvis, and we see a café on the beach; it's like a fifties diner and it's got a picture of Elvis, so Keith's now had something to build him back up, and he says, "Let's go in!" Keith loves to eat. I love to eat, too. And we both love burgers.

They do a peanut burger in this café, and both of us are like rubbing our hands and going whoa yeah! It was called the Elvis Burger, and it was two layers of hamburgers; cheese, hamburger, cheese, hamburger, peanut butter. And I mean a lot of peanut butter. The burgers come over and both of us are like, oh yeah! And we eat these. We got curly fries; they're absolutely delicious. Both of us are now, man, I'm stuffed. And Keith says, in some Memphis, Tennessee voice, "It's the way the king wouldof wanted it." Both of us are now reasonably happy that we've found this place. Newquay is still pissing us off, and looking outside we're asking ourselves, do we really wanna go back into it? And then it's like, hell, let's go to the pub.

Bad idea.

We go to the pub and it's, oh no, some crappy bullshit Oz-themed pub. You go in and again it's like some Disneyland of pubs. You know what I mean? 'Alright, cobber?' I mean, just shut up. You're not Australian. Just stop it now. You know? What've you got? 'Fosters.' Oh yeah, yeah. Alright. Don't especially want it, but it's cheap. So we sit down and both of us are saying, I don't wanna go back out there, I hate heat, I don't even like sunlight; no, I don't like heat or sunlight either, what the hell are we doing in Cornwall? You know? What are we doing in Newquay? It's just so totally inappropriate. We shouldof just gone, I don't know, to some dreary place with pubs. We'd've been happy and OK. Not here.

38

Mona's with her friends and I send her a text saying, I'm down here, why don't we meet up? And she texts OK.

Fucking mistake.

Never ever follow a woman you've just met anywhere, especially halfway across the country, especially when she's going on holiday with her friends. One, you look desperate and, two, it's just never gonna work. But I was obsessed. But you've got to see there's some kind of learning curve here. I do learn from these mistakes. Also I have that sense of adventure; I have that sense of, I wanna see where this takes me. It's exciting. And I have got a certain element that's, as long as I don't die, as long as I don't end up in prison, I'm willing to take a certain amount of emotional pain and a certain amount of whatever to see this through. You know, I'm not going to be happy about it; but if I get a story out of it, and I feel alive for just a split moment in time, then maybe it's worth it. However, I'm coming to the conclusion now that maybe this isn't the best theory in life. Anyway.

There we are, we're drinking the beer. Another one? Yup. Another one? Yup. We're like drinking non-stop from around two in the afternoon. We've got hardly any money and we're spending it quickly. Very quickly. And we're hating it. And then we start doing that typical thing, you know, 'Lend us a tenner and I'll give it to you when I get back.' Stupid. Because he would say it to me and I would say it to him about an hour later, so these exact same amounts of money were just being exchanged back and forth. And then it was, you know, 'I have got the bank card.' 'Yeah, but how much you got in there?' Keith was always a great man for debt-management, in terms of he doesn't manage it, he just spends it. So he's like, 'Yeah, fuck it, it doesn't matter.' Because he's had beer now. 'I DON'T CARE!' Do you know what I mean? So with Keith there, money wasn't that big a problem. And with him prompting me I took out more than I shouldof as well despite my worrying about it a bit more. So we ended up exceeding our budget on the first afternoon.

We must've had about eight pints each and it's now about nine o'clock in the evening. And we are wasted. You know, ahmmmaa goinnnn AAAARRRLLILLOWWILLLA. Keith's wasted. I don't actually feel that wasted. I remember sobering up as soon as we went outside and that sea air's hitting me and I'm thinking, I'm gonna have to sober up now cos we're gonna go and meet 'em at a pub.

Keith's not very good at talking to women when he first meets them. I'm not being horrible to Keith. Even though he doesn't talk to me any more, and even though he doesn't like me any more, I actually miss Keith. I miss talking to him. I miss hanging around with him. I liked his philosophy on certain things, and I liked his sort of, fuck it, I'm gonna make it, even if nobody else wants me to make it, and even if it's gonna put me in serious debt, I'm still gonna get the job done. I respect that, because I can't do that; Keith can. I didn't like the porn films he made; but I respect anyone who just goes, sod it, I'm doing it anyway. So I do miss Keith.

Anyway, if truth be told, Keith's not the sort of boy that's going to be instantly attractive to eighteen-year-old girls. He's not trendy, he's balding, he's slightly overweight. Right? He's funny, but girls that age don't want funny, you know, you need some sort of appeal at the beginning. He's not particularly great at talking to women, and not only that, he's drunk, and he doesn't want to talk to women. Cos Keith's quite bitter. He'd probably go, 'Ah, ya stuck-up bitches!' And that's not gonna go well. Do you know what I mean?

So we get there. There's Mona. She's happy to see me – kind of. Right? You can tell the instant sort of disappointment in these girls' faces, one with meeting me, and two with meeting Keith. And you can tell there's just this atmosphere and we're thinking, we're fucking out of our depth, these girls don't want us here. And Mona's acting a bit weird. She's wearing this sarong thing and little hot-pants, flip flops, you know, part swim and beachwear, part walking around. She's looking great, but I pick up some vibe from the get-go. The girls she's with are not the sort of girls I would normally hang around with. Bitchy, pretty. You know, no talking film or culture. Nothing. This was just like, what bag did you buy?, and didjaknow Pete fancies whatever? You know, the opposite sort of women me and Keith needed.

Anyway, they drink, we drink more, and then eventually they want to go to a drum 'n' bass place. I hate drum 'n' bass. Keith hates drum 'n' bass. These girls are miserable. They don't want to go to drum 'n' bass, they're having a bad holiday, not because of us, they're just having a bad holiday anyway, but they're taking it out on us slightly. We get to the drum 'n' bass and this place is like DUM DUM BOM. I've never been anywhere like it. It is loud. Whack yourself on the side of the head every three seconds – that is what this place is like. No lyrics. Just BOM BOM BOM. Can't talk.

"WHAT'RE YA DOIN', MONA??!" It is literally just like that.

"WHAT??"

"WHAT??"

You literally just can't talk. You're just standing there like a lemon in a half empty club with BOM BOM DUM going on.

"SO WHAT'RE YA DOIN' FOR THE RESTA THA WEEK???"

"WHAT???"

"DOESN'T MADDER!!!"

Do you know what I mean? It's just useless.

"SO WHADDABOUT THE RELATIONSHIP? D'YA THINK THERE'S ANY KIND OF FUTURE WITH US???"

"WHAT???"

This is not the sort of place you wanna try and build anything. Keith's like "I'M GOIN' 'OME!!!"

"WHADDYA MEAN YOU'RE GOIN' 'OME??? YA CAN'T DRIVE BACK TO THE CAMPSITE"

"I'M NOT DRIVIN' BACK TO THE CAMPSITE. I'M GOIN' 'OME!"

"IT'S ONE O'CLOCK IN THE MORNING!"

41

"I DON'T CARE, I'M GOIN' 'OME!"

"OHHH GOD!" And Keith leaves. Just disappears.

"KEITH'S JUST LEFT. I'M GONNA HAVE TO SEE 'IM!"

"WHAT??"

So I go out but I can't find Keith. I'm thinking, he's got my car keys, he's gonna steal my car. But Mona comes out and I snap into some semblance of control.

"Alright, how're you doing?" In a nice easy-going voice, you know, trying to sober up a bit. "Is everything going OK?"

"Can we sit down?"

And I'm like, OK. But instantly I know. So we sit down on the grass. I'm going to be open and frank with you; I knew what was coming and I wasn't going to take it well.

"I don't think there's any future with me and you."

Now I'd slept with Mona about a week before at the warehouse. She came on to me big time. So this was a shock. I think this was one of the reasons I fell for her in a big way. She really was coming on to me which previously, at that point, I'd never had any kind of exposure to anyone like that. I was the one that's always having to put the groundwork in. I'm the one that has to pursue them. This was totally the opposite. This girl called me; she hunted me down. And this was what was giving me mixed signals. Cos up to this point I was thinking, bloody hell, this girl must be keen, she must be into me cos she's chasing me. I'm always having to chase women, but this woman's chasing me. So my head's a bit messed up. I'm thinking, this girl's keen; but something happened on that holiday, and I'll tell you what did happen on that holiday before I ever arrived. Before I ever arrived, it was doomed. Mona realised that she was missing her boyfriend. She missed her boyfriend and wanted him back. He'd already found someone else. And all this, amazingly, was gonna be my fault.

What happened was she'd dumped her boyfriend and he'd had two weeks of what am I gonna do? I'm really depressed. And then he slowly started to come out the other side of it because of this other girl he knew, OK? Mona hadn't had the depression, because she'd been hanging around with me for two weeks. So she'd been high; he'd been low. He was beginning to peak up; she was beginning to peak down. OK? She's away on this holiday; a holiday she would normally have gone on with him, and she was thinking, I miss him, if it hadn't been for YOU, I would have realised I missed him earlier; you know, not the sort of thing you wanna hear when your heart's being broken. Because it was. Do you know what I mean? She was not just ripping it out, she was stamping on it. It was like, 'It's your fault that I can't get back with him, because if you weren't there keeping me happy and keeping me occupied, then I would have realised I'd made a mistake.' I mean, what can you say to that? You can't say anything.

So I'm crying. Heavily. Sobbing. She doesn't know what to do and just goes back into the nightclub. And I can hear the sound of the nightclub going BOOM BOOM BOOM. It's just taunting me. I'm not being aggressive in any way; I'm the total opposite, completely beat up and crying. And then Keith re-emerges. "What's up, Matt?" And I'm kinda blubbering and can't really make more than basic noises, but Keith guesses and says, "Ah, fuck her." You know? This is Keith's normal way of dealing with such situations. "We'll find some others." And then I smashed my phone. I suppose I wanted to put some kind of emotional full stop to the whole thing.

Keith scrabbles around and recovers the pieces and then just says, "Let's go 'ome!"

And I croak some kind of barely audible reply like, "Yerp lessgorome," and we go back to the car.

Keith says, "I'm driving."

And I say, "No, we can't drive back. We're a mess. Let's walk back."

"I can't walk back, I'm too tired. I'm driving."

"You're not driving, give me the keys. You're wasted."

"I'll get us back. I'll get us back."

"Look, Keith, it's not a good idea. Let's call a cab."

"I 'aven't got any more money."

43

"I 'aven't got any more money either. Let's just walk back."

"No, I'm not walking back."

"OK, let's sleep in the car. Put the seats back, sleep in the car, people do it all the time. It'll be fine. At least until we're sobered up."

"No, I'm driving back."

"We're not driving back."

We get into the car. I'm wasted. And Keith goes, a bit kinda annoyed, "Ohh, OK, let's sleep here." How much of an idiot am I? I'm an idiot. I fall asleep. No word of a lie, next thing I hear, no, not hear, you know when someone goes like that, shining a torch into your eyes when you're asleep? It's blue and red. I'm coming round now, slurring a bit.

"Whath's 'appening, whath's 'appening?" And all I can see is Keith just sitting there looking at me like his world's about to end.

"It's the police, Matt."

"Whaddya mean it's the police?"

"I tried to drive us back. You know, I tried!" As if he had gone down in a hail of bullets or something.

And then I remember, coward that I am, that I said, "I'm asleep," and shut my eyes again. I remember saying: "I'm asleep", just like that. RATTATTATTAT on my window. Again. RATTATTATTAT. I'm awake; but I'm not awake.

I can hear Keith going "Uhh ummm what's wrong?"

"Well, we watched you and you went round that roundabout three times." Quite a nice calming voice, really. "And there was a vast quantity of smoke coming out of the vehicle, that was obviously the clutch burning."

"Oh yeah, I'm lost. I'm trying to get back to the campsite."

"Oh. Have you been drinking?"

You know, you can see where this is going. Can you breathe into this. I'm afraid you're under arrest for drink-driving, and dangerous driving, and for an unroadworthy vehicle. Have you got your driver's licence?

"No, I haven't got a driver's licence."

44

"Do you mean you haven't got a driver's licence, or you haven't GOT a driver's licence?"

"I haven't actually passed my test."

"Right. OK. That's another thing."

And they open the door now and they're shaking me and I'm back to my groggy, slurring, "Uhh? Whath's 'appening?" They bring me back round and I smile and laugh about it now, and even Keith smiled and laughed about this, because we were friends for quite a while after all this happened, but I look up and I see Keith, and he looks so... he's balding and he's sitting in the back of this police van, he's cuffed, and he's looking at me, he's not even angry, it's just the look, sort of like a man whose face has run out of expressions.

So the police say, "Come on," and lead me through it. I'm hamming it up a little, you know. They lead me to the back of the police van and put me in. They don't cuff me. And I just sit there. And you know what? They only go and give me a lift back to the campsite. No exaggeration. These are the nicest coppers I've ever met!

"Keith, what're we gonna do?" We're whispering now.

"I don't know. I think I'm in really bad shit, man." Keith says 'man' a lot when he's worried. "I think I'm I'm I'm fucked, man. Yeah. If I don't see you in the morning, don't call my mum about this. Just don't call my mum."

Keith's mum's Irish and she'd've killed him anyway. She'd've gone down there and broken into the prison just to have killed her own son for doing this. You know what I mean? He'd've rather been under lock and key than have his mum ever find out. I'm like going, "You'll be alright, you'll be alright," thinking, 'You're fucked'.

Then the policeman who's driving says, "What campsite you at, fellas?" I tell him and he says OK then, and I tell Keith, look they're taking us to the campsite, it's gonna be alright, it's gonna be alright. We get to the campsite. How embarrassing is this? A police van, with police lights, passing all these camp-like people in tents.

45

It's us two, right? Then the policemen come round the back, open the back of the police van, and one guy goes, "Come on then," and Keith goes to get up, "No, not you," so Keith then sinks back down again, crushed.

I get out and the policeman says, "Is this your tent?"

"Yeah, that's my tent."

And then I can't get the zip. But the policeman, I swear to you, is the nicest policeman I've ever met, and he says, "I'll get it, I'll get it for ya." And he goes like that and I get into the tent and he comes in with me! Then he goes, "Is this one yours?"

"Yeah, it's mine."

And he undoes the sleeping bag for me, and then he goes, "Oh, take your shoes off. You don't wanna go to sleep in your shoes." I take my shoes off. I lie down. And then he zips me back up. No lie. He zips me back up in my sleeping bag, and he goes, "Have a good night's sleep and you'll see your mate in the morning."

I'm like, "OK, yes officer," a bit shakily.

And then they go and I fall asleep.

The next thing in the morning, I don't know if you've ever been in a tent, but the sun is beaming down, and I feel the lining that stops the moisture from getting in SLAP, SLAP, SLAPPING me in the face, you know, like a Rottweiler's tongue, sticky and hot. I open my eyes and there's Keith, shoeless, sitting there, hungover, looking like he's just been to Baghdad or somewhere, most sombre face ever, looking at me like he's gonna shoot me, just relacing his shoes.

I'm like, "What happened?"

"They took my shoes off me and they took the laces out." Cos obviously they didn't want him to hang himself. So there he is, just sitting there, lacing his shoes and looking at me sombre-faced. It was one of the funniest images I've ever seen.

Basically what happened was the policemen were really nice to him when they got him back. "Do you want a cup of coffee?" Gave him a black coffee. "Right, we'll come back for you in a minute and we'll put you on the ol' big machine." Cos I don't know if you've ever been tested? Essentially you blow into the tube and that gives them what they call due purpose, or cause, that's it 'due cause'. So you blow into it. You're over the limit. But that won't stand up in court cos it's not accurate enough. So they take you back to the police station where they've got a big machine. I've seen them on TV though not in real life. This big machine's got a much more elaborate tubing system and you blow into it four times and they take an average from the four readings. This machine is a helluva lot more accurate and it's the one they'll use in court if you're over the limit.

Anyway, as I said, these police were really nice to Keith. I think they could see we were just two guys, it was late at night, no one's got run over, the car's obviously a piece of shit, we've had a really bad night/evening. I can only think they took pity on us. So they asked Keith where he was from.

"I'm from Kent and I'm never ever going to step inside your county ever again, officer, I promise." You know?

And Keith can be quite a hustler when he needs to be. He probably threw himself on the ground and clasped his hands to heaven, like a Louisiana Baptist preacher or something, begging and saying his mum was Irish and she'd kill him. Keith studied performing arts and, you know, he can turn it on when he needs to.

Anyway, what they did was they kept saying, "You're lucky we're busy, you're lucky we're busy. We can't do it yet. You're lucky we're busy. We can't do it yet," you know, putting it off and off. And then one officer says to him, "You may wanna try and sort yourself out, OK?" And basically what he was saying to Keith was, try and sober up, drink some coffee, walk around a bit, while you're waiting, you know? They were really nice to him and in the end it took like two to three hours before they took him to that machine. They said OK and did it four times, and he was something like 0.1 off a prosecution. They basically said to him, you're under the limit. Just. You've had alcohol in your body but you're just under the limit. How the hell? We'd been

47

drinking all day. How the hell he managed to do that I'll never know. But if they'd've done it as soon as they'd got back to the station, he'd've been fucked, basically. They still had plenty of other charges to throw at him, though: driving without a licence, driving in an unroadworthy vehicle, careless driving, or whatever it is, they're quite major, and driving without insurance. But he did manage to escape the drink-driving rap. They told him there was gonna be a court date and he would be getting a letter, then they let him go.

So now we need to get back home, but we can't get back home. Luckily I've got AA cover and, no lie, two AA men towed us all the way from Newquay back home. We went Newquay to a halfway point service station, where another AA man picked us up and took us back the rest. It took eight and a half hours and the whole way back Keith's just sitting there with the worst hangover in the world, quietly saying in this, like, plangent voice, "What have I done? What have I done?" But I did feel by the end that me and the AA man had built some kind of a relationship, because of the time we'd spent together. He'd been a sheep farmer on Andrew Lloyd Webber's estate with a quad bike and two sheep dogs that stank when it got wet. Cool guy and he even came in for a beer after he'd dropped us off.

Anyway, the letter comes through a couple of months later, saying Keith doesn't need to appear at this court date but it would be beneficial if he opts to do so etc., etc. Keith's like, fuck it, I'm not going back to Newquay, so he writes this long, apologetic letter, which again it says you can do, about how it was a one-off, how I was highly distraught having just been dumped, you know, he laid it on thick. They gave him a six-hundred-pound fine and banned him from driving for five years; but, as Keith said, since he didn't have a driver's licence anyway, the ban, which started from that date and not any date when he eventually did get a licence, didn't really affect him. It was still quite a punishment, but it couldof been worse. Luckily he's one of those people that doesn't drive.

48

You know, Keith tried to make me pay half of that six hundred quid? In the end I was scared to go round cos his mum eventually found out, as they always do, and he, of course, came clean after her sustained interrogation. Then she turns on me.

"Whoit sorta troubl've youse bun gettun ma sonn unto?"

"Um, I don't know what you mean, Mrs O'Neill?"

"Youse gowin ta be payin half o' this foin then?"

"Um, um, um."

"Cuz oi really thank ya shoold ba."

And I'm looking at Keith, and he's looking at the floor, and I'm just going, um, um, um.

"Cuzit really was yewer fult, wasntaht?"

I didn't pay Keith any of the money. Because it really wasn't my fault. Maybe I shouldof taken the keys off him, maybe we shouldn't have slept in the car, maybe we should've walked back, maybe we shouldn't've been drinking all day. Maybe Mona shouldn't've dumped me. You know what I mean? But at no stage did I ever say to Keith, here are the keys, drive me home now. You know?

Chapter Six
Mona Part One

Lovers and madmen have such seething brains
(Shakespeare, *A Midsummer Night's Dream*)

I'm aware that I should be telling you about how Mona and I met before and not after we split up. But I've decided upon reverse chronology, like in that film *Memento*, because I kinda like the sense of doom. It suits my take on life, and especially women. You could argue that what I'm doing is more like a *Star Wars* prequel, because we're only talking about releasing prior information on a one-off basis, rather than adopting a whole retrospective narrative strategy. And J-J, who was my movie guru, always hated films like *Memento*, and said it was just smoke and mirrors trying to hide the fact that the story is a non-story lacking plausible forward-moving dynamics, and you conceal this fact by telling it backwards so no one will notice. J-J can be harsh in his judgements, but I can see where he's coming from, and, as I say, he knows his stuff. However, I have some issues with *Star Wars*, which I'll go into later. So maybe the best parallel is with *Annie Hall*, which J-J used a lot in his video classes, and which begins with the fact that Annie and Alvy have broken up forever, and then shows you how they met, which makes the scenes between them more poignant, I think. Especially the ones where they're really happy (not many of those, it has to be admitted, and maybe that's why I feel it's more truthful than your average romantic comedy). Anyway, it's the perspective I favour when I think about Mona. The pain first; then the fleeting pleasure. Mona was the second girl I made love to; but she was the girl to whom I lost my virginity. I'll explain.

Like I say, Mona was incredibly attractive with an amazing figure. It's really hard for me to find the words to describe her overall, especially her face, and the best way I can sum her up is to say, think Natalie Portman in the *Star Wars* movies, i.e. when she had long hair. If you looked at Natalie Portman and then you saw Mona, you would know what I mean. The face, the eyes, the whole thing, but especially the face. It's a freakish similarity. And it's the reason I can't watch any film with Natalie Portman in it any more; and I mean any more, ever again, ever. That's the honest truth.

We met at the birthday party of a girl called Zoë that I used to take photos of. She was very tall with blonde hair. I think her mother was originally from Sweden or the Netherlands or somewhere Nordic like that. She was very photogenic in a *Dazed & Confused* sort of way, which is the style of photography I was heavily into at the time; you know, messed-up teenagers presented in a cool way, not glamorous or arty, but not seedy either. Natural and yet at the same time highly posed. I can't really explain, you'd need to look at the magazine. Anyway, I sold a couple of photos and there was some interest in my work on the net, probably because the photos were, surprise, surprise, a bit dark and twisted. Maybe I'll go back to my photography someday, because it's a talent I have, though I would now use a different style and I've taken all my old pictures down from my room. I also had to sell my Mamiya large-format camera to finance my trip to the States. But I digress.

Zoë's birthday party was at the Mandarin Chinese in Southfield. Sitting next to me was Mona, and we got on really well. In actual fact I had my eye on another girl who I thought at the time was the prettiest one there; but that's always the way it goes. Because you've got your eye on someone else, you end up acting cooler and more in control to someone who's got their eye on you. It's like, even though I know I'm a beautiful girl, this guy is acting like he could take me or leave me, so he MUST be something really special, because all the other schmucks go gaga when they see me, so this guy is no schmuck, and therefore I find him more intriguing and desirable than the others: in short, I want to get to know this guy BETTER. This is how the minds of beautiful women operate in my view; but, as you can tell, I'm not exactly knowledgeable on the subject.

I didn't think anything much of what happened at the party, but a day later and to my great surprise I get a text from Mona saying she'd got my number from Zoë and hoped I didn't mind etc., and would I like to go out with her and a couple of friends for a drink? It was obvious she liked me a lot, so I said that would be cool and picked her up on the Friday night and took her to the Star Tap, which is where I used to go a lot in those days. I remember she looked stunning. Long, straight hair with ringlets at the end, and she was wearing this amazing outfit which was a kind of corset but with the ribs on the outside. You could tell she'd really made an effort. Seems the friends had backed out, so there was just us two.

We talk and talk and things are going really well. We have some drinks, but not too many. We're certainly not wasted, mainly because I've hardly got any money, and around eleven o'clock she leans in to me and says, "I really want to kiss you," just like that. I can't remember what I said back, but something along the lines of, "Well, I've got no problem with that." But then she suddenly changes her mind.

"I don't know. I've just broken up with my boyfriend."

"OK, fair enough." I don't know why I was so reasonable about this. You might have expected me to trash him. It's not that I wasn't keen; but I didn't want to come across as sleazy, and I was also feeling sympathetic towards my unknown rival, or ex-rival. Probably I was just trying to act in that cool, take-it-or-leave-it way which had brought me thus far. "Obviously

I would like to, and I think that would be a good thing, but I can understand where you're coming from, so I don't want to push you into anything." Whatever. Again I don't remember the words exactly.

We talked some more and then danced a little bit, and I don't dance, but I made the effort. And the place was getting busier and busier. Now I was known at the Star Tap at this moment in time. This was like the Golden Age. Now I go there and I'm some schmuck. But in those days, me and Joe, we ruled those streets. You know, we knew everybody, everyone treated us with respect, we never got kicked out, we got let in and we got free drinks. We were made. Now I go back and it's just like I've been in a jail term. No one knows me. The mafia bosses have all changed. It's like I've been away for too long. But at this moment in time, I'm like a made man. I know everybody, the bar staff know me, so I'm looking popular.

We go to sit in this alcove by the stairs and Mona slides up to me and puts her hand on my inner thigh. Then she starts to bite my ear. Next thing I know she's kissing the side of my face and before I know it I'm kissing her. No discussion. It's like she just crept up on me. And now I'm getting off with her. Passionately. And we're acting like there's no one else around. And then the place starts emptying as the bouncer starts clearing everyone out, but because I was known at the time, I just look up at Jez, the barman, whose real name is Steve, and he says to the bouncer, "They're all right, they can stay," meaning us, which made me look incredibly cool, because it was a lock-in, where only a select group were allowed to stay, and me and Mona were in that select group. So we stayed all night at the Star Tap until six in the morning. We then caught a taxi back, but since I only had enough money to get us to the lip of Southfield we had to walk the rest of the way to her house.

We get to her front door and start kissing all over again. I've got no money at all and I've got to walk back home through the badlands of Lower Street at seven in the morning, so I kiss her

53

goodbye and go on my way. She can't invite me in, even though her parents are away in Spain where they've got property, because her sister is indoors, and Mona doesn't want to wake her up or get into any complicated discussions about who I am, etc. And in fact it was lucky she didn't invite me in, because the previous evening her sister had run into Mona's old boyfriend when she was out with friends in Southfield, and, as he had nowhere to stay, let him sleep in the house. So all the time I'm kissing and getting off with Mona outside her front door, he's inside, probably listening. Mona was really pissed off when she went up to her room expecting to find an empty bed to go to sleep in, and lo and behold, there the fucker is! She woke her sister up, kicked her out and told her to sleep on the couch while she slept in her sister's bed. She just said, "I didn't want him back here. You brought him back here and put him in my bed. You can sleep on the sofa." Fair enough, I say.

Anyway, a couple of days after this Mona went away to Spain for four or five days to meet up with her parents. I heard nothing from her; no phone, no text, nothing. And by this time, needless to say, I'm hooked. Line and sinker. Any kind of nonchalant 'Nah, yeah whatever' has gone completely out the window. There ain't none of that no more. I'm champing at the bit for her to get back.

When she does come back, alone, i.e. without parents, etc., she's different. Distant. I'm like, what's wrong? And she's like, quiet, don't know, feel a bit ughhhh, don't know, nothing's wrong. You know the sort of thing. I'd met her by accident, as it happens, when she got off the bus from Heathrow or wherever with her backpack on and looking jet-lagged, despite the minimal time difference. We went for a drink and I asked her if she wanted to meet up tonight, and she said she didn't know, but didn't really want to meet up, felt a bit tired, etc. I could tell something wasn't right and this was throwing me off. This girl had been pretty keen before and now nothing. She'd called me, chased me, initiated the kiss with me; what is this? What the hell is going on? This is hurting my head. And then, when

54

she'd finished her drink, she just said, "OK, I'll meet up with you this evening," and that was it.

I pick her up at half seven or eight o'clock and ask her where she wants to go. She says she doesn't really want to go to a pub.

"Take me somewhere different. Take me somewhere you don't take anyone else."

So I decide to take her to the warehouse, because I still had a key back then.

We get to the warehouse and I open up and she is well impressed. I mean, not many guys could take a girl to a place where they can have the run of a space the size of an aircraft hangar and full of antiques and furniture.

I remember she was wearing a white, summery mid-thigh-length dress and one of those crop tops with thin straps so you could see the beginning of her creamy-white bosom and a little bit of bra. We sat down on this old-fashioned wooden couch with very little padding. I'm lying back at an angle on one corner of the couch with my arm hanging casually and limply over the rest like I'm in some Noël Coward play, and she's lying at the other end, also at an angle, with one leg on the couch and one dangling over the side, so that her dress is falling down unevenly over her thighs; and I don't want this to sound like some really bad erotic novel, but the next thing I know she's sliding this dress up. And I know this sort of tantalising revelation of flesh never happens by accident, but I'm also like, nah, whatever, because she was acting distant with me about three hours ago. But I knew she could tell I could see her knickers. That was the whole point. And then she crawls over to me and asks me if I want to kiss her.

I'm a bit hesitant, to tell the truth, and say that I'm not really sure what's going on, because three hours ago she seemed so distant. But she then explains that that was only because she'd just got back and was feeling a bit tired and disorientated by the flight and sudden change of scenery from Spain to here, which I could relate to. So next thing I know I'm getting off with her. Again. But this time we're on our own and it's getting heavier.

Then she looks at me and says, "Do you want to have sex with me?" Those were her exact words. Mona was a very direct girl and didn't believe in beating about the bush.

"I haven't got any condoms with me." Me being Captain Sensible.

"Don't use any. You don't need to use any."

"There's no way I'm not using any." You know what I'm like.

"Look, I'm on the pill. It'll be fine, don't worry."

"It's OK, I may have some in the car in the glovebox. I'll go and get them."

Then I swear to you she grabbed my wrist and said, "If you go and get them, we're not doing it." That is exactly what she said. And it freaked me out. I mean, this was an opportunity, and I hadn't had sex in a while. At least a year. This was a very beautiful girl, a girl that I was slightly obsessed with, offering. I had to make a decision there and then and there was no way I was turning back. I may have gone, you know, are you SURE you're on the pill? etc.; but she just said yes and remained adamant about how we were to proceed. It may not sound cool, but I then told her in all honesty that I'd never had sex with anyone before without a condom. She then became quite gentle and reassuring. "Don't worry about it, it'll feel better, it'll feel like we're closer." And so in the end I went with it.

I was thinner than I am now and I'd been working on the lorry a lot, so I was stronger and could move heavy stuff around. So I was able to push two of these large leather sofas together without great difficulty. However, once we started, you know, getting it on, the sofas moved and we fell through the middle. This was highly irritating. So then I had to go and get two wardrobes to put either side of the sofas as blocks to make them interlock and keep them from moving around.

So we're getting it on and Mona slides her dress off. She was very in control. There was a lot of moving about as to who was on top, but there was no question about who was leading things. The lovemaking was slow with protracted, very protracted, foreplay, which of course made me look quite skilful and experienced, and

56

not some randy twenty year old; but the truth is I was in no hurry to penetrate her for the simple fact that, one, I was worried shitless about it for reasons of health and disease and two, I was continually asking myself, is this girl really on the pill?, because I don't want to be the father of her child. So simply to avoid putting it in, I was inventing a lot of other stuff which was making me look like a tantric master. However, the truth is it was fear and paranoia that was driving me to this high level of restraint and creativity. And I'd had a lot of practice in learning how to do other things as a result of my experiences with S., who second time around never wanted me to do anything else.

I remember looking at Mona's breasts and thinking they were amazing. I've seen a lot of breasts, both in reality and in printed form, but these were nice, everything about them, and it was a really hot summer and both of us were naked, so we didn't feel like we needed any kind of rug or whatever. Then she said, "I want you, I want you," and next thing I know she's on top and I'm inside her.

She's now going way fast; a bit scary fast.

"I want you to come inside me. I want you to come inside me."

Now this may have aroused many others; however, in my case it was just fuelling my paranoia that this woman is using me for something, so I'm holding out. And if there was ever a method of avoiding premature ejaculation, being paranoid about this stuff is it. Cos every fibre in your body is WILLING you not to do it. So I'm going for ages and I remember her saying, "Are you not enjoying this?" Maybe I had some sort of unhappy grimace on my face or something, I don't know, but I'm enjoying it, I'm really enjoying it, and fifty per cent of me is loving this moment and thinking, *I haven't had sex in ages, this girl is hot, she's got the best pair of breasts I've ever seen, she's leading the way, it feels amazing.* But the other fifty per cent is going, *What the fuck is going on right now? Three hours ago this girl didn't want anything. I'm not using a condom, but every sex education film I've ever seen has warned me against this. This is a case scenario where every health professional would be telling you this is not what you do. You don't know where this girl's been. She's just come back from a foreign country. She could be just using me so that I impregnate her.* Everything. So it's Doctor Jekyll and Mr Hyde.

I'm focusing but thinking all this, and now I'm on top. And although this sounds like I'm lying, or being big-headed, I swear to you it's the truth. I don't know why she said it; maybe she thought I wasn't enjoying it and needed encouragement, but she goes, "My boyfriend could never go this long." She couldn't have known, but this was not a good thing to say to me right then, because it only put me off. Because her boyfriend was the last person I wanted in my mind at this time, plus the fact that she was thinking of him at this very intimate, and for me tense and rather stressful, moment, which didn't exactly enhance my confidence in what was going on.

Anyway, to cut a long story short the inevitable did happen. She was on top of me at the time. Whether she came or didn't, I don't know. She definitely made a lot of noise and went through the motions; but whether that was just to build up my ego I'll never know. She said she reached climax; but whether she did or not, I've got no idea. And also, for what it's worth, and again I've got no illusions about this, she was probably bullshitting me to make me feel good, but she said she'd never ever reached climax through doing it this way; normally her boyfriend (AGAIN the mind games) had to go down on her. Whatever. Part of me took it all with a pinch of salt, thinking, well, I just got laid, I can't complain. But nonetheless these things are always in the back of your mind.

Now I don't know how graphic you want to get, but having never at this point had sex with a woman without a condom before, I'd never had to go through the whole thing of, OK, we need tissue. So I'm lying there and, like an absolute idiot, going, "Why do we need tissue?"

And she says, "Well, it's going to come out in a second." It just never ever crossed my mind. So I say OK and grab a vest I'd previously been wearing and hand it to her. She climbs off, and as she does so the jism just drops out of her SPPLLLUURGH. It's disgusting, and I am slightly grossed out by this, because it is not the most pleasant of things to see. And my vest is being used as a mop. But then again it didn't gross me out so much that I wanted to go home and have a shower.

I remember telling my head doctor about all this when I was about six or seven months into my treatment. He told me that nothing good could come of this relationship. He told me I needed to find a nice girl, one with whom I could build a relationship; not one that you just sleep with like that. His view was, and he was careful to let me know this was his personal opinion as a human being, not a shrink, but he said that this just sounded like a one-night stand, and he felt that a relationship should be more, you know, he was a bit schoolteacherish, and I can kind of see where he was coming from, and I do agree with him, but for him, in terms of a meaningful relationship, what I was describing to him was not the best of beginnings. And he also asked, do I really want to be hanging around with girls like Mona?

The fact is he was right. I mean, don't get me wrong, I like flesh on flesh, breasts are nice, I can feel when something is enjoyable. But with most of my sexual experiences, I've never felt an emotional connection. And although this sounds like the kind of thing my shrink would say, the reality is I didn't trust any of them, and as a result never really felt comfortable. And a lot of the girls I've been with, even the ones that come from stable homes, have always had issues, because their boyfriends or someone else has always done something to them before. 'Don't do that, I don't like that.' Do you know what I mean? It's weird.

Anyway we laid there in the warehouse for what felt like ages, then we kissed and parted and went home. We never had sex again. Five days later Mona went down to Newquay.

59

Chapter Seven

Boston

Wine Spodiodi

I arrived in Boston on a Greyhound bus I caught from Times Square. I always intended to travel across America by Greyhound bus, so I had purchased a ticket for six hundred dollars in NY that would take me across the States as I'd originally planned, and Boston was going to be my next stopover on account of it being on the way to JK's grave in Lowell. I mean, I wasn't hoping to see the America that Kerouac had, or anything like that, because I knew it wasn't there any more. But I did want to see his grave, wanted to see his hometown, and his house. My own little pilgrimage, if you like.

Some family friends who lived in Boston had offered to put me up for a while, but since they all had jobs I had to amuse myself during the day. So I spent a lot of time on Duck Tours which were really cool. There's this boat they invented in World War II. It's basically got wheels and can drive straight into rivers and just go along. It doesn't need any kind of levers or conversion; you literally drive into the water; off you go; drive out of the water: off you go. It's a really good way of seeing Boston, cos they take you on a land tour then they take you onto the water and then straight off again. Duck Tours. There's one in London now; don't know whether it's the same company. But it all originated in Boston.

I also found myself visiting a lot of bars. I love the bar culture in the States. It's so much better than over here. Here you go into a pub and everyone looks you over and gives you evils, like, 'you ain't from round here'. Whereas over there, especially in cities like Boston, you could be a single person and sit at the bar and you wouldn't look like a loner. And even if you did look like a loner, people seemed to respect that. And you could sit there and the barman or barlady would talk to you; it wasn't like you ever felt like you were imposing on anyone. They'd be like, where you from?, and you'd start a conversation. So even though I was on my own, it never felt like I was on my own. And it is handy being English, because everyone wants to talk to you.

I would often end up buying everyone a drink, because when I get drunk I get very generous; the opposite of what I'm like in normal life.

"Do you wanna beer? Have a beer. Do you wanna beer? Have a beer."

And I'm handing them all out. This pissed off the people I was staying with. I think they thought I was showing them up. But I was having a good time. Bostonites don't drink any beer other than Sam Adams, a beer they only make in Boston then ship around the country. You can't get it over here. Boston's where it comes from, cos that's where the brewery is. There was also IPA which some people had, but Sam Adams was the one; if you're in Boston, that's what you have.

So I ended up drinking a lot of Sam Adams in Boston. But I was also going through my wine spodiodi phase, which was always a bad era. If you read *On the Road* and listen to Kerouac's recordings, you'll see he mentions it. A wine spodiodi, and this is slightly my interpretation, because I have to bring it up to date, is the ultimate get-drunk drink. Basically it's a pint glass and a small glass of white wine. Has to be white wine. This is a Jack Kerouac drink. He actually says somewhere that everyone was drinking wine spodiodi, a mixture of white wine (he may have said port, but white wine's what I remember), whisky and beer. I had to interpret it from that, because he doesn't give the exact mixing. It's basically a glass of white wine, two shots of whisky and then topped up

61

with beer and stirred anticlockwise (I added the anticlockwise). And honestly it goes down smooth. You would think it would be dreadful, but it drinks really easy and will get you messed up after one. It costs you about ten dollars, but after that you don't need any more. So I had a couple of those. The most I've ever had is about three or four, and you do not ever want to do that. I was mega-ill after. So to every American I'm meeting I'm saying, "You gotta have a wine spodiodi. You gotta have a wine spodiodi."

"What the hell's a wine spodiodi?"

"You mean you don't know what a wine spodiodi is? One of your most famous authors used to drink wine spodiodi! Here, have one."

"What've you done to it?"

Which is classic Boston, cos people there are paranoid about friendship. You offer them a beer or something and they're instantly suspicious. Not like in LA. There you offer drinks and everyone goes, 'Yeah, give me ten!' Not Boston. They're like, 'Why do you want to give me a drink?'

"Nothing. Just have it!"

"OK ... I'll give wine spodiodi a go ..."

I reckon I bought around thirty drinks. And people were doubling up. You know, someone would say, no thanks, and the next one would say, I'll have his as well. It cost me a fortune. I even had to take more money out from the ATM. But I was making everyone happy.

But in America bar staff can be sued if you get alcohol poisoning, or you get so drunk you die, or you get drunk then drive and kill someone. I'm not joking; there have been cases. Vicarious liability or something, they call it. So bar staff get very careful and they don't like giving you wine spodiodis. And you've also got to remember that in America a bartender is a career. Not a part-time job like over here. You take tests and exams and all sorts to be a barman over there. They don't have optics; they pour it out for you. It's amazing and it's so much better. A hundred times better. They tip out the individual shots, none of this optics stuff; it looks so much cooler.

So they don't want to do wine spodiodi. But the get-around is to say, OK, I'll have two shots of whisky, a pint glass, half a pint of beer and a glass of wine. There's no way they can say no to that. And they've been sensible: they've served me all the drinks individually and I'm the one mixing them. A lot of them were cool with this; some of them told me to leave. Only once, though, as far as I remember. The rest were just intrigued by what I was doing; you know, they're bar staff, they like drink. They were impressed that this crazy English boy was drinking this crap; and not only that but they'd never seen this drink before.

So everyone's drinking wine spodiodis. And everyone is always pleasantly surprised. They're like, yeah, that's actually drinkable! Don't ask me how it works, but it is drinkable. The whisky's not got that kick to it, the wine's mixed with the beer. It's arguably not the best drink in the world, but you can drink it. So I'm buying them and mixing them and everyone is really happy. Someone says, "It tastes strangely of coconut." Then someone else says, "Yeah, it does taste strangely of coconut." So everyone's just having a good time. And the cool thing is the bars don't shut till two, and it's quite normal not to arrive till ten thirty, and no one ever goes out until the bar closes, even in Boston, even on a weeknight, and even though they've got to go to work the next day. Don't ask me how they do it. None of that ding, ding, drink up at eleven. I know things have changed a bit recently, but even so most pubs over here still shut at eleven.

Anyway, I'm now in an Irish bar in Boston called O'Brien's or something; big, diner-style layout but with a bar in front, recently opened, new black and white tiled ceiling and décor with walls showing painted faces of people sitting down and having a conversation in a diner but laid out like a film strip; not Irish at all really, probably wasn't O'Brien's. Anyway, it was next to a comedy improv club in Charlestown near the Brown University M.I.T area. I remember it had a weird toilet. You walk out the back and turn right, and now you're into open brickwork, and there's one toilet which is male and female, so it doesn't matter who goes in there, and you have to wait and queue up, cos there's only one, no urinals or anything, like in an airplane. A lot of bars have toilets like that in America. Anyway, I end up at this place and I'm getting kinda half drunk and mixing a wine spodiodi for a black girl. She was twenty-seven/twenty-eight, frizzy hair but not afro, about five-five, sorta slim, not fat but not anorexic-model thin; a normal person, really, and she had freckles, which you don't often see on a black woman. She was wearing a black leather jacket and top and black jeans, and she had a cool bag. It was like a huge lunchbox made out of metal. You know, those old tin lunchboxes that kids used to have? Now imagine it enlarged. I think I commented on it at the time.

"That's a cool case."

"Yeah, I bought it in New York."

She was using it as a briefcase and opened it up and there was a DVD box in there.

"Oh man, what film's that?"

"It's my film."

"Really? Can you buy this?"

"Yeah, yeah."

She let me take the DVD out the case and I looked at it, and that got us started on a conversation about how she got the movie made.

Quick list of topics that we covered: her movie, how it was made (not sure if that counts as a separate topic), funding, what her job was before she got into movies, her new movie, how many people she worked with. Did she like living in Boston? Would she ever want to move to New York, and other stuff I don't remember. Her name was Tremayne and she used to be a copywriter before getting into movies. She was in the bar with this man; don't know who he was, but he was tall, goatee, cool-looking like a jazz musician. So I start talking to them. And I have to be honest, I had the impression that some people found it a bit strange that I should be talking to this girl and this black man, that they might be a bit dodgy or something, you know? But I suppose when you're a fish out of water you don't know who is dodgy. You just think everyone is nice, which is the danger, and which is why what happened in Vegas happened. By then I'd met so many nice people that I'd lowered my barrier.

Anyway, Tremayne asks me how come I'm over here, and I say I'm on holiday, then I ask her some more about the movies, she says she's a director now, oh really? I've always been interested in etc., yeah, I've just directed this film, oh really? My range of responses is narrow, but I'm genuinely interested. She says she's taken this latest movie to Sundance, and I'm well into this. Then she says, "I'm going outside to smoke a joint." The weird thing is, she doesn't invite me, but I just follow her cos I know I'm allowed.

So we're outside now, smoking the joint. And I'm aware that in America they're a lot stricter about this kind of thing than over here. Over here you get a slap on the wrist. In America you're talking prison time. So I'm a little nervous, but because I'm drunk it isn't really showing, and in fact she has to tone me down a bit, saying, "Calm down, white boy," cos I'm getting a bit too blasé about things and gonna get us all arrested. Anyway, the black guy says he's going home and splits, and so it's just me and Tremayne, and she says, "Where shall we go on to now?" I say I don't know and we start walking.

Next thing I know we're walking along and I see this fake plastic deer in someone's garden. I jump the garden fence, jump the deer and start stroking it. She's shouting, "Don't do that. Come back, come back, you're not allowed over there!"

But I'm going, "I love the deer, I love the deer." Then all of a sudden she says the cops are coming and there is a WHRRR WHRRR of cop car noises. So I jump back over the fence and there's a KKRRSSHHHHEEE and the whole inside of my jeans rips.

I should tell you something about me and clothes. I don't care what I wear really. But if I buy something for myself I want it to be good. If people are buying it for me, I just don't care. I'll go, yeah, I've got a pair of jeans, whatever. I mean, I want something to look OK, I want it to be respectable. But I don't care whether it's a certain make or name. It's like the shirts I buy. If I told anybody the make of them, they wouldn't know who that was. I just worry about quality and whether I'm gonna look stupid. If my mum or dad are buying it for me, it's not about who makes it; it's whether it fits and I don't look like a fool. When I'm buying it, I want it to be decent but I don't give a shit who makes it. But the clothes my mum and dad buy me are pretty good anyway; you know, don't get me wrong, they're up there. It's just that the clothes I do buy I can't normally buy many of, because they're usually very expensive. They're not designer. I mean, I like black shirts, good black shirts, not shit black shirts. The most expensive black shirt I've ever bought for myself was nearly two hundred quid. The cheapest black shirt I've ever bought was seventy-five. Of course I've had black shirts that've been worth a tenner; what I mean is the best black shirt I've ever had was a hundred and ninety-five quid and it was fucking amazing. But I could take you to places where you could spend three or four hundred on a shirt. There are plenty of shops in Bluewater like that. In fact my mum won't go shopping in Bluewater, because she says there's no point in going there unless you've got enough money to buy something special, so she'd rather go to Lakeside.

I used to buy expensive jeans too; but I've noticed that with jeans, unlike shirts, the difference between a hundred-and-seventy-five-pound pair of jeans and a fifteen-pound pair of jeans is very small. So today I only wear Dickies workman jeans. They've got triple-stitching on the seams and basically they're like a tank in terms of jeans. Rock solid. The material they're made out of is double-hard. And they're also comfortable. They have shitloads of pockets, so you can do lots in them and look OK. They cover every aspect. I mean, over here, people see you in a pair of Dickies jeans and they think you bought them from a specialist skateshop and you've spent, like, fifty quid on them. So it's a double whammy. Not only are they durable, not only do they look decent, but people think you've actually spent a fair amount of money on them. Yet

66

the jeans I'm wearing now as I write this I bought in America for less than a tenner in Walmart. I mean, can you imagine anyone over here saying, 'I bought my jeans in Asda?' People do, but they wouldn't go around boasting about it.

But the jeans I ripped jumping the fence that night in Boston happened to be a hundred and seventy-five pounds. Who knows why they cost a hundred and seventy-five pounds? Probably they were made in some fancy limited edition, you know, only a certain run of them. That's what I mean. Piece of fucking shit. So, anyway, I'm flapping about in the street in these ripped-open, eviscerated hundred-and-seventy-five-pound jeans. Tremayne's laughing, I'm laughing, and she tells me I need to get out in the sun more because I am so white. Then I run into a door and collapse and she takes a picture of it, cos she always carries a camera with her everywhere. You know, this woman is a twenty-four-hour seven-days-a-week trying-to-get-a-movie-made lady. Not like me. Maybe I just like the idea of it more than actually doing it. Anyway, let's not go there.

Next thing, all of a sudden, I start going up to total strangers who are just out walking down the street, shaking their hand, saying, "Nice to meet you. We're working for a magazine called *Now!*", bullshit, bullshit, bullshit, just out of nowhere, ripped flapping jeans and everything. And the amazing thing is, Tremayne backs me up the whole way. She is brilliant. "This is my photographer, Miss Jones."

"Nice to meet you, sir."

"Nice to meet you."

They shake hands.

"Man, this is a wind-up, isn't it?"

"No, this isn't a wind-up, sir. We're doing an article on happiness in Boston for next month's edition featuring street interviews with real Boston people, and we were wondering if you could possibly spare just a couple of minutes of your time."

And slowly the guy is turning and turning, and he's gradually buying it. Maybe the English accent is helping, I don't know. We even lean him up against the fence, write down his name,

Tremayne takes a photo and then he leaves, glad that he decided after all to walk down this particular street at this particular time on this particular evening. We made his day. Then when he's gone, Tremayne looks at me and says, "What the fuck was all that about?" But this is the thing; she also said, "Man, that's the best hustling I've ever fucking seen in my life."

And the truth is, I love doing that shit cos it's amazing, like dicing with death. You know, am I gonna get caught out? am I gonna get caught out? am I gonna get caught out? And I'll push it and push it and push it, until the back breaks and someone turns around and says, 'That was just wrong.' But it's cos I just wanna feel that I've really done something. And it's also a control thing. It's like you don't know whether what I'm saying is true or not, real or not, whether I'm joking with you or deadly serious, and I'm enjoying and wallowing in this level of control at this moment in time. And it's also, like, are these people gonna hit me, are they gonna hit me, how far can I push 'em before they turn around and hit me?

And S. told me that was my form of self-harm. She basically said that I wouldn't cut myself. I'd go up to a bouncer in a pub and go URRYYER, URRYYER, URRYYER, URRYYER, agitate, agitate, agitate, agitate, agitate, agitate, agitate, agitate, agitate, agitate, PPPSSHHH, 'Ow, ya git!' It would be like that. And a lot of people back away cos they don't understand me and think I'm a nutter. And the truth is not many people can handle it, so I guess that's why I don't have many long-term friends.

Anyway, next I go, "I need sweets." Just like that. So we go into what Tremayne calls a candy shop and I fill this plastic carrier bag with every sweet in the house. CHNGG CHNGG CHNGG CHNGG CHNGG till the bag is nearly splitting. Then I grab a plunger, the largest one I can find, don't know why. A big QUUWWWWWCKK plunger. She says, "What're you doing?"

"I wanna buy a plunger."

"OK have a plunger."

And I go up to the guy behind the counter and buy it all. She's examining all this, wondering again, 'What the fuck?'

68

Then we go to a bar, which is absolutely packed, and I'm hiding this plunger inside my jacket. I am really drunk. She gets us in but tells me not to hide the plunger like that because people will think I'm carrying a weapon. And in fact I do get stopped by a bouncer and he asks me what I've got. I show him and he asks me why I've got it, and I just say it's for when I go home, and he's kinda OK with that, though everyone's looking at me like I'm an absolute psychopath. So I then go up to the bar and go GGDOOINNNGGG with the plunger and shout out, "Wine spodiodi!"

The bartender's laughing his head off, cos luckily he can see the funny side of it all, and Tremayne's laughing as well. Bartender serves us some drinks, and then before we walk away I spend five minutes trying, and I mean really trying, to pull this plunger off the bar, which causes even more merriment all round. Eventually we go and sit down at the back where there are some seats and I stick the plunger on the table. Everyone's laughing, Tremayne's still laughing, though I think she was also a little embarrassed. We drink some more and then they start shutting up shop, so I pick up my plunger and we leave. Much to my annoyance I forget the sweets which really pissed me off, because after you've had all that alcohol you want some sweet food.

We catch a cab back to hers. A flat in a tower block. Not a posh area; we're not talking ghetto, but not upmarket either. Normal, I suppose you'd call it. Don't get me wrong, it was still a nice flat; over here you'd pay a lot of money for this flat. Anyway, we go inside and she puts on Radiohead's *Hail to the Thief*. I'm thinking, this isn't out yet, and she says she downloaded it. I say, "Oh, I really enjoy downloading things", not in any geeky way. I'm thinking, *This girl's cool. She likes pirated material.* In fact it was a famous album cos it was leaked at least a month before it was released, so everyone was like I've got it, I've got it. If you were cool you had that album early. Though of course the die-hard fans were going, 'I don't want to listen to it, it's not mastered correctly' and all that crap.

We talk and talk and then she goes and gets changed and when she comes back I'm now on the sofa and then getting off with her.

Just petting, as it's called (I've no idea why; I thought that's what you do to domesticated animals), and kissing. I'm not sure how the transition from not kissing to kissing happened, but I'm kissing her kissing her kissing her, getting it on getting it on getting it on. Now at this point in my life I've only ever slept with one woman. So I was, even though I would never have admitted it at the time, really kinda like, I don't really know what I'm doing. I mean obviously you know what you're doing, but you don't KNOW what you're doing. Now I'd be a helluva lot more confident. But back then I was not as self-assured as I would be now because my experience was not that high. And so I have to be honest with you I was quite relieved, bearing in mind my lack of confidence and also the germ thing, when she said, "I really want to sleep with you but I'm afraid I can't because it's my time."

However, me being drunk and an absolute moron, I said, "Whuut djoo meen?" So she explains and I say OK and nothing further happens and she goes to bed.

I wake up in the morning on the sofa, hungover, not feeling great at all. She's still in bed so I go to her bedroom down the corridor and knock on the door. She's still lying there in some nightdress thing and says, "Come and lay with me." Her room is very white; white sheets, metal-framed bed. The décor is Bohemian, arty, but the overall look is clean and white. Her kitchen wasn't like that. It had green and vibrant colours and lots of pots hanging up, and you could see she liked cooking. In fact the bedroom was the only white room in the flat. The lounge, where I'd slept, had bare wood flooring sanded smooth. It was not that stuff that you lay down to look like wood; it was proper polished wood. It also had this, again, not hippy but arty feel to it. I don't know if you need all these details, but I'll give 'em to you anyway. The sofa had a suede throw on it, there was a nice stereo, knick-knacks, rugs, TV, not plasma or anything like that, pictures and photos and masses of books on wall-to-wall bookshelves which hit your field of vision as soon as you walked in. I also remember going in her bathroom and sticking the plunger on her wooden flooring cos it had really good suction.

Anyway, I lie down with her, and we both fall asleep again. I do remember her waking up and stroking my hair. It was nice. I slept with my clothes on, naturally. I mean, it wasn't gonna go no further, and she knew that. I remember saying something like, "I promise," something or other, and she instantly got annoyed.

"Matt, don't promise me that. Don't promise me anything. I don't want you to promise me nothing." It was weird. It was the only thing she was uncool about. Everything else she didn't care, she would roll with any punch. Not many women would back you up all of a sudden with some kind of crazy magazine crap. This girl could hustle. But the only thing she did have a problem with was when I said, 'I promise'.

Anyway it got to about four o'clock in the afternoon and she said, "Look, I'd really like to lie around with you all day, but I've got to get up and do some work, so I'm gonna have to kick you out."

"Oh. OK."

She then says, "You know, you're cute, but you're an overthinker."

"How do you mean?"

"I watched you sleep for ages. Man, you've got some troubles."

"Why is that?"

And she told me that all the time I was sleeping I was twitching like a motherfucker.

"What's happening in your dreams?"

"I don't remember any of it. Why?"

"Man, you were like this," and she demonstrates some kind of palsied Tourette spasmodic twitching thing, exaggerating for effect. "Man, I can tell you're an overthinker." Then she added, "And you're incredibly mischievous as well."

"No I'm not, not really. It's only when I'm drunk."

And then I start to worry, "Oh man, what did I do last night?", you know, why did I do that, why did I do this, why did I do that, why did I do this?

"That's what I mean. You're an overthinker."

71

"Whaddya mean?"

"Well, man, you've done it. Did you have a good time?"

"Yeah, but why did I do it?"

"Why does it matter why you did it? You did it anyway, and it was entertaining."

And that was it.

Oh yes, one other thing. In the lounge I'd seen lots of pictures of her with all these other men, and suddenly I thought, *Oh no I've got AIDS.* But then how could I have got AIDS? But that worried me for weeks afterwards. Cos I had this cut on my lip when I'd been getting off with her, and suddenly I'm thinking, *Man, what if some of her blood had got into that cut?* It is a possibility, but apparently it's not high and therefore not worth worrying about. The chances are slim. But, you know, you could go for ten years with AIDS with nothing happening, and then all of a sudden… It was not like it was gushing blood. It was just a cut. It wasn't oozing and pussing blood everywhere. It couldof been no more than a cracked lip. But it hurt when I touched it with my tongue. And it had been bleeding before. And I mean you could shake someone's hand and be unlucky. If you've got an open wound, that is. My head doctor told me a while back that once the saliva has mixed in with it and other stuff, there isn't any real chance of infection. But I didn't actually mention this specific incident. So I think I'll have to ask him again next time I see him.

We parted badly, really. I don't mean we fell out or anything; but it's always awkward when you've slept round someone's house and you don't know them. It's always that thing like, are we gonna see each other again or not? I mean, it's obvious you're not gonna have some kind of relationship with them, because that's not what the whole thing's about.

Anyway she calls a cab, takes me down to the door, I hug her, she kisses me goodbye, I get into the cab and the cab drives off. After we've turned the block the cabbie asks me, "Wuz that yer girl?"

"Oh no, only met her last night."

72

"Good for you, kid. Dja sleep with her?"

"Kinda."

"Great. What's with the plunger?"

And that became our next major topic of conversation. I mean, he was a crazy mother like all taxi drivers. You know, "What's the plunger for? Is that for your girlfriend? Did you fuck her with it? I tell you how to have sex with these women."

"How do you have sex with these women?"

"You treat them nice. You take them to a nice restaurant. You don't want no girl you sleep with on the first date." And he gave me the whole advice thing.

One other thing I remember about Tremayne. I was talking to her about my film script, *born2run*, which I said had been rejected by about fifteen hundred producers, despite all the effort I'd put in and the number of places I'd been to and people I'd hustled and pitched it in front of, etc., etc., and she was not sympathetic at all. It was like, "You've done fucking nothing. You've walked just this far up the mountain to success. Man, shut the fuck up and just get on with it. Stop being so soppy and just suck it up. Fuck that. Fuck them not liking it. Just get on with it." She was a tough lady. She'd taken her script to Sundance, been introduced to Tarantino, and he had cut her dead. But it didn't bother her any; she just went ahead and made it anyway. I don't know if it was any good or not – but that's not the point. She taught me a lot, this Boston lady. I mean, who's to judge if this script or that movie or this life is any good or not. So stop whining and just get on with it.

Chapter Eight

Willin'

Destroying history

I've had a history of shit jobs. I've always worked since I was young and the first job I ever had was when I was twelve, washing cars on a Saturday morning in a garage down the road. Start at eight, finish at two. It was pretty rubbish; I should have seen it as a sign of things to come.

When I was fourteen I had a job at an antiques warehouse shifting furniture around and loading and unloading the lorry. Twenty pounds a day cash in hand. I didn't particularly like going to work; it was boring, especially in the summer holidays when you want to be out doing other things, and the pay's not particularly great. So one day, I must've just been sixteen at the time because it was right after my GCSEs, I took along my cousin, Louis, for company. I thought we might have some fun. I checked it out with Sam, the manager, who was really the owner, but he was like, no, we don't need him. So I asked if Louis could come anyway, and eventually Sam said OK, but he won't get paid. Louis wasn't doing anything and the money lack of didn't worry him, so off we go.

We get to the warehouse. Louis was the same age as me but skinny, not as stocky. There was another guy there at the warehouse called Gerry. He was sleeping with Sam's sister hence had a job there. He was a Goth, mid-thirties, slicked-back greased jet-black hair, sort of eighties skinny jeans, really tight, like they'd been sprayed on, and big black boots. This is his dress code every day. Gerry was a sadistic bastard. He'd say to you, "Take that up those stairs," knowing full well you're never going to be able to do it, and he'd just stand there and watch you suffer. You know, like the big single chair in a three-piece suite; you have to have it so that the bit you'd normally sit down on is facing you, then you lift it up onto your head, so you're basically wearing it like a hat, and then you carry it. That's the technique, the key to which is the head as support. But at that age these things are bloody heavy, and the stairs were steep and narrow.

So there we are. We've got to unload the lorry. We unload the lorry, the lorry goes off then comes back later on, and we need to load the lorry back up. And Gerry goes, "It's the chest of drawers five rows down." Now in the warehouse everything is stacked three or four high; wardrobe, chest of drawers, roll-top desk, glass-front display cabinet, you know, something else, something else etc. So it's high and the rows are only about a metre and a half wide. Everything is packed in. So we go five rows down and of course Gerry is like, yup, it's the bottom thing.

Now here I am with my cousin who has never lifted anything in his life trying to pick up this stuff, and his little muscles are proper straining trying to move it at all. Deathtrap waiting to happen really. We get the top thing down and we have to shift that out the way. Other thing down; shift that out the way. Then we've got this final thing, a three-drawer chest of drawers, solid wood, weighs a ton. We both try to pick it up. I'm picking it up; I'm struggling like hell. Louis is groaning out, "Can't do it, can't do it!" and puts his end down. I say, OK we'll PUSH it. So I'm now pushing it, but he's getting nowhere. So I say to him, OK you push and I'll drag, cos he can't get it round this corner. We come to the end and he jumps over, I jump over. And I'm now dragging this thing round the corner, but he can't get any leverage to push it.

I remember the next sequence like it was all in slow motion. He puts his hand on the chest of drawers, then puts his hand on the coffee table behind him, then he goes to push the table one

75

way, but it doesn't move that way and his hand instead moves it the other way. I remember it all vividly. It started with the table going clck clck clck clck clck then the thing on top of that going crck crck crck crck then just going PPPRRWWW PPRRWWW PPRRWWWWWWWW and then it was literally just CRASH after CRASH after CRASH for fifty seconds. CCCKKKKR-RRRRRRRR CRRWWWCCCCKKRRR KSSHHHSHHH-HSHHH. Smashing glass, splintered wood. You could hear it CCCCCKKKKEEEEERRRRRRRTCHTCHHHHHHHH!!! It was like one of those stunts in the movies where the director says; let's get this one right because we're only going to get one go. You know, let's cover it with fifteen cameras, because we're only going to be doing this once. It was on that scale.

Then I remember, painfully I have to say, and I'm not even adding this for effect, the noise finally stopping, and I'm feeling, at least it's come to an end at last, I can now breathe again, you know, and I was almost sighing out loud with relief at that point. And then I saw a final thing, a little pot cupboard, poised on the edge of falling, go clck clck clck clck, checking out the options, before finally selecting pot-cupboard oblivion, and taking as many other things with it as it could, with a CCCCCKKKKEEEEERRRRRRRTCHTCHHHHHHHH, setting the whole place off in motion again for another fifteen seconds. And I'm just looking on helplessly and thinking, *NOOOOOOOOOO!!! WHYYYYYYYYYY????*

Sam runs out and goes, "What the fuck was that?"An atomic dust cloud has appeared inside the warehouse, hovering over the strewn wreckage below. Louis is now crying and he's gone and hidden in the lorry. Sam's scared the crap out of him. I'm just standing there like a slack puppet whose strings have all been cut except the one keeping him upright, incapable of the simplest motion in any part of my anatomy, but stuck with a stupid, embarrassed smile that's frozen on my face. "What the fuck have you done? Get the fuck out of my sight." Sam normally never loses his temper; but I've just destroyed half the warehouse.

76

Eventually Sam goes, "Get in there and sort it out." And me and Louis start trying to clean it all up with potato sacks and a shovel. That's all we had. It took us ages to tidy everything up. It was just bag after bag after bag, and throwing it all into the skip, cos this furniture was beyond restoration. It was just splinters, shards of glass, dust, and we had to scrape everything up. Everything. It was like someone had just dropped a bomb in the middle and there was this blast area within a twenty-metre radius of the epicentre, which was where me and Louis had been standing. Wardrobes with glass fronts smashed, gone. The structural integrity still there, but the doors all splintered and broken through. Eight-by-six-foot gold-framed mirrors smashed in. I probably got about a hundred years bad luck that day. The smaller items obliterated, unidentifiable. You know, you'd look at it wondering, what was this once? It was a war zone. Legs everywhere, crushed and snapped in jagged fragments. Drawers pushed out and lying in bits on the floor. It was epic.

The problem was things falling onto things, you know, the little thing falls down first, then a bigger thing would fall onto the little thing, knocking something else off which falls onto another thing and knocks something else off; the whole domino effect. I can remember at the end of the day Sam came up to me and said, "You've ruined five grand of stock." And I knew this was no exaggeration. I mean, I was the most expensive employee of the day, if not the year, chewing up five grand of stuff. But I think he could tell I was distraught, and he maybe even felt a little guilty, because I was a mess. I mean, I wasn't crying; because I was too shocked to cry. I was just, you know, 'Fuck.' This was, like, the single worst thing I've ever done. It was bad. And it was mega. Some of this furniture was probably nineteen-thirties; so I'd destroyed history as well as money.

I went home early because Sam was obviously very angry with me. Mum was really angry with me, too. Sam wouldn't speak to Mum when she came to pick me up, cos I didn't drive at the time. But then, after the calm had set in, Sam came up to me and said quietly, "I'm never going to fire you, Matt," because he was, you know, a friend of my dad's, and also I think he knew I was really upset. I mean, I was only a kid; if Gerry had done it, for example, or one of the other men, I think there would've been more hell to pay.

And in fairness to Sam he's a very laid-back guy. He's one of those people who'll be angry with you for a day; you'll go in the next day, and everything's fine, it's all forgotten. Maybe he took into account that he had two fifteen/sixteen-year-olds trying to lug huge furniture around, and we were only trying our best. Losing five grand of stock must have hurt. But it wasn't like we were grown men throwing it about and causing an accident. I don't know why he was so cool about it, but he was. Probably just wrote the loss off. Maybe thought, I've got some space in here now. You know, every crisis is an opportunity, and all that crap. I don't know. I got a lot of stick at the warehouse though, and from that day on my name was Smasher. 'Alright, Smasher?' 'Smasher, come on we're going.' 'Smasher, get the other end of that.' But of course it was the kind of environment where nicknames were a big thing; everyone had to have a nickname.

Working at the warehouse was something I did in the summers to earn some quick money, but after I left college I didn't work there for a while. Then I found myself experiencing a liquidity squeeze and went back, but this time Sam put me on the lorries at thirty pounds a day. I liked working on the lorries, because I got out and about, and because I was with Arthur. Everyone called him 'Art', or 'Artie', but I always called him Arthur, cos I've never liked nicknames, especially with mine being 'Smasher'. So as a mark of respect I called Arthur, 'Arthur'. 'Course he still called me Smasher; but nonetheless I felt I was making my stand against the dominant culture.

What happened was I was on the dole and needed a job. I'd just bought myself a Mamiya 645 Pro 120 film camera, and that had taken up the last of my savings. Because of my age I qualified to go on this thing called New Deal, which was basically some bullcrap thing where they send people along to learn how to write a CV and I did not want to be going to this. And not only that, they'd send you to things like numeracy and English classes which I knew was just going to be a bunch of people that didn't want to be there; you know, it was not going to be the highest of educational experiences. So there's no way I'm going along to that. I say to the lady at the unemployment office, how do I get out of this? And she says, the only way out of it is if you stop claiming. So I just say, OK, done. She looks a bit surprised, so I repeat, I don't wanna go to this, so sign me out. She just goes, ohmmm. She was really not expecting my response. It was one of those things where I was doing it cos I wanted to win the argument; but afterwards I was like, crap, now what am I gonna do?

So I went to Sam and said I was desperate for a job, told him the whole truth about why, and my not wanting to do this New Deal crap, said I only wanted to make roughly what I was getting on the dole, so, you know, even if he could only give me one and a half days' work a week I'd be able to survive. Cos I had no overheads at the time. Not like now. Didn't have car insurance, phone bills, any of that, so I could live very, very cheaply. So he said, OK, I'll give you one day a week, which was thirty pounds, which was about what I was getting on the dole. And then one day soon turned to two days and two days to three days. And what also happened was slowly I moved from working in the warehouse to being on the lorry with Arthur.

Arthur wasn't getting on well with his driver's mate, who just moaned all the time; you know, I don't get paid enough, I hate this job. 'Course I can now see how one comes to that cycle, cos that's how I eventually became. But, anyway, Arthur picked to go out with me more than this other guy for the simple fact that the other guy just irritated him. And I looked up to Arthur in a big way. He was one of the best and most honest people I've ever met. Maybe not honest in terms of how he gets his job done, but what I mean is he would never do anything to hurt anybody, and it always seemed to me that he would look out for me. And not only that, he had an enthusiasm for life that I enjoyed. He would always want to chat and talk about stuff; you could talk to Arthur about anything. I don't think he was the best-read person, you know, he didn't have the best of education; but you could sit down with him and tell him about Kerouac, and he'd be interested. He may never ever read any of JK's works, but you could sit down with Arthur and go, I'm reading this book, and you'd tell him about it, and he'd say, oh, sounds quite cool. Whereas you know what some people are like; oh, what's that fucking bullcrap, what ya reading that for? Arthur wasn't like that. Or we'd talk about movies. Again, a lot of the films Arthur was in to I wasn't in to; but that didn't matter, cos it was just like an open discussion. He was into sorta comedies and kung fu and violent films; but I kind of enjoy those films at a certain level as well anyway.

And where I overthought everything known to man, Arthur didn't. He could break things down in a way I couldn't. You know, I'd go to him totally headdone about some girl, and he was the best cure for headdone. Seriously, I swear to you. A girl would be messing with my head in a mega way and literally an hour in the lorry talking to Arthur and I'd be like, how the fuck did I not see that? He'd just break it down into, this is why she is doing this, and that's why she needs to do that, and even if he was wrong he sounded so damn sure that he was right, without being arrogant at all, just very clear-headed, that I found it just incredibly reassuring.

And Arthur also got me on to hamburgers. Again I worry about everything, whereas he'd worry about very little. And one of the things that he enjoyed was roadside cafes. And I would be afraid to go to a roadside cafe. One, they look scary, and unless you've got a lorry you don't kind of feel right about going in, and the customers also look a bit scary; but not only that, the knives and forks in there aren't too clean. But I enjoy fry-ups as such, and after you've been lifting furniture all day it's the best place to go ever. And Arthur would know. I always said to Arthur he should write the book of Kent Cafes. And he would write the ultimate guide. Because it's like a secret underworld society. There'd be a shack he would pass every day, and unless you were a lorry driver you'd never know it was a roadside cafe. It just looked like a container. It was a container. But inside there'd be two fat ladies. And they'd have names that suited. Arthur'd go, OK, let's go to Mean Jeans. And I'd go, Mean Jeans? And it was because the two ladies in there were called Jean, and they were mean. Both of them. So it would be Mean Jeans. Or he'd say, let's go to Mercury's. And I'd say, what's Mercury's? And it's because the guy in there behind the counter looked like Freddie Mercury. It was this bizarre world of cafes that Arthur introduced me to and it was fun and amazing.

But when we couldn't find one of these cafes we'd wanna burger. And Arthur was always on the bizarrest of diets. He'd have a hamburger and just eat the meat. And he was convinced and swore to me that that was OK, because he didn't eat the bun and the cheese. I can see the logic; very Atkins. You know, cutting out the carbs. But I said to him, it's still a McDonald's burger; I'm sure it's still not good for you. And he'd just say, shut up. But he wasn't overweight or anything. He was stocky and he'd always say that me and him were the right sort of size for lifting work. You know, low centre of gravity. You don't wanna be too tall, cos you're gonna get back problems. You wanna be short, large, thick legs and bulk up here. You know, like the English archers at Agincourt. And we were about the same sort of size, so that made me feel a bit better about my body image. The other guys that worked on the lorries were tall and lanky, and you could tell they weren't the carthorses that me and Arthur had the physical shape of.

For someone who lifted furniture all day, Arthur was typical sort of broad, thick arms, balding, so with shaven head, and about five-nine. Short and stocky. You wouldn't wanna fight him; he'd rip ya head off. That was the other thing I liked about Arthur. He had this sort of calming, straightforward, nice nature; but if you upset him he'd whack you over the head. He didn't ever do it to me, but there were several times when he would get angry and I would worry it was gonna kick off. Mainly with other antique dealers. Arthur was very protective over that lorry. And he would get annoyed if someone tried to load something onto it. He'd say, what the fuck d'ya think you're doing? And the other guy would go, Sam said it would be OK to put this on here. And Arthur'd say, well I haven't heard from Sam, and I've already got stuff to put on there. Anything you put on I've got to take off, so unless I hear from Sam that it's going on there, you're not putting it on there. Oh come on, get out the way, Art. Don't you tell me to get out the way. I'm not having it put on there because I'm the one that's got to carry it off. How much are you going to pay me to take that there? It's petrol we're using up. You're not fucking putting it on. And it's escalating, escalating, escalating, and there were several times where there would be some pushing and shoving. And as I said you wouldn't wanna fight Arthur; honestly, if he smacked you your head would fall off. I would muckaround fight with him, and every now and then he'd wind me, and I'd be like, Jeeeesus, Arthur! And it'd be like, OK, OK, I don't actually wanna play this game any more. Cos you'd think you were pretty quick, then all of a sudden he'd just go BANG and you're instantly doubled up wheeeeeezing and fighting for breath. Every now and again he'd just show you that you don't even know what you're playing with, cos if he wanted to he could hurt you.

On a typical day we'd turn up at the warehouse and the lorry would be empty and we'd load it up. And again it was like a very straightforward mindset that Arthur had. He'd see it all like a game of Tetris. You know, you have all these shapes that you've got to interlock. So on the lorry there would be all these different bits of furniture that he would get to interlock and fit. Arthur was very good at that. I mean, I'd just be like, let's put this and this on there and there, and get going, and he'd be like, no, slow down, then he'd start visualising how it all went together to pack it in and tie it together, with the rope passing round the outside of this cabinet, threading through that settee arm and looping through the leg of that rolltop desk, before hooking onto one of the wooden ties attached to the lorry's inside lining. And he'd also have to factor in the day's delivery schedule and make sure the last drops were

82

at the back of the lorry and the first ones at the front. You know, it was quite a mental task. It would've been a helluva lot easier if everything had been on pallets; but you can't put furniture on pallets, because it's all irregular shapes, and that's why it was like Tetris. No pallets and no forklift truck; everything had to be loaded on, arranged and secured, and loaded off by hand. It was almost an art form and Arthur was its Picasso.

If the drop-off was an auction house that was nice and easy: drive to one place, unload it, half done, go to another place, unload it, done. And at an auction house you could take it off more quickly than if you had to go to customers, which could be more of a pain in the ass, because you would be dropping off at individual locations which could be anywhere from a council house to the biggest mansion you've ever seen. And that would be a different dynamic, unlike when we went to auction rooms to, say, pick up, because obviously we were sometimes picking up furniture loads from auctions, and that could be quite stressful and hard work, because you've got a queue of other lorries picking up for other antique dealers, so there's no dilly-dallying. You gotta be getting it on there quick, cos other people want to get into your spot, load up and go home. But when you went to a house you had to be on your best behaviour and more things could go wrong, and if they didn't it was only because Arthur was so good at it.

I remember one time we had to drop a sideboard off at a house where this guy lived with his wife who was an opera singer, quite a successful one, cos the house was automatic-gated and palatial, even though it was out in the sticks. He was Italian and his dad was some Scottish ice-cream maker. You know, his dad was Italian and obviously came over to Scotland. So he had money and his wife had money. And this sideboard cost thousands. It had this enormous ornate mirror piece on the back and it was solid; this was not a cheap piece, and it weighed an absolute ton. And not only that but the house was spotless, so we really had to give it maximum care and attention.

I remember we had to go up the staircase and there was this bend. The ceiling was really low, making it even harder for us to manoeuvre. And it was just the sheer breaking point of the pressure of you can't drop it, but you really want to, cos you're dying, and I would always go upstairs backwards, and I remember groaning and just being like, I'm gonna drop it, I'm gonna drop it, and Arthur saying calmly, you're not going to drop it, you're not going to drop it, keep going, keep going, and me saying, I can't hold it, I can't hold it, and him again, don't drop it, don't drop it, and sweat literally just pouring off, and your muscles telling you, let go of it, let go of it, let go of it, and you are just willing yourself, saying to yourself out loud, can't let go of it, can't let go of it, can't let go of it, because one, you'd squash Arthur, who would've been instantly flattened under the weight, and two, you'd be in deep shit; and then you finally get up there, put it down, and you're just kind of amazed. Because it's been so stressful, and yet rewarding. All you've done is move a piece of furniture fifty feet or whatever; but you know that you've beaten something. Your own body was saying you can't do this and you need to put this down; but you overcame all that and countermanded the instruction. I mean, you ached all over, especially the next day, but somehow it had been worth it; you felt good about yourself. You'd come through.

Eventually I fell out with Sam when I asked for a pay rise. After working about a year on the lorry I called up and said, and this was not unreasonable, look, I'm only getting thirty pound a day; I can't live on thirty pound a day; I want thirty-five. And he said, nope. So I said, then I'm not coming in. And he said, so are you coming in tomorrow then? And I said, nope. And he said, we need you tomorrow, we're really busy. So I said, thirty-five pound a day. Nope. I'm not coming in then.

And Sam didn't talk to me for that for longer than when I smashed up all his furniture. And I'm talking months. He'd come round and we'd be like:

"Alright."

"Alright."

And that'd be the end of our conversation. He was mighty pissed off about it. And my mum was like, you've really upset Sam.

"Well, he shouldof paid me thirty-five pound a day."

"He was already doing you a favour giving you a job."

"He wasn't doing me any favours paying me thirty quid a day, was he?"

"It's better than nothing."

"Yeah, but I was working hard and it was below the minimum wage."

You can see how the argument went back and forth. In hindsight, maybe I was a little rash. And maybe I shouldof said, OK, but tomorrow's gonna be my last day. Maybe I shouldof said, I can't live on this, I'm gonna have to find myself another job, thanks for giving me this job, but unless you can give me thirty-five pound a day I'm afraid I'm going to have to call it quits. But I didn't do that. I did it the Matt Pearce extreme way, all or nothing, tried bargaining, tried the, you need me, pay me thirty-five pound a day, and he was willing to say no, and I weren't willing to back down.

So, yeah, in hindsight I do regret that. Sam was nice enough to give me a job when I needed one. But when I think it through properly, there was an element in me that felt I was being a little taken advantage of; well, not that exactly, but he wasn't a good payer on time. By that I mean that if I worked a full week, I'd say I need my money, and he'd say I haven't got it. He would be like that. Even though I'd worked my week at the agreed thirty pounds a day and only wanted what I'd earned. I mean, I wasn't saying, can you lend me some money, or can you give me the week that's coming's money? I just wanted what I was owed. And I wanted it for the weekend, naturally. But every week this was a mission, and that became a major stressor. I mean, it was a physically demanding job that I didn't particularly like anyway; I wasn't getting paid that much, and to cap it all off I always had this thing in the back of my mind about whether I was actually going to get paid on Friday, or was I gonna get fobbed off with, you'll have it next week, you'll have it next week. And the dangerous thing was to give in and say, OK, for fuck's sake, give it to me next Friday, because now they've got double the money to give to you, so they are even less likely, one, to have it, and two, go and get it. I remember many times it was like, I need my money, oh, I'll give it to you Monday, no, I need it now, oh we haven't got it now, then we're gonna have to go to a cash machine, I'm too busy to go to a cash machine, then I'll wait. And I'm waiting and waiting and waiting until eventually they get bored of me sitting there and they have to take me down to a cash machine to get my money just to get rid of me. And all this even though they always carried wads of notes in their pockets, cos it was very much a cash business. Yet still Sam'd say he hadn't got it. This is what I could never fathom. You've got fucking money; I need my money, I've worked my week, so give me my fucking money.

So, yeah, even though I say I do regret it, if I look at all the elements involved, there was a build-up. I was getting more and more pissed off. Every week I'd be like Lee Marvin in *Point Blank*; you know, give me my money, give me my money, I just want my money. Once, they handed my money to some other guy to give to me, and he wouldn't give it to me, you know, holding it back just for fun, like in the school playground. I got so annoyed that I jumped on him and put him in a headlock, and Arthur just stood there laughing, like he was a spectator at some grindhouse wrestling floorshow. I got my money in the end; but you shouldn't have to go through all that just to get paid, should you? So in actual fact, once I take the build-up into account, I don't feel that bad about it.

As I say, Sam reacted far worse to my attempt at pay negotiation than when I wrecked five grand's worth of stock. Cos for Sam the warehouse incident was understandable, whereas this was not understandable. It's one thing to smash up the warehouse; it's another thing to ask for more money. In this world, asking for more money, you don't do that. You're crossing a boundary. Breaking a Mafia code. Accidents happen; but asking for money's not an accident. You need to have made a decision and crossed over that line. You know, knocking a piece of furniture over, you didn't think that through. That was accidental. But to actually sit down and go through the process of thinking, I'm getting fucked over here, I want more money, and then to even bring that to the table; that's not something that you do. You know, I'm already doing you a favour, and you dare ask me for more money. See what I mean? Even if they are underpaying you, that doesn't matter here or there in that culture.

Sam and I get on a bit better now. He comes round, we talk. A little. It's not exactly all forgotten, though, even after all these years.

"Alright."

"Yup."

It's not quite as bad as that, but there's still some tension there. We're not really friends. Something has been lost. And he made me give him back the key to the warehouse.

"I want the key back then."

That was quite major really. Cos now I couldn't take girls back there any more.

Chapter Nine

I Think of Jack

If you want me again look for me under your bootsoles
(Walt Whitman, *Leaves of Grass*)

"Hi, I'm looking for—"

"Jack Kerouac."

The lady in the visitors centre at Edson Cemetery instantly knew as soon as I got there. The cemetery was easy to find because it was massive, probably the largest I've ever been to, and it was the only cemetery in Lowell, half a mile or so outside the town centre. Just inside the wrought-iron gates was a larger-than-life bronze statue of Passaconaway, Chief of the Penacooks, a Native American who supposedly died at the age of 122 and was, according to the plaque, 'a friend of the white man', which must be why they built a statue for him, complete with sculpted feathers and necklace of bear claws, though it was all now greened over with copper carbonate and minus left arm (they got graveyard vandals in Massachusetts, too). There were lots of other posh memorials, including one of a deer, that were really kind of amazing in comparison to the basicness of Kerouac's, which didn't even have a gravestone, just a marker on the ground. But that's probably how JK would've wanted things anyway. If Keats's name was writ in water, Jack's was printed on souls and footsoles. His mother, after all, worked in a shoe factory, so he had the walking gene alright. If he were a painting he'd've been van Gogh's old boots.

Jack's house in Lowell wasn't at all what I was expecting. Don't know why, but I thought it would be like a museum; not Graceland or anything like that, not a tacky shrine for beat pilgrims, but something that would contain some small particle of his spirit within its walls. But in fact it was just a non-descript wood-fronted semi-detached house. It wasn't a typical Lowell house, because Lowell's a shipping town and very brick and Boston-looking. You know, urban and industrial. But Kerouac's house was wood. It wasn't a shack or a cabin. There was brickwork underneath probably; but from the outside all you could see was creamy-white wood with brown window ledges, porch and deck. The door was whitewood with panes of glass and netting. And there was grass and trees all around. It was more like a New England building, which is in fact close by. But there was nothing to say it was Jack Kerouac's house, and all the houses looked the same. I mean, I knew the name of the street (West Street) and the house number where the house should be; but maybe I was looking at the wrong fucking house, who knows? Maybe it had been knocked down and redeveloped, I don't know. It was inhabited, and I didn't wanna go up and knock and ask. That would've been embarrassing for everyone. All I can say is that it was not a posh house; it didn't jump out at you in any way, or make you want to live there.

Don't ask me why, but it kinda reminded me of the house in *Psycho*; you know, the one at the top of the hill behind the Bates Motel. Maybe it was because of the wood and the little porch? Maybe it was because of the unhealthily close mother–son relationship, in JK's case with Mémère, who knows? Maybe I'm just a weirdo.

I got a lift to Lowell from one of the guys I was staying with in Boston. Everyone in America seems to have a nice car. Even the people you wouldn't imagine to have nice cars, they all had brand new ones. They seemed to have them on a lease. You know, they would ask me what car I've got and I would tell them about my Fiesta, and they would ask what year's that?, and I would tell them it was around ten years old, and they would say, WHAT? To them it was unbelievable to drive anything over three years old. It was like the second-hand car market in America just doesn't exist. Obviously they have classics over there; but it's very rare that anyone has a banger. In fact they didn't even know what a banger was. I said, when you get your first car, you always get a crap one, and they were like, no, I got a brand new one, you know, my dad got it for me. But this wasn't just the rich people who were like this; everyone seemed to be. It was like when you got to the point where you wanted to trade your car in, which was after three years max, you traded it in and got a new one on lease. So you were always in this cycle. 'Course, there is that Bruce Springsteen song about driving really crap old cars on *Nebraska*; so maybe things are different in New Jersey. Or Nebraska. But even there the point of the song is that this isn't the perceived norm, which is why you write a song about it in the first place. Could you imagine writing a song about driving an old Fiesta in Freetown? I mean, who doesn't?

Anyway, I got my ride to Lowell and found the cemetery, and, as I said, JK's grave marking wasn't flash at all, just a plaque on the ground surrounded by notes that people had left there along with pens and notebooks and alcohol, even though that was the last thing he needed. I wanted to take some grave dirt away with me and, I know this is a bit gay, but I felt that if I was gonna take that I had to leave something that I had brought along behind. J-J had given me this blue lapis lazuli for good luck before I set out on my travels. It was a cool gemstone, so I thought fair enough. So I dug out the grave dirt and put the stone into a small film canister, as a gesture of, you know, I've taken something out I'm gonna put something back, and also as a way of leaving my mark that I'd been there. I really dug that blue stone deep into the ground and covered it back up. In theory it should still be there.

You feel kinda sombre when you visit someone's grave, so I wrote a little note 'To Jack' and stuck it into the ground, then held a minute's silence in which I just thought about the life.

I'd always known, from J-J and from *On the Road*, that JK had a certain reputation with women; but the letters to and from

Joyce Johnson opened my eyes a bit. I suppose at first, and I hate to use the term and I wouldn't use it now, but I just thought, you know, Kerouac's a cool guy, and he quickly became something of a hero figure for me; but after reading the letters I could see the man had many flaws, and one of them was possibly his treatment of women. He could be harsh and pretty cold towards them; you'd have to say he wasn't particularly nice, even though they all seemed to like him (but isn't that always the way, I find myself wondering bitterly?). But what made it even harsher is that he wasn't consistent in his coldness, which would've made some sorta sense. Instead he'd be really horrible and then instantly like, 'Oh I miss you, I love you', and so on and so forth, and then it would be like, 'Go away!' So in one letter he would lead them on, and then in the next he'd be, like, you know, the opposite. I remember one letter would be about his love for this Joyce Johnson, how he misses her and how he can't wait to see her again, she is just this amazing whatever, and the next letter he sends would be about how he'd just slept with two prostitutes in Mexico and how that was a fantastic soul-connecting experience. And as she points out, it's a kinda weird thing to do; you wouldn't think to send that letter straight after sending the previous one. I remember her saying that one minute it was like he was talking to one of his buddies and the next minute they were lovers, and the next minute they were buddies, and the next minute he's horrible to her, and the next minute he's telling her, oh, you're amazing, I love you. So he was all over the place.

And you can tell it from his books. I mean, he's not a particularly young man; I'm not criticising him, because, you know, I'm not a young man myself any more, and I still live at home, but what I mean is he's well into his late twenties/early thirties and throughout his life he's always got this central home base. A lot of his friends and a lot of the women he's been with have always said he would never ever cut the umbilical cord. His mum was always and forever the only one woman in his life. A lot of women would say they would get to feel close to him, feel that

91

they had a connection, but they always knew underlying it all that they'd never be as close to him as his mother was. You know, if he were ever in dire need it wouldn't be them he'd go to, it would be back home to his mum. And they would never be invited. And that comes across in the letters as well. He always promises Joyce Johnson that he'll take her to see Mémère, but never does. But he'll go there for a three-week recovery. Like he'll go to Mexico, go crazy, travel the country; but he'll need that three weeks back home in the comfort and the safety of his mother's arms. I don't mean that literally; but to a certain degree that's what it amounts to. William Burroughs once said that Kerouac's biggest problem is that he will never cut loose from his mother's apron strings. He was always a mother's boy; never took after his father at all, apparently.

And also, I think it's got a lot to do with the fact that he had an older brother that died. Jack grieved like crazy, even though he was only five years old. Normally you'd think a small child would just get over it – well, not get over it exactly, but handle it better than if he truly understood the ramifications of a close family member passing away; but JK really felt the loss and wrote a book about his brother, *Visions of Gerard*, who was nine when he died. And the gap in age between Jack and Gerard was about the same as that between Jack and Neal Cassady, and Jack is always referring to Neal as his brother. So Jack was deeply affected by Gerard's death in, as he puts it, an almost spiritual sense, and after that period his mother became the major centrepiece in his life. You know, from that point onwards the connection he had with his mum intensified, along with his relationship with his cat. He really loved that cat with a passion; in *Big Sur* JK describes Tyke, the cat, as his second brother.

When you first read *On the Road* you think of this easygoing, relaxed adventurer; not relaxed in the sense of can't be bothered, but full of energy, full of life, nothing can get him down, hit the road whatever. But as I've read more of his books and also done research into the man himself, I began to realise that for quite a lot of his life he was just a depressive drunk. So quite the opposite of how he appears in *On the Road*. But the weird thing is he doesn't lie in his books. Maybe that was just how he was feeling at the time in *On the Road*; full of YES!, full of hope, full of dreams and yearnings. Yet as you go through his books they get more and more and more depressing, and full of more and more alcohol-related stupors. Full of woe and no. And in reality if you read *On the Road* carefully you can see he's actually got a depressive view throughout, and he's also a bit of a git; I mean, what about that Mexican girl he lives with and then just gets up and walks away from, washing his hands of her? That's another confusing thing. He talks about how he could settle down in Selma and marry Bea, but in the end he realises that's all bullcrap; he's just living in a fantasy. When push comes to shove he's like, fuck this, I'm off. And he does, doesn't he? And in the end it's kind of insulting to those people that work day and night, and he's like, I could get used to this, you know, picking cotton in the blue morning air, chorus of birds singing, the beauty of the sere brown crop, bending to it beneath the snow-capped mountain, kneeling down in the earth, I knew I'd found my life's work etc.; and you think, get real, Jack, you're not a man of the soil, and they ain't doing it for the fun of it, or the holiness of it, or the poetry of it, or whatever. They're doing it cos they ain't got nothing else they can do. You know, give them a choice; they probably wouldn't be doing it. But he insists on finding some kind of this-is-the-promised-land feeling to it all; and you think, come on, grow up. You know, they're doing this because they gotta; not because they necessarily wanna, or because they believe it's the right way to live.

And yet despite all this you come away uplifted; and not only that, you come away with, yes, yes, YES, I wanna experience life. I don't think you come away with that from any of his other books, though. So I think of Jack as a one-book novelist, even though he wrote loads more. I know: I sat down at a ramshackle formica worksurface in a Portakabin just off a two-mile section of the London-bound A2 and read through them all, one by one.

I think of Jack Kerouac as a child all his life. He says somewhere in *On the Road*, that everyone starts off as a sweet child and then

93

the nightmares of life break in around you, when you least expect them, and the rest is just managing the trauma. JK knew all about that, which is why he drank so much, why anyone drinks so much. To block out the memory and the pain. But he was also the tenderest of mothers to his own sweet child, which, like a Mémère of his own, he would nurse through every crisis, never give up on, always forgive, and never abandon, because that child carried all his hopes and dreams, without which he would have been truly lost and forsaken, whichever kind of road he travelled down. And that sweet child was his soul, which, as Henry Corso says on a DVD about Jack, is a tough, tough baby. The soul is made of stronger and tougher material than anything mankind can possibly imagine or manufacture. It endures everything, survives everything, surpasses everything that life can throw at it, including death. But you have to care for and keep tender with that baby, nurture it always like a plant. Cos all that you've got is your soul.

And that reminds me of something J-J once told me. J-J said that life is sort of lived backwards. Do you know what I mean? Maybe you don't. Nor did I at first. Apparently it means we're perfect before we're born, with all the wisdom of the cosmos, and then we pass through that birth canal and forget everything, instantly, which is why you get traumatised and spend your life trying to go back. And all your life you desperately keep trying to relearn what you once knew, before you were born, and have now forgotten. And you never do. But the trying is everything. I explained all this to a pretty evangelist girl I met on one of my long-haul Greyhound bus journeys across the big, sprawling American Midwestern night, a travelling speck moving-yet-not-moving along a vast red plain. She didn't believe a word of what I said. But I was just passing on to her what I'd learnt from J-J, my source of wisdom in all things spiritual.

J-J also told me that the reason we are limited in what we can learn in this life is that we inhabit a fallen world. It was not created by God, but by someone else. Not the Devil, exactly, but someone called the demiurge, who thought that he was God, and

94

probably had the best of intentions, but just wasn't up to scratch. And that's why the world is such a botched job. You know, as Woody Allen said, the best you can say about God is he's an underachiever. This is known as the Gnostic heresy; but it isn't a heresy at all, it's fucking common sense. I mean, look around. Does this world look like the work of the hand of God, or a bodge job? Apparently a lot of cool people like Alfred Hitchcock and Christopher Marlowe believed in this theory. Martin Scorsese kinda does, too, but concludes that we're all fucked anyway, so get used to it, which I kind of think is a cop out, but I ain't gonna disagree with him. As J-J put it, all you can do is keep your own tiny spark of light burning, that single still-glowing ember that is like an almost extinct but tenaciously clinging residual memory from your timeless cosmic consciousness, the faintest of whispers, the faroffest of echoes, the smallest of microdrops of spiritual fallout, that sweet child, your soul, no matter how much darkness the world tries to bury it in.

I think JK was an eternal child, not always sweet, but what do you expect? Kids will be kids. Hence his weird relationship with Mémère. I mean, he was a hopeless parent himself; a non-existent father to his only real child, his daughter, Jan. But you can't really blame him, since he could never be anything other than a child himself all his days. And she probably understood that, cos she became a writer, too. And a substance abuser as well, unfortunately.

I think of Jack Kerouac as a sad person. I mean, look at the life: dead at forty-two, drunk, living at home with your mother. I'm not one of those people who say, forget the life, look at the art. I say, give me a good life every time. Like my head doctor says, a good life doesn't mean millions – which of course Kerouac eventually made, or wouldof. I read somewhere that his estate is now the richest in the world. But when life deals you a loser's hand, as it did JK, then you have to have compassion for whatever it takes and took to survive. Cos he had a bum hand all right. But who knows who dealt it? God? Karma? His own soul? Who

95

knows who deals out our lives? All of us carry somewhere inside something of Jack's pain as well as his heavengoing yea-saying yawping exultation. It's in our DNA.

So I just stood there for a quiet minute bending over his plaque in the soft Lowell rainfall under a pearl-grey April sky, as a tender wind blew gently off the sweet Merrimack River, thinking of Jack Kerouac, thinking of Jack Kerouac, thinking always of Jack Kerouac.

Chapter Ten

Shit Job #2

Of the four types of alienation in labour under capitalism, the first is the alienation of the worker from the work he produces, or from the product of his labour
(Karl Marx, *Economic and Philosophic Manuscripts of 1844*)

Finding the time to read JK's books was down to another of my shit jobs: keeping an eye on three multi-camera-setup CCTV screens, eight hours a shift. I had to watch out in case of car breakdowns along a stretch of roadworks where the traffic had to be kept flowing at all costs. It was quite literally a shit job, in that many of the guys who also worked there had an unusual preoccupation with that particular excretory function, which I suppose eased the boredom and offered distraction from a routine of otherwise almost total sensory deprivation. Horizons shrink in that kind of ambience, just like in prison. As for me, I had *The Dharma Bums* and *Big Sur* to get me through my captivity.

It all came about once again through my experiences at the Jobcentre. I go down there; get in the queue. I tell you what, it's not like what you see in *EastEnders*, *Coronation Street*, *Brookside*, *The Bill* or any of them TV programmes. They're actually nice people behind the counters. And to be honest with you, they don't really care that you're unemployed, except for the keen ones who love their job and see it as, like, must impress, you know, this is my job and I need to be seen to be carrying it out properly. The people I like going down there and seeing are more like, ah, no work this week, doesn't matter, bye. But the keen ones are like, we have this new jobsearch. And you say to them, but we're not gonna find anything there, are we? That's not the attitude, dear boy. Then they go and look; nothing there. And I'm like, what did I say? They: worth trying though, wasn't it? Me: no, you just wasted twenty minutes of my life. And then you leave. Whereas the people I like are, ain't no point, really, is there? No. You know, those people, they're just cool.

The best is old ladies that don't know how to use computers. You know, you sit down, act ultra-polite. Cos this is the thing I don't understand. People go in there like, fucking 'ell, got me outta bed, didn't ya, mate?, fucking 'ell, ain't never gonna find me a fucking job anyway, are ya? And of course what they get back is: 'labouring work, really hard, yours.' And they go, aauugghhhh! Whereas if you go down there, wait, duck and dive the queue a little bit, you know, you go first, you go first, no, you go first, until there's an old-lady-free moment, and then whooosh you're in there.

"Hello, how are you?"

"Nice. How are you?" And they're shocked with the politeness. You see them almost fall off their chair. "I haven't seen you here before. Are you new?" You know, get her as far away from looking for a job for you as possible.

Get her talking about what she had for dinner last night or whatever until she suddenly goes, "Oh no, the computer seems to have crashed," partly due to the fact that I've been distracting her for the past ten minutes. It hasn't been that long, but what I mean is, it's better to be in there for ten minutes talking about something else than ten minutes trying to find you a job, cos that depresses the hell out of you, and you wanna get out of there; you know, you wanna pretend that you're not there.

So you're talking to her and she's like, OK, right, BOOMP, BOOMP, the computer's crashed. "You probably know more about this than me, ha ha!" And I'm just sitting there thinking, yup, yup. So time's ticking, time's ticking, no time for a jobsearch, keep running the clock down, until she goes, OK, just sign here. Done. Took me ten minutes. Not twenty-five. Not thirty, as with the keen ones. That's a bit harsh. I mean, they're not arsy or anything; they're nice and polite. But they're keen; and you don't want keen.

They always come up with mad stuff. One lady that I quite liked when I went in there said, "We've had a couple of people like you. In between contracts?" and I'm like, yeah, and she's like, "It was four people we had. Three of them have found work in television and the other one I think still comes in." And she seemed nice, not horrible or anything, not looking like she's thinking, you're scum, or anything like that, and so I'm like, OK, and she's like, "OK. Right, shall we bother with a jobsearch?" And I'm like, ummm, because I'm kinda feeling GUILTY now because she's done that 'shall we?' thing, and I couldn't find it in myself to say no. Because she's given me that power, and I just didn't want to let her down. So I just say, "OK, let's do one," in the smallest voice I could find, but not so small she couldn't hear it at all.

And she says, "Probably not gonna find anything, are we? OK, let's not."

And I'm, "No, let's do it," like the tiniest dormouse now, and she goes CHTTT, CHTTT, CHTTT, CHTTT and types 'television'. 'Television' leads to 'entertainment'; 'entertainment' leads to 'VIP.'; 'VIP.' leads to… 'BODYGUARD'. You know, cue urgent, hushed, bassy negroid American voice-over, Whitney Houston in pointy silver bra and Kevin Costner looking coolly paranoid about his next pay cheque.

"I think I've finally got something for you." This woman is proud of her find.

"Really? What is it?" And I'm genuinely surprised.

"Hang on," and she's giving it a build-up. Now she's like show-woman; she's gotta sell this to me. So she goes off PAT, PAT, PAT, rips off the printout, waves it in the air triumphantly, like ahhh

99

haaa, some tonic chord ringing out in her brain, sits back down, really pleased, slides it across to me. I pick it up and I crack up. I just laugh. She's hurt.

"What's wrong?"

"I've never done this sort of job before."

"Really? It says 'VIP'. It says 'Important people', 'Entertainment industry'."

"Yeah, but normally I'd be, e.g. photographing them, or directing them, or working behind the scenes. I don't normally take bullets for them."

And the woman's like, OK, fair enough, but I could see she was really hurt. So I read a bit more, and it talks about being based in Ireland and offering 'international travel'.

"This doesn't look safe," I finally say, looking like I've weighed it all up, done a SWOT analysis and everything.

"I don't think it's Northern Ireland." She makes one heroic last-ditch stand; she's almost pleading. "Cos it says Dublin."

But I'm immovable now and just block it, but politely, almost apologetically, saying it really isn't me.

"Well, look into it." She's finally conceding defeat. And I agree I will, meaning of course I won't, and then I leave.

When I first went down the Jobcentre I had to think pretty hard about what I should let them put me down for. It had to be in the media, cos that's always gonna be hard to slot Freetown people into, and after all, I had done a media qualification at college; not that that means anything, like all qualifications these days. I knew if I said 'cameraman', they'd probably get me to do some assistant camerawork for some dodgy guy and his wife. So I said, put me down as a television director. And instead of questioning this, or pointing out that this would seriously narrow down my options, they just went DOOOPP, done.

But of course this is the classic thing; they don't understand what a director does. They see it as a company director. You've no idea how long it took me to try to explain. And this is what happens, because they get bored as well. They're only human. And the computer is so stupid. It can't think sideways, it only thinks in a linear fashion; this to this, this to this, right? So I say to the lady, yeah, I direct. Oh, what company? And I give her the name of a video production company J-J and I set up in a moment of madness, called Spirit of 68. We had letterheads, business cards, everything. Even had a website. No product; but that was where my movie script came in, if we could just sell it. It was all J-J's idea; technician, spiritual guru and tyro entrepreneur. J-J is able to get his head around a lot of the worldly things that I just can't be arsed with. Initially I thought he'd named this company after some crap Bryan Adams song; and I don't mind admitting that for a couple of seconds the high esteem in which I had hitherto held J-J took a serious plunge. But then he explained that it wasn't that at all (I was confusing it with 'Summer of '69'). It wasn't hippies and Woodstock; it was revolution and the streets of Paris and being realistic by demanding the impossible, and that if voting changed anything they'd ban it, and cool ideas like that, so I was with him at once. Anyway, back to the lady.

"Right."

"Yeah I've done a bit of this, bit of that, you know?"

"I see. So have you been in business long?"

"No, I don't run my own business."

"No, I mean working with other businesses."

"I don't understand." And now she's looking at me like I'm special needs; and I'm looking at her the same way.

"No, I direct. Like a director of movies, or a director of television, you know, something like that."

I remember now that I had previously at some point said 'editor', but oh God, once I said that things went downhill in a big way. You can imagine why: oh, so you're a newspaper editor? No, VIDEO editor. Oh dear, we've got no category for video editing, I'm afraid. How about magazines?

Eventually she searches through 'Arts and Creatives' and finally finds me, like, some creative-stroke-artist-stroke-such-and-such grouping, and that's what I was fitted into. But no TV

101

director. No, like, category for TV, commercials, advertising, that sorta thing; just creative artists whatever whatever, and I had to go into that category. And, you know, that's the one category where the jobs don't come up very often. So the lady then says, OK, we need an alternative in case after so many weeks we can't find you anything, and I'm like, shit, shit, think, think, OK, TV executive. And she just says, "All right." Just like that. And that's how I got my professional profile.

The other thing about the Jobcentre is the characters you queue with. It's a little bit like prison: no eye contact. And you don't really understand what a traveller is till you see one down there. I mean, like, real gypsies with weird faces and weird hair. It's like they've been set back in time. They've got, like, fifties' hair on a young man's body. You can see they live in that community and come out of it only when they need to go to the Jobcentre. They sit there as confident as anything, looking like they hate everybody; but you're never ever gonna take the piss out of their hair. But the thing is, they almost pull it off, cos they don't look self-conscious and they're not trying to look fashionable. It's just the haircut's like father to son, father to son, handed down. Also when you're queuing you've always got guys saying, can ya hold the space for us, mate, while I use the phone?, and they don't expect a negative reply and being polite you say OK and end up queuing for them, while they're just outside having a fag or a natter with their mates, anyway doing something more enjoyable than queuing, and then they come back in, one before their go, and say, thanks for holding the space, mate, and then they go straight in front of you.

The other thing is you have to become a master forger. You're meant to write a record of the work you've been trying to find? I always did mine the night before. Looked in this magazine, looked in this magazine, did this, did this, did this, gonna look that up, sent off a CV, got reply back, none available. Again keen lady; sweating time. PHEW. You know she didn't read it all the way through; but she looked. Another lady, you hand it over, and I couldof written, you know, the Jobcentre's crap, the Jobcentre's crap, the Jobcentre's crap, the Jobcentre's crap; all it seemed that she registered was the fact that there was writing there and there were dates: done. She could see that I'd bothered to write something down, and that was it. They always check; but they don't always read. Cos it's not the dole any more; it's Jobseeker's Allowance. I am not unemployed; I am a, you got it. And to be a jobseeker, I have to fulfil my part of the contract, the contract they make you sign the first time you go down there. You know, are you able to work? Yes. Are you able to work in the next twenty-four hours? Yes. And if you fail either of those two questions, instantly you can't have any money. So you sign all this stuff. And that was classic. The lady says to me, so how often you going to be looking for work? And I have to sit and pause awhile to think about this.

"Once a week?"

"All right."

"And how often are you going to network?"

"What do you mean?"

"You know. I suppose, maybe, asking someone in the pub if they've got any work? That's networking."

"I'll do that."

"Three times a week?"

"OK."

So there's a whole list of supposed you must do this, you must do this, you must do this, OTHERWISE you will not get your MONEY. The form's obviously got some government guy going, we must scare the shit out of them; but the problem is it loses its sting when you've got some lady going, ah, don't worry about it. I mean, when you first see this form you're shitting your pants: omigod, they're gonna come round my HOUSE; they're gonna check I'm doing something. And they probably would in Germany. But over here they don't bother. JK wouldof said the nice ones are lazy and tender. I would just call them human beings.

And I did some research on the Internet and there's a whole movement of people, mainly a mass of guys in Wales, trying to get rid of the Jobseeker's Allowance, saying, this is taking away our freedom and rights, why should we have to do jobs we don't wanna do? Why should we have to sign a contract when we're unemployed? You know, how the system's bringing them down when they're honest folk, and they don't need to sign no contract saying they're actively looking for work, why do they need to be told they're actively looking for work, when that's why they've gone on the dole, because they couldn't find any in the first place? You know, they are mighty pissed off about it. But apparently if you go in there on the right day, or your auntie works there, or you manage to get someone lazy and tender, it's legally OK to put, actively seeking work how many times a week? Zero. Actively networking: zero. Actively doing this: zero, zero, zero, zero. There's nothing that says legally that that person being seen has to put anything particular down there. So all that contract you've signed is saying is that you will do zero job-looking, zero networking, zero everything, so in the end it's like not signing it, and you're allowed to do it, according to the website, and these people seemed pretty pissed off, so I think they'd know. It's never actually been known to have zero, zero, zero; that would be pushing it. But it has been known to have, actively seeking work, once a week, networking, never, thingy, never, thingy, never, thingy, never, how many job seeking tasks? One. So in a fortnight you'd have two entries: looked for work; looked for work. And that would be it.

Anyway, one day I went to the Jobcentre and went over to the machine with all the jobs that get downloaded on to it every day. My criteria were: short hours, easy, and nothing below five pound an hour. And I found one that fitted the bill: Auto Renovations – Keeping the Roadways Running. It was me that found this, incidentally, not the people at the Jobcentre. They were finding me things like 'Weapons Technician' and stuff like that. Anyway, I rang up this place and talked to a lady called Lynne who seemed quite nice and we arranged an interview.

I get there a quarter of an hour early. Sit down. Lynne basically asked me whether I had two arms, two legs, I said yeah. She also kept saying to me: you know, it's boring, it's not very exciting, it's not a good career move. Basically she's not really selling it to me, but she's a nice lady, honest person; she couldof been like, this NEEDS somebody, she couldof given me bullshit, but she told me the truth: this job is boring, but at the same time not very stressful. These days any job, no matter how low down the food chain, specifies non-monetary motivation from the applicant, you know: why are you applying for this position? Well, since the age of four I've always had an interest in industrial cleaning. Lynne wasn't expecting that, and I liked her honesty, so I said, yup, I'm up for doing it, and she said, OK cool, start on Monday. She did ask me why I wanted the job, and I said that I used to make promotional videos for different places, colleges, prisons, whatever, and I wouldn't mind getting back into that field, but at this moment in time I couldn't find anything in the industry, and she understood. And I told her I'd been unemployed a long time and needed to keep my car running, and to be honest I'm seeing this as more of a part-time job than anything major, and she was like, that's fine with us, because it's either a job for old people trying to top up their pensions, or bored and needing something to do, or it's students who wanna earn a bit of extra money and have plenty of time to think about their exams and whatever like that.

The job itself, she said, was three screens, eight cameras, and basically I have to wait for someone to break down. The most exciting part of the job is when someone breaks down. The rest of the time I could, like, do whatever I wanted. She said if I had a PlayStation, bring that in. Whatever I wanted to do was fine as long as I kept one eye on the screens. And so, apart from the occasional DVD and F1 replays on a portable TV I brought in after I'd been there a week, reading is what I spent my time doing, a lot of, in between a few well-spaced-out breakdowns. And that's how I got through the complete works of Jack Kerouac.

The induction was memorable. Turned up on the Monday and cos I was a little late the security guy goes, you ain't coming in. Really stern and all. So I can't get in and I'm scared that I've fucked this job up already, but another guy comes by and says, don't worry you can come along to another induction session on Wednesday instead, see you then. So I come back again on Wednesday, getting there early this time. It was so boring. I'm being taught by a guy with a nasal voice about how, when you're digging a hole, you've always gotta check for electrical cabling. I'm like OK. Then they showed these people who've got blown up through hitting an electrical wire. And I have to sit through all this even though it's not what I'm gonna be doing, cos they've only got one induction pack to cover everyone. And some of it was, bloody hell, well bad. I mean, if you drill through an electrical wire it's like a flamethrower blowing up in your face. I mean, man. They showed you an example and it is vicious. It's like someone having an enormous blowtorch and letting it off on to your whole body for three seconds. You go WHOOOSHHH like that. It's a sudden thing that just happens and you're charred instantly. Then we get to hear about all the birds, like, don't shoot any, don't run any over, if you see some voles, don't touch 'em, just let them run free, and if you see any rats, report 'em, cos they need taking out, because apparently Weil's disease was quite bad.

Then another guy steps in, and he looks at us intensely, saying what a key job we're gonna be doing for the rail-tunnel link by keeping the roads running. And then he did the speech: "You keep the motorists motoring." You know, classic American style. "You get husbands home to their wives. You get men to work in the morning." So in the end it's like, 'I control the roadways.' "Traffic reports on the radio? That's you they got that information off of. People want to go and see their daughters? You're the ones that get them there on time." It was like a World War II propaganda docu-short by Frank Capra or someone. Then he just went back to saying, "But don't hit any electrical cabling with a hammer." And then there was another shock-treatment video-nasty, true story apparently: a guy with a sledgehammer whacking a pole, the hammer breaks and the guy throws it away and uses another one. Later on in the day when he's gotta bang an iron post into some concrete he unthinkingly grabs the faulty sledgehammer and it slips and his fingers get caught between the hammer handle and the metal post, and the guy talking us through all this is taking great pleasure in saying, "Yeah, popped like a melon. Three fingers crushed to a pulp." I had to sit through all this even though I wasn't working in construction, because otherwise they wouldn't let me on the site.

I'd been forewarned by the interview lady that the recovery men were real rough and ready. When one of them gets to a car that's broken down, the guy or girl in it's like really relieved and glad to see them, and the recovery guy'll take great pleasure in going, 'OK, see that lay-by down there?' pointing about a hundred yards down the road, and s/he goes, 'Yeah,' and he'll go, 'Do you think your car can make it?' and s/he replies, 'Yeah, but I think there's something wrong with the brakes though,' to which he'll then say, 'OK, let's see if you can make it down there on your own?' 'Why?' 'Cos that's as far as I'll be taking ya.'

Most of the breakdown guys were gypsies. I don't mean to be disrespectful calling them that, and I know I'm supposed to refer to them as 'vulnerable and resource-poor members of the travelling community' or something, but whatever, that's basically what they were, living in caravans all the year round. The shifts they worked were horrible; I wouldn't wanna be on call twenty-four hours a day, seven days a week. They were paid a set rate whatever and whenever and they never knew whether they were gonna get called at one o'clock in the morning to pick someone up, or whether they were gonna get three days off. In fact they didn't actually pick anyone up; just dragged them a hundred yards to a lay-by. That's what was meant by 'Keeping the Roadways Running': getting people out of the way. Not trying to help them out. The broken-down driver would just have to sort out their own car rescue. Originally I thought we took them to a garage, but no, we just got them to the nearest lay-by, out of everyone's way. The traffic's gotta flow.

On my second or third day I'm reading *Visions of Cody*, or trying to, cos I always found Kerouac's *Visions* books the toughest

107

to get through, and I notice a toilet roll on the work surface. At the end of my shift a guy comes in to take over, picks up the roll and announces, "I'm going for a crap." I reply, fine. He leaves, comes back and then puts the roll back down on the table with a contented yeeaghhhh!, obviously taking great joy in this crap he's just had, then says, "You can borrow some if you like. Double-velvet. Have to give it back though." Moment of unshared laughter. Then more seriously, "They only leave industrial strength out back. Like the Black Hole of Calcutta it is. I'll leave the tour till after you've had your vaccinations." Noting my fewness of words and anxiety of expression, "You don't say much, do you?" Head shake. "Good thing around here. I reckon you'll be all right. Just try and keep it inside as much as you can." Thumbs up sign. "May as well be off now, son."

He was a nice enough guy. Most of the CCTV watchers were pretty pissed off. And watching cars go by in long-shot for eight hours, even from three different angles, is not gonna lighten your mood any. I remember one of them saying, "Bloody hell, this is so boring. I could be at home right now shaggin' the missus. I may even start doin' that."

I'm like, "Why?"

"Been here four hours; fuck all's happened. I coulda been PAID to BE AT HOME, SHAGGIN' THE MISSUS."

"Right."

Then he had some fat-man gag. "And to be honest with ya, ya'd wanna be getting paid with my woman. She's even balder than me. From all the hair I've pulled out. Ha ha!"

However, this rough-and-ready crew of follicly challenged, anally unretentive missus-shaggers found themselves one day recipients of a visually and orally explicit lesson in the erotic arts, for which they were entirely unprepared; as, I daresay, were the other beneficiaries of this workplace educational initiative, aka continuous professional development – namely their pleasantly surprised spouses and partners. And it was all thanks to my old friend Joe.

Unlike me, Joe doesn't have to try that hard at all with girls.

There are, like, the legends of Joe: Joe goes to a bar on his own, leans on the bar and a girl comes over and gets off with him. No effort. Didn't even look around. She just came. Walked over; hello. She chatted him up; he got off with her. Due to the sheer fact that he knew what he was doing, stood a certain way, leaned a certain way, put himself in a certain position; and it worked out. Classic Joe. The other thing is he always tells them what they want to hear whenever; but then those sorts of guys always do. Although he's not good at talking to women at all, which is why he hates taking me along. They talk to me, get off with him, then talk to me again. Joe says he doesn't know how to talk to women the way he wants to talk to them, while I talk to them like they're my friend. But I think that's just because I haven't got his looks, so I've had to develop another way of getting their attention, whereas he's never had to work that hard and so has ended up not knowing how to talk to them at all.

Joe is the kind of guy who sets out; sets out to get drunk, sets out to get wasted, sets out to get laid. He's a Method man. He's got an underground network of women that he's slept with before, and knows he can go up to them and bingo; but sometimes the Method falls to the wayside, he gets pissed and desperate, and then he'll take whoever. And he's got no standards at all. I mean, he knows what's good and what's bad, who's attractive and who isn't; but he's totally equal opportunities.

Joe's oral skills are legendary. I know this from some of the girls he's been with. Joe once told me that right from the beginning he concentrated on developing his oral technique, which is now apparently world-renowned. But other than that he's rubbish. A girl called Danielle who worked at the Star Tap once found herself lying on the floor at a party with him. He went down on her and, even though she now hates Joe, she told me about his consummate skills. Said it was amazing; the best ever. And he doesn't have to do anything else. That's it. In fact when he does try and do something else, you know, genital to genital, he's pants. Can't keep it going for more than a minute. The fact is, with Joe, its oral or nothing.

109

Not that they were complaining.

Joe's technique is never to go out and get it; you'll only see him do that in desperate situations, and I have seen it a couple of times, and he's been less than impressive, cos obviously he's not had that much practice, so when he tries it, it's bad, you know, I-really-fancy-you, awful, drunk and slobbering like some horny Mongoloid. What he normally relies upon is putting out the vibe thing and then going in for the kill. He won't go up to a girl and say, hello, my name is, whatever. He'll stand in her vicinity for half an hour, an hour, as long as it takes, looking cool, occasionally making eye contact. Setting the scene. Then he'll go in. And he's not a smash & grab sort of guy, doesn't go BOOF, bang, bang; he's not like that. He lays foundations, almost psychologically in the back of their mind, like, I have seen you this evening, haven't I? Know what I mean?

And Joe does this amazing thing. He'll work a room. He'll start at one end and he'll walk the whole thing just bumping into people, and he told me that bumping is a major technique you have to learn, not like ZOOOSH SMACK but gentle, like, oh sorry, so they turn around and catch a glimpse of Joe and his image is embedded in their brain, not for there and then, nor for him to suddenly go, hello; that'd be too cheesy BANG, a bump, hello, right? More bump; sorry; off again. Bang; he's off on the rounds again. Bang; hits another one. Bang; hits another one. Bang; hits another one. And all these girls are just catching glimpses of Joe. They know they've seen him, but they haven't spoken to him, or the only words he's ever said have been hello or sorry. So when the evening's coming to a close, all the girls that are left with no one remember Joe. They either walked into him or they said hello. They remember in the back of their heads, that kid seems cool, you know, he didn't come straight out and ask me or anything, and Joe will do the standing thing now and at the same time he's watching to see which women are any good, checking off those that have got someone and those that haven't. He's casing the whole room all the time.

Now the end of the evening is in sight and he knows he's gotta get some. That's when he'll start going over. But that's what I mean. He's not going over cold; he's worked this whole room. Generally he doesn't even have to do this bit; as the evening finishes he'll move in closer, perhaps with a drink, perhaps he'll start dancing, whatever, but he rarely does this, not being much of a dancer. Most of the time he'll just lean. And a girl will come over; I saw you earlier, didn't I? See what I mean? It's given them an excuse to make the first move. 'I bumped into you earlier, didn't I?' How easy is that for a girl to start a conversation with? Otherwise she's got to come over and what's she gonna say? But cos he's laid the foundations, they've now got an excuse. He's made her life easier. She can say, bumped into you earlier, what's your name? Bang, bang, bang, he's getting off with her. Bang, he's in bed with her. Joe always does this; it's a technique he always uses.

Joe will also use oddities for conversation openers, like, do you want a Palma Violet? You know, those sweets that are purple and taste of soap. He always buys something that will remind them of their childhood; something that's very sweet and kind of comical. Like Palma Violets. You don't eat those every day and you very rarely see them. Or Black Jacks; but he doesn't use Black Jacks any more cos you have to chew them and they make your tongue black.

But you have to remember Joe's good-looking, and that's the only reason he's so successful. His methods won't work if you're ugly. You have to operate in a different way. And the other thing is Joe always says you have to try twenty times and be prepared for nineteen rejections; but the twentieth makes it all worthwhile. I personally don't like to be rejected even once, cos of the underlying fragility of my self-esteem, so I can't do that; but then I'm like most people, and most people don't get laid like Joe, and never will. Cos he'll just go, fuckit, next, fuckit, next, fuckit, next, fuckit, next, bang. He's hardly ever offput.

As I say, Joe hates talking to girls and can't. Maybe that's why he's trained his tongue for other uses, who knows? Basically Joe just wants to sleep with women. He only wants conversation if

111

he's drunk; and then it would have to be about books or film. He doesn't want to talk about crap; and that's all girls wanna talk about, according to Joe.

Anyway, I told Joe one day I was having some trouble getting things right with S., you know, had some concerns about the quality of our sexual relationship, mainly from her perspective, and he said he had just the cure. It was a DVD. Joe watches a lotta porn. This wasn't porn; yet it was, he told me, the most explicit thing he'd ever seen, and for Joe that was saying something. The women in it weren't fit or anything, but Joe said not to worry about that, just watch and learn and then go away and apply the strokes as demonstrated. He offered his highest possible recommendation: lesbians rate it. I was a bit concerned that this DVD might be a bit advanced, but I was not going to argue with Joe in view of his Jedi-like mastery of this subject.

The DVD was called *Fire in the Valley: the Art of Female Genital Massage*. It was totally illegal of course; but Joe, who considered himself a pleasure activist, said that was only because the government and sad bastards at HM Customs enjoyed curtailing the erotic development of the masses. I was a lot more worried about my mum, to tell the truth, so I opted to view it undercover at work, slipping the disk in between *Desolation Angels* and 'Mexico City Blues'.

And, man, did I learn some stuff. Everything Joe had said I would. How to be aware of what women like, how to be attentive, how to listen to breathing, how to gently pinch and squeeze, stroke and blow, circle and rub, tease and pull, always keeping it interesting and new, varying the pressure, varying the direction, constantly checking the feedback, providing just the right amount of sexual nourishment so she stays hungry. How to move inside and outside, inner lips, outer lips, working the clitoris, locating the spongy area where the G-spot is, taking it slow, developing a conscious-aware touch, visualising it, playing her body like a violin, or doing a Hendrix, depending. Quite a lot to keep in your head while you're supposed to be enjoying yourself. I'd never before realised the requirement for this level of effort and focus.

You'd wanna be paid. I can see why prostitutes consider themselves sex workers. This was love's labial labour.

But it was also totally like the complete opposite: formless, structureless, go-with-the-flow, improvise, get mystical; all about meditation, attention, placement, rhythm, freeform, cosmos, singing the body erotic, honouring it, celebrating it, here and now, coaxing it gradually then instantly into shifting out-of-body, warpdriving to there and eternity. I tell you, JK on his lifelong Buddhist journey, which he never quite completed, but I guess you never really do, unless you live like a Tibetan monk, wouldof definitely approved.

I learnt all about Crescent Moon, Temple Gate Tease, Rocking Around the Clock, Twisting and Shouting, Ring Around the Rosie. After I'd finished the Tour de France, I was suddenly aware of an audience behind me. I turned around and saw a group of about a dozen recovery men and CCTV guys. But they weren't grinning or anything. They were, like, seriously into it. There was this hush like when Jonny Wilkinson shapes to take that kick that's gotta go between the posts to win the World Cup.

"Not bad. I'll have to give that a try with the missus."

"Where'dja get hold of this, Matt?"

"Mate gave it me."

"Can you get it from HIV?"

"HMV. No. It's illegal."

"Oh right. Why's that, then?"

"Dunno."

"Do they do one about massaging men's bits?"

Instantly we all look away from the screen and eyeball the last speaker.

"For the missus to watch."

Sigh of relief. Actually it was a fair point. In my experience, limited as it is, girls don't take half the trouble with us that we put in for them. It's like we're just there to keep the rhythm going. And this was especially true with S. Anyway must avoid sounding bitter.

113

"I'll find out."

In fact there was a 'brother version' called *Fire on the Mountain*. And you can guess what that was the art of. Joe had a copy of that, too; but he said the problem was it was for gays only – he'd never been able to get a girl to watch it without laughing. Naturally it was made before the female sequel; gays always getting in there first.

"Can youse do us a copy of that one?"

"No problem."

"And one for me."

"No problem."

"Can youse do one for all of us?"

"No problem."

"You're a good kid."

Huge mitt patting my shoulder. I avoided reflecting on the viscous brown contents of its palm. It couldof been oil.

I ended up doing copies for everyone and quickly earned the reputation of a likeable subversive, which wouldof pleased Joe. I think the DVD mustof helped me in my own development, because S. gave me some rare positive feedback at one of our periodic we-need-to-talk-about-the-relationship reviews. Naturally there were also plenty of areas for development. Like my tendency to get emotional. My apparent dependency on alcohol. And my undisguised hostility towards her dopehead boyfriend. I argued that these were essentially all the same weakness; but she disagreed. I then pleaded I was doing my best in working towards the required goal of continuous improvement etc., if only she would just give me one more chance. And I did try.

But shortly after this the sexual dimension of our relationship shrank to a vanishing point; and I had a lot more serious things to worry about.

Chapter Eleven

Alice

The pleasures in love are always in proportion
to our anxieties
(Stendhal, *On Love*)

Even to this day I'm not sure if I ever went out with Alice. For instance, I was never allowed to hold her hand in public. When I asked her why this was, she said, 'I don't want anyone to think we are together.' It was as harsh as that.

Alice and I had met briefly around college, but it was at a party, where I got completely wasted and we ended up sitting on a bed together, that a connection was made. A few minutes earlier I'd got into a fight with this chav who'd been following me around, baiting me, calling me 'four eyes' because of the thick-rimmed black glasses I was wearing at the time, and generally taking the piss, thinking it would impress his mates to be seen to be taking the piss out of someone and earn him plenty of value-plus points in chavdom. He and his mates were cousins of the person giving the party, and prior to their turning up it had been a really nice atmosphere, everyone happy, knowing everyone else, being cool. I mean, we were all media students, a little bit kooky, a little bit different. And then these cousins arrive, and for whatever reason one of them takes an instant dislike to me, you know, alright four eyes?, look at that fucking four eyes. And him and his mates go hohohohoho. I just ignore this but later on he comes up to me

115

and says the same sort of thing again, and this time I'm like, wha? And he goes 'these', pointing at my eyes and pushing, flicking at them in the air, going like that, like that, getting closer and closer, while I'm walking up the stairs. Then he goes like that again and flicks my glasses clean off my nose, so I look, you know, weak, like a prick. Why did he do that? I dunno. Why does anyone do anything? So I turn and say to him, what the fuck are you doing? And I notice for the first time he's got this pink top on. A lot of chavvy men wear pink, and I've never understood why. It's not a gay thing; they just seem to like the colour. So I say to him, you're mocking these (my glasses) and yet you've got a fucking pink jumper on. Instantly he doesn't like that. He grabs me. I grab him. We end up tumbling down the stairs and rolling around on the floor, wrestling with each other, me punching him in the ribs and his mates laying the boot in, as mates always do. So I've got people kicking me while I'm rolling around in beer and all sorts; but I'm also shouting, "Where are my glasses? Where are my glasses?", cos I'm worried someone's gonna stamp on them.

Then someone goes, "I've got 'em", you know, like considerately freeing me up to direct the whole of my attention to this erstwhile ruckus.

Eventually it gets broken up. I've got a ripped shirt and I'm like a wild man.

I mean, I'm wasted but I'm also a ball of rage. This motherfucker needs taking down. "I'm gonna kill you, I'm gonna find you, I'm gonna rip yer head off, I'm gonna kill your family, I'm gonna kill your mother, I'm gonna kill your father." I have lost it totally. "I'm gonna track you down. I'm gonna kill everyone you've ever known." I'm Joe Pesci angry, partly because I've been made to look so weak. This guy's mates are just like, fuck off, you know. The truth is I'm actually calming down now, though no one realises it. And then I do this weird thing. As ever, I've seen it in a movie, don't know which one, maybe *Fight Club*, and it always freaks people out. I start punching myself in the face, shouting, "I wanna fucking punch you so hard," and all the while I'm punching myself in the head, hard, proper smacking myself with a round-the-face right hook. For me, it's like I'm saying, look, I can fucking beat the shit out of ME; so just imagine what I'm gonna do to you. That's my interpretation anyway. Other people, however, just find it freaky.

Three people are now holding me back, two pinning my arms. I'm straining to get free. Girls are screaming. It's mayhem. Someone tells the chavs that it might be better if they just left, and after demurring somewhat they agree to go, without any of the politeness that implies. And now I'm like whhhooorrrr whhhooorrrrrr deep breathing, so some people take me outside, give me a drink and then in a fingersnap I'm back to normal. I apologise. Say sorry to everyone. I've drunk too much and those guys upset me. Those kinds of people always irritate me. Trying to justify it. Don't get me wrong: I'm not trying to glorify what I did in any way. I wish I hadn't done it. But it was one of those things that happened. I mean, I would never track the guy down and kill his family, whatever. You know, I'm sitting here writing this, and there are no dead bodies anywhere on my account. But at that moment in time I meant it. And as with a lot of this stuff past movies were playing into my head: *Platoon*, *Taxi Driver*, millions of Vietnam films, Korean gangster flicks, everything. It was like, if I die today, I'm taking you down with me. It's not just going to be me. I don't know which movie that's from, but that's the mentality I had going: if I have to die killing you, that's good enough. It'll be worth going down, if I can take you with me. Cos I'm not leaving this planet unless you're leaving it wimme. You know, that sort of kamikaze style. Not good mentally. But it was that level of extreme. The Klingon mindset of, today's as good a day, you know what I mean? Not healthy thinking. But this is how it gets when I'm wasted. My head doctor has warned me against adopting this philosophical position which holds great appeal when I've been mixing alcohol with my Seroxat. These days I've learnt to control it enough usually to be able to press pause. But we're talking then, not now.

117

Alice, understandably, is not impressed.

"I didn't think you were that type of boy."

This was later on when we were taking a timeout on a bed in the spare room, both of us a bit worse for wear. She seemed pretty upset.

"I'm not. He was just following me around everywhere, pestering me, I had a lot on my mind and it just sparked me off. I've been under a lot of pressure. Things have been going on at home."

"What sort of things?"

"Stuff with Dad."

"What sort of stuff?"

"I don't really want to discuss it."

"Please. Please tell me."

Then she began to cry. More. Heavily. So I told her my dad had had a bad accident, near death, there'd been some litigation, and I'd ended up with a post-traumatic stress disorder.

"Man, how fucked up are you?" Which was kind of a straight question.

"Well, not that fucked up, but obviously something like that's gonna affect you."

"OK."

And then, seeing as I was clearly losing this battle, I went down on my knees, genuflecting, holding her legs and putting my head on her lap, saying, "I'm sorry. I'm sorry." Quite pathetic, really. But at the same time, I was so out of my head I didn't feel I could communicate my situation very effectively, so I thought I should do something physical, like begging. And it kind of worked cos she started stroking my head.

"I've been through some bad stuff as well, you know."

And I'm thinking, OK, death of a granny, Mum's lost a leg, something like that.

"My dog died."

Given my irrational but deep-seated dislike of dogs on account of their relaxed approach to hygiene, this to me was not the greatest of tragedies; but in fairness I can see how you can love a dog like a best friend. Then she began to cry so heavily she couldn't even talk, and I sat back up and put my arm around her. But it was a bit weird cos most girls feel sort of right, you know, they fit; but Alice weren't fitting. She was rigid and non-relaxed. When you hold someone they normally meld to you; but that weren't happening. It was like holding a large cube. Not that I'm saying she was a cube or anything; it was just uncomfortable and didn't feel right. Finally, she stopped crying.

"Could be sick at any moment."

"Right."

"Cos I'm really pissed."

"Right."

"How long've you liked me?"

Shit. I hate that sort of question. "Ages."

I'm thinking OK, just go with the programme. I'm wasted anyway. She was drunk, too. But a weird kind of drunk. Not LLLAAYYALLLLLLRRRFF. Her speech patterns were fine. It wasn't like double-vision and slurring. She may have been a little bit wobbly, but not like a wino in the street. It was just that more emotional honesty was pouring out of her than normal. A couple of layers of the onion had been peeled off.

"I've liked you for about a year and a half. I've told everybody about you. Everybody at work. My mum and dad."

That was a bit scary, and I'm thinking omigod; but then a certain vain part of me is also like, hey, you know? So I'm sitting there thinking, this is quite cool.

"And then when you went out with S. (but she didn't say 'S.') I was well jealous."

"Really?"

"Yeah. Couldn't handle it when I saw you and her together."

"I never even knew you liked me. Whenever I spoke to you at college you seemed offish."

"I can't flirt with people I like."

"Whaddya mean?"

"Well, say I hate you, I could flirt with you easily. But anyone I do like I can't flirt with them because I get frigging nervous (she didn't say 'frigging'). So if I seemed offish it was me being scared."

So I'm thinking, right, this girl's liked me for ages; I'm at least gonna get off with this girl this evening. Natural thinking. A year and a half, I'm here, she's willing. Supposedly. This could be good. So I lean across and move in; I'm a bit drunk so I'm going for the direct approach, straight for the lips. WHOOOSH hand instantly comes up. You know, the classic gesture like you see in one of those old 1950s Hollywood films.

"No."

"What?"

"Nothing is going to happen this evening." This is clearly non-negotiable. And then, "I'm not sure if I even like you any more."

Now I'm like wha?

"You've liked me for a year and a half and now in twenty minutes you're not sure if you like me at all?"

"That was before you had your head shaved. And before you had the fight."

I forgot to say I had recently gone the mohican route to save on barber's costs. I was going through a Travis Bickle/Vietnam vet phase and foolishly allowed a friend to modify my normally thick and wavy locks with some clippers when we were both drunk. I ended up having to go to the hairdresser anyway to get the ensuing disaster retrieved into a quarter-inch crop-cut, which I suppose did give me the appearance of an East German SS enthusiast.

"Yeah, but my hair grows back. It doesn't matter. The hair doesn't matter."

I mean, I was quite liking the idea that this girl's liked me for a year and a half; and now that she's saying she doesn't, I'm trying to grab it back. "The hair doesn't matter," I'm imploring now; and I have to admit that if there were ever a strategy for getting me suddenly to open up and get emotional about how much I like someone, this was it. I was like, man, I'm not gonna lose this if I've had it for a year and a half!

"Yeah, but my dad won't like you."

"Whaddya mean?"

"Last person I brought round had purple hair and my dad said he was in a cult."

There was no real answer to that. "The hair'll grow back. The hair'll grow back." Desperate but emphatic at the same time.

"Yeah, but I'm not even sure if I like black hair."

And now I'm like, WHA? "But I've always had brown-black hair!"

"Yeah, but now I'm not sure."

"OK, putting the hair to one side if we can for the moment, as regards the fight thing, forget that ever happened. It's not like me. I'm not aggressive. I don't normally lose my temper ever, ever, ever, ever, ever, ever, ever, EVER."

"OK."

Massive pause.

"But you look like a skinhead. A thug. Someone who would start fights."

And now I'm starting to get pissed off, so I try the, well, if you don't like me because of my hair, perhaps it would be better... you know, I gave it that one.

Another big pause of silence, and I'm just sitting there.

Then she asks me how many girlfriends I've had. I say five, taking girlfriend in its broadest sense and reaching back into primary school, and she doesn't look too pleased.

"What, you've had five women?"

"Well, some of them were girls, cos they weren't women at the time, they were like, you know, sixteen."

"Right." She didn't really get that. I think she thought I was some sort of paedophile, so I explained that I was only sixteen at the time as well and she was then OK. I then ask her how many boyfriends she's had, and she says three. I'm now thinking, well, maybe this girl's not a virgin, you know, because

I'm interpreting 'had' as 'slept with', and so that came as a bit of a surprise.

"One for a week, one for two days, one for a day."

"Tell me about the one for a week."

Turns out it was the guy with the purple hair. She was still in love with him, of course. She'd known him about a month; but the weird thing was they had never been alone together, because he had a female friend, an 'ugly cow', as Alice put it, that used to hang around with him all the time, making Alice jealous. And in the end it was more like Alice was having a relationship with the girl, because she would get more phone calls from the girl than from him. The girlfriend would be the messenger, and it would be she who would phone Alice and say, we're gonna be here if you want to meet him, like she was his PR agent or something; you know, he will be available for a book-signing at such and such, he's got a window at such and such. So this threesome thing was all very odd. And Alice said she would ask, "Are you two doing anything?", and he would say, "I'm not even going to dignify that with an answer"; obviously meaning yes. In the end he joined the army, but Alice said she still wasn't over him and started to get tearful, so my head's now back round to the virgin thing.

All this time I've been aware of a massive crowd gathering outside the door, which is like a wooden shack door, cos there've been lots of eyes looking in through the slats, no doubt intrigued by the presence of this psycho in their midst. Then the door opens and George and Jenny walk in and sit down on the bed.

"How are you two?"

"Fine."

And Jenny then asks, "How are *you* two?" Meaning, heyyyyyyyy! I just say, "Fine," but give a sideways look that says, 'I ain't getting nowhere', and Jenny laughs. Then Jenny and George start getting off with each other, and Alice and I end up watching and listening. We weren't, you know, hmmm, that's a good technique; it wasn't like that. We were just lying down and they were sitting at the end of the bed. But even though we were lying down, Alice was still about three feet away, or it felt like that. We weren't close, anyway. I'm now thinking, *What shall I do, what shall I do, what shall I do?* but the next thing I know she's holding my hand, which feels a bit odd, like I'm thirteen. And then George and Jenny lie down as well, transversely across the bottom of the bed. There's all this QUUACCKKK, QUUUACCKK SSLLLLPPP going on; maybe not quite that bad, but it sounded like it at the time. Jenny's now on top and George is leaning up, and they're getting off heavy. And I can't help thinking to myself, *Man, they're getting shitloads and I ain't getting none!* Then Alice laughs; and I must admit there was some humour in the situation and the noises, and I start laughing as well, then George and Jenny start laughing, and soon there is this mass laughter everywhere, until Alice finally says, "I'm trying to sleep."

George and Jenny say, "Go and sleep elsewhere." But this is the comfy bed, and Alice and I've got squatters' rights; there's no way I'm going downstairs to lie on the floor, whatever. Alice shuts her eyes and I'm now lying there, looking across, while George and Jenny start getting off again. I don't know if this was pervy, but part of me was interested in how they were getting on.

So I'm watching George and Jenny, and in the process my own motivation starts to increase, so I look across to Alice and she's still got her eyes shut and she's looking fit. In the darkness the light from the door was creating this soft illumination of her face. Her hair wasn't tied back; it was down and it looks good that way. She was looking nice. And she has got the flattest stomach I've ever seen. So I move across, move across, move across. I don't know quite how I did it, but I managed to get close enough to her face to lean in and lick her ear. She doesn't move. An inch. If anything she went more rigid. Eyes pressed firmly shut. So I then kiss her cheek, moving down, moving down, kissing her neck, moving up, moving up, getting ready to attempt the lips. She must've known this was coming, cos her head raises a bit, and I'm thinking, hey, this must mean she wants to do it. So then I'm gently kissing lips, slightly open, which must've lasted about ten seconds, and then I initiate the tongue.

Suddenly she goes, "No, I'm sorry," but softly, apologetically, and turns her head away. So I'm back to lying there again and listening to SLLLRRRPPPP QUUCCKKK QUUUCCKK; and now I've got pissed off.

"You're making too much noise. Me and Alice are trying to go to sleep." Jenny looks at me and smiles coyly, but I'm standing firm: I ain't getting none; they ain't doin' it. "There's a bed down there," I say, politely but forcibly, meaning of course the floor.

Then Alice lifts herself up: "Yeah, and I can feel you keep kicking me. And it's not nice."

Jenny says, "But I can't help it," and we all start laughing again. Alice and I weren't unpleasant in how we said it, but we were sticking to our guns, so Jenny and George eventually got off the bed and lie down on the floor.

Major goop noises now. I'm lying there listening, cos I can't get to sleep. Alice has got her eyes shut. So I again lean over her while she's laying there and start looking at her, wondering if I like this girl or not. I mean, it's not often you get to stare at someone and feel comfortable about checking out every angle of their face, so, like a photographer or cameraman, I'm kind of going, yeah, seems OK from this angle, let's take a look from here. I'm even assessing the lighting source and the diffusion. I'm looking for ages, checking every feature and angularity, symmetry, smoothness of line and shape, slopes and declivities, surface undulations, anfractuosities, granulations, skin tone; and I don't know whether it was because I was horny at the time and there was kissing and other stuff going on on the floor, but Alice was looking better and better at every single moment. So I moved my hand and started to stroke her hair to see what it felt like. It was thick and curly and felt really soft. Then I start stroking her face, not in a pervy way, but gently with the back of my hand, running slowly down her nose; I thought this would feel quite good. And previously when women have done this to me it felt alright, you know, a bit weird, but only cos it's like someone is stroking your face, which is not a horrible thing, even if it doesn't happen every day. Alice starts to laugh, however, then turns around so I can't do it any more. Then she turns round again, takes my hand and holds it. And then she passes out, and I fall asleep.

Next morning I wake up. Alice is about to go but whips out her phone number and gives it to me while I'm half awake. I mumble thanks but she doesn't say a word, just leaves. I put the number on the bedside table then go back to sleep.

A couple of days later I get up the courage to call her, thinking I'm probably gonna have to be doing some apologising over my behaviour at the party. I mean, I was wasted. She tells me she didn't like the earlicking; but the rest was fine. I insist that earlicking is not a sign of weirdness; I mean, I didn't lick her whole ear or anything. It wasn't as if it were a dog lick. It turns out she has discussed this incident already with a couple of girlfriends, and they have confirmed that, in their view, it is an acceptable and indeed pleasurable interpretation of foreplay. One even went as far as saying, 'Earlicking's the best.' But this hasn't persuaded Alice to change her viewpoint, which is that it is strange and not something to be repeated.

One of the funny things about Alice is the way she speaks. One minute she can have the softest, like, nervous way of talking, then she'll suddenly say, 'How fucked up are you?' And there are no transitions. It's like smooth boxing, smooth boxing, smooth boxing, you're thinking this is an easy fight, then suddenly BOOSH! power-punch. And she'll tell you stuff and won't protect you. You know, anyone else would say, 'No one's talking about you at college. Don't worry about that. It'll be fine.' And you'd keep the fact that no one's talking about you as something to hold on to, even when they then add, 'I don't wanna go out with you any more, I'm afraid; but don't worry about college, I guarantee no one's been saying any bad things about you,' despite the fact that this decision to dump has been made precisely *because* people at college are talking about you. But with Alice it would be like a constant stream of consciousness, as her thought process totally unfolds to you. 'Everyone's talking about you at college. They're calling you a psycho. And that's sort of making me not want to go out with you. Yet when I get home, I do want to go out with you. But then when I get back to college, they're all saying that you're nuts, saying weird things about pills, and I don't want to go out with you again, but then when I'm at home I'm thinking that I do like you.' It all comes out like that, but slowly and calmly, like, yeah, they hate you, and they're talking about you as a psycho, very softly spoken; but she's getting nothing of you squirming at the other end of the phone, emotionally wrecked and feeling like, 'They hate me at college! They think I'm a psycho!' And because it's so weird, you just have to be like, 'I don't care.' You have to be non-sensitive, like fuck them at college; but really you're like, aaahhhh! So that was another oddity about Alice. But she did it in a very shy way so you couldn't be horrible to her. And at least you always knew what she was thinking.

Alice and I met up a few times after that and I started to get really into her. My head doctor noticed the improvements. I was getting more relaxed, my mood was lifting and the obsessional thoughts were almost non-existent. I mean, we were doing a lot of proper kissing now; serious levels of saliva were interchanging. But I hadn't gone down with anything, not even one time when she had a cold. So the cleanliness stakes were gradually diminishing. I managed to cut my handwashing down by half, and soon there was no clear definition between the parts I was washing and those I was non-washing, and my skin wasn't constantly cracked and bleeding from dermatitis as a result of the excessive scrubbing. I didn't have to go and stand on the edge of the carpet any more, or do this weird thing in doorways, taking two steps forwards and two steps back. No idea what all that's about. Hypervigilance, according to my head doctor. A need to create a safe environment through ritual. Which also explained why I was always going around checking (three times) that the bolt on the front door was locked, light switches off, plugs taken out, gas turned off, kettle not on: anything I saw as a potential hazard. I mean, I'd be brilliant if I had to look after the Queen.

It was all apparently about my not wanting another accident to happen, like the one that happened to Dad. My head doctor told me that this kind of hypervigilant, hyperaroused behaviour is common with ex-military like Gulf War and Falkland vets, who still go on patrols at night round their neighbourhoods and hit the ground whenever a car backfires. It's more unusual in civilians, except when they suffer a post-traumatic stress disorder, which he tells me is my condition. Of course I pointed out to him that twenty-first century life is pretty much like a war zone anyhow, especially in Freetown, so my hypervigilance could come in handy in certain situations; but he just told me I had seen too many movies. He was, however, really pleased to see me sobering up, because Alice stopped me mixing alcohol with my Seroxat, cos she didn't want any repeat performances of the Wrath of Matt Khan.

It was my head doctor who told me I should tell Alice about my seeing him. I'd been worrying about this a lot, how best to approach it, but I was really dreading doing it, so one day when we went to a cash machine in the high street I just blurted it out.

"I see a shrink." Just like that. No preamble or anything. Get it over with.

"Right."

"Here's his card. Lansten. Still go."

"How often?"

"Once a month for a check-up." Then, "No, I'm lying, I see him every week. Well, not quite every week. Every now and again. Sometimes once a week. Sometimes once every two weeks. Changes."

"Right. Anything else?"

"No, I've finished now."

"Right." Long pause.

"Have you got a problem with that?"

"No, why would I?"

"So you don't wanna go home?"

"No. I suppose it's quite a fashionable thing to be doing."

127

I think she was just trying to make me feel better; but I appreciated her being cool about it.

"It's probably not something you wanna advertise to my mum and dad, however. But I haven't got a problem with it."

Our more intimate moments still held major challenges though. I was always doing my best to get her to remove some clothing, but without any success. There was this one time in my bedroom, listening as usual to The Smashing Pumpkins, which was the only music of mine she liked. I was kissing her, then we'd stop and talk, kiss again, stop, talk, and I've, like, got my hand and I'm exploring areas, or trying to, stroking her arm, progress to the breast area, get moved away, down to leg area, get moved away, kiss again, getting off with her.

"Could you lie down?"

"Why do you want me to lie down?"

"Just, please, lie down."

"I don't wanna lie down."

"It's just that, at the moment, when I kiss you, I'm lying down and you slide down, and eventually I end up like eating my own chin." She laughs. "So it would help a lot if you just lie down."

"I don't wanna lie down."

Kiss again. Getting off with her again. But I'm like aaeerrgh straining all the time and my jaw's about to dislocate.

"Please lie down."

She now lies down, eventually; but sideways.

"Why are you lying sideways?"

"I wanna lie sideways."

"Right."

"Is there a problem with that?"

"Well, it's just that I'm trying to kiss you, but now you're, you know, sideways on, and it's difficult and uncomfortable and I'm gonna rick my neck."

'Why do I have to lie on my back?"

"Why not?"

"Hmmmm."

In the end she does lie on her back, very rigid and limbs firmly clamped together. But it's better. Now I'm getting off with her and I've got my hand there and I'm sliding down, sliding down, sliding down, sliding down, boomph, hand gets taken and put back to where it started. Kissing her, kissing her, kissing her, stroking her arm, stroking her arm, stroking her arm, stroking her arm, kissing her, kissing her, kissing her, getting near breast area, arm gets taken, kissing her, kissing her, kissing her, and I put her arm over to one side and shift my weight to press down on it a little, hampering its freedom to move, kissing her, kissing her, kissing her, stroking her face, stroking her face, stroking her face, kissing her, kissing her, kissing her, move my hand down, I'm on the outside of her leg now, going like that, like that, like that, getting away with it cos it's the outside of the leg, hand moves over onto stomach, I can feel her arm starting to move, my hand speeds up, slides downwards, WHOOSSHHH, intercepted, hand put back up to original position. I put her arm back, almost wedging it against the headboard, getting off with her, getting off, getting off, getting off, getting to breast area, her arm's not easily able to move, I'm thinking I'm gonna do it! I'm gonna do it! WHOOSSHHH hand intercepted, by her OTHER hand.

"Man, you've got hands everywhere!"

"Whaddya mean?" And she gives me the coyest look.

"This hand wants to explore. And it just CANNOT DO IT!"

"Whaddya mean?"

"Well, it just wants to go on adventures. But everywhere it goes, it just cannot GO there! Like HERE and HERE and HERE." And I'm touching her in those off-limits places to make my point, and each time she's like UURRGHH recoiling. "What is it?"

"Nothing."

Kiss again then stop. Something needs to be discussed.

"You've got nothing to be shy about or afraid of. We won't do anything you don't wanna do."

"OK."

"I mean, you gotta understand that when I'm kissing someone,

129

it's not abnormal for them to wanna, like, touch. You know, in the relationships I've been in before, girls I've just met, when I've kissed them, there's a certain level of touching (I nearly said 'groping') and it's, like, natural."

"I know it's natural. But I just don't feel comfortable with my body."

"Well, it's not like we're getting naked."

And she went UURRRGGHH again; this was not an image she wanted in her mind.

"It's just that I'm trying to touch you. You can understand that, can't you?"

"Yeah."

"Well, why don't you touch me?"

"I'm nervous."

"Just try."

I'm thinking, fuckit, if she doesn't wanna touch me, she doesn't. But she does start stroking my face, only it's a bit like a seal's slap.

"That feels good." You know, build up her confidence. "How's it feel to you?"

"Well, it's a bit boring."

And I'm thinking, well, you can go other places, but I just say, "OK," and start stroking her hair. "I'm sorry if I made you feel uncomfortable."

"No, you didn't. Well, you did a bit."

"What do you mean? When?"

"On Friday."

"Is that why you didn't stay?"

"Yeah."

"Did you think I was trying to have sex with you?"

"Yeah. Would you have done?"

"Naah. Never entered my mind."

"Don't lie." And she now looked at me real serious.

"OK. I'll be honest with you. Of course it entered my mind. But it wasn't as if I thought, 'Get-Alice-in-bed, sleep-with-her,' in some Teutonic Terminator voice, cos I never think like that. It was just that, like, I kiss you, then I see where I can go, you know, just progress from one stage to the next. It's not as if I go kiss-sex, kiss-sex, kiss-sex." I was trying to put across to her that I'm not some bastard who just wants to get her into bed, strip her off, then leap on her. So I'm now stroking her face again, and really apologising, overly so, cos that's what I always do. "I'm not gonna jump on you."

"Hee-hee." But nervously.

"I was just wanting to see the natural progression. If at any point you said no, I would've stopped."

"Yeah, but you don't, do you?"

"Whaddya mean?"

"Well, like now. Every time I moved your hand away, you tried again."

"That wasn't a 'no'," and now I'm upset but trying not to sound so.

"Well, what was it, then?"

"Well, it was just my hand being moved away. If you'd've gone, no, I wanna go home, you know, if you'd've said that, I wouldn't've, like, held you down and said you're gonna fucking..." I was trying not to scare her, cos as you know I can turn instantly scary, "I wouldn't've done anything like that, and you've gotta understand I'm actually getting quite upset. I'm beginning to feel like some dirty rapist, trying to do something with you that you don't wanna do."

"No, you're not being like that."

"But it's beginning to feel like it, the way you're putting it."

"I don't mean to."

"So I haven't upset you?"

"No. But you are pushing your luck."

"OK, I'm sorry if I've upset you." Now I'm overdoing it, I'm sorry, I'm sorry, I'm sorry, you've got nothing to worry about, and when I try to do that stuff it's just me getting into it, I can't help it; but as soon as you say no, definitely not, I would never pressure you into doing it.

131

"Yeah but you push your luck!"

"It's just me… it's… it's what we DO! But, you know, if you say no no as in no, no, I won't do it. OK? I won't touch you again."

"Oh."

"I won't."

Then I go to touch her hand. "OK? Are we cool?"

"Yeah, we're cool."

"I feel uncomfortable now."

"I feel a little bit uncomfortable as well."

"Is this why you didn't stay on Friday night?"

"Yeah."

"OK. Do you wanna go home? Have I upset you?"

"No."

"Did I upset you on Friday?"

"It was a bit annoying that you kept asking me to stay and stay and stay, and that you wouldn't come downstairs and just stayed in your room hoping I'd come back, and you didn't see me out."

"I did in the end. I was just pushing my luck."

"THERE YOU GO. You push your luck."

"Yeah, but only in a playful way. I never wanted to make you feel threatened. I would never do that."

"OK."

"Do you want me never to kiss you again?"

"No, I want you to kiss me."

"Would you not want me to touch you?"

"I would want you to touch me, eventually."

"Do you not want me to have sex with you?"

"No, I wanna have sex with you."

"Then WHY???"

Bad move to shout like that.

"I'm sorry."

"Just not yet."

"OK. But you're not like Sarah?"

"What do you mean 'like Sarah'?"

132

"Well, you know, can't have sex before marriage."

"No, I'm not like Sarah. Would it be a problem if I was like Sarah?"

"Not at all. Look, I'm sorry if I upset you."

"No, it's OK. But I really don't feel comfortable with my body."

"What do you mean?"

"I don't like the way it looks." And then she said, "But you wouldn't go out with someone who was ugly, would you?"

"No, I wouldn't."

"Right."

"Why did you ask me that? Is that one way of proving that you're not ugly? That if I'm going out with you then obviously you can't be ugly, cos I wouldn't be?" I'd never normally use a word like 'ugly', even indirectly, but I was, you know, falling in with her terminology.

"Yeah."

"You're not unattractive. You've very attractive. I find you very attractive and I know that other people find you very attractive."

"Who?"

"Let's ignore that. Lots of other people find you attractive."

"Yeah but."

"You're not fat, like Annabel." I felt an example was called for here. You know, bring other people down so that me and Alice can feel better. I then told Alice that her legs were 'nice'. Not 'nice', but NICE! I remember going through her body parts and saying how good they were: legs, stomach, breasts, arms, neck, hair. I wasn't like that guy that was amazing with women, Don Juan, or whatever his name was. It was more modern day, cos when I began to use words like 'beautiful' and 'attractive' these were obviously not corresponding with the words in her head, cos it's like they've been diluted over time, you know, you read about it in fairy stories, you've seen it on TV, coming from the mouth of some horny, sleazy French fucker with a moustache trying to get it on with Marge Simpson, and these words begin to mean nothing, you know, they aren't the words of here and

133

now. And she's beginning to see it as if I'm trying to make a schmuck out of her. If I'd've gone, 'Ah Ma-donnnn-a, yoo urrr sooo buuuteeefuuullll,' it would've been like you've seen in so many comedy acts where some greasy Greek is trying to get the middle-aged English housewife out of her knickers. And this is the thing, and it worked, and you can mock me all you want, but I started to use words that weren't announcing any intent to seduce and also worked with the words that she could relate to. I said 'fit', 'nice' and 'cool'. And I made a joke out of it as well. I mean, you gotta understand this was quite a tense thing, but I was trying to lighten the air.

She started talking about this surfer guy, someone she met and nearly kissed at Glastonbury, and was mocking the way he spoke, like, 'yeah man, cooool,' and so I'm like, 'I don't know how to say this, and what I'm saying might sound cheesy,' and now I'm as if I was this surfer guy, saying, 'Man, your legs are well cool' and 'your stomach's amazingly fit'. And I'm meaning it in true honesty, but so that we both feel comfortable with what I'm trying to say, almost giving it a third-person outlook. Right? I just thought, fuckit, I'll do it how he would do it. So in the end it's light-hearted, but she knows I'm being honest. So it was 'fit', 'cool', 'well fit', 'well cool'; just variations on a theme. Occasionally I might throw in 'amazingly' or 'awesome' or 'very, very, very', but that was obviously adding more humour.

"So what is wrong with your body?"

"I don't like my feet."

"Let me see your feet."

"No."

And so I tried to grab her feet and we ended up playfighting while I tried to get to see these supposedly hideous peds.

"There's nothing wrong with them feet." I mean, she had small feet, a girl's feet. There was nothing wrong with them at all. "So what else don't you like?"

"I don't know. Just all of it."

And then I explained again how good her whole body was.

134

"Well, I dunno, haven't you got anything you've got a problem with?"

"Not really. Can't think of anything."

"There must be."

"Ummmmmmm nope."

"Oh."

And I could see this was upsetting her, so I said, "Errr, I don't like my chin. Nose is horrible. My eyebrows are bad. And I hate the lips."

"So you hate your face?"

"Yup, I hate my face."

"Oh."

And that shot me to fucking flames. No 'but I like your face', or anything like that coming back.

"So?"

"Yeah."

She didn't actually say, I can see what you mean. That wouldof been too harsh, even for Alice. But it was almost. And I was like, doh! Can't win.

But we start to kiss again and me to fondle. I will say she wears the largest of bras. I mean, this bra is UltraBra. This ain't no frilly fucker; this bra is old school. A nun's bra. I've never seen it, but just from feeling it through the clothing, it's got straps everywhere and serious levels of support. Everywhere there could be support, there's a strap. But I could see my attention to this area was starting to concern her, so I told her that her breasts were well fit. I can't remember exactly, but I was just trying to reassure her in a non-cheesy way.

Then we slowed it all down and just talked and she said she'd better be leaving.

"You're not leaving because of this?"

"No."

"Tell me if I've pushed it too far."

"No, it's OK. But I've really gotta go."

"Stay longer."

135

"That annoys me as well. You're always asking me to stay longer. You're always pushing your luck."

"But I like spending time with you. It's surely not so hard to understand. I mean, it's not like I want to leap in bed and fuck you." I didn't say it like that, of course. But I wouldof thought she wouldof seen it as a compliment that I wanted to spend more time with her; but she was getting annoyed about it, like I was putting her under too much pressure and she was gonna get into trouble with her mum. And I know what I'm like, I do push my luck. So we go downstairs. I remember kissing her, but only quickly, cos she moved her head away, so I think hmmph, OK. She gets into her car and I go to kiss her goodbye but I only kiss her on the cheek, and she gives me one of the weirdest looks, but over ever so quickly, like hmmph, why hasn't he kissed me properly?, then she went.

I never gave up on trying to remove Alice's clothing, and she seemed to quite like my trying, but only up to a point, beyond which she would get annoyed, withdraw privileges and launch an inquest into the defects of my personality; e.g. my inability to respect boundaries. The exchange of views which followed could get quite emotional for both of us, and in the end we decided that the only way forwards was for us to draw up some rules of engagement.

Basically we were sitting in the car outside my house, arguing. I'd been trying to come on to her and she got irritated and said, "I don't find you attractive at all any more." Oh, OK, thanks Alice. That's nice.

She: "Oh, I may as well just go home, it's not gonna work out, is it?"

Me: "No, we need to sit down and talk about it."

She: "Yeah but we go in circles."

Me: "Come indoors for a cup of tea. We'll calm down and then try again."

She: "Look, I really want to be friends with you."

Me: "OK. I don't think we should just throw it away like that."

She: "No, I agree."

Me: "But we are gonna, like, throw it away if... we don't sort this out."

So we went indoors and ended up sitting on my bed, sipping tea in a kind of uneasy silence, until I had a bright idea.

"Why don't we come up with some rules?"

"OK."

And then I took it one step further. "Let me write these down; do you mind?"

"No, I don't mind."

"Why don't we turn it into some kind of treaty? You know, if any of these are broken, the organisation falls apart."

"Right, OK."

And this is what we wrote down:

1) No talking about girl/boyfriends, but can tell each other that we have got one, no details. Then we amended this slightly: 'Allowed to tell each other about a boy/girl we may go out with.' What this meant was, I'm not allowed to say to Alice, man, I saw this girl the other night; man, she was fit. I really liked her. Her name was suchandsuch; I talked to her. Not allowed to say that. I'm allowed to say, 'I'm going out for a meal with suchandsuch.' Not my girlfriend yet; but I'm going out with her. OK? And I'm allowed to say, I've been out with her a few times, and we're now boyfriend and girlfriend. But not allowed to, like, talk about people that we just saw and fancied. Cos what's the point? It's just pissing each other off. You know, fair enough; you've gotta like communicate to the other one that you're now with someone else, cos it may begin to look a bit weird that you can't do things certain nights. Right.

That was a discussion.

2) If invited, allowed to come; if not, do not invite yourself. Then in brackets: 'no hard feelings.' This was obviously directed at me.

137

3) No holding hands in public or in private, i.e. so we don't look together. Why? Because she wants to be available for other boys. It's as harsh as that. She don't cut no corners. No, like, being careful with feelings. 'I just don't wanna look like I'm with you.' Thanks. That makes me feel nice.

4) No kissing, unless on cheek, or special occasions: e.g. present-giving, like birthdays, Christmas; haven't seen each other in a long time.

5) No pleasuring of each other in a sexual way, i.e. she wanted to put something down in the treaty, which she knew I would never be able to upkeep.

Signed Matt Pearce, signature, signed Alice Howell, signature. Dated first of the seventh two thousand and two.

We had hoped to stick to all these rules; but thirty/forty minutes after we'd written them down, number five was already broken. But I've still got that treaty somewhere, you know, held on to it, like Jedediah in *Citizen Kane*, for the sake of history.

Chapter Twelve

On the Road

In America if you've got any kind of
intelligence, or you have a questioning attitude
towards authority, you do stand up

It's a weird existence on a Greyhound bus. And you learn tricks. Like when you get on at your first main depot, e.g. New York, first destination Chicago, final destination Las Vegas, Los Angeles, wherever; and that's where you've got to set your seat. And it's gotta be the best seat, cos you're in that seat for a long time. You've got to be selfish in the respect that you know that you're going to be one of the only ones that's gonna ride this thing through, and you wanna be comfortable at all costs.

On your first few journeys you're green and you sit close to the toilet, thinking, that's a convenient place to be situated. Mistake. You don't wanna sit next to that toilet for three days, cos by the third day it's gonna reek, it's gonna smell of shit, and if you're trying to get to sleep someone's always gonna be passing you. Where you wanna sit, and where I learnt to sit, is just behind the driver. Not directly behind the driver, but the seat just behind the first seat behind the driver, cos that's where the wheelbase is. For whatever reason when they designed these things the wheelbase causes that first seat and that next seat to be a lot further back, and you can quite literally put your legs out. And you wanna stretch out; and this is the only seat on the whole bus on which you can achieve that. So that's one of the first seats you wanna get in. The other thing I learnt is, always make sure you're wearing a pair of sunglasses when you get on. Cos when you first get on, you haven't met anyone and you don't wanna talk to anyone, and, you know, you don't wanna, sort of, bother anyone, plus you don't wanna be bothered by anyone e.g. sitting next to you, cos they're gonna annoy you and want conversation. So what you do is, you get on that bus early, you claim that seat, put your bag down beside you, put your sunglasses on so no one can see your eyes, and lie up against the window, kind of half-asleep. One, nobody wants to ask you if you can move your bag so they can sit down, because you look like you might be asleep, plus it is important to have that bag beside you so you can get stuff out of it without having to be like, excuse me, excuse me, getting your bag down and sitting hunched up with it on your lap, or by your feet, and that's no good; and two, you don't know them, so they're gonna be inclined to leave you alone. And nine times out of ten that works. People just keep on moving by. It's almost like you've got a sign: 'Keep on moving. Keep on moving.'

That's one of the first things you do. Another is to go to the toilet. There are no washing facilities in the toilet. All they've got is little wet handwipes smelling of lemon in silver foil packets, like they have in KFC and Chinese restaurants. Again it sounds selfish, but by the second to third day there's none left in there. None. None. You go for a pee or even worse, you ain't gonna be able to wipe your hands, and then you're not gonna be able to eat them delicious crisp cookie things I'll tell you about in a second. And you're gonna worry about it, especially if you're me. So after you claim that seat and put your bag down, you wanna go to the toilet and PLPP flip off the top of the container and take as many wipes as you can. Screw everyone else. I mean, I don't like being like that, but I'm on this bus for three days and I want clean hands. And you wanna make sure you don't get seen, cos other people know this trick, too, which is how it all goes so quickly of course. So it's CKKK, CKKK, CKKKK, load up, load up, load up, go sit down and slyly distribute them back into your bag. That was the routine I got into when I rode the bus.

Once you're settled in, for the first few hours it's all optimism: quite interesting, nice, you know, new people, you're fresh, you feel clean. By the end of the first twenty-four hours, however, you're like, fucking hell, I stink, I'm sweaty, uncomfortable, don't feel like I'm getting anywhere, a kid's crying, you know, beginning to do your head in. Forty-eight hours: you're acclimatising, kinda liking it, getting used to the rhythm of the day. Plenty of time to read, stare out the window for hours on end. You find strange amusements in, you know, looking forward to the next stop. And I got addicted, and I'm amazed at how much time this used to pass, this is so sad, but anyway, there were these crisps over there, and of course this is the land of the most junk food you've ever seen, and these crisp/cookie things came in medium-sized packets. They were like hard corn with in the middle a soft, sorta pasty goo. It was a savoury snack, you know, like cheeseball puffs, those things you bite into and chew at Christmas with the soft cheesy goop in the middle but hard outer shell. Like dog treats, crunchy outside and in the middle a soft savoury goop, not gooey-gooey, but you could push your finger through it. And I don't know, but there's not a lot to do riding a bus, so I would drop one of these crisps in my mouth and I would just sit there and purposefully suck it, TSSTTT TSSTTT, CLKK, CLKK, just suck the goop out, and this took a while, until you'd be left with just the hard shell, you know, like an insect sucking out the inside of its paralysed prey, and then you'd go NGGU NGUULP. Next one: TTST, TTSST CLKK. And the whole packet would take about forty-five minutes to an hour. You'd just sit there eating them really slowly and taking great pleasure in making one last longer than any of the others. There was just very little else to do.

Eventually people would start to bring down some barriers, not that they had that many anyway, and start talking to each other. This would begin after about a day, because you'd weeded out all the people taking the shortish journeys, and now you're onto the hardcore that are in it for the long haul, the final destination.

However, the lessons you learn come from the mistakes that you make; and I made a big one at Chicago, e.g. when I was still new to the bus system. It begins when I'm at Boston and check my bag in, which has got my name on it, get on the bus, show my five-hundred-dollar universal ninety-day pass, take a seat. Don't think anything more about it. You have to remember these aren't like two or three-hour journeys; these are epic missions. You get to know the people on the bus. That's part of the trip. But I get to Chicago and my bag isn't there. My kickass bag's been kicked off.

How it works is that you write on the bag where you're going. You have a ticket thing. I didn't do that. I thought that when you get off the bus, you go, my bag's in the hold, they find Matt Pearce, and give the bag to me. And the whole time you don't ask for the bag means it gets left on the bus. I mean, that's how it would work in England. But it doesn't work that way in the States. Over there what happens is, at every stop, they look through the bags and find all the ones marked for that stop, and then kick them off. If there's a bag that hasn't got a ticket on it, it just gets thrown off at the first stop, cos they think that's where it's going to. That's the default. You have to label it, and I didn't know you had to label it. I thought, and you would think this wouldn't you, you know, you get to a stop and you would go, my bag's on there, oh what's your name? Matt Pearce. None of this labelling stuff. Anyway, that's what happened. And the thing is, I'm seeing the bags getting unloaded all the time and thinking nothing of it. Probably watched my own bag being unloaded and left on the ground, but thought, well, these people are getting off cos they're getting their bags, but mine's still in there, because I'm not getting off yet. And you do see them getting off and going that's my bag, that's my bag. And because the journey's so long, it's nearly a day later before I realise what's happened, cos basically that's when I get off and the guy says, "You ain't got no luggage."

And of course they don't wanna help you at all, cos the bus depot people, predominantly black and Mexican, are a section of society that is low paid, no motivation, and they are basically like, you know, go away. Lost everything, all my clothes, maps, books, toothbrush, everything except what I'd kept in my small rucksack on the bus, which luckily included my money and my copy of *On the Road* which I was re-reading at the time. Also lost my film script, *born2run*, so if I ever see it one day up there on screen or straight to DVD, I'll know which motherfucker to chase down.

This involuntary downsizing probably predisposed me from the get-go against staying any length of time in Chicago, and matters got worse when I found myself in a real dive of a place. The guy in charge was brilliant; he had one of those throat vibrator things that made him sound like a Dalek, like 'Hiiiiii', but it was a proper down-and-out place, really cheap, ten dollars a night, which is a fiver or something. There were people staying there for long periods of time and it was the kinda place Bukowski might have holed up in during his *Factotum* period. But it was not the most hygienic of accommodations. I took pictures of a stain on the bed cos I wanted to document it in case I had to work out what the hell I'd caught when I was put into intensive care when I got home, cos in the States, without medical insurance, I'd've been left on the sidewalk. A photograph of a stain probably wouldn't have helped the surgeons much in pinpointing the virulent super-bacteria wasting my immune system like something out of *28 Days Later*, but it felt comforting at the time.

This all came about because when I first rolled into Chicago I had no idea where I was gonna stay, because I never really knew where I was gonna stay wherever I went. And being now bagless and scriptless, I was not in the best of moods. In fact I was even thinking, you know, I wanna go home; but then it was like, I ain't going home, I can't give up, and I kind of pulled myself together and went over to this board in the bus depot, which was one weird board. It had all these places on it: places to stay, restaurants, hotels whatever, and you pushed a button and it rang through.

Now bus depots are not the best locations to hang out in. Real deal down-and-outs in bus depots, like big time. Cos if you ain't got no money, you go by bus. I even saw some Amish people, this white family with, you know, the hat and everything, and I'm thinking, that's weird, but obviously they can't go around on horse and cart everywhere and they've gotta travel somehow. So anyway, I'm in the Chicago bus depot, huge population of black people, as you would expect, and I'm kinda standing out like a sore thumb, cos there are no Amish brethren for me to try to blend in with. Everyone seems friendly, but there's an element of, you know, this is a bit dodgy. So I go up to the board and push a button, which activates some kind of intercom that calls through, like speed-dialling on some freephone system wired up to facilitate business. Someone answers. I'm like, hello, I'm looking for a room. We haven't got any. I get this response about ten times; then find a place that says 'Rooms for Ten Dollars a Night!' and I think, that's cheap! so I press the button, get directions and call a cab. But before I can get into the cab this bum comes up to me.

"Come on, brother. Give us some money. Give us some money. Come on, help ya brother out." He was a black guy; polite but persistent.

"Uhhhh, uhhhh."

"Get in the cab! Don't give that motherfucker anythang!"

"Ohhhh."

"Man, don't give 'im anythang!" And then the cab driver, who's also black, turns to the bum, "Get away, you, get away!"

"Come on, man, come on." I'm getting full-on pleading now.

"Ahhh, I really gotta go..."

"Get in the car! Get away, get away. Don't give 'im anythang!"

In the end I give the bum a dollar; and proceed to get berated by the cab driver for the whole of the journey.

"Ah can't believe ya gave that motherfucker a dollar," in proper, you know, high-energy Chicago blues and rap, even though he's quite an old guy. "Who's drivin' ya? Who's drivin' ya to this place? You gotta give ME money. Not that motherfucker. 'E never did nuthin' for ya!"

"I'm sorry. I won't do it again."

Seeing the genuineness of my contrition the cab driver relaxed a little.

"Ah don't mean ta be goin' on. Ya do whadya like. Beh. Ah just don't wanna see ya being cheated. Don't be cheated." He was still angry but I could see he was also concerned for my material and spiritual wellbeing.

"OK. I'm sorry."

We finally arrive at the ten-dollar-a-night hotel which is in some dingy street in the middle of nowhere, and I climb out.

"Remember. Remember what ah said."

"I'll remember, I'll remember. I promise. I promise."

It was a roughish area, you know, I instantly picked that up; but whatever. There was a Starbucks on the corner, and whenever you see one of those you know you're still in civilisation, not that I'm a big fan, but you always know that at least you're not in Beirut, though there's probably a Starbucks there as well. Anyway, I go inside and the proprietor's behind a bulletproof glass screen. It actually says 'manufactured bulletproof' whatever. And he's really old and got this phlegm-soaked croaky voice that you can barely understand. And even though he has the throat vibrator, he doesn't use it all the time, so sometimes it's just 'HRRRRRGGG BAAARRRRRGGGG GGHRRRGGGGG' very low-decibel, so all you can do is nod and hope that's the right response. But he was over the moon at my arrival, cos I don't think he got to see that many English tourists during his average working week.

"How much is a room?"

"Wherrrrregghhhyagghhfffffruugghom?"

"Freetown. England."

"Ohhhggghhhhhh!" You know, really excited.

"I just wanna room."

"Dja wanna paaay baaa thaaa weeeek?" He's using the throat vibrator now, producing the black Dalek tones.

"Pay by the week?"

"Yeah, yaa caaan paaay baaa the weeeek."

145

"No, I'm alright. I just wanna stay a couple of days."

"Okaaaay." Less excited now. He then explains about some special offer where you can pay by the month, and I'm thinking, I don't wanna pay by the month, what sorta fucking hotel is this?, and repeat that I'm only looking to stay for a couple of days, then he goes BZZZZZZZZZZZZ and I'm thinking, this is weird.

"Gotaathaadooor, gotaaathaaadoooor." BZZZZZZZZZZZZZZ.

And this door opens and I go through. Door goes CLNNK behind me, and the guy pops out of the room he was in.

He's short and his skin's more olive that I'd appreciated, so probably Puerto Rican. But really old, and with the voice you could tell he didn't have the finest bill of health.

"Ahhlll showyawhereitissss."

And he takes me along the corridor.

"Vennnnnding macheeene's there. Get yaself a snaaaack."

"OK. Thanks."

"Roooom's thisawaaaay."

I follow until we get to my room.

"Here'saaa keeey," and he undoes the door. I'm thinking, you don't see many hotels with keys these days, you know, normally it's a swipe card, but he's now inside giving the tour.

"Ya gotta showerrrr therrrre. Caaan't haaave a baaaath."

"OK."

"TeeeVeee."

"Thanks."

"Beeeed." You know he's pointing out the obvious.

"Yup."

"Yeaaaah."

"Yeah."

An uncomfortable silence, and I'm wondering what's going on, but finally I oh of course realise I've gotta tip him and give him something; not a lot, cos I'm over my hundred-dollar-tipping by now and beginning to get an idea of the value of things, but enough, about five dollars, though even that was probably way too much, I don't know, but I couldn't give him just a dollar, cos that

146

would be weird, just like fifty pence, you know, here you are, go and buy yourself something nice. Anyway, he seemed happy and shuffled off.

So I'm in this room now and I've got no stuff to unpack, just a couple of items in my rucksack, so I start checking the place out.

Begin with the bathroom; it looks rough. Hasn't had a clean-out or new décor in a decade. In fact, looking around, everywhere feels grey and brown. Carpet's a bit sticky, not clean, hasn't seen a vacuum cleaner in yonks, brown-coloured, you know, pooey. TV is on this crappy wooden stand; sort of MDF fibreboard built, but with some shit oak stuck on the front of it, so it looks reasonable, but if you were to CLKK CLKK tap it you could tell it was not solid. Funnily enough it was just the sort of thing that Sam's antiques warehouse would load onto a container and ship out over to America. The TV's old, not like the ones you normally get in hotels, and the once-white phone is yellow from nicotine stains. In fact there are fag stains and burn marks everywhere. The pillowcase has burn holes in it, where someone has obviously been smoking in bed. The whole place just seems worn-in. Incredibly. The bathroom has big brown tiles and is really badly lit. There's no window in there, just an extractor fan which makes an awful WHOOOOAAAA noise. It's the sort of place where when you take a shower, even though the opposite wall, where the sink is, is only a few feet away, you have trouble seeing the shadowy corner at the bottom. It's got a light phobia and steams up incredibly quickly. You can imagine cockroaches falling on your head. The only window is in the bedroom, and it's one of those long, thin high-up ones with slit panes that creak open amidst great protest to an angle of about thirty degrees when you pull a tatty lever; so you ain't getting a view in this joint. And you ain't gonna be bringing no one back here, neither. It's dim, brown, drab, worn-in, dull; but it is what it is. And I'm thinking, well, it's cheap, only ten dollars. But it is the sort of place that you drag the stand with the TV on in front of the door every night before you go to sleep, as I did, cos the door's only got a latch lock on it, which can be kicked

147

in instantly, and although there is nowhere to run to, if I am about to get shot, it will give me a few seconds to work out if I've got any kind of plan to get out of this situation. Of course maybe it would be better to die in my sleep rather than get woken up and then shot, I don't know.

I take a look at the bed cover and think, fuck. There are burn marks including this mega one that really starts to piss me off; but luckily it is only at the end. Then there are the stains, one in particular, about nine inches and in the shape of Africa. Everything's now going through my mind: looks like a blood stain, looks like a blood stain, maybe it's a semen stain, even worse. I'm trying to rationalise it, you know, if I get into the bed from the other side, stay well away from that region, maybe it's doable. I chill myself out, relax and decide to go out to get some food, cos it's still the morning and even though I'm exhausted I know I need to eat something.

As I leave my room I see a rough-looking woman in the room opposite, cos the door is open, and her room is full of stuff; clothes, huge boxes, everything. This woman is not travelling light. And I soon discover that this place is for people that've got no money, you know, they've defaulted on the last payment of their house, or something like that, and they've gotta get out quick. So it's like a halfway house. I've not ended up at a hotel at all. And this was why the guy was trying to offer me a long-term deal. This is a place for people to stay while they're trying to get their lives back on track. But it was different and dirt cheap, and better than a hostel, because at least you had your own room, for a similar hostel price. I mean, yeah, you pulled the TV in front of the door, and you heard arguments through the walls, people shouting at each other and stuff; but you got used to it.

When I return to my room after a couple of maple-syrup pancakes, almost to piss me off further, when I pull the bed cover completely back, BOOOM, another stain, very similar, reveals itself on the actual bed sheet itself. So I'm surrounded by stains, and now I'm like omigod how am I gonna get around all this?

148

You know, I'm tired and whatever and I really need some sleep. So in the end I just get in and purposefully try to fall asleep on the side without the stain on the sheet; but of course I know that during the night I'm gonna move around and there's just no way of avoiding it. So that's when I decide to take the photos. And cos I was knackered from this massive journey of getting from Boston to Lowell to Chicago I slept through the whole of that day from midday until the following morning. Twenty, twenty-two hours' sleep.

When I woke up around 10 am the next day I was a bit disorientated, as you would be, you know, what fucking day is it? I was so beat. I got up and went over to the vending machine and bought a packet of pretzels and sat back down thinking, there's nothing I can do now. The whole of my first day in Chicago had just gone, wiped out.

But there were still important things concerning personal hygiene to address. I mean, here I am and this place is not the best, but I'm trying to keep it together; however, I need to clean my clothes, having lost my entire wardrobe, and I haven't got any detergent or anything. So I proceed to develop this system where I have a shower but I put the plug in and take my clothes off, in the shower, turn shower on, have shower, lather everything up so it builds up soap suds in the water, and while I'm in the shower stomp all over my clothes, like a grape treader, working the soap in, washing the clothes and me at the same time, getting everything clean. And then I'd get out of the shower and give the clothes a bit of hand washing. Then I'd take the plug out and rinse my clothes out with cold water and then hang them over anything I could find. But I'd have to do this before I went to bed, cos I've got nothing else to wear at this point. So I go to bed naked, praying there's not going to be any kind of evacuation, cos then I'll have to put wet clothes on. In the morning most of the time the clothes would be dry; put them back on and start the cycle again. In the end I performed this ritual every night. Not always the jeans and the shirt, but definitely always my vest and underpants.

149

Chicago itself was great. I really liked it, even though I didn't get to see too much of it, being trapped in this washing cycle and gripped by the fear of going down any day with typhoid fever. And also I was starting to become more of a night owl; this is one of the habits I picked up on my American trip. Because if you're gonna meet people, you meet them in bars, you meet them in restaurants, you meet them at shows, and it seems a bit strange if you're out in the day and you're going, hello, how are you?, and all that, whereas in a bar at night you can get away with it. So I don't really remember that much about the days; I just sorta walked around, took in the streets, went to museums. I caught the bus out to the Shedd Aquarium which was one place everyone said I had to go. I was expecting to find, you know, a four-by-four wooden thing with goldfish in it; but it was massive and had gigantic tanks of every kind of fish you could imagine: octopus, barracuda, stingray, all moving slow and graceful, perhaps a bit mournful. But to be honest, to me an aquarium's an aquarium, you know, just a place with fish, so I didn't stay long and walked all the way back, where I mustof seen about a million Mexicans working on landscape, central reservations, hedgerows, stuff like that.

I know it sounds cheesy, but just like everyone says, Chicago's a windy, windy city. Don't know why but it blows all the time. And it was never sunny; just drab and overcast. It's also one of those places where you only have to travel a little way out and then you can look back and really get a sense of a city skyline. I mean, you only need to be a couple of miles out and it's nothing, nothing, nothing, road leading in, then BOOM: city. No gradual build-up, like, say, London, where the housing gets denser and denser; Chicago is just suddenly there. From the angle I looked at it from at the Shedd Aquarium, probably no more than about five miles out, as you kept looking in that direction you could almost see the yellow brick road, as it were, leading to the golden city, and then BAM there it is, the city of Chicago itself.

Maybe it was the time of year, but the whole city seemed to me grey and dreary. One thing about Chicago that I thought was incredibly cool, however, was the elevated transport system; the e-train or whatever they call it. Just like the underground, only overground. You know, like in *The French Connection* car chase, where you've got trains flying over above the cars. That film mustof been shot in Chicago, being Friedkin's hometown. And you can be, like, at a payphone and look up and there's all these stilts and then a train goes by. You see it while you're walking along; CHKK, CHKK, CHKK, CHKK as it goes past. That is so cool.

When I was in Boston everyone told me that when I got to Chicago I had to go to The Second City, which is where all the great stand-ups started: John Belushi, Chevy Chase; OK, they all went downhill, but back in the day, when there was Dan Aykroyd, John Candy, Billy Crystal and all these guys from the late seventies/early eighties, not quite sure of the timeline, but THIS is where they started. THIS is the place. Back then there was only one Second City and it was in Chicago; but, like everything, they started a fucking franchise so you can go to a Second City in San Francisco, Second City in New York; but THIS was the original. So I found it and bought a ticket to a show.

I've always loved stand-up. For me it's the purest form of comedy. And only the Americans can do it. I can't listen to British comedians; they haven't got the gene. British comedy just makes me squirm in embarrassment, like British movies; no balls, no talent, no edge: and above all, no intelligence. Completely dumbed-down. You'd think that adjective would apply more to the US than anywhere; but remember they were the ones who came up with the term in the first place, meaning they identified the problem, recognised it, named it. We didn't even have a name for it in the UK, until the US lent us theirs, which is like them lending us their intelligence. Cos that's what it's really about. And in America if you've got any kind of intelligence, or you have a questioning attitude towards authority, you do stand-up.

The first stand-up I began to appreciate, enjoy and respect is Bill Hicks. Bill Hicks to me is the ultimate stand-up: one, because he's fearless; two, he says whatever he wants; three, he doesn't give

151

a shit about pissing anyone off, especially his own paying audience. And what he was talking about, even back in the nineties, is still perfectly relevant today, especially with the Gulf War and whatever. He didn't care. He would question anything, things people just do going about their normal lives, thinking to themselves, oh yeah, that's the rules, I'll do it. He wasn't that sort of person. And nothing was ever taboo. Pregnancy. Abortion. And he wouldn't do it in a shit, cheesy way, though; it was always clever. He'd bring up religion, advertising – 'Anyone here from advertising? Just put up your hands. Right. Go home and kill yourselves. No, I'm not joking.' – American politics, world politics. If he were around today he would be taking issue with Islamists just as much as with George Bush. He wouldn't care. 'Course there'd be a fatwa out on him, so he'd be dead; but he wouldof said it anyway, in the same way that some rednecks broke both his arms and strung him up on a tree for taking Jesus' name in vain.

"You caan't saay thaaat 'bowt Jeesus!"

"So you're a Christian?"

"Yeeupp, prahd of it."

"Then forgive me."

And they'd look at each other like, wha?

"I mean, surely that's the very foundation of your religion. Forgiveness and understanding?"

But the good ol' boys couldn't get it, so they beat the crap out of him.

That's the kind of guy Hicks was. And I suppose I also kind of like him for his mental instability, and the fact that he was like an evangelical preacher. I mean, he'd get out there and he'd be sweating, laying it down with such a passion it was like he was channelling lightning; inspired but scary. People would say it was frightening to see him up there, cos they would be taken aback by his gusto. He was in the zone. Like some of those old blues guys that sometimes don't even seem able to sing, only groan, howl or chant; but you gotta listen to them, cos they are somewhere else, man, somewhere beyond, somewhere amazing. That was Bill

Hicks at his best. Giving it all he had. Rage, bitterness; that was the man. One pissed-off motherfucker. He was maverick, as edgy as they come; he was never gonna be tamed into a cutesily psychotic cartoon animal voice in some U-certificated Disney Pixar movie.

Bill Hicks smoked like a chimney, had a drink problem and was well into his drugs; but that's the thing about stand-ups. Just like the blues guys, they're shamans that need the peyote or coke or whatever to get the visions and the gift of tongues. And that's why they either give it up, you know, flip a switch and go into movies, like Robin Williams or Eddie Murphy, or die, like Lenny Bruce, John Belushi or Bill Hicks. Cos it's not sustainable, which sorta adds to the penumbra of edge and scariness that surrounds the spotlight they're in. They're all addicts, obsessives and fuck-ups at some level; but that just feeds into the oddball humanity of their material. I mean, profound psychological problems just get recycled into the act, as with Woody Allen, the neurotic granddaddy of them all. But there was one weird fucked-up story about Bill Hicks that I particularly liked, cos for obvious reasons I especially could kind of see where the man was coming from.

As with this type of person generally, Bill Hicks was shit with women but got obsessed with one. One day he comes back from LA to find that this girl he'd been dating and then broken up with had started going out with his best friend. This pissed him off royally; especially when he then found out, cos he'd never ever been able to sleep with her, that she had slept with the friend, and, to make things even worse, the friend had not used a condom. So this is bothering Bill big time. Now he's back from being away, she gets to know him again, they're a little bit older, they end up dating once more, and eventually make love. But their relationship is doomed because he can never ever get this thing out of his mind, this is the kind of guy he was; he felt that when he was going down on her, I mean, the guy's fucked up, right, he felt that, even though it happened ages ago, it was like he was going down on the friend. It was like, that guy's semen has been inside of her; how could all the crevices inside of her vagina have been thoroughly cleansed of the

153

remnants of his semen? E.g. I could be down there and something decides to fall out at that moment in time and BAM it's in my mouth if I'm going down on her. This is what I mean; quite gross. And he couldn't handle it. Very obsessive, very looking into the fine detail, but totally irrational at the same time; so quite OCD. It's not that he was afraid of the germs; he just didn't like the idea that someone had been where he wanted to have gone first.

However, I'm not expecting to see the next Bill Hicks at The Second City, but that's cool cos I'm as equal opportunities about comedy as Joe is about women. I'll listen to anything even though I may not like it all. Generally I prefer black stand-ups like Eddie Murphy and Chris Rock, cos they're a bit raunchier and get away with more, maybe cos they're black, talking and walking with jive and rhythm and screaming out in their high-pitched whining-assed 'Ah'm pissed off, motherfucker' voices about rap, sex, women and chicken, you know, using their own culture and turning it inwards because they've got the licence to and white guys don't. But I can also listen to right-wing redneck stand-up like Larry the Cable Guy, with his proper southern 'gitterduunnn' which kills audiences every time. I find it all interesting at some level. And it doesn't have to offend anyone, or be political or full of anger, rage and bitterness like Hicks to be funny. It can just be stupid everyday stuff, like parking and shopping and the 3-F staples of food, family and fornication. I'll listen to David Cross, Lewis Black, Jim Gaffigan, Demetri Martin, George Carlin, who's almost ninety, Mitch Hedberg, who died of a heroin overdose, Sarah Silverman, who died a death onstage in the UK with her Jewish grandma gag – sure it's dark and twisted like a David Lynch movie, and you wonder at times if it's even funny; but that's what makes it a high-wire act.

So I've got no preconceptions as I go inside The Second City; whoever's there can be black, white, yellow, male, female, trans, gay, straight, bi, Jewish, Christian, Muslim, WASP, ethnic, New York liberal, good ol' boy from the swamplands of Louisiana, whatever. They just have to make me laugh.

154

It was a typical American comedy club: dimly lit, small round tables with a candle on each one, curtains opening and closing on a wooden stage, everyone sitting around smoking and drinking, orders being brought by waitresses to the tables which are arranged on two tiers separated by brick steps and a metal railing. On stage there's a troupe, you know, group performers doing skits like, 'OK you've got three friends and they run over a deer on the way to the wedding of one of their mothers', that sort of thing. Someone comes out, sets the scene, then skips off, a bit gay, and then the performers act the scene, ad-libbing and using props like chairs to represent a car, etc. A bit like Monty Python, you know, sketch-based, silly and kind of surreal. It's the first time I've seen this kind of comedy performed live, and even though I'm not a big fan I'm glad I've come. However, it's not stand-up, and I'm not laughing my head off.

As I say it's dark in the club and I'm on my own and fit waitresses are walking around, and by now I've had a few to drink, so I'm starting to feel a bit confident. One of the girls, attractive, you know, not ten, but I wouldof said eight, a little bit older than me, twenty-three or twenty-four, comes up to me and says, "You're on your own?" Again I think it mustof been the English thing that got the ball rolling; that always seems to be a conversation starter.

"Yeah, I'm over here on my own. Been staying with some people back in Boston."

"Oh, Boston?" And then we start talking a bit, you know, the usual stuff, where you from?, where you from? However, it wasn't customer service type talk; she was genuinely interested, cos she had to get back into character at the end of it with, "I'm gonna have to go back to work now. What drink did you want?"

"I'll have a Jack Daniels and Coke please."

She gets me a large JD & Coke and when she comes back, because I'm, like I say, confident, I just say, "I'm looking to get something to eat after this," and this is so cheesy, though kind of smooth, but I would never do this in England, never ever, never dream of it, would never have the confidence, wouldn't even

155

think of it, fear of rejection, whatever, but maybe because I'd had so much Jack Daniels, maybe because of the success I'd had in previous places, maybe because I was getting on with her so well, I then asked her, "What time do you finish?" And I don't know whether it was because I seemed so confident or what, but she said, "Oh I finish at eleven, meet me in the Irish bar over the road."

"All right." And I'm so cool I'm not even sounding that bothered.

"All right then."

I eventually leave, having seen enough of the dead deer and the mother's wedding, and go over to the Irish bar, thinking she's not gonna show. I'm hungry now so I order and start eating the Chicago equivalent of bangers and mash.

"All right?"

"All right." Thinking who the fuck's this?

"You don't recognise me, do you?"

Turns out it's her, but the place is so dimly lit, and she's not in her work outfit any more. But even with this cue I still can't figure out who she is, which is quite embarrassing.

"Wha ... what's your name?"

The penny finally drops, and we laugh about it and start chatting.

"How long you in Chicago for?"

"Not that long. Where's the best place to go? I wanna see something special."

"Well, you're in Chicago, you've gotta go to the blues club."

Again back in the day this is where all the famous blues musicians used to play.

"I've got no one to go with," again, you know, I'm playing up to it. "Why don't you come wimme?" I mean, I've got nothing to lose.

"Oh, I don't know…"

"Come on, let's go now."

"I can't go now, I've got work tomorrow."

"What time you gotta start work?"

"Two o'clock."

"Man, you can have a lie in. We can go. Come on. Lessgo, lessgo, lessgo."

"OK, OK, OK."

So we go, but not before she says goodbye to some friends of hers, and as we leave she says that she's worried that, man, they're all gonna think that, I can't remember the term she used, but basically we were gonna go off and fuck. That took me aback.

"Really?"

"Yeah, they're gonna think I'm loose."

"No, they won't." And possibly I'm thinking, I may be getting laid here. But I'm trying to act cool about it, although a little bit of me is getting excited like, you know, Englishman abroad.

We get there about midnight. The club is in a basement down some stairs off the street. You walk down the steps and there are two rooms, one to the right and one to the left. We go left. On the walls are old posters of blues and jazz musicians who played the venue in the seventies and nineties. Inside there's wooden floorboards and a bar at the back stretching half the length of the room. By no means is the joint flash and swanky, you know, no posh lighting and leather seats. It's well worn and dimly lit, as you'd imagine a blues place to be. The seating reminds me of church pews: long wooden benches with worn red leather padding lined up facing each other with a table in front. The walls are bare red-brown brick; not plaster-boarded or anything. The bar is long and wooden-fronted, with a metal foot rail and barstools, wood with red leather seats, and old-fashioned green-tinged lighting over the bar staff, so you can see the drinks on offer. One of those places that you probably wouldn't want to see in the day; the dimmed-down edginess and coolness only seeping through around midnight.

There were only about twenty-five people there cos it was a Wednesday night. On the stage, which was wooden, nothing too fancy, was an ensemble of three guys, one singing and playing guitar, another on bass and another on drums. And cos there was only this three-piece there tonight, for whatever reason, they had to switch between the two rooms, which were identically laid out. On a Saturday no doubt both rooms would be full with music playing; no idea how they worked out the acoustics, cos there was only a wall and the bar dividing the rooms, but they obviously did. The singer and guitar man was your stereotypical black bluesman: big, slightly overweight, weathered and in his fifties at least. He looked like he'd lived and he probably drank a lot of whisky and smoked ten packets a day, cos he had a cigarette in his mouth most of the time. You could tell he was old school. He wore an open red lumberjack shirt with a white T-shirt underneath, jeans and workman's boots. The other two were more trendy, being quite a bit younger. One of them had a goatee; they looked cool, content to have this old-timer leading them. But they were there, getting old and ready to take the lead when their time came.

I didn't recognise any of the songs, but it was blues music alright; standard twelve-bar stuff with jams that went on for ages. And it worked. It was what it was. Reminded me of a stripped-down version of R. L. Burnside, you know, chnka chnka diiiing chnka chnk, well I'm sittin' down lonely, lonely as hell, chnka chnka diiing chnka chnka, drums in the background kicking in. And the singer-guitarman's foot would be stomping away, and sometimes they would be going for it, the singer getting himself worked up, the footstomping getting faster and heavier, and the bass and drummer speeding up. And they'd keep up that tempo for around seven minutes. None of the songs ever really came to an end; they just merged. In fact it was only when the leader said, "Going over ta tha other room. Pleeze join me in fave minutes," that you knew there some sort of closure was on its way.

And he was always nodding. He'd be playing and then turn and nod to the bass, which was obviously a cue to go off into something else, and same with the drummer. They were all really into it, especially the leader with the cigarette in his mouth, jamming away nodding to the others so they could have a go, then he'd beam a smile and say, "Thank you very much," and everyone would clap, even though as the night wore on there were only about four of us left so the clapping wasn't deafening; but it was late now and you could tell these guys were hardcore, doing a six-hour stretch, and they didn't look like they were stopping, you know, you could tell they loved it.

I don't know what money they were on; I can't imagine it was that great, on account of there being so few people in there, but it didn't seem to bother them any. Every half hour they'd take a break, pack up their instruments and move lazily over to the other stage then BAM they were straight back on it. Whether I was pissed enough to not realise they were playing the same track over and over, I don't know. But it worked and I enjoyed it and was proper getting into it, lying there with my bag and jacket and a beer on my chest, thinking, yeah, even though it mightof looked ridiculous, you know, this white boy and these black musicians going MMMRRRRRRR moaning and groaning about cotton-picking, while there's me thinking, yeah man, I can feel it, I can relate, not to what they'd been through, of course, but in terms of the pain. And by around two in the morning people would get up and go nuts dancing. Some crazy woman pretty much danced all night, on her own, drink in hand, up there on the dancefloor doing her thing. She was a white lady, weathered, you know, you wouldn't call her attractive; anywhere between thirty and fifty, difficult to tell. And the band would pick up tempo getting quite a bit rocky at times, as the guy put overdrive on his guitar and the drummer kicked in, whipping the high-hat, and the bass gathered pace while the leader howled out in his deep, gruff, moodful bluesman's voice, sweating and getting into it big time. You couldn't work out a thing he was saying, it was sound and fury; but that was all part of it.

The girl I'm with is listening and also drinking, but not too much, whereas I'm drinking, drinking, drinking, and getting more and more wasted, though I'm relaxed as hell. I'm lying out on one of the wooden benches, just listening to the music and I'm into it big time, you know, heeey, this motherfucker's got soul, and because it's now three in the morning he and his

159

ensemble are only performing for me and about three others. There's no one else there. She's sorta enjoying it and we're talking a little bit, and then she says, "I've gotta go home, I've really gotta go home now."

"Stay, stay, stay."

"No, you stay. You stay."

And don't ask me why, I just said, "Alright. I'll stay."

So she left and I'm now there on my own. And this place doesn't shut till seven in the morning. I just lie there with this Budweiser on my chest, listening to this music, and periodically the guy would, in a deep bluesy Chicago voice, do the 'I'm now gonna go over ta tha other staage. You can join me in tha other room in faave minutes,' thing. So the ensemble would traipse over to the other room and the other stage, and I'd get up and follow them, find myself a comfy seat, sit back down, shut my eyes and listen to the music. Lady would come over every now and again, 'Can I get you a drink?' 'Yup.' 'Another Budweiser?' 'Yup.' Budweisers over there don't cost much; booze in America really isn't all that dear in comparison to the UK. It's only when you start cracking out the wine spodiodis that it starts to get expensive; but because of the lack of amount of those that you can drink, it kind of averages out.

So I'm sitting there, drinking and drinking, really enjoying it. It was probably the worst blues in the world, but I'm into it. And there's no fear, maybe because I've drunk so much, I don't know, but I'm just in there with maybe two others. Come half six I sober up a little bit and get a cab, go back and sleep the next few hours.

RING RING RING RING. I've given this girl the number to my room, thinking, she's never gonna call me, never gonna call me.

"Uuuuurrghhhh." It's midday and I've just woken up.

"You just got up?"

"Yeahhh."

"What time did you stay till?"

"About half six." Mind's starting to clear a bit.

160

"Hope you enjoyed yourself. Did you have a good time?"

"Yes, thank you for taking me."

"Do you wanna meet up for lunch?"

We arrange to go for a pizza, and afterwards she says she has to go back to get her work stuff. So we take the e-train back to her apartment. She lives just down from Wrigley Field, which you can see at the end of the road from her apartment.

"When you come back through Chicago, I'll take you to Wrigley Field. There's no game on this weekend but I'll take you, I promise I'll take you."

"OK."

We talk and the whole time I'm thinking, I may be getting some, I may be getting some, I may be getting some. We're sitting on the sofa and she's got these tight white trousers on. I get playful about the whiteness, saying I need sunglasses, and we joke a bit. I think we maybe kissed a bit, too. You know, there's always that awful uncomfortable bit where you're sitting on the sofa and you think, do I make a move? Or do I not make a move? Is this the right time, or not the right time? In the end I decide to make a move, but as if by magic a friend turns up, freakishly skinny girl, says hello to me, but otherwise doesn't show me any major interest, and obviously I can't make a move now. Friend eventually goes, but the mood has now gone, too. We do end up kissing, but it's not the most amazing kiss in the world. I stay another forty minutes or an hour, just kissing, stroking, whatever. It was one of those times where you know there is never going to be any progression to anything else. She asks me if I want to come back with her to work, and I say I will cos I need to find my way back into the city. It was, you must have been in this sorta situation, where you aren't overly disappointed there isn't going to be anything more; but at the same time you're not going to dwell overly on the fact that you kissed her, you know, cos it was not like we're boyfriend and girlfriend now. It was what it was. It was enjoyable. And that was it.

We caught the e-train back into the city and when we parted she reminded me of her Wrigley Field promise and told me to give her a call on my travels. But I made the mistake of calling her up when I was pissed in Vegas, and that ruined everything. You don't wanna be calling a woman in Chicago when you've just been to a Vegas strip club and you're drunk, if for no other reason than time-zone differences. Because while it's six o'clock where you are, it's three in the morning where she is.

So that was the last I saw of her.

Chapter Thirteen

The Best Day Ever

Body Worlds

One day Alice and I were chatting outside a country pub a couple of miles from my house. It was sunny and she was drinking orange juice and ice. The ice was kinda forced on her by the barman, who was one of those cheeky chappies that loves to hold forth. "What, only orange juice? You want more than that! You want more than that!" You know, looking around and smiling and winking at everyone, and they're all grinning back, and Alice is now embarrassed in front of all these strangers staring at her, so when he then asks if she wants ice with the orange juice and she says no, just to get out of the conversation, he reacts theatrically with extreme disappointment, "What? No ice? Oh no, I was really looking forward to scooping that in," so she instantly collapses under the pressure and has the ice. I give him a look and ask for a pint of Guinness Extra-Cold which apparently contains nutritional qualities, and I haven't eaten all day. We take our drinks outside because it's warm and because Alice is clearly struggling with this inbred Old Vic overfamiliarity with customers.

"I thought you'd be not as nice as you are."

"What do you mean?"

"Dunno. You're just nice."

"Don't you want me to be nice?"

"No, I want you to be nice. I don't want you suddenly to be horrible to me."

"I really don't understand what you mean, Alice."

"I dunno what I mean."

"Right."

"I just thought you wouldn't be as nice as you are. You're just a nice person."

"Yeah? Isn't that a good thing?"

"Yeah. But I just didn't think you'd be as nice."

"What do you MEAN?"

And then it got dropped, because she just couldn't explain what that meant. But she did say she'd been quite into the idea that I wouldn't be as nice. However, whenever I did do something slightly not nice, she moaned at me. So what is that?

Anyway, I just said OK and she said, "Don't be horrible to me now, though." I really had no idea what this girl was all about. Then she said, "I'm going to London tomorrow."

And she said it like, you know, one of those lines like, 'I'm going to the cinema tomorrow. Do you wanna come?' It was one of those do-you-wanna-come ones.

So it was, "I'm going to London tomorrow."

SSSWWWSSSHHHHHH.

An Impreza WRX drives by, piloted by a guy in a baseball cap, arm dangling out of blackened window and flicking a cigarette.

SSSSSSSSHHHHH.

A Lexus LS600 sweeps past, smooth hum of V8 engine fading slowly down winding country lane and returning the meadows to birdsong, grazing sheep, lowing cattle and the swish of corn ears swaying in the soft Kentish afternoon breeze.

And the 'do you wanna come?' never comes.

So I'm just sitting there, and in my mind I'm thinking, fuck me, I've gotta do something cos I wanna go. I'm bored out of my skull, haven't done anything in ages, I'm not sitting indoors, my head doctor says I gotta get out more, fuck it, I'll invite myself. If she says fuck off, she won't, but she might do, I'll

"What are you thinking about?"

"I think you should invite me to London."

"No." Instant.

"OK." Inside I'm like ohhhhhhh reeling from this. "Why?" meekly.

"It's just me and Harriet going and I'm driving and it'll be stressful."

"OK."

But later it was, "You can come if you want." Probably cos by then I was in a mega-sulk.

"Why don't you want me to come?" And then I did the whole, you know, if you don't want me to come I won't come thing.

"No, I want you to come."

"Oh, it don't matter." And then, "The only reason I wanted to come is cos I wanna see the Body Worlds exhibition." So now it's looking less like I want to go on a trip, and more like I can mix my thing in with your trip, you know, genius stroke.

"What's Body Worlds?"

"It's an anatomical exhibition by some Professor Gunther von Hagens in Germany who basically preserves bodies, and it costs thirty-five thousand for each body."

"Preserves bodies?"

"Yeah, it's for scientific reasons and the guy's trying to create some sort of art as well."

"What, it's real body parts?"

"Yeah." And I explained to her about the guy holding his own skin and stuff.

"Why do you want to see that?"

"It's interesting and I've got some photography ideas that it fits in with, like two people getting off with each other, making love and kind of tearing each other's body apart. Literally. But I'm having difficulty making it less gruesome, cos I want it more beautiful. And I'm hoping the exhibition will give me some ideas to make it more softly softly, cos every time I try and think of it in my head it always looks gory and I don't want

165

it to look gory, so this is a good time for me to be going there, you know?"

And of course I'm just making it worse.

"That's odd."

"Yeah it's odd, but you don't have to worry; it's just something in my head. It's not an idea I wanna do. I mean, I don't wanna stab someone or make love to them in a pool of blood or whatever; it's just something in my head, sort of like a Francis Bacon painting."

"Alright. Cool." And by the end she was actually getting into the idea of having something creative in your head rather than some fucking bullshit shit. "OK, I'd go. But I'm not sure what my mum'll think."

"Mum?"

"Yup. She's coming, too."

Alice's mum was actually quite a nice, jolly, optimistic sort of person. She ran some meals-on-wheels company for the elderly, you know, yet another outsourced social 'service' which osteoporostic granny only gets to access if she pays cash on the barrelhead, lady, cos, like my head doctor says, it's the Wild West out there now, so she ends up paying for it three times, you know, once in a lifetime of taxes, once with her savings and once with the tax from spending her savings. Them government bastards have as usual got it all down; beats me why anyone would vote for any of them. As J-J always said, why vote for your own oppression? Anyway, mustn't go off on one. Mum did all the driving in the end because Alice lacked a bit of confidence and was worried about me being critical, although I'm not mean like that. But London's not the best place for underconfidence.

Mum was a pretty good driver, if a bit right-footed, late-braking, last-minute overtaking and crunchy through the gearshifts ('Sorry!'). The motor noise of her high-end Ford was constantly brrrrrrrr da-BBRRRRRRRrrrrrr, DA-BRRRRRRrrrrrrrr pfhtphtphtphtphtphtphtpht, Sorry! BRRRRRRrrrrrrr. I found myself gripping the back seat a lot and was giving Harriet, who had a bandaged thumb on account of getting it trapped when

166

slamming some other car door (how on earth do you get your thumb trapped in a car door?), a few we're-all-gonna-fucking-die glances; but she seemed unfazed, obviously immune to it all now having survived her own personal car trauma. Harriet was chattier than Alice and doubly chattier than the mum who barely spoke to me the whole time. In fact when I first got into the car it was just, "Alright." "Alright."

And that was it. But later I found out why this was.

"The only person who can speak to Matt the whole day is me. Don't ask him questions. Nothing." Harriet obviously cracked; but the mum found a way round Alice's strictures.

"Alice, ask him what he does. Alice, what does he enjoy? Alice, what are his future plans?"

It was that ridiculous. Some of the questions got through; some Alice screened out. I think the only thing the mum ever said to me direct the whole day was, "Do you want a cup of coffee? How many sugars?"

We parked up at Alice's nan's somewhere on the South Circular. The nan was a really nice old lady in this white smock thing, really laid-back and welcoming, you know, 'Hello?' 'Come on in'. She had quite an arty house, with sketches of horses in different poses and a massive upturned Vitruvian Man on the walls, which was cool. She had lodgers staying there with her and a dog that kept sniffing my nuts. This was where Alice's mum asked me if I wanted a cup of coffee; though she checked first with Alice that this was OK. The dog keeps bringing me this rubber toy which it wants me to grab, and everyone seems like they expect me to, so I grab it and now it's like grrrrrrrrrrr grrrrrrr, digging in, leaning back and pulling hard, all the time looking me in the eye and expecting me to give up, not instantly, but after a couple of hard tugs, but I'm pretty competitive and not overkeen on dogs anyway, so I ain't gonna lose this game. And now everyone's watching intently, like this isn't the programme to follow, and the dog is like GRRRRRRRRR GRRRRRRRRR and I'm like AARRRRRRRRR, proper straining myself, and eventually I do win, and the dog kind of whimpers

167

away and goes over to Alice looking well pissed off. And I can see it's thinking, 'Bastard, doesn't understand the rules round here!'

Mum then says, OK we need to get going, and now we're off again quick-marching to the Tube to get to the V&A where there's an exhibition she wants to catch. It's a photography exhibition of chairs, quite boring, still lifes, portraiture, other stuff; good pictures but nothing amazing, though having said that, I couldn't do it. There was one I recognised; Lewis Morley's famous picture of Christine Keeler sitting astride the back of an Arne Jacobsen chair, and next to it a parody of the same signed by Matt Groening in which yellow-skinned Homer Simpson with his excess adipose tissue and XXXXXL underpants sits on the back of a plastic red schoolchair like they have at college, sucking his finger in babypose. Nearby they'd also put out a replica of the Arne Jacobsen chair, in case anyone else found themselves seized by the urge to strip off, but fortunately there were no takers. Alice complains there are no buttons, you know; I want interactive, I want video clips, I want shit to happen. And because I'm talking to Alice and Harriet and making them laugh, which seems to be one of my main roles in life, people keep looking at us, like what are you doing?, and the ones running the show frown and go shhhhhhhh! But I don't understand why you have to be quiet at these sorts of things. I mean, it's not like you're in church. And when those guys first showed their pictures at their original exhibitions, there wouldof been people there pissed up and all sorts. So I don't think the artists themselves wouldof minded people talking and discussing their work.

Mustof taken us about an hour and a half to get round the exhibition, and afterwards we sat outside on the steps and ate some marmite sandwiches which Alice's mum had brought along. There was a bit of a debate about going to Body Worlds, cos the mum wasn't too keen and I could tell she wanted to bag the idea.

"There's a mummy in the science museum. He can go and see the mummy."

"I'm not interested in just any dead body."

168

"Yeah he is," says Alice.

"I'm not. I don't wanna go on some tour of, like, seeing every dead thing in London, you know, a squirrel or a pigeon or whatever. I'm only interested in this other exhibition. But it doesn't matter. Doesn't matter."

And I could tell Alice was wavering, maybe because of this intermediary role she was playing, relaying the mum's point of view, which she was now starting to adopt herself. Fortunately Harriet chipped in and said she was really up for going, so the mum, who remained unkeen, suggested we three go on to the Body Worlds exhibition without her and all meet back up later at Nan's.

The mum now leaves, and as soon as she's gone, Alice is instantly much more relaxed and talking to me like I'm a friend. Harriet's even more relaxed, and the whole day starts to go a lot smoother. We're now really talking and joking around as if we've been let off a leash. Me and Harriet start picking up heavily on this smell of gear coming from some French kids sitting nearby and smoking it big time, and Alice is like, can't smell anything.

"What?"

"You know, ganja."

"What?"

"You know, snffffffffff, that smell."

And Harriet's like, "Yeah, I can smell it."

"What?"

"You know, marijuana."

And finally Alice is like, oh yeah, I'm slow aren't I? But Harriet's like, you probably wouldn't know the smell anyway, would you Alice? And Alice was like, no, I wouldn't. Cos she had never been exposed to it.

We caught the Tube to Aldgate East and after temporary disorientation, where we were pointed in the right direction by some guy in his thirties with no legs, which kind of set the scene nicely, walked a mile or so to the Body Worlds museum at the top end of Brick Lane, which is less of a lane than a long, wide

169

boulevard like they have in Paris, but more Bangla and Brixton feeling, queuing halfway down because so many people wanted in. This at least proved that my interest in seeing Doctor Gunther's expo was not just the result of my personal weirdness. Or if it was, then this weirdness was widely shared.

It's not every day you go and see dead bodies on display, cos that's basically what Body Worlds was. Alright they've been through the plastination process where they inject plastic into the actual body bits; I don't know the exact science but that's the gist of it. It was one of the most hyped-up shows in town, and I know this might sound cheesy but it was a bit like it was a naughty thing to go and see, not like rude, but kinda like it weren't for everyone. I mean, you did have to be reasonably open-minded. The average person, like Alice's mum, would be like, why the fuck do you wanna go and see that? So there's an element of that, and not only that, but you never know quite how you're gonna react, cos all the media's going it's GORE!, you know, and BODY BITS! and there's a MAN HOLDING HIS SKIN! And you're like, Jesus, am I gonna puke or something? Obviously when you get there you don't puke. It isn't actually as bad as you ever thought. But unlike any exhibition I've ever been to see, I have to admit I had butterflies in my tummy before I went in. There was an anticipation and an excitement about going to see it. And that was quite cool. In fact I was amazed that Alice wanted to go in at all, cos if there was ever anyone that would be quite outspoken about I'm not going in there you crazy bastard, it would be her. But she was up for it big time.

So we go in not knowing what to expect, and then you're in there and the next thing you know you're looking at these bodies. And the weird thing is, well, I don't know about you, but I had trouble even imagining that they ever once lived and breathed. They looked so fake; I mean, they were obviously not, but they looked so preserved, like even if you had a body floating in formaldehyde, for some reason, to me, it wouldof felt more real. The fact that they'd drained it of all the blood and, you know, it looked like a really, really realistic fake. Do you know what I mean? Whereas if it had been a shark in a pickle jar, you could be like, well, I can still see that that flesh is flesh and moist and supple. Whereas these were like drumtight, you know, and I'm touching them, even though you weren't supposed to, but I couldn't help myself, I just had to, and it felt plasticky. And the colour didn't look quite right; it all looked a bit too polished. You'd imagine there'd be several shades, but it was almost like, that's a muscle, it's red. It was weird. Don't get me wrong, I was impressed; this is not something you would normally see. I remember specifically there was one guy who'd been stripped of all his skin, so you could see all of his muscles, and he's got his arm out and he's got his skin draped over his arm like a cloak. And I remember just tapping and pinching with my thumb and finger on the skin, just like that, and it going BRONBRONBRONBRONBRON, flapping, and that was quite disgusting, cos if you got really close to it you could still see the hairs attached to the follicles.

So that was quite cool and we had a good time. The only bit I did find quite repulsive, again, whether it was right or wrong or not, I don't know, everyone made a big fuss about it, and it was impressive to see, but maybe there's an element of, you know, is this morally correct?, was the cut-out section of a pregnant woman who died during childbirth. Whether she actually died during childbirth I don't know, but her stomach section was cut away, just like you would see in a normal science manual or anatomy book, you know, and there's the baby; you see it. And nearby there was a plasticised deformed foetus, and, that was a bit weird, cos, you know, I'm sure that foetus didn't sign up for it. But I suppose surgeons and people doing autopsies must see this kind of thing unplastinated all the time, and that's probably a lot worse.

I'd like to say we came away from it with a greater understanding of the human body, but I don't think we did. It was a freak show, basically, and I went to see it as a freak show. I'm not gonna lie to you, I went for the excitement, for the eeriness, for the shock value of the whole thing. Maybe I did learn something about muscle

171

structures and the length of veins; but if I did, I can't remember it now. The thing that's stayed with me is the freaky, ghoulish nature of the whole thing. And I'm sure the guy that runs it knows that that sells, otherwise he wouldn't be going around talking like Dracula and wearing a long leather coat and leathery cowboy hat. You know, he's this doctor saying, 'I want to enhance the people's vision of the human body,' but he sounds like he's come straight from Transylvania, and he's got the whole image going on, you know, long black coat and give him a lightning flash and he could be Hugh Jackman's Van Helsing. 'This is not a freak show,' but he looks like 'Well-come', you know; if he'd been there at the door, going 'Come right in and see the flayed man carrying his own skin,' it wouldof been perfect. That's what it was like. Showtime. But I enjoyed it. Funnily enough it wasn't the human beings that struck me the most, but the horse. The horse stripped of all its skin, standing there with its muscles, humungous, with the flayed guy riding him and holding a whip, like one of the Four Horsemen of the Apocalypse; that was the most impressive. It was just huge, the size of it, but not only that, you know, bloody hell, a horse must be incredibly powerful, because there you see side by side the man and this structure of sheer power; you know, even if you worked out every day and became some freaky steroid addict, you're never gonna get legs like that horse, you know, it's obvious really, but you ain't ever gonna get near that level of sheer awesome power.

We discussed amongst ourselves whether we'd sign up for this plastination thing, and I said yes, no problem, for the simple fact that I feel that once you're dead you're dead, you know, and if there is any kind of spirituality or soul or whatever, you wouldn't need your body anyway. That body has served its purpose, and it's only going to sit in the ground and rot anyway, so if I could live on and, being what I'm like, I wouldof said at least then I wouldof done something with my life, cos I'm probably never gonna do anything anyway, so at least sticking me in a museum so people can poke my skin, at least, then, in DEATH, I've done something. But Alice was like, oh great, no thanks. She wasn't up for it. She said no. She didn't want people touching her. I said, yeah, but they're not going to be touching YOU, you're dead.

"Yeah, but I don't like the idea of it."

"But you won't have any idea of it, cos you'll be dead."

But she said no. Which I can understand.

Then Harriet said she's seen something scary on the Internet about some underground movement where you can pay and go and have sex with a dead celebrity. You know, as soon as a celebrity's dead the mortician or night warden or whatever puts out the word, you know, we've got whoever, and for a couple of thousand you can come and poke around. Honestly, this takes place, apparently. Alice doesn't believe it, and even I, for whom the Internet is the font of all wisdom, am a little sceptical. But you think: sick things happen. So it probably does.

We decided we wanted a change from expos and I suggested the Pepsi Max ride at the Trocadero, so we hopped on the Tube to Piccadilly. I tell them that I know where we're going, but when we get there I can't remember where the Trocadero is. However, Alice and Harriet had been there before and they point the way. Get there. See this thing. Fuck me, I'm worried now. It goes right to the top of the Trocadero Centre. To the roof. Must be fifty feet at least. And then it goes WHOOOOPPHHHH. And I'm like, where is it? Turn around. WHOOPPHHH. When's it gonna happen?

"It already has."

Alice and Harriet aren't happy.

"We're not going on it."

"Come on."

"No."

"Please, just watch it."

Then Harriet was like, "No, let's just go on it. Come on then."

"No." Alice wasn't moving.

So I then flipped a coin; heads you go on it, tails you don't.

It's tails.

"Heads. You gotta go."

Harriet sees it but backs me up. "Yeah, you've gotta go now."

"Do it one more time."

Flipped the coin; tails again. Harriet again says, "You gotta go on it now, you lost."

"OK, come on then."

I take my glasses off, cos there's no way they're gonna stay on my face when dropping at sixty miles an hour, and put them, along with my wallet and everything from my pockets that's gonna come out, in Alice's bag. Can't see a thing now and I tell her she's got to guide me around. We're walking towards it; but now Harriet changes her mind.

"No, I'm not going on."

"Come on, Harriet, you've gotta come."

"No."

Alice says, "I'm not going without you. You've gotta come if I'm going."

Then I offer a solution and say, "OK, I'll go twice, once with Alice, and when she comes off it alive, you can go on it, Harriet."

"No."

"NO! She's gotta come with us!"

We've arrived at the place where you get on now, and Harriet's still trying to get out of it, using her thumb as an excuse, so I ask the big Jamaican guy there if you're allowed on with a damaged thumb, and he says, "Yay muuun."

Harriet goes, "Shit, man. Shit, shit, shit, shit, shit."

The Jamaican guy goes, "You needa shit?"

"No, no, I'm just saying shit, I don't wanna go on it."

I'm laughing now.

"You needa shit? Toilet's over there, muuun."

"No."

"She's just scared."

Eventually we hand the guy the money and now we're all strapped in.

"I HATE YOU, I HATE YOU, I HATE YOU. Can't believe you made us do it."

"Let's just do it."

"I hate you. I hate you." All the way up there, screaming.

174

Then the Jamaican guy goes, "Five…" does that thing, but immediately goes DNKKKCHKKK. "WHOOAAAAAAAAA!"

Even I went, "OOEERRRAAAAAAAAAA!"

You can't help it. You're reaching sixty in about one point two seconds, cos the whole thing's ten seconds and you've gotta slow down in that as well.

All the way down they are SCREAMING. But when it hits its highest point, the screaming just stops. It's like, "URRRRRP!" Abrupt silence. "URRRRRRAAARRRRRRR!" And I asked afterwards why they stopped screaming, and they said they didn't know; it was like it got so bad they couldn't scream any more.

Then this woman, quite fit, comes out and says, "Another go?"

"Nah, it's alright."

"Free?"

And I'm like, "Yeah, alright." And I'm already strapped back down and locked in. But when I look up after doing this, Alice and Harriet are on the other side of the glass, smiling. I'm waving them in, but they ain't having it.

Then the guy that runs it comes in and goes, OK, I'll go, and we go up. As we're ascending he says, "Man, you gotta look down, you gotta look down." I ask him how many times he's been on it, and he says one thousand five hundred. "You gotta look down, you gotta look down, munn, it's the scariest." I start looking down but then it just drops and I go whiiiiiiiiing like that, and the guy goes, "You didn't look down," almost angrily, and takes me right back up so I'm now going for a third time. And we go WHOOOOPPHHH. This time I look all the way down and I can see why it's so scary, cos the glass bit looks like it's gonna chop the top of your head off as it hurtles towards you. Obviously it's never gonna do it, but it LOOKS that way because it's so fast. If I'd had a fourth go it wouldof been nothing because I'd just've got used to this. And I did ask for another one, but the guy said, no, that's enough now. So we left. And where there are pictures of you on the screen showing photos of EEE ARRR, there was only one of Alice and Harriet; but there was me in three different poses going NNNUUGGH, UURRRRGHH, AAAGGHHHH.

175

And afterwards Alice and Harriet were like, are you proud of us?

"Yeah, I'm very proud."

"Are you pleased we went on it?"

"Yeah, big time. It was impressive."

"Thanks for making us go on it."

They were really grateful and pleased that I'd made them do it. They were like, "Man, now when I come here again, I won't ever have to go on it cos I can say I've been on it already." I don't think they actually enjoyed it, but they were on a buzz for having achieved this supposedly death-defying feat.

Then we went into a shop. Alice bought a T-shirt; Harriet got some tops. I bought some combats. This was easily the best part of the day. It was as if we now knew each other quite well. Going through this super-high-velocity drop had brought us closer together, bonded us, and the whole day seemed cool after that. We went into this other shop off the Tottenham Court Road and I bought some new trainers which kick ass. No laces nor Velcro neither. They're like bungee cords; man, they're well good. You can wear 'em for everyday streetwear, but also skateboarding. And they're made in Nam! So I'm now wearing these Nam shoes, which are massive and made by Acupuncture, a really good make. It took me about eighty hours to choose them of course. Previously my chosen footwear had been these shoes where part of the sole swivelled round to reveal a groove which enabled you to slide down railings. OK, limited usefulness. But they were still cool. But these were even better. When I got back Mum said they looked a bit like stormtrooper shoes, in terms of *Star Wars*, cos the front's high and you look like you're about to go into some kind of futuristic battle. But these shoes are cool, and Alice liked them. It was the most relaxed I'd ever seen her. When we got back to the nan's Alice was happy and not as nervous anymore. I think she even said this was the best day ever.

My head doctor told me Alice was good for me because in my world she was 'safe', and so he cut my Seroxat down from fifty to forty mg. About a week later Alice dumped me.

Chapter Fourteen

From A to B in Two Weeks

Women are manipulative, unpredictable,
shallow, irrational, out for themselves and cold

This is my cousin Gary speaking, the bitterest person I know. And yet Gary's good-looking, so in his case the bitterness isn't linked to unattractiveness. I think it comes instead from his being a romantic, which, contrary to how this is generally portrayed in the media, is always gonna be your downfall, cos in my experience women are actually not all that romantic themselves; they just like their men to be. Sure they can talk the talk, when they feel like it or need to. But that's as far as it goes. They have a practical take on life and know what happens when you walk off a cliff. They understand gravity. A lotta men, however, still believe if you flap your arms fast enough you might fly. Or they can be persuaded to believe it.

Me and Gary share a great deal in common; Gary loves films, I love films. I don't know many people who would sit down with me and watch a Hungarian film about speed-eating, you know, *Taxidermia*. Not many women are gonna want to do that. But Gary has. And he likes books; I like books. And although he's now doing well as a customs officer, he's had his fair share of shit jobs, you know, selling concrete, data-inputting for the NHS, and has had many a period of unemployment; so we've got that in common, too.

177

When Gary was growing up he would read obsessively and get through books in a couple of days, you know, Stephen King, loved Stephen King, would read one title after the other; Dean Koontz; he would devour these books, which are not slim volumes. Now he's moved on to authors like Chuck Palahniuk, you know, strangely bitter guys which kind of fits where he's at. Loves Charles Bukowski, which I introduced him to; also kind of fits. But he'll also read sci-fi: Philip K. Dick, William Gibson, J. G. Ballard, and older, more classic stuff, like Aldous Huxley and George Orwell. Gary is a genuine lover of anything and everything. I mean, he knows good movies and he knows shit movies; but he will quite happily watch any genre. If it's shit, it's shit; but he's not the sorta person who would say: I'm not watching romantic comedies, I'm not watching fantasy. Not one of those. Foreign language movies, Japanese, Korean, Russian: he's up for anything. We watched *Diva* the other day, and he loved it, cos he's open-minded enough not to be bothered by something that's got subtitles or is in black and white, which a lot of people, and I've met many of them, refuse to look at. And he's got taste. I mean, we sat down the other day and watched *Death Proof* and *Planet Terror*, which I'd downloaded illegally of course, and I was telling him that I quite liked *Death Proof*, thought the cars and the stunts were cool, liked that whole seventies look, but Gary watched it and said it was rubbish, and after *Planet Terror* I found myself apologising, cos I could see he was right, both films were truly awful, and *Death Proof* only marginally the less awful of the two. But at least he watched them before coming to that judgement.

Gary's weight goes up and down like a yo-yo. He's one of those people who when they go on an exercise regime, really get down to it, and he'll get himself down to around twelve and a half stone, really toned. He's the same height as me, five-nine, so this is his optimum weight. He'll go down the gym, hammer it, run four miles every other day, and after three months he'll be mean and lean. At the moment, as he'll admit, he's big-time overweight: and I'm talking sixteen stone. And that's how it always is: twelve and a half stone to sixteen stone to twelve and a half stone to sixteen stone. I've told him this is not good for him; but it's the way he is, cos he loves eating shit. He loves kebabs, fried food, pizza; and he doesn't eat a little, cos like me he has a big appetite. We're a similar body shape, so the appetite thing may be genetic as well. But whereas I'm a pretty steady fourteen stone short and stocky, he's either twelve and a half or sixteen with the weight going upanddown, upanddown. However, these fluctuations are always connected to women.

"Ah, I lose all the weight, get down, and it doesn't do any different."

"What do you mean, doesn't do any different?"

"Well, I'm still not successful with women. And when a woman does come along I'm like this, sixteen stone." Cos he's back in his fat phase again.

When Gary does his running and stuff, he's obsessive. I mean, I can't run four miles every other day; the man gets up there. But now he's a chubber, sixteen stone; he's big. The thing is these sorts of regimes are tough; they work, but they're not sustainable. The minute you break them, you never want to go back to all that pain again. And even when Gary's on these regimes, he's hating every minute, it's a mission – he doesn't wanna be running; he wants a kebab! And he sweats. I used to go to the gym with him and I've never seen a man sweat so much. Even when he was at his height of fitness you could wring his T-shirt out at the end of it.

It is the women Gary has known that have affected him this way and made him bitter. He was a late developer; didn't have a girlfriend till he was twenty-two/twenty-three, I mean nothing, no whatever. You know, he's a book reader, likes movies. And his other problem was he would go out and get pissed, and was shy and didn't know how to talk to women. I still don't think he does know how to talk to women, in fact. Part of his problem is that he's a nice guy. I mean, I'm a nice guy, too. You're probably a nice guy. But me and you both know that there comes a point when you've gotta close the deal. Comes a point where you've got to be

179

pushy, you've got to lay something on the line and embrace the possibility of rejection. That was something that took me a while to learn, and it was probably only through Joe that I eventually saw how it could work. But Gary could not do any of that, and as a result he just did not clinch the deal.

Gary's first exposure to women came when he had this thing with a friend's girlfriend. You gotta realise this is someone who's never had anything, and here is a girl offering herself to him on a plate. I mean, he's not gonna say no, is he? Yeah there's the friend; but he's not a good friend, so Gary tells me. She's alright-looking, not brilliant, and comes over to his parents' house, talks, gives him a few blow-jobs, introduces him to the world of three-dimensional erotic pleasure. Over time he gets a slight pang of guilt; but he's also like, I ain't getting none anywhere else, you know? And the girl's like, I'm not happy with Chris, I wanna be with you, Gary. But at the same time Gary doesn't realise; or he does realise, but for whatever reason won't draw the obvious conclusion. I mean, I know the type of woman that I'm into; I want her to be arty, individual, free-thinking, open-minded, and attractive, obviously, cos you don't want no moose. But Gary, partly because of the friends he's got, cos Gary's one of these people who's got friends who aren't into the same things as him, you know, they wanna listen to Icon dance music, Gary always ends up with chavs. The sort of women I like, I know I have to go to the places where that type of woman hangs out, you know, the hunting ground where these women will be available: arty, different sort of women, maybe not individual, free-thinking, cos that would paint some amazing picture, but at least a little bit unusual; so I'll go to the Star Tap, Sensonics, etc. But Gary won't do this. He'll go with his friends, and he's got a group of friends who've known each other since school, meet every Friday, meet every Saturday, then maybe meet once in the week, very strong brotherhood; they're nice guys but they all wanna get pissed, watch football and go down Icon, do you see what I mean? Not watch movies, not talk about books, or art, or whatever. I respect Gary's strength of character; he can still read books, watch movies, listen to Nine Inch Nails, and at the same time, somehow, I don't know how it works, still keep very good friends with these people who aren't into that stuff. But he always seems to end up going to these places where you're not gonna meet the right kind of woman.

And this girlfriend of this bloke, this friend, is not the right kind of woman. She wants a man that drinks beer, watches football, drives a nice car, dresses nicely, has his hair perfect, and is eventually going to have a good job, nice house and, you know, look after her. So it's what car you got?, what clothes do you wear?, how much money do you earn?, what music do you listen to? Nothing out of the ordinary; nothing free-thinking. No creativity involved. Do you know the sort of women I mean? They're basically into squaddy types; guys who spend hours at the gym lifting weights and toning their pecs. You know, why are you reading books when you could be working on your physique? Lads. And I wouldn't say Gary is a lad, even if he does dress like one.

So here's this girl and she's telling him everything, you know, I wanna leave him, I'm gonna leave him, and Gary's getting his penis sucked which can be quite persuasive, you know, so he's like bloody hell, I'm on to a good THING. I LIKE this! And this goes on for months, and eventually he falls in love with her; cos she is his first woman, after all. And what does she do? I don't think we should really do this any more. The guilt. I'm so bad. Why have I done this? I'm not sure we shouldof done this. And Gary's like, fuck! He doesn't know how to handle this. You know, he's gone in with probably the hardest relationship you can ever start off with, and it fucks him basically. He's like, aaaaarrrghh. But I thought you wanted to be with me? I'm not sure I want to be with you. Maybe I was just going through a difficult time. You can imagine the sort of thing without being there. There he is, having been promised the world and fallen in love with the girl, and she pulls the plug.

So Gary goes into a deep depression and everyone's worried about him, and I say to him, "Look, man, you've gotta find a

181

NICE girl," you know, basically repeating what my head doctor said to me about Mona; 'she wasn't the girl for you, you were getting involved with the wrong kind of girl'. I shouldof followed my own advice here but anyway, "You need to find someone that shares your interests." Anyway, Gary sort of recovers, as we all do eventually; but it leaves him with a bad taste in his mouth. And still he hasn't, you know. He's had his dick sucked and explored and felt around a bit, so he knows some, more than he did before, and his parents, even if they don't know what's been going on exactly, know that he's been having some kind of gender-opposite relationship at last and are probably thinking, you know, thank God he's not gay; but he still hasn't penetrated.

Gary changes job and starts dating a new girl who he works with. You know, office romance and all that. Starts getting to know her. She's, again, chav; into money, into cars, not into the sort of music Gary is into. You can see the pattern here. One of the stories he told me about her is that he was lying in bed with her after they'd just had sex (at last!) but she's not very good. I'm wondering what he is basing this on, and he says she doesn't get involved.

"What do you mean she doesn't get involved?"

"Well, you know, she's there. I just thought there would be more to it."

And I remembered what J-J once said about what he called the W-factor; that some girls had it and others didn't, but it had nothing to do with class or education, cos some highly respectable girls had it and some slappers didn't. And if you had it, it meant you would enjoy sex, be passionate, creative, mutual and proactive in your lovemaking, exploring, pushing boundaries, trying out techniques, giving and receiving new sensations, boldly and bodily going wherever; and if you didn't, you would just lie there, you know, fulfil your role but not feel anything particularly special, not exactly bored and thinking of England, but not on fire either. And you had to be born with this W-gene, the 'W' in question being wickedness, which J-J said even some of the nicest and loveliest girls were born with, and which should not be confused with promiscuity, which is just a same-old same-old condition that never evolves into anything interesting. And if you aren't born with the W-factor, you can never ever acquire it, cos even the greatest teachers, you know, tantric masters or whatever, can only do so much. They can repair and nurture; but they cannot put in what God, in His wisdom, has decided to leave out. So I'm thinking this girl must therefore not have the W-gene, and that is why Gary is thinking, oh, is that it? But at the same time he's not gonna turn it down.

So the relationship goes on for three or four months, and he does his usual: he changes. He always tries to change for them. I suppose we all do to a certain degree; but, you know, he's trying NOT to listen to the music he wants to listen to; trying NOT to watch the films he wants to watch. He's trying to back away from the person he is. And he's going to all these nightclubs he doesn't wanna go to, and getting drunk to handle it. Sounds familiar, right? And then eventually, as you would imagine, the relationship ends. But this is how; and they always end this way with Gary. She ends it. But say this is A and this is B. With a man you would have A.1, A.2, A.3, A.4 dadadadadada: B. And A is, the world is fine; everything is going OK. But with a woman it's A, and then, like a freight train hitting ya, BOOM, here's B. And you're like HOW THE FUCK DID WE GET FROM A TO B? B being, I don't wanna be with you any more. And this especially seems to happen to Gary. He's happy; everything's going OK. The sex may be a bit weird; maybe they're a little bit off some days. Women are like that. Then all of a sudden, out of nowhere: BANG. B. They're gone. Don't wanna see you any more.

And he's still gotta work in the department with her.

A week goes by. Gary sees her starting to hang around a little bit more than usual with another guy in the office; someone that he considered a friend. Word goes around; this motherfucker's now dating her. Gary starts to add things up: maybe she was kind of seeing him before we were... you know, was she doing anything with him before? Couldn't've been, cos we were together a lot, so there would never have been that… were they emailing each other? All this is playing on his mind, as it would. So BAM there she is, every fucking day, seeing her, like some nightmare, and them giggling together. Luckily she soon gets another job and leaves. But this whole experience pisses him off: how the fuck could we have been together for four months? I cared for that girl; I had feelings for that girl; she dumps me, and within a week she's with someone else. So therefore I meant nothing to her. That is gonna make you bitter. But the man still doesn't learn his lesson.

Gary has a dry period of about a year and a half. As we know, over time, you get a little bit more desperate. A new girl starts at the office, on the floor above him. They get to know each other at a work do and start dating. She's got some weird illness where she has to take these pills and stuff which destroys her sex drive. I've never fucking heard of this, but anyway. She's chav; like they're all chavs, even though, and I think even Gary is coming round to realising this, chavs are not the sort of girls he wants. I think it's basically that Gary likes the look of a chav; but he wants the mind of something else. That's the catch. His girls are all good-looking; all blonde, all nice pair of jugs. Tall, blonde, big jugs. He wants Page Three, but with the mind of an English Tripos graduate. And you can't get that, unfortunately; or I've never seen it. Gary wants the chav look, but with an interest in rock music and whatever. That is the problem. But as I keep saying to him, there are nice girls, they do exist, and I'm, like, turning into some kind of Jewish mother now, 'nice guurrls,' you know. Anyway, she's got this pill thing; they go on a couple of dates. He takes her for dinner, they meet up for lunch, BAM he's going out with her. He's horny, of course, he's trying it on, they get off, she whacks him off, sucks him, you know, whatever. But when he tries to do something for her she's like, nah, I'm not interested, nah not interested. Not even digital. This woman must really have no sex drive, cos she's not even asking for anything else. She's giving him stuff, probably thinking, well, if he's gonna be my boyfriend I'm gonna have to give him some relief. Who knows how the female mind works? So he's getting that, and he's not complaining; but at the same time he's like I wanna make love to you, you know, he's not done it that many times.

Then it happens. And this is gonna make a man that's already bitter positively drown in authentic pissed-offedness, not scary, but real and raw. Gary is with this girl for six months. It's his longest relationship. He has sex with her once; but she's on these pills and she's got this illness. He sees her taking these pills; he knows it's not bullshit. Something's going on. Then, like a freight train, BOOM. Six months; bam, it's over. And like a throwback to the past, she starts dating another motherfucker from the office, this time not within a week but within two days; two days of dumping him.

This would piss anyone off. But then one day he's sitting there in the staff relaxing area, eating his lunch, and he overhears some girls talking. They mention something about this girl he used to go out with and the new guy. Naturally Gary's ears prick up. They start talking about this sex thing the two of them did, you know, something graphic and detailed, and it makes his stomach turn. And now he's thinking, I only had sex with this woman once, this guy's only been going out with her for a week, and I only used to get blow-jobs and hand-jobs, you know. Gary's eating his tuna sandwich and thinking, this motherfucker's already getting more than I ever got. And he's like, hang on a fucking second, cos he can't handle this, and he steams into the office.

"What the fuck is going on?"

"Look, this isn't the place. We're at work. Leave me alone."

Then he sees the guy, and I think he wouldof gone over and knocked the guy out there and then, but fortunately he was saved from himself by the manager who calls him into his office and accuses him of industrial espionage (how cool is that?), cos he's been advising old ladies not to buy the company's useless overpriced hearing aids, cos he doesn't like ripping grannies off. So of course the management take him out. Gary finds himself suspended on full pay with immediate effect.

Fortunately he has a new job lined up; but that doesn't stop him from being pissed off that this girl has dumped him for no apparent reason and has started going out with someone else immediately after, and he knows she instantly started having sex with this guy after she had made Gary wait six months, and then he only ever got it once. What cuts most deep, however, is that he can't find any explanation for any of this. None. None. All he can do is ask himself, what is wrong with me? Why didn't she want to do it with me? As you would.

Gary goes dry again for another six months. Then a friend of his starts dating a Norwegian girl at the art college in Southfield, and because of this Gary starts hanging around with arty student types. Here is a glimmer of hope. These people are a little bit more like him. And they're fit. Norwegians. He likes Norwegians, cos he likes fit women. And he begins to realise the advantages of actually speaking to women and sharing mutual interests. I mean, they're taking him to places he's never been before, like Sensonics, where he finds they play his sort of music. Alright some of the people there are a bit freaky; but he's having a good time and he's happy. Turns out this friend's Norwegian art student girlfriend has a female friend coming over to stay with her for two weeks. They decide to go to the National Gallery. Gary comes along and meets the friend; instantly he's smitten. She is stunning; I mean, it's almost ridiculous. This girl is a Norwegian goddess. And she seems to like Gary. And he's at his peak at this moment in time: twelve and a half stone, four miles every other day, toned; he's made.

Gary and she start going up to London alone together, visiting galleries, the Tate Modern, the National Film Theatre, Shakespeare's Globe. He's only got her for two weeks; but they're seeing each other all the time every day. The friend that she'd come over to see is getting pissed off cos this goddess is spending all her time with Gary. He's taking her out, they're going to dinner; they're seeing each other pretty much every day. Gary's dad's jaw nearly hits the floor when he's introduced to her; you know, he can barely speak. Even Gary's mum is like, Gary, you're punching well above your weight here.

Anyway, Gary ends up, as he would call it, 'banging' her in his bedroom; and apparently she was 'filthy', it was like nothing he'd ever seen. She, like, had the W-gene in every part of her body. She stripped off, laid on the bed and said, do whatever you want to me. And Gary's like, what the fuck, what have I done; you know, I've served my time, I've had some serious pain, and now I'm being rewarded. Anyway, he said it was amazing; and man he performed, he performed OK. You know first couple he was pretty quick, cos after all he'd been dry for a period. But he was soon up to game. He even called in sick. I mean, Gary's an all or nothing kind of guy; he calls up sick and doesn't go to work for three days. This is a job he likes, he doesn't want to fuck this up, but everything's going out the window. This girl's stunning; he's in love with her. He's literally living in his room with her. They're getting takeaways, sleeping together; it's like some love affair in a book. It's only two weeks; but there are big similarities between Gary and the Norwegian goddess and me and Mona: condensed, intense, passionate, beautiful girl, throw everything out the window, cos THIS is what I'm focusing on. I've never seen him so happy.

After a while she's like, oh yeah, I'm bored with my boyfriend back home (here we go), I wanna come over here, I wanna stay here; you know, Gary, you're so different, and whatever, you know, this sort of stuff. And Gary's like, I'll come over there, you know, you're amazing. Mistake, as we know. Don't do that early on, cos you're only gonna shoot yourself. But he's into her, whatever: they're together; they're going out all the time, two weeks, full-on, unimaginable.

Finally the two weeks come to an end, and Gary drives her to the airport. He's taken another day off work. He's nearly in tears. She's nearly in tears.

"I'll text you, Gary, I'll text you."

He kisses her goodbye. She gets out and goes into the airport. He drives home, his heart aching for this woman. Texts her. She texts back.

187

"I'm on the plane. I'll text you when I get back to Norway."

A 707 flies overhead; Norwegian Air, similar to the one she's travelling on.

Gary waits. And waits.

It's gone.

She's gone.

Text never comes.

Ever.

Gary tries everything: calls her, texts her, tries speaking to her friend.

"Oh, she's like that. She does this."

That's it. The end.

Gary's still cut up about it two years later. It is also the last time he had sex. On his MSN Messenger profile he says, I was once a boy and now I'm bitter. Gary still wants a girlfriend, wants female company; but he's afraid of being burnt again. Doesn't understand women; doesn't understand them one bit. He's had a lot of time to ponder it, and he thinks she was up for a fling, told him what he needed to hear to get him to take her out, show her a good time and get a little fantasy going together. But she knew it was a game, and he didn't. He ended up spending a lot of money on her, taking her out for dinner, taking her to galleries and plays; she wasn't paying anything and he was, like, her meal-ticket for two weeks. I said to him, it's a shame, because all she needed to say to you was, I'm here for two weeks, show me a good time, I think you're attractive, you think I'm attractive, we can fuck all day, do whatever you want. And he wouldof been like, fair enough. You know, do you wanna go to the theatre?, yeah I'd like to go to the theatre, cool, I haven't got much money, do you mind?, no I don't mind, done. He wouldn'tof had a problem with that. I mean, this is a fabulous-looking Norwegian woman.

But she didn't play it that way. All this, I wanna be with you Gary, I'm not happy with my boyfriend back in Norway; that was how she played it. She played with him instead of being honest with him, and she broke his heart, cos she led him to believe she was interested in him, then got back on that plane, flew back to the fjords, maybe thought once or twice about whether she'd get back in contact with him, maybe did want to see him again, but then saw her boyfriend, thought fuckit it's gonna be way too much hard work, you know, Magnus is here, Gary's over there; so she deleted his number and that was it.

Obviously she mustof liked Gary cos you're not gonna put in all that effort if you don't; clearly she found something attractive about him; conversation, they got on, he made her laugh, you know how it works. She thought this is someone I'd like to spend two weeks with. But she mustof also thought, you know, he's single, he's got money, a nice car, BMW, you know; it'll take me out of my ordinary, mundane Norwegian life, show me a bit of England that I'm never gonna get from some tour guide. I mean, she's on holiday. And she's done this before. Why Gary's friend never warned him about her, I don't know; cos surely his girlfriend said something to him. But I suppose Gary would never have listened anyway.

Gary still likes women, cos after all there are certain needs that only a woman can fulfil. And Gary's a guy that needs pootang. But he's got such suspicion now; why should I do anything for you cos you're only gonna fuck me over? So he won't go the extra mile for them anymore. And he's become a really big porn fan, cos he ain't getting any anymore. In fact now I come to think about it, it was Gary that put Joe on to *Fire in the Valley*.

Gary's been with chavs and arty types and found that the only difference is conversation. He's become bitter as a result, because he was expecting it to be love. A romantic. I, however, gave up believing in love after Mona, and especially after S.; i.e. when I discovered that women just don't have the same take on it, and some of them aren't really that bothered about it either. So even though Alice and I had a really good time together, when the phone call came I was, to tell the truth, half expecting it. But still the brutality, the sudden whoosh from A to B, took me by surprise, even though Alice was never one to beat around the bush, which was a quality I liked about her, but which naturally didn't take the edge off the knife corkscrewing into my heart.

I was meant to go over to her house one Friday night, but I was really tired. I'd been working long shifts as a runner at the Beeb, and being keen, believing, foolishly, that it might lead to something more than making tea, I was putting in extra hours and effort just to, you know, get myself noticed, be seen as keen and enthusiastic and interested. So I didn't fancy driving all the way over to Pensdown and suggested she came over to mine instead.

"Do you wanna come over here?"

"No, I can't come over. My parents are in. Why don't you come over here?"

"I'm not sure." I mean, I was really tired and didn't feel like driving through twenty miles of icy, dimly lit winding country roads. "What would we do?"

"Watch TV with my mum and dad."

Great.

"Ummmmm, maybe. I'll give you a call back."

"OK."

I lie down for a minute to consider the options; but what happens? I fall asleep. Deep sleep. REM sleep. Permasleep. Hours go by. I wake up about quarter to twelve. Too late to ring back. I don't have a mobile phone at this point, so I can't text her or anything. So I leave it.

Next day the phone call.

"Hello."

"Hello."

"I'm really sorry I didn't call you back last night but I fell asleep."

"Yeah, I think that was a bit out of order. You shouldof called me back." You know, not screaming or shouting or anything; but I can tell she's in a really bad mood about it. "I stayed up late expecting you to call or come over. And I told my parents that you were going to come over."

"I'm really sorry, I was really tired. Seriously, I'm really sorry."

190

Silence.

"Do you want to do anything today?"

"No."

"Do you want to meet up next week?"

"Nnno."

"Oh. Well, when do you want to meet?" I mean, I'm being given nothing to work with here, but I'm still trying.

"I'm not sure I wanna meet up."

"What do you mean?" Of course, I know perfectly well what she means; but, you know, you need to hear it.

"I don't think I want to go out with you any more."

"Oh."

I absorb this.

"Is this just because I didn't call you last night?"

"No. Lots of things."

"Like what?"

"You're not who I thought you were gonna be."

That hurts.

"Well, what do you mean?"

"I dunno. You're just not who I thought you would be."

And of course I'd known from previous conversations that she'd been talking about me to her mum before I ever asked her out, and she'd built up this character of Matt, which I've still got no idea about; but you wouldof thought she'd've realised after the incident at the party that I was possibly not that character.

"Oh right, OK. Do you still wanna meet up, just as friends?"

"No. I don't think that's a good idea."

"OK."

And the tone was sort of cold. Reminded me of *The Godfather*, like, this is business not personal. You know, OK, we've done what we've done but it's ended now. You know, very little emotion. It's not working out, you know, the decision has been made. The boys have looked at it, thought about it and decided, you know, you've had a good run, the arrangement's been mutually beneficial, we've enjoyed doing business with you, there've been some good experiences along the way, but now it's over. And as we know, when a woman makes a decision, that's it. No point in discussing. It really isn't anything personal; I mean, obviously it is, but it's not your fault, this just needs to be done. Business is business. This is the way it is. It's over now, and you need to leave town. Twenty-four hours. OK? Now get out of my sight.

I saw Alice again years later by accident in the Star Tap. She looked totally different. Long hair, make-up, which she never used to wear, dressed more like a woman than a girl. Before, she wore jeans, T-shirts and jumpers; now she was in a black dress. She looked more feminine; clearer skin, no spots any more. She'd grown up. I'll be honest with you, she looked good. She wasn't with anyone, just some friends from uni.

"Hi, how you doing?"

"Alright."

"What are you upto?"

"Not doing photography."

"Did you not finish your degree?"

"Yeah, I finished it but I learnt I didn't want to do photography. No good at it."

Alice was never happy; but never miserable either. Just always like, it is what it is: neither great nor whatever.

"You with anyone?"

"No."

"OK, see you around then."

"See you around."

And that was it.

But I felt good about seeing Alice again. I mean, she'd made it, in spite of her issues. She'd come through and grown up into a lovely woman. And it always amazes me when gauche and gawky teenage girls, with all their shyness and lack of confidence, undergo this fabulous metamorphosis in their twenties. It gives you hope. You know, the system sometimes works.

Chapter Fifteen

Evangelista

Now abideth faith, hope, charity, these three;
but the greatest of these is charity
(Corinthians 1 13:13)

Apart from sucking crisp cookies hyperslowly, one thing I did a lot of when I was travelling across America was listen to 'Millionaire' by Queens of the Stone Age, which had come out just before I flew over. It's pretty heavy and I had it on repeat, which probably indicates a bad state of mental health; but it was good to be on the road and moving to this song, cos it sounds like a train, and I'd have it full blast in my headphones. I especially love the bit after ten seconds of intro when the power kicks in. I mean, you've got to imagine being on a Greyhound bus, things flashing past you, and listening in your headphones to this thundering locomotive bassline with squealing riffwork arpeggioing over the top of it and the singer splitting his vocal cords and screaming his lungs out. It's, you know, unrelenting, unrepentant, non-stopping. And another Queens of the Stone Age song that for me summed up this period of my life perfectly was 'Feel Good Hit of the Summer'. Quite a long title, really, but it was massive, and it was S.'s favourite song for obvious reasons, if you know the lyrics.

On the journey from Chicago to Des Moines there was this pretty girl; slim, brown hair, shortish, not a bob, cos that sounds dreadful, but I don't know women's haircuts; anyway, she's sitting on the seat in front of me and over her shoulder I can see this huge book she's reading, enormous like some educational textbook, massive, about that thick. Not a novel, more like a science year workbook, you know, the sort you would have at school; big but portable and soft-covered, like some RT Network manual. It was not a light-looking book. Turns out it's a modern-day illustrated evangelical bible. I think to myself, that's fucking weird, which leads me to want to say hello or that sort of thing; and not only that, I'm not going to lie to you, but she was pretty. Very. When you're on the bus, and you're on there a long time, a lot of people will introduce themselves to you, Americans being the way Americans are, and you very rarely have to start a conversation. But this girl was different. And so we're sitting there and going along, she's reading, I'm sucking crisp cookies and listening to Queens of the Stone Age and occasionally peering over her shoulder and wondering how you strike up a conversation with a nice-looking evangelista.

On the Greyhound there are stops every now and again to get food, and because of the crazy bus schedules, sometimes you would be stopping off for a dinner break and it would be like one in the morning. They'd be like, 'Food time!' and you'd be like, God! But there wouldn't be another break for eight hours after this, and you're kind of hungry, but you're also tired, so it's this weird middleground where you're a little bit peckish, not ravenous, cos you've gone past hunger now, but you're also knackered; but me being the chubber I am, I'm gonna eat, and that means a full meal. And there was this one time where we stopped in the middle of nowhere. I was probably passing some of the greatest country ever, but it was nighttime so I couldn't particularly see, and there were all these weary, travel-worn, Greyhound stinky bus people, cos everyone's sweaty and hot and uuurrrrrgghhh. It was a bit like that movie *It Happened One Night*, you know, black and white and thirties depression kind of feel, but in smell-o-vision, and without any sense of upturn, just some long journey into the night. I remember some black guy and this strange couple who looked like

194

your stereotypical runaway couple. The boy had a shaven head and was wearing this white vest. He didn't look aggressive, not muscle-bound or anything, but definitely the sorta guy that would rob you. Not a tough guy, just a bit of an urchin. Neal Cassady type, I guess. His girlfriend was reasonably pretty, but messed up, a bit drugified, you know, heroin chic. But they seemed really sweet together. And this black couple as well, pregnant girlfriend, but he was a real smooth talky; you could tell instantly, cos he was chatting to everyone, cracking jokes, cool guy, loud, not overly obnoxious, but you could tell he was confident. He was a good-looking guy, smart clothes, confident in himself. I did think it was strange for him to be catching the bus. But there we all are and we get off in the middle of the night and go into this diner.

It's a proper American diner; one of the only proper American diners on the roads I came across when travelling. But again it was like so much of my trip in that it fitted into the stereotypical idea I already had before I got there, which part of me loved, because it felt like this is real as well as stereotypical, but at the same time not Disney; you know, the waitress in here DOES look like she's too old to be a hooker any more, and she looks like she DOES go out the back and smoke fifty fags and says, 'Thair's ya dinna, honey,' you know what I mean? Some hick town right out in nowhere and here we are in the middle of the night and there's the sheriff, with the badge and greenish shirt and modern standard-issue cowboy hat, sitting over in the corner with his cop buddies waiting for a call to come in and talking to the waitress, who then comes over to me.

"What kin ah get ya, honey?" Nice, but firm.

"Um, um."

"D'ya need help pickin'?" Again nice, but, you know, rushing yer at the same time.

"Uhhh, I don't know."

"This here is good."

"Er, what is it?"

"Chicken 'n' patata, honey."

"OK, I'll have one of those, please."

When it comes over I look at it and think, this is fucked up: the rankest looking Kentucky fried chicken sort of stuff you've ever seen, you know, like something out of *Eraserhead*, with some really bad mashed potato and gravy you could peel off it's so solidified. And I'm like uuuurrrrrrrr, but I'm hungry and I'm eating it, I'm eating this chicken, but then the waitress comes over again.

"You not eatin' that patata?"

And I mumble no and shake my head.

"Dja not like it?" You know, kind of challenging my taste preferences.

"Well, errrrr."

"Eat it." She says it in a playful way, but in a way which is also, you know, someone MADE that. So I eat it cos I don't want to piss her off. It was like I was round her house for dinner, you know; like I was gonna offend the chef if I didn't.

There was a group of Mexicans on the bus, cos like I say it's the cheapest form of travel, and when I come out of the diner these Mexicans are chatting amongst themselves, quite lively and animated, and suddenly this pretty evangelist girl goes up to them and BAM starts up a conversation in fluent Spanish. And even the Mexicans are taken aback because here's this white girl, travelling alone, youngish, nineteen or twenty, straight off the bat chatting to them in their native language. They're kinda like, huh? But she has an air of real confidence, almost arrogance, which was understandable, I suppose, cos she was untouchable, you know, like, I'm on a mission of God and I can talk to my people. So you felt that she was quite happy to travel alone, cos what's gonna happen to her? She's got this aura of, if it happens it happens, you know, nothing bad can befall me, and even if it does, it's what God wants. Everything is what God wants. She didn't ever express it in those terms, but this was definitely the feeling I got later when I started talking to her.

We sat back down on the bus. I was still a bit taken aback that she spoke fluent Spanish, cos it's quite unusual to see a white and reasonably wealthy girl, not trash, not like the boy in the white vest, travelling alone and speaking with Mexicans in their own language. Turns out her mum and dad were missionaries down in Mexico and she was raised there for many years, so she knew Mexican people and many different cultures, and felt comfortable, you know, cos if you're brought up there, probably not the safest place in the world, as well as in America, you're not gonna be a run-of-the-mill shy nineteen year old; you're gonna know things and you're gonna be a little bit streetwise, although she didn't give off a streetwise vibe. The man in me was a bit kinda like, you know, you need to watch yourself, there are some dangerous people in the world, whereas she didn't seem to have that at all, though I'm sure she could look after herself.

Anyway, there we are back on the bus. She's still sitting in front of me. I'm looking over her shoulder while she's reading the book, and I think, fuckit, and lean over, avoiding subtlety, as is my way, which sort of makes her aware of some activity behind her, so she turns her head round and looks at me.

"Alright?"

"Yup." Not unfriendly, but not a 'how'ryadoin?' or anything like that.

"What you reading?" You know, I'm bored. She smiles and says such and such. I think she said it was like a religious textbook. She's answering my questions politely, but there's no sense of, let's chat.

"Sounds interesting. What's it about?" I'm not easily deterred.

"It's the Bible."

"Oh right. Are you very religious?" Being very careful not to sound like I'm looking to have an argument or anything.

She nods.

"So what are you actually reading about at this moment in time?" I mean, she has to open up a bit with that one.

She starts telling me all about the more detailed version, cos any version's gonna be more detailed than the one I know, owing to the slimness of my religious knowledge, of the Adam and Eve story; i.e. how God created these two trees in Eden, made Adam out of dust

197

and then cloned Eve from one of Adam's ribs, so they, like, shared the same DNA, and everything was cool, except no eating from the Tree of the Knowledge of Good and Evil, which of course as everyone knows they go ahead and do anyway, cos you're always gonna end up breaking the one rule your parents tell you never to break, that's just the way it is in fairy tales. So God punishes them by making them mortal and forcing them to live in a world of pain outside Paradise, to stop them ever trying to eat from the other tree in Eden, namely the Tree of Life, which is divine-only restricted access.

I have some questions, which I deem it wise to keep to myself for the time being in order to build rapport, about why knowledge of Good and Evil is such a bad thing; though I can see how if you're in Paradise this knowledge could be seriously troubling and create unnecessary complications which, given the amount of free time you've got on your hands, might easily lead, as it would in my case, to obsessional thinking, which is where problems begin. And it's also gonna destroy any idea you might have that you're immortal, which, as my head doctor says, is one of the key beliefs hardwired into us when we're born; so basically you're gonna be fucked, you know, welcome to the world of adulthood: this is what happens when you start wanting to know things. So God mustof had solid psychological reasons for it all. And because He also intends for Adam and Eve to break the rules, because He wants Adam and Eve to be mortal, as part of some bigger project, He is not actually quite as pissed off about what they've done as He makes out.

But Adam and Eve also decide off their own bat to wear fig leaves, which God did not originally intend, and He is not overly pleased with this. I mean, He's set things up for them to run around naked and free in holy innocence and not be ashamed about it; but they've now gone and eaten from a forbidden tree, taken issue with the nudity thing and covered themselves up in embarrassment, just like shy teenagers suddenly super-sensitive to their own bodies. And I recall J-J once telling me, after we'd watched some awful gothy GNVQ (Guaranteed Non-Viable Qualification) intermediate pop video set amongst tombstones with lots of DayGlo rubber snakes dropping down all over the place to lamentable hiss FX, that the serpent incident in the A&E story is just Eve having her first period, snakes being, apparently, symbols of fertility, while the expulsion from Paradise is simply what happens to you at puberty when you find yourself forced to leave childhood, aka growing up, just like me in my two photos. J-J studied anthropology for a year at uni, and as you can see has a lot of surplus knowledge as a result. Either way the fig leaf is seriously screwing with the original Genesis design template, which is why God has some concerns. But He still has it all under control; or so the pretty evangelista is telling me.

"So where you headed for?" I kind of felt throughout that it was always me leading the conversation, asking the questions. She didn't wanna know anything about me. But after being on the bus for so long, any conversation's better than nothing.

"Evangelical college in Massachusetts." This was in the direction I was travelling away from, coming from Chicago and headed for Vegas; but she had to first stop off and see her grandmother somewhere near Des Moines before going back east to this religious school, while her mum and dad were still down in South America.

"Have you always been religious?"

"My mum and dad are missionaries."

"Oh, whereabouts?"

"Somewhere in Mexico."

"Were you brought up down there?"

"Yeah, I was home-schooled. But now I'm going to religious college."

There was no getting away from this topic, so it was time to get down to specifics.

"I consider myself to be a good person," you know, I'm getting cockier, wanting to see how far I can push it. "Not particularly religious, but at the same time I feel I've done no real evil in this world. What do you think that's gonna mean? How do you think I'm gonna fare?" Half joking; half not.

"Well, when God comes back," and she's looking at me seriously now, and I'm obviously not realising this at the time, but it's soon clear that evangelical means quite literally if it's in the Bible and it's worded that way, that's what it means, "when God comes back, there's going to be hellfire, brimstone," you know, we're talking mega. "And God will take those that have been righteous and have chosen the right path and send them to Heaven," whatever, I can't remember the exact details, but the crux of it being, any of those that are deemed bad are damned to Hell.

"Yeah, but I don't consider myself to be on the righteous path, or a mass murderer. So what about me on the line?"

And then she made the evangelical point, and I don't know if it's just an evangelical point, but nevertheless it seemed harsh to me: "Being in the middle is as bad as being against."

"How do you mean?"

And she was like, through your ignorance you've failed to acknowledge the one true whatever. You know, that's as bad. And she meant this one hundred per cent. This is the way she believed. I mean, she wasn't gonna kill me; but nonetheless I was a bad person, I was not following the teachings of God, I didn't believe in God particularly, and in her eyes that was as bad, you know, ignorance of the law doesn't make you any less guilty. Turning a blind eye to God and being like, well, I haven't really looked into it, not really that interested, I'm not gonna go and kill anyone, just be here in the middle: that is no excuse, you're still gonna have to pay the price; i.e. brimstone, fire, damned to Hell, devil's gonna get me. Which I thought was a bit strong.

"Oh right. That's a bit bad then, isn't it, really?"

"Well," and again she wasn't apologetic about any of this at all, "that's the way it is. You've chosen that path."

"So do you dislike me?" I mean, you know what I'm like, always pushing it. "Do you think I'm a bad person?"

"That's not for me to decide." She was very preachy, but understandably, her mum and dad being ministers.

"What do you mean?"

"Well, if that's the way you want to live your life, then who am I to say any different? But this is what I believe, and I think, a hundred per cent, to be honest with you, that, you know, you're doomed."

"Oh, right." Again I got the sense that she wasn't being horrible; but no way were we ever gonna be friends, cos I was a sinner in her eyes, no matter how much I pointed out that I'd never killed, shot whatever, done anything.

"Well, what can I do?"

"You can change the way that you're living your life, by all means. Come over to God."

"But what if I find out that I don't particularly agree with it?"

"Well, in the end there is only one belief."

And even though I can see I'm on dangerous ground, "But what about other religious beliefs?"

"They're on a wrong path."

"Buddhists?" And I'm thinking of JK, even though he wasn't exactly a dharmic success story.

"No."

I then mentioned a few other faiths but the reply was always the same: they've not followed the right path; they've chosen to believe something that's wrong; they're doomed. Again, in the middle. You know, they may not be mass-murderers or anything; but they're still fucked.

"Roman Catholics?" JK again, more of an adept in this, especially the guilt. I'm still rolling them off, but it is no, no, no: what you've got to understand is, THIS is the teaching of God, THIS is the Bible, THIS is what is written, THIS is it. Anything else is bullshit; though of course she didn't use that word. So I'm talking to a proper hardcore fundamentalist, wrapped up in a very attractive, friendly looking, intelligent, fluent-Spanish-speaking, young girl's body. Quite a scary combination.

"Do you think you'll ever get married?"

"I don't know. I might never get married. I want to concentrate on other things." She wants to be, again, a minister down in one of those South American countries and doesn't think marriage is necessary for her, doesn't believe a lot in boys, sex, not that we mentioned that, but I was getting at it. None of any of this is preoccupying her mind. I mean, this was someone who had focus, whether you agree with that focus or not. But in my mind I'm thinking, yeah, I wanna see what happens when boys come along, let's see how it works out then. Cos in a way I'm thinking she's sort of a bit like Eve in Eden peeping through the gates at the outside world. You know, she's still inside childhood, cos she hasn't met a snake yet. I mean, it's an all-girls school she's going to.

"Do you think you'll ever have children?"

"I don't know." Again you could tell this was not on her mind; or at least she said it wasn't. All a bit scary, in some ways, but interesting. Don't get me wrong, she wasn't like a crazy bible-basher; I don't think she wouldof introduced me to her parents, and I don't think she wouldof invited me to go out for a drink with her and become friends. She had beliefs, she was confident enough to tell me about them, and confident enough to tell me that I was on the wrong path and she was on the right path. Nonetheless she was telling me that I was damned. And that's the thing that made her really scary: cos of the strength of her fundamentalist beliefs, she had this tendency to see non-believers as less worthy and almost subhuman, do you get what I mean? And I was of course a bit taken aback by this; but then I just thought she was extreme. I wasn't like, you know, you'd better give me that book, I need to do some reading; it was more, fair enough, there's a lot of unrighteous people going down then. But you gotta remember this was a helluva conversation to be having on the way to Vegas. I mean, if I weren't damned already, I was soon gonna be.

She was the first person I'd ever met with beliefs that strong. But at the same time I wasn't like, bloody hell; and much to my surprise it didn't spook or freak me out. Maybe that just shows how shallow I am. But it all seemed too extreme to me. I mean, you've gotta realise that at this point some fucked-up things have happened to me. Dad had his accident; my reason for leaving for

America wasn't the greatest; and I'm thinking, well, as a kid, I never did anything fucking wrong, you know, I was a good person, I may not have been going to church every day, but I was still a good person; and fucked-up shit still happened. And I see plenty of bad people getting away with bad things. So how the hell can I believe in half of the stuff that she's telling me? You know, I feel that I've been punished for not doing anything. So if there is this God that's gonna descend and strike many of us down or whatever, it seems that He's laid a bit of it out already. But I didn't say any of this to her, of course.

Maybe I wouldof been more taken aback if she had been more of a manipulator; but she just laid it on the line. She wasn't like, there are benefits to this. She didn't try to sell it to me. So I give her respect for that. Didn't try to convert me; wasn't a knock-on-the-door whatever. She didn't even try to scare me. It was just, well, that's your choice; this is what I believe in. I'm right; you're wrong. You're doomed; I'm not.

The conversation ended, politely if not brilliantly, and I leant back in my seat. She got off at the next stop; I was in for the long haul. So it was back to the unrepentance of Queens of the Stone Age and sucking the goop out of cheese-middled crisps.

Chapter Sixteen

ABC

Neurotics choose to endure the pain of their
symptoms because without them life would be
unbearable
(C. G. Jung)

I like telling stories. According to my head doctor telling a story helps the mind to work things through, and that's what the mind is there for. It's not just a tape recorder to take information in; it's also a mouthpiece, so we can talk about how we feel, cos otherwise we just bottle everything up. And when you bottle things up, your emotions just get left behind, which is not healthy. So telling stories, especially ones that contain some kind of catharsis, even if it ends up as a crying session, as many of my sessions with the head doctor did, helps the mind get the files in order, you know, like a computer on standby filing stuff away, doing the work.

I read somewhere that we are more influenced by stories than by anything else, especially numbers, which is why so many people do the lottery, cos the idea of becoming rich overnight makes a better story than the odds of fourteen million to one. Some economist called this 'irrational exuberance', where something inside you makes you ignore the probabilities and just do it, you know, like having unsafe sex. Seems all of us are hardwired to be irrationally exuberant somewhere in our makeup; and those who aren't know how to press the buttons of those who are – you know, advertisers, politicians, con artists; the smart operators in this fucked-up world.

Some stories, however, are not easy to tell, like my going crazy at that party, for instance. Or Dad's accident. Or S. They are a source of confusion, shame or unresolved anger, incompletely processed, tears without catharsis, sensations that don't make sense. They can't be worked into a neat and tidy narrative with beginning, middle and end. Acts One, Two and Three. A before B which is followed by C. Hook, conflict, delay, turning point, climax, gratification, resolution, credits. All that crap. Can't be made into a joke or candified into a Richard Curtis movie; more like some French new wave film, like *Pierrot le Fou,* where the plotline malfunctions due to accidents and cause and effect and characters coming unstuck. The fact is some stories are not designed to be told at all; just lived through and endured.

My head doctor, though, would disagree. He would say that they can be talked through as well; just not neatly and tidily. They need to be told in fits and starts, with pauses and hesitations, ramblings and digressions, circularities and non sequiturs, sentences begun, stopped, redirected in midstream, chopped off and cut loose to voyage on their own, adventuring out, sinking fast, getting lost or abandoned, the way I usually talk, in fact, which is how most people think their 60,000 thoughts a day; jumblings and scramblings, fragments thrown together not always adding up to a whole, process without closure, pixels without picture, attempts at expression, improvisations, verbally and grammatically and orthographically and politically incorrect, episodic and picaresque, like jazz, like stand-up, like a Godard movie, bending, twisting and breaking rules, transitioning abruptly, syncopating, being clever, inventive, creative, imaginative, spontaneous, disconcerting, revolutionary, live, putting self on the line, crossing boundaries, continents, conventions, speaking profanities, offending decorum, risking disapproval, ignoring taboos, diving into streams of conscious and unconsciousness and fishing for whatever's there, pearls, eyeballs, or the souls of men, running the gauntlet, embracing incoherence, postmodernity and digitilisation, yet still ABC, just about, but not necessarily in that order, so ACB or BBC, with ellipsis and hiatus and gaps in between; then coming up for air, bursting and busting the straitjacket, jumping and running backwards and forwards, speaking in tongues repetitive and redundant, progressive and regressive, articulate and aphasic, dysfunctional child and adult, dazed and confused, rapture and rupture, Cassady and Kerouac, eloquent in half thoughts and mid-sentences, non-linear mind scribblings that tail off abruptly under the pressure of pain and memory, raw emotions, multiple perspectives, ghost writings and guilt, things that might have been said and unsaid, and the urge to revise, with words amputated from syntax but crackling with nerve endings, electric-alive with interactions, interpretations, interrogations, interpellations, feelings, raw and undigested, straining imperfectly to describe something real and felt, yet evasive and refractory, symptomatic of something unutterable, perhaps repressed and necessarily so, best left alone and worried over, a mental haunting of some kind, beyond exorcism, a bit like this sentence.

"I'm mad," were my first words to the head doctor.

"No, you're not mad."

That was mildly reassuring. But what else is a head doctor gonna say?

Dr B. was plump and chubby-faced, overweight really. Not that he was supersize; but he needed to lose some weight, as he often said. He loved gardening, was religious, Catholic, never ever pushed it on me though, but would tell me about it if I asked him. Late forties, non-smoker, though he used to when he was in the RAF but quit when everyone else quit, tanned cos he was born in some Mediterranean country and had that tone of skin as well as a slight accent, not trendy in any way, wore a suit but nothing flash, even though he earned a shitload of money, glasses, seemingly inevitable in that profession, but not designer, slightly shorter than me, short black hair, not cropped or shaved or anything, just combed and tidy, ready for work but you could tell he'd had a haircut to keep it under control; not like mine all over the place. I'd really like to see him again; but unfortunately I can't afford to.

Whenever we chatted he would talk about his cooking, cos he liked to cook, and he loved to grow his own vegetables: cabbage, carrots, potatoes and tomatoes. That was his thing, and he did it one, to unwind and two, for a little bit of fitness. And he would always swear that everyone needs something like that in their life. It doesn't really matter what, not got to have anything to do with their work; just something they can do to relax and chill out. That was what he did. He didn't care whether the potatoes grew; he'd try again next year. It weren't the end of the world. You know, if it grows, it grows; if it doesn't, it doesn't. That was his outlook on it. You could tell, though, that the man loved his food; but don't get me wrong, he was not obese and he didn't eat shit. He would talk about nice food, good wine; he wouldn't be like, I wanna fry-up, you know what I mean? He was a foodie in the respect that he liked good food, Italian, Indian, Chinese, everything; he wasn't large because he had, like, three McDonald's a week. He would never go into a McDonald's.

You could also tell that he was a skilled professional cos he was always in control, always monitoring himself as well as you. I would try and drag him into conversations. You know what I'm like. I would try big time. And he knew I was trying. He realised that I needed to engage with him on a friend-to-friend basis; but he was skilled in keeping it shrink–patient. But he would allow me, I know this, to feel that we were more friends. And I think he liked me, and knew that I liked him, although I also knew we weren't buddies. He was definitely aware that we needed that fifteen minutes at the end or the beginning to talk about his gardening, to talk about the fact that he was once in the RAF; cos I didn't wanna fucking tell everything to just anyone: I needed to know a little bit about him. And I think that's understandable, you know, who are you?; if I'm gonna tell you all this shit, let me hear a bit about you. So I'd ask him about how he would deal with a lot of the patients he sees, you know, it must be quite depressing, and he would tell me, we would chat, and a lotta people would say, why are you wasting your time doing that?, it's costing a lotta money; but I honestly feel that was as useful as the other stuff. And also I'm of the school that, you know, I'm not taking advice from someone I think's an idiot. I need to know that this person isn't stupid. Cos if I think they're a monkey, why should I listen to them? In a sense they've gotta earn my respect. That's my patient's charter.

Dr B. was a jolly person, never miserable, wasn't like a shrink that's like, hmmmm, you know, wasn't like that; a genuinely nice guy. Wife, kid, talked about them occasionally. Always incredibly rational. I wondered how his approach would work with irrational people; but he'd done that line of work before, you know, after the RAF, when he was working with proper crazies, forensic psychiatry or something, so he was no one-trick pony. I would wind him up by saying he was working at The Mansion for his pension, you know, this was his payday, this was where he racked up the euros. He would laugh, but he left The Mansion soon after my treatment ended and went off to work as head of some prison psychiatric unit with people who had either committed or were going to commit crimes due to their psychological disorders, you know, real bad cases. So a major change. Said he wanted to get back to working with people who definitely, definitely needed help. Not that he thought I didn't; just fancied a new challenge, I suppose. I don't think I had anything to do with that decision. He just wanted to go and help the really sick, you know, the ones that wanna go out and stab people. A lot of those around these days, unfortunately.

Dr B. had a million letters after his name and had written stuff on post-traumatic stress which had been published. He lent me a couple of articles once and I took them home but couldn't understand a word. I liked the fact, though, that he wasn't Freudian or anything; didn't zero in on the sex stuff. He knew what he was doing and I truly believe he had a genuine love for it, you know, he wanted to be the best he could be. Some you just think are in it for the paycheque, taking the easy route; but I genuinely felt that Dr

B. was always pushing his own knowledge. And as a person I liked him. He's likeable. You wouldof got on with him. And obviously he was smart. Probably wouldn't share our taste in music and movies and so on and so forth; but you could tell he wasn't silly.

The first thing that struck me when I went to see him was how different the approach was from the previous medical interventions I'd had the displeasure to undergo. All the other head doctors, and it sounds poncy, it sounds stuck up, but the simple fact of the matter is that if there was ever proof that you get what you pay for it's when you have a head doctor. Maybe I got lucky, and I'm sure you can pay a helluva lot of money and see some bastards who don't know their shit; but Dr B. knew his stuff and this sold him a long way for me, you know, I'm seeing the fucking best and this guy's a good guy. Whereas a lot of the people I'd seen before seemed to be reading from a script, you know, you could tell they really didn't want me there and we were always on a very tight time-frame. The NHS guys would never look you in the eye, never do anything but take notes, ask questions and when you asked them a question it was, 'We're moving away from what we've really got to focus on.' Foveal vision; nothing peripheral. At times Dr B. would also do that and bring us back on track; but I always felt that he understood that for me to really get to trust him there needed to be a period of getting to know each other and I needed to be able to ask him questions and find out about him. I mean, he never gave that much away but he would talk and the others never did. So I just felt that this guy knows what he's doing, whereas with the others I just felt I was a test study, you know, we're all juniors here and you're our first case.

The diagnosis of the NHS guys was OCD and nothing else. OCD, done. And the way forwards was exposure therapy. Work through the anxiety. They had this theory, which they loved, which is that the body can only sustain a high level of anxiety for a certain amount of time. So you push yourself into a situation where you're anxious for as long as your body can sustain it and then, through the physiology, so the theory goes, you can no longer be anxious, cos your body's all anxioused out. You know, your body produces adrenalin, your heart beats quicker, pulse gets faster, whatever; but this can only be sustained for a certain amount of time. Some people it's sixty minutes; other people it's forty minutes. It varies. Where the hell do you think they found all this out? Where do you think they saw this taking place in real life? Correct. Prisons. Internment. Experiments carried out by Nazi doctors in Auschwitz. People put under high degrees of stress with no control over it, and the studies showed you could do the same thing to them over and over again and they would become more and more blasé about it. You know, their bodies weren't reacting to it in the same way. So this, worryingly, took a major leap to, well, we know that you're not going to die, right, and we're gonna make you do something you don't wanna do. OK, I may be telling this a bit hardcore, but this is what it was; you're gonna feel uncomfortable about it, but you know that you're gonna feel uncomfortable about it, so as long as you know that you're gonna feel uncomfortable about it, that's OK. You're not gonna like it; but that's part of the process. And unlike the internment camp, unlike war, where you have a real reason, as they would put it, to be anxious, your anxious worries are being triggered inappropriately (they are big on 'appropriate' and 'inappropriate'), so we need to retrain your body to be able not to be triggering these anxious anxieties, when there is no need. If you're getting shot at, if your car's being blown up, you need to be fucking anxious, right? But if you're eating a sandwich, right, you don't need to be anxious. If you're in London and you need to touch something after you've touched something else, you don't need to be anxious. So with that in mind, you need to push yourself and do these things. So get on with it.

In my view this is a ridiculous theory. Because the simple fact of the fucking matter is, you are anxious, no matter whether it's appropriate or not, cos it feels appropriate at the time. Every part of your body which has been designed over hundreds of millions of years, whatever, is telling you, don't do this, don't do this, don't do this; and yet they expect their telling you to be enough to override that. So it's kinda like, oh, my shrink said it would be alright, so I'm just gonna really be anxious for forty minutes. And that was the other thing; they had this chart and you were meant to fill it in, like, on a scale of one to ten, how anxious were you at this moment in time and then the next moment straight after and all that? It was really stupid and I kept telling them that.

"This is stupid."

"No. You've got to stick to it."

"But it's stupid."

"You've got to stick to it. How did you do?"

"I'm not doing it at all. It's rubbish."

"Hmmmm."

You know, they didn't wanna talk about it, discuss reasons and methods. They were all about the solution rather than the cause. There was no talking about why I'd got to this situation. No talking about why they felt I was doing it now. It was like, this is the problem, let's sort it out, and this is the way to sort it out. Put yourself into these situations; fight the fight, feel the burn, ride the rapids, work on the triggers, and come out the other side. They didn't use those terms but that was pretty much what it was.

Classic example: eating in a fast-food place. I've been out in town, I've carried bags, I've opened doors, I've done all these things. Go and have a burger. I can do that now easily. I mean, if I've got the opportunity to wash my hands, use a wipe, I still will, cos that's fucking common sense; but if I haven't and can't, I'll still eat it, right, cos I'm a chub and I'm hungry. But back then I was a helluva lot thinner and the reason I was thinner is cos there was just no way I couldof done it. I mean, it is crazy and it's like looking back on someone else; but say we were out and we go to McDonald's and you buy me a burger and say, there you go, instantly my adrenalin wouldof kicked in: one, I don't want to embarrass myself cos I don't wanna say to you I can't eat this because of this reason, you know, I'm gonna look like a nutter, more anxiety, more anxiety, so I'm trying to work out how I am gonna get around eating this without looking like a fool, and

211

also like there ain't no way around it cos I am gonna look like a fool and I don't wanna look like a fool; and two, I'm gonna catch something, we're in fucking McDonald's, burger's probably dirty, my hands are dirty, how am I gonna get it from here to here and then eat that bit? It's not gonna happen. So my anxiety is going up and up.

Their theory was I just went and did it. Basically it was, you know, go and do it, expose yourself to it, exposure therapy. I mean, there is more of a science to it than this, but you gotta remember this was a long time ago I was told it and I'm just giving you the gist, which is the gist of how I saw it as a fourteen/fifteen-year-old boy. So if I can remember it as good as this now, that's probably as well as I understood it then. And I had this little flowchart where I was to mark down my anxiety over a forty-minute period; you know, after five minutes he was at a level ten, cos they love this, NHS shrinks, 'on a scale of one to ten, one being not anxious at all, a calm, relaxed state, possibly lying in bed, ten being very anxious, heart beating loudly, fast pulse, whatever, where would you be?' So it would be, 'When I first went in I was a ten. Ten minutes later I was a nine.' This was how it was meant to be. But I was like, 'I was ten the whole way fucking through.'

"You can't have been."

"I was."

"You can't have been. It's not physically possible."

"I was."

And my argument was, it wasn't like one event. It wasn't like, 'I'm really anxious, I'm really anxious, I'm touching this burger!' cos there would then be other things going on and my point was that, surely, they were separate anxiousnesses? You know, that one's gone; but now here's another. Where was this written in science, or in a manual, that you couldn't? I mean, it's a bit like, I don't know, you could compare it to this: some men, I imagine, have sex, BAM, do what they do, ten minutes later they're ready to go again, whereas another person might be an hour. I'm sure it's the same thing with anxiety. Some people get really anxious and

212

then maybe their body isn't able to make them anxious again for an hour and a half, I don't know. But with me it was like anxious, drop a little, BAM, anxious again; this is what they could never seem to understand. I would say to them, "I understand what you're saying, but there are a lot of environmental things coming in that just kick off the anxiety again."

"What, so close to when you were at ten?"

"Yeah."

"Oh, it must be because it wasn't sustained over a period of forty minutes."

"Wha? This isn't making any sense at all."

"Hmmmm."

They didn't wanna know at all. The very questions you'd ask wha? wha? about, they were just like, no, this is right, this is right, just carry on, carry on. And because they were cognitive behavioural therapists, they didn't wanna talk about the past or why you had got to this point. You know, whenever I said something like, when I was such and such I did this, they were just like, 'We're not here to talk about that.'

But Dr B. was not a cognitive behavioural therapist; he was an analyst. However, he didn't badmouth any of those NHS guys even though I gave him plenty of chance to. He even said we may do some cognitive behavioural therapy. But we never did. Like we were gonna do some exposure therapy, but never did. We didn't do that stuff. Maybe because I'd spoken so negatively about my experiences in the past. But he wouldn't criticise. Like I would say, "Oh, those NHS punks, they were crap."

"I'm sure they did their best."

I gave him the opportunity to say, I'm a legend, they were rubbish; but he didn't, and wouldn't even nod when I gave him the cue.

When I first turned up at The Mansion I'm thinking, man, this place is pimp; like The Ritz. I mean, I was used to going to some two-up two-down in some dodgy Freetown backstreet; but this was a real mansion set in bucolic countryside, huge, white

213

and posh with Arcadian pillars. It was like a retreat or something. There were all these skinny girls, cos it was a residential place, not just for day visits, and these girls were suffering from anorexia and bulimia and all that stuff. You'd sit in the waiting room and you got free drinks and whatever. Eventually this little secretary came up, "Hello, Mr Pearce," and she'd lead you to this lift that was always dodgy, never worked well, cos it was really old and they were always trying to get it fixed, and they'd get it fixed but it would still break, and I'm walking along and seeing all these people's rooms, proper rooms with beds and stuff, not like a hotel, but not like a hospital either, and you'd go up and there'd be this waiting area and then Dr B. would come in.

"I need to lose a little bit of weight," you know that was the only thing he was a bit morose about, but in a jokey way. But he wasn't massive, not like Jeff Garlin in *I Want Someone to Eat Cheese With*. You could see he had a belly, but he didn't have this going on, you know, it wasn't that, but you could tell he had a gut. So I go in and he shakes my hand; again totally unlike the NHS guys. "OK, let's talk about what you want to achieve in coming to these sessions." And that's when I told him I was mad.

"You're not mad. You've just come up with coping mechanisms."

"Yeah, but nobody else does them."

"Yes they do. All the time."

And he then told me about rituals, which is the first time anyone had ever explained this to me, where the idea comes from, how you only have to look through history and see that people have used coping mechanisms all the time. You look at people out in Africa or native America or wherever, rituals have always been put in place when that human society or individual has got no control over the chaos around them. So the purpose of a rain dance is to lower anxiety levels. This was his theory anyway as a doctor, others are not going to agree with it, you know, they're gonna believe in a certain mysticism about the rain dance and its possible cosmic resonance whatever; but he saw it as, you know, for these people if their fucking crops don't grow they're all gonna

214

die. They're gonna worry about this a lot. They wanna feel better about it. There ain't nothing they can do to feel better about it, except one thing: perform a ritual. You know, you go out and do a rain dance and then you think, I've done that ritual, so now they feel they've been able to control something that is, from a rational point of view, totally uncontrollable. And Dr B. said it's always exactly the same; tribes live on the base of active volcanoes and know that volcano's gonna erupt, but if they think about that every day it'll do their heads in, so they do rituals to stop the volcano from erupting. And it was the same thing with me and my rituals: the handwashing, checking and rechecking locks, standing on the edge of the carpet, double-jigging through doorways, etc. I could see what he was saying. One thing he didn't like, though, was when I turned this round to praying.

"So are you saying exactly the same thing about praying to God?"

"What do you mean?"

"Well, there's nothing you can do about these things, you know, such and such has got this, or such and such needs money for this, so you pray to God, therefore you lower your anxiety levels."

He didn't quite agree with that and scooted around the subject a bit. I didn't pursue it any further cos I didn't wanna upset him.

The first session was a consultation, I think he called it an assessment, and again, cos this is obviously something they love in the psychological world, there was the, you know, one being this, ten being this; I suppose it's the only way you can gauge what people are feeling at any one time. So we did that bullcrap. But he was polite and genuinely interested and I got to ask questions as well so it was kind of like a conversation of sorts, like those Socratic Q&A sessions Plato writes about, but lower-powered, obviously. It was definitely no one-way street.

"Do you think we can work together?" Not, OK, you've been assigned to me, see you next week. There was an element of choice which was again unlike the NHS.

215

"Yeah, yeah. I like you."

"You don't need to like me."

"Maybe not. But for me, I do need to like you."

"Why is that?"

So I laid it on the line. "Why the hell am I gonna trust someone I don't know or don't like? I mean, if you're gonna be telling me all this stuff that I've got to go out and follow and possibly feel anxious over, I've gotta trust you, and if I've gotta trust you, it helps if I like you."

"You don't have to agree with everything I say."

"I won't. But I can tell you're a good guy."

"Well, if you like me, you like me. All the better."

Which was cool.

"So what do you do?"

"I do trauma."

When I look back on my time with Dr B. I think about what I learnt. I mean, I couldn't do everything he told me to at the time. And I often disappointed him by mixing alcohol with my Seroxat and engaging in the kind of disinhibited behaviour he strongly disapproved of, you know, throwing a pint glass with beer in it at some huge guy in a bar who was pissing me off, then eyeballing him and saying, go on, go on, hit me, I know you want to, go on, stab me in the eye, go on, then freaking him out by punching myself. Dr B. said I could get seriously beaten up or worse if I kept doing that; and when I told him that that was the point, that I WANTED someone to hurt me and if it put me out of my misery, so much the better, he increased the number of our sessions to twice a week.

"The thing with alcohol is that it will make all your emotions much more raw, and exaggerate them. You will feel more in touch with life; but you won't have control. So we need to work through the cause of your anger before you're allowed to drink. We can change the medication if necessary to find something which does allow you to drink, but I believe this is the best medication for you."

"You make me sound like an alky."

"You're not an alky, but you use alcohol to excess, like the vast majority of young people your age. You're in this phase of your life."

"I don't really like going to get drunk, but I go because my friends go. I mean they wanna get pissed. That's what they do. I don't like them because that's what they want to do; I just like them for themselves."

"How old are they?"

"Nineteen. Same age as me."

"So what's it like to be a nineteen year old these days? Does everyone have to go and get pissed?"

"Yeah and it's horrible. I mean, I don't go out to try and get drunk. A lot of the time I stay at home and do other things. But a nineteen year old today, from my socio-economic background, right, would go and get drunk on a Friday and Saturday and try and forget about the rest of the week. Seriously. That's the state of play for my generation at this moment in time."

"Well, it's a phase. Because in my generation, which was not so long ago, that was also the state of play. And it lasts until your friends get girlfriends, and then you never see them again."

"Sounds harsh."

"It's not harsh. It is what it is, as you would say. People pair off and there's no need to get drunk with your mates any more. It's not exciting any more; it becomes boring."

"I find it boring now."

"Well, some people find it boring to start with and don't really engage with it."

"I know. I know."

"It's a waste of money, anyway."

"And I can't even communicate with those people."

"So why are you doing it?"

Dr B. was always using the 'why?' question, you know, the ultimate head-doer. He would usually produce it as an end point to our mini Socratic dialogues. According to Dr B. the key was always ABC: antecedent, behaviour, consequence. That was one of his mantras. Antecedent, my thought; behaviour, what I do;

217

consequence, my feelings about my life. This first came up when I told him I was struggling to find a good reason to get up in the mornings. I was what you might call seriously depressed at the time.

"I mean, I'm thinking, you know, what's the purpose of life?, and staying in bed is simply a natural evolution of that thought. And whilst it's not a brilliant option, at least it's thought through, whereas other people are getting up not thinking about it at all."

"But you need to question these thoughts; challenge them."

"But when should I do that?"

"In the antecedent phase. Antecedent is, I'm thinking, ruminating about whether I should get up. Behaviour is, I stay in bed, because there's no point. Consequence is, I feel depressed, useless, pointless, etc. They all link. Your behaviour dominates how you feel, which is unhappy."

"So how is it working in my ten-year-old brother's head, who seems to have no problem getting up at all?"

"Antecedent, I'm awake, here I am, hooray! Behaviour, I get up. Consequence, I do well at school."

"OK. Right."

"You don't think hooray; but you could. You could get up bouncing for joy, you could say, thank God for another day, that's fantastic, I've got another one to use, instead of oh no, not another twenty-four hours of misery!"

"I don't want you to think that I'm not aware that it's not good what I'm thinking, or that I'm complaining that I'm alive knowing there are plenty of people that would probably wanna be alive, but are dead."

"I don't think that, no. I'm not judging you. You judge yourself."

"But what if I'm bouncing for joy and then something goes wrong? Surely I'm then back to square one, and it wouldof been better to have stayed in bed?"

"That's life. Life is a risk."

"Hmmmm."

"What happens when David Beckham misses a penalty for England and they lose and go out of the World Cup?"

"Everyone hates him."

"So what if he gets too scared to take the penalty?"

"He looked pretty worried the last time."

"What if he'd chickened out? No risk? Here, Owen, you take it instead. And Owen misses. How would Beckham feel then?"

"Guilty."

"All right? You've got to take a few risks in life."

"But what if Beckham takes it and misses?"

"He says to himself, I'll try and do better next time."

"Even with everyone looking at him and hating him?"

"Even with everyone looking at him and hating him."

"Even with the newspapers trashing him every day? Fans booing and hurling missiles at him every week? Everyone slagging him off left and right? Insulting him and his family and sending death threats?"

"Even with all that. Do you want to stay in bed all day?"

"Not really. I just lie there and worry."

"So your antecedent is, you fertilise this worry, you feed it somehow, your behaviour is, you stay in bed, and what is the consequence?"

"I get more depressed and do nothing."

'Such a waste of time. How many days out of ten are you doing that?"

"A lot."

"Five?"

"Umm."

"Half the time."

"Yeah."

"What time do you get out of bed?"

"In terms of total slobs, they'd probably see it as quite early, you know, I'm getting up around half ten to eleven; but then I won't go to bed until around one or two in the morning."

"And what are you doing until one or two in the morning?"

"Thinking."

"Where? In your bedroom?"

"Yeah. Sitting in my arm-chair."

"What are you thinking about?"

"Everything."

"Worrying."

"Worrying, thinking what's the point?"

"The point of what?"

"Everything."

"Frankly, I don't know what you're worrying about, because we all have a finite number of days. I might have three hundred left; you might have thirty thousand. Every day we tick one off. The next might be our last, we don't know. So why waste your time?"

I should probably back up here and tell you about the 'inciting incident' to all this, the event that supposedly kicks everything off, the reason why I'm here talking to a jolly-faced, slightly overweight, highly intelligent, likeable and top five per cent wage-earning shrink; namely my dad's accident. Car accident. Like most accidents that happen to people these days. If it was an accident. Dad was a good driver. I mean, I take my standards from the unsurpassable Neal Cassady, and Dad obviously wasn't quite that good; but he was up there. In *Big Sur* JK writes about this other driver, Dave Wain, cos JK is always having to be driven around, not being able to drive himself, which I always think is amazing as well as ironic, since he writes about driving better than anyone ever before or since, better than Springsteen's fuelly headed ramrodders and Hunter S. Thompson's flashy technical bullshit. JK says he thought that Dave Wain and Neal Cassady were the two greatest drivers in the world, even if Dave sometimes lifted at corners, which Neal had issues with, since for Neal this was the ultimate taboo, and JK also says that, even though he always felt safe with Neal, he preferred Dave's driving, cos with Neal there was always the danger, not so much of an accident, but that the car would suddenly take off and soar skywards; you know, as JK puts it, it was always a crisis about to get worse, right up to the point when some miraculous and unforeseeable solution is pulled out of the hat by Neal's overdrive thinking, lightning reflexes and supernatural dexterity, whereas Dave just made the wheels stick and the engine purr. And my dad used to drive like Dave. And when he put his sunglasses on and let the top down on his gold and black fur-trimmed custom Mark1 Ford Mexico RS, cos he always said the Mark1 handled sweeter than any of the other versions, no one looked cooler. Didn't need no stereo; he could make that car sing by itself.

Dad needed all his skills on the M20 when a Vauxhall Cavalier travelling in front of him had a blowout at seventy in the fast lane. The Cavalier's rear offside exploded, causing the tail to swing and bang into the central barrier, spinning the car one-eighty and nearly taking my dad's Mexico with it, before slewing across all lanes for two hundred metres and ending up facing the wrong direction. My dad being my dad didn't hesitate. He parked up, jumped out and went to pull out the Cavalier driver, a woman in her fifties who was unconscious at the time. Her glasses were all smashed and there was a lot of blood. She was pretty mangled up. And then suddenly BOOM. Dad finds himself flying through space. Cut to black.

Another angle. Jump cutting. The driver of some speeding blue car, who considers his time to be more important than my dad's time, or this smashed-up woman's time, or the time of anyone else in the whole goddamn universe, zigzags through the wreckage without lifting and clips my dad as he opens the Cavalier driver's door, catapulting him twenty feet in the air. Skywards. Heavenwards. And he never really comes back down again. Close-up eyewitness, saying the blue car mustof been doing a hundred and ten and didn't slow at all on the impact; if anything it went even quicker. You know, flashback, a bit of wheel lock, smoke, downshift, power on, traction, rubber down, upshift and away. Fuck you, suckers. I'm fast and furious. It was a guy driving, but no description, no age, no number, no nothing. Couldn't even tell you what make the blue car

221

was, officer, it moved so quick across the lanes, and then was gone. I'm sure it was blue. Couldof been green. Or grey. Maybe a Ford. Possibly a Nissan. You know, it just went by so fast.

Dad was in hospital for six months, and when he came out he had no memory and I had OCD. My little brother was too young to realise what was going on; and anyway when you're only five years old you accept catastrophe, seeing it as sort of part of the normal run of things whose logic you haven't yet worked out but are sure you will one day when you're older. But I was older and at a deeper-thinking age, so I needed to work the whole thing through, which I couldn't, because in my world, which, despite my age, was still a young world at the time, although that was soon to come to an abrupt end, bad things didn't happen to good people, and that's why I developed what my head doctor called a PTSD, aka post-traumatic stress disorder.

To say my dad came out with no memory is a bit of an overstatement. What he lost was his short-term recall. He's fine at remembering things that are on a longer time frame; just not what happened yesterday, or an hour ago, or five minutes ago, and sometimes thirty seconds ago. In computer terms, as you know, hard drive is long-term memory; you wanna store something, you wanna archive something, you put it on a hard drive, yeah? The things that happen in the here and now, the things that need to be accessed immediately, conversation, or you read one page of a book you turn over, but you need to remember the previous page to make sense of the next one; this doesn't need to be put into long-term storage. You know, if I were to ask you what happens on page thirty-eight of Jack Kerouac's *On the Road*, unless you're some kind of freak, you ain't gonna remember. But you need to remember page thirty-eight by the time you get to page forty, otherwise the story's not gonna flow. That's the area of memory that my dad's got wrong: his RAM, random access memory, the one that's refreshed all the time; that's the one that's not functioning properly. However, you could also say that a certain chunk of his long-term hard drive storage has also been corrupted. I mean, let's

222

call it ten gig rather than ten years; say you've got like a fifty-six-gig hard drive, you know, one of those gigs for every year of my dad's life: from the moment of that accident ten gig on the platter of that hard drive disk was wiped off, erased. Everything before it is still there in long-term storage; but with everything that's written from the moment he wakes up after dropping back to earth from the sky, it's like the hard drive isn't booting up a hundred per cent correctly immediately. This is where it gets complicated, not black and white. Cos my dad's random access memory, the stuff that's being refreshed but never logged into long-term memory, isn't so great: but if he accesses that short-term memory again and again and again, over time it can be stored into long-term memory. But it needs to be repeated again and again and again.

For example, whenever Alice used to come round, Dad would know who she was: that's Alice. But when she first came over, if I were to ask him about it the following day, he wouldof been like, someone came over, didn't they? Yeah, but who was it, Dad? And he wouldn't remember. It's only after she'd been coming around for some weeks that the memory had been refreshed enough to be logged: that's Alice. It's like you've got that random accessed memory and it needs to be refreshed, refreshed, refreshed, God knows how many times, and then at some mysterious point, it's like CHNGGACHNGG; and once it's made that leap, it's locked in. How it goes from here to being here, I'd be a millionaire if I knew.

And it's made even more complicated by the fact that he can remember things he wants to remember, which can be really irritating. Especially where money is concerned. Like if I borrow a pound from the pot for parking, he will never forget it. I mean, he might vaguely forget it, and it might be a week before he'll suddenly go, 'You've gotta give me that pound back you borrowed.' And I'm like, 'You remembered that?' I mean, he didn't remember the day after or the day after that; but eventually he remembered. Maybe it's cos he saw the pot and that triggered the memory, who knows? And things that annoy him, he remembers. I mean, when his social worker takes him to see a film and you ask him about the story when he gets back, you'll get the most jumbled, not so accurate description. You'll get the gist but… However, if you ask him who cut him up on the way back and who he was shouting and swearing at in the car, cos he's still got a short fuse like me, you know, a touch of Italian, I think, he'll remember. Or if they go into HMV and the assistant addresses the social worker rather than the cripple in the wheelchair, you know, what's he want?, what was that he said?, he'll remember that alright. Sometimes I think if we just piss him off all the time he'll remember everything.

One thing Dad was always hot on, however, was having the most comprehensive automobile insurance going. So five years later, when all the details of his claim were finally argued out and sorted, I was awarded six months' treatment with a specialist psychiatric consultant. And that's how I got to be at The Mansion with Dr B., who normally only rock stars can afford to have a consultation with.

"Do you think there are *any* benefits to thinking too much?"

"None. Look, we know that these obsessional thoughts are pointless. They once had a purpose, they were useful, these thoughts, when there was fear and worry and serious problems in the household with Dad being ill. But the use is outdated, outmoded and it should be discarded like a 286 computer. Just throw it from the highest building and say, I can fit this 286 into my pocket now. When you think too much, you become over-cautious, worried, anxious, preoccupied, you can't concentrate properly, you waste your time, you think about stupid things as well as important things, you don't know what's important; it's confusing. But it's not your fault; it's automatic. You've trained yourself to do this."

"But why have I done that?"

"To cope with the trauma."

"But the weird thing is, if you're an idiot you don't think so much."

"But idiots do stupid things, don't they?"

"Yeah, but what I mean is, perhaps it would be better to be stupid so you couldn't think so much, and then in the end you'd be much happier."

"But are you being clever by thinking so much, or are you being stupid?"

"I'm being both. Because I think so much I'm stupid."

"Let's try not to personalise it with words like 'stupid' or 'clever'; it's just a condition that is hampering what you can do, preventing you from getting on with your life."

"So what you are saying is, even if I wake up and fail, at least I will have tried."

"But you mustn't be impulsive. You mustn't get pissed and go around throwing pint glasses at strangers. You need to be responsible. Do what is responsible and good as far as possible. Don't do impulsive and stupid things, and don't procrastinate, and you'll feel a lot better."

"But how will I know that I'm doing the right things?"

"You'll know. If you switch your thoughts, and become clever at that, you'll be cured. That's the secret. The medication will help a little, but it will lose its effect. What you need to do is challenge your thoughts. You need to be me. You need to hear my voice. My name is Challenge, OK? You need to remember me and think, well, would he stay in bed for three or four hours wasting his time?"

"No."

"No. He'd be out in the garden or doing some work."

"But sometimes I have difficulty working out what is a waste of time. And then I worry about whether it's a waste of time or not, and then in the end I don't do anything."

"Give me an example."

"Well, the other day I was gonna sit down and draw. Normally I draw storyboards and stuff, but this time I just wanted to draw in a way that was unconnected to anything. And I went to do it; but then I thought, this is a waste of time. It's not gonna get me anywhere, it's not gonna gain me anything. So I didn't do it."

"But your logic is wrong. What you should be doing is drawing for its own sake."

"But doesn't everything have to have a benefit to it? Like even if it's just improving my drawing skills for a time when I'll need to do more advanced storyboards?"

"You can do things for fun, you know. Cos you like it. I mean, if I didn't do things for fun I'd be miserable."

"But this is the thing: I can't remember how to do things for fun. A part of me is always saying, there's no point. It's not gonna get me anywhere in my life. Not gonna get me any extra money. Not gonna do this, not gonna do that."

"You don't have to be all goal-directed. Let's look at a slob. Someone who doesn't do any work but enjoys his life."

"But is that good or bad?"

"He likes it."

"But is it good or bad, though?"

"His aim in life is to enjoy himself."

"But he hasn't, like, found a cure for something; he hasn't been into space."

"He's a good person."

"He hasn't been into space."

"He's a good person."

"But he hasn't done anything!"

"He enjoys life."

"Yeah, but he hasn't DONE anything!"

"What's life for?"

"I don't know."

"Is it to achieve something all the time?"

"That's what everybody thinks it's for."

"But things that are worth achieving are material things, giving pleasure to yourself and other people and doing good things."

"So, say I did nothing all my life but was happy; would you see me as a bad person?"

"I wouldn't judge you. But if you were happy, I would say, well, you're doing things that make you happy."

"You wouldn't think I was a good person, though. The shrugging means that you wouldn't."

"Maybe but …"

"You'd judge me."

"You judge yourself. And you're judging that if you're not doing something at this minute you're wasting your time."

"That is how I see myself."

"And that is very obsessional. You can't be goal-directed all the time."

"But that's what everybody's always taught me."

"Yeah, but you've listened to that."

"Cos I thought it was true!"

"Be good at school, don't worry your mother."

"Exactly."

"Pass your exams, don't worry your father."

"That's it."

"Be a good boy, achieve what you can, do your best all the time and don't relax ever in your life."

"That's right."

"But that's wrong advice."

"But that was the advice the teachers gave me!"

"Well, it's wrong."

"You should tell them."

GETTING ANNOYED NOW.

"They're wrong. You should be balanced. They should have said, play sport, go out, enjoy yourself, have hobbies and achieve well at school. That's balanced."

CALMER.

"So I shouldn't feel guilty about just doing things for fun. Even if it isn't gonna benefit me."

"What do I do the garden for?"

"But there is a point to that."

"What?"

"You're growing things."

"I could easily buy onions. I don't have to grow them; it's a waste of time, isn't it?"

"No, it isn't, though. Cos you're gonna get them for, like, free."

227

"Not at all. It costs me a fortune in time and effort. I can make more money by using my time seeing people. I'm inundated with people wanting to see me."

"But you can't do that all the time otherwise you'd go mad."

"Ah! What do you do then?"

"Ah!"

"I do it for fun. I don't have to grow onions."

"Yeah but there is a benefit to it, though."

"The benefit is, I relax. There's no other benefit. I relax; I see the fruits of my labour. But it's not goal-directed in terms of making money or achieving an objective. The objective is sheer enjoyment of doing it for its own sake. And that's what you've lost."

"I can't even remember the last time I did that. My friend and I used to make films for fun when I was like twelve/thirteen. But now I can't do it for fun any more; it's become my work."

"So you haven't got anything to do for fun any more. But you need to do things for their own sake; to enjoy them."

"But I get obsessed with everything I ever try to do. I mean, say my friend, Joe, were to sit down and relax, he might do something like draw that chair. Don't know why he'd wanna draw that chair; but he's gonna draw that chair. He'll draw that chair and then go, OK, done. And I'll look at it and I'll go, but the arm's crooked, the back ain't right. Even things that are supposed to be relaxations for me I get obsessive about. I won't do anything unless it's gonna be perfect. And maximum effort. For example, today I was gonna do something on my script and I had quite a lot of time to plan it, six hours to start doing it; but then I thought, there's no point, because I've got to go out at four. So I thought, no, I need a whole day. Twelve hours. Or even twenty-four. So because of the fact that I had to be interrupted after six hours, I wouldn't do it. That's madness. But I was always told you've gotta put a hundred per cent in otherwise it's not gonna be any good."

"If I put a hundred per cent in all the time I'd fall apart. Sometimes ninety per cent is good enough."

"No it isn't."

"Yes it is."

"But everyone keeps saying to me you've gotta put in a hundred and TEN!"

"I don't know who these people are. Who are they?"

"Teachers."

"What do they do that's a hundred and ten per cent? That's so good? Tell me. What have they ever done? Which films have they produced? I don't mean to be horrible to teachers; but why are they going to be your role models for life?"

"They're the ones that you're meant to look up to."

"You've done that. Now you're older, more responsible and more mature. You don't have to take what they say at face value any more."

"But what about my little brother? We should be getting him in now and telling him all this."

"Don't worry about your little brother. He sounds more balanced than you are."

"Yeah but that's because he's ten and doesn't think."

"You need not to think. Your problem is you think too much."

"But why is that?"

"Because it's safe. Trying to problem-solve everything. I don't think you think all the time because you want to; it's because it's safe and keeps your mind occupied, yes? Whereas if I'm feeling fed up I just think, well, where's the nicest beach I've been to?, let's just go there and relax. But if you've got a problem, you think what's the next job I can do to avoid feeling uptight? But don't feel bad about this, because you wouldn't have reached this stage unless you'd coped the way you have done. The way you've coped is quite an automatic way of coping; there's no way you could have been taught or known how to cope differently. So don't castigate yourself; you need to be your own best friend, not your own worst enemy."

And I told my head doctor that, before my dad's accident, I used to think, as he said a lot of kids do, that good things happen to good people; bad things happen to bad people. This is what

229

we're taught at school. But as adults we know that that's not the fucking case at all. And he would say to me, you have to remember that things aren't black and they're not white. It's not just one. It sounds cheesy, but it's true: it's grey. And I would say, how do you mean? And he would reply that behind every choice, behind every event, behind everything, you know, the decisions that people make aren't always determined by whether it's a good thing or a bad thing. Sometimes you have to opt for the grey selection in order to keep life ticking on, and for people to do what they've gotta do and whatever. It's the same with court cases and crimes, whatever. People would like to be able to say, 'You're bad because you did this.' But if you look at the background behind that crime, maybe they did kill someone, maybe they did run someone over, maybe they have made mistakes; but if you look at what led them there, very rarely will it literally be they were a bad person all the way. There is that grey area where, yeah, they did do this, but that was only as a result of this and then this. And I would say to him, but that's just making excuses. And he would say, you could say the same thing about a lot of the decisions in life. It might look like excuses; but life isn't as easy as black and white, good and evil.

And that was one of the biggest lessons the head doctor ever taught me. I have not put it as eloquently as he wouldof; but that was basically the gist of it.

Like I say, I learnt a lot from Dr B., and not just about the need to use some irrational exuberance to get my ass out of bed. For instance, how bad things do not only happen to bad people, and God will surely know all this, and if he's any good at his job he'll take it all into account when he's weighing up souls. Which is why I couldn't accept the reasoning of the evangelista on the bus, even though she was really pretty. Cos it seems to me that her take on religion was no more than a coping mechanism, just a bit more elaborate than usual, and one which a lot of other people have bought in to; however, I definitely would not want to be the one who points this out to her, would you?

230

Chapter Seventeen

Vegas Part One

Vegas, baby

I arrived in Vegas at night. The evangelical girl had got off the bus a while back, and I got speaking to the black guy, the one with the pregnant girlfriend. You remember: charismatic, reasonably good-looking guy, confident. Mustof told me his name, but I can't recall it. Maybe I've repressed it, who knows? Previously at other stops, him and this other guy would be smoking a joint. They'd offer it to me, but I'd be like, no, no, I'm not interested. But in a thank-you-but-no polite sort of way; not in a kind of like, you know, I ain't touching that shit. Then I started talking to him on the bus. His girlfriend was there; she was very quiet, good-looking, if not a little pregnant, do you know what I mean? As I say he was like real, ah yeah, you know, he was very confident. And you could tell he was a hustler; nice guy, but not everything he said I believed. Nonetheless he's company; we're talking.

"Ah yeah, we're going over to Vegas to see my sister. Gonna stay with her for a couple of days. I was over in Chicago doing dadada." I couldn't quite work it out, something to do with sales, sounded very dodgy though, right? "Yeah, waiting for my paycheck to come through. Having a bit of trouble with some money. Wanna try and set ourselves up in Vegas. Been travelling around." And his girlfriend is nodding and agreeing. "What's it like over in Britain? I'd love to go over there one day. Wanna go to Manchester."

231

"Right."

Loads of questions, we're talking, whatever. He seemed cool.

"When we get to Vegas I'll show you a good time. I'll take you to some of the best places."

You have to remember the whole time I've been in America everyone that's said this to me has been a stand-up, regular, nice person, yeah? So my guard has been lowered. So I'm kind of like, yeah, sounds cool, sounds good.

"Where you gonna stay?"

"I really don't know yet."

"Huh? You don't have a plan? Don't have a plan? Man, that takes some balls. So where you gonna stay? It's expensive, you know, it's expensive."

"It's OK, I'm gonna treat it as the most expensive part of my trip, you know, I've kind of taken all that into consideration, and I'm only gonna stay a couple of days, cos, you know, I'm probably gonna blow more money here than I have anywhere else."

"Ah. So it mustof cost you a lotta money, this trip?"

"It's cost me a little bit. My granddad left me some money, you know, it's sort of a once-in-a-lifetime thing."

"Oh, that's cool. That's cool." Then, "But you gotta stay with us! You gotta stay with us." And I could see his girlfriend was a bit like, what's going on here? "Yeah, yeah, it'll be fine, it'll be fine, it'll be fine."

And she was like, "You sure your sister won't mind?"

"Yeah, yeah, he's only staying a couple of nights, it'll be fine."

A little while goes on and I'm thinking, I'm not sure I wanna stay with these people, I don't know them. But I don't want to hurt their feelings. However, at the next stop he comes back over.

"Not sure you're gonna be able to stay."

"Oh, really?" Sounding disappointed, but thinking thank fuck.

"Let me sort you out somewhere. Let me sort you out somewhere."

232

Now I'm like, what does he mean? I don't wanna stay with one of his buddies I don't even know of.

"Don't wanna stay on the Strip. Don't stay on the Strip. Those hotels, those fairygroundy places, they ain't real Vegas. And it's gonna cost you mega money. I know some places. I can get you a room. It'll have a kitchen in it, it'll have a toilet, it'll be a nice place, off the Strip. You'll have to get a cab to some of the spots, but it'll be a helluva lot cheaper. We're talking a hundred and twenty five dollars for three days. And that's cheap in Vegas."

I'm thinking, hmmm, alright, OK, fair enough. I've known him for a little while now, forty-eight hours maybe, and in busworld that's a reasonable amount of time. But at the same time there is a niggling feeling. But I'm thinking, you know, this is just you being British. Everyone I've met so far has been nice, I'm being an idiot, just go with the flow, you're having a good time, why would he want to screw you over? You know where this is going.

We get there, and I'm kind of now following them, right?

"We gotta go see my sister first. Then I promise you, I'll sort you out and I'll take you to a place. I know someone who works on reception. I'm sure I can get you an even better deal."

He's a nice enough guy.

We get to his sister's. It's way off the Strip. Kind of rough area. Not a ghetto, but at the same time I'm getting a feeling that it looks a bit dodgy round here. And the house is not posh. An apartment, two-storey, gated thing.

Sister comes to the door.

"Who the hell's theez?", sort of thing.

"Oh, this is my buddy. We met on the bus."

"Oh, hi!"

Shakes my hand. I put my bag down, the only luggage I have left now, as you know, containing CD player and headphones, couple of pairs of pants and vests, a T-shirt, and that's it. Oh yeah, and a toothbrush.

As I say, this place does not look posh at all. I'm not being horrible, but it's like a one-bedroom apartment, and I'm thinking, these two have come here to stay, his sister don't look particularly keen, what's going on here? And why didn't he get paid from his last job? It all seems a bit weird. And I forgot to tell you that earlier he'd asked me for five dollars, cos he wanted to get himself a drink and he promised he'd sort me out once we got to Vegas. Yeah. But he's smooth, he's quick. He's talking to me, whatever.

"Let's go for a drink. Let's go for a drink. We'll leave these two to catch up."

OK.

"Shall I leave this here?" Meaning my bag.

"It's up to you. It's up to you."

"I think I'll bring it with me."

We go for a walk.

"There's a bar just over here."

And we're crossing roads you're not even meant to be crossing, cos you can't walk anywhere in Vegas, and we're crossing roads, scrambling over hedges and wire, cos you just can't cross anywhere.

Eventually we get to this bar.

Go in.

Immediately this guy's hitting on every woman in sight. "Ah, let me have your number, baby."

I'm like, this guy's got a pregnant girlfriend, something's not right.

No, no, no. Another voice inside me. She's a waitress for God's sake in a bar; she can handle it.

He's a smooth-talker, though.

"Ah, c'mon," and he's sort of coming out with lines; white girls, black girls, he's hitting on anything that moves.

I'm buying the beers.

"You any good at pool?"

"No, I'm not particularly great at pool."

"Let's have a game of pool."

He thrashes me at pool.

There's a dartboard.

"Give you a game of darts."

234

"I ain't never played darts."

"That's fair enough, cos you thrashed me at pool."

I thrash him at darts.

We sit down at the bar. And at this bar there's even a fruit machine built into the counter. We're having a couple of goes at that. We're losing money. He's talking some more to the waitress.

"You worked here long, honey?"

He's chatting everyone up. I mean everyone.

"Do you like pussy?" To me.

"Yeah, you know. It's alright," sort of thing. And all the time I'm thinking, why are you doing this? You've got a girlfriend. And then it's like he's reading my thoughts.

"Oh man," more quietly now, "you know, me and my girlfriend, whooough, you know, you seen her. I'm not sure if I want this baby."

Fucking hell, why are you telling me this? You haven't had that many.

"You know, I don't know. Maybe I'll stick around. Maybe I won't."

I'm now thinking, this guy is dodgier than I thought. But at the same time I'm also thinking, well, he's not doing me any harm. But this is all getting a bit heavy, I'm not sure I want to hear this, and he's hitting on everything that moves. He's a bit of a player.

And I'm paying for everything.

But I'm not gonna lie to you. I'm only twenty-one at the time. And I don't know quite how to get myself out of this situation. I can't sort of say, look, I'll find my own place, thanks for everything, but I'm off. I don't know what he's gonna do. But this is when I shouldof realised something was suss.

"Man, I need to make some money."

"Really?"

"Yeah, I'm waiting for this paycheck to come through."

"Right."

"How much money you got on you?"

"Not that much."

"But you've got two hundred, right, to pay for this place to stay?"

"Yeah, I've got two hundred for a place to stay."

"Good, good."

Sips his drink.

"And you could get more if you needed more?"

I'm telling you this all in hindsight. At the time everything's happening and I'm just thinking this is just some weird line of questioning.

"Yeah, I've got more if I need to get it. I haven't got loads, but I've got more if I need to get it."

He leans in really close.

"If you give me a hundred dollars, I know some people where we can triple or quadruple that."

"Nah, nah, I'm not interested."

Closer.

"Look, man, I just make a few phone calls. Seriously. I buy some stuff; I sell some stuff. I can easily double it. You know, you take a share, I take a share."

"No, seriously, it's fine, it's fine."

"OK, I don't wanna push ya, don't wanna push ya," even though he is. "Only if ya wanna."

We leave the bar.

"I'll take you to a casino near where you're gonna stay, cos they won't have started their shift yet."

"OK."

We go in.

I'm now buying him fucking dinner.

We're sitting there. I'm hungry so I'm buying dinner. I'm trying to be friendly, I don't wanna be getting involved in anything, but I'm thinking, he's an all right guy, maybe he's got some strange habits, but many men hit on women, and I know people back home that probably buy and sell drugs, you know. I'm here, it's an experience, I'm not involved in anything; just take it for what it is. So I'm constantly trying to keep myself level, telling myself, don't get worried, don't get worried, just don't get involved in anything, but at the same time, keep it cool. You know, what a story to tell, sort of thing. And anyway, you know, it's not like I'm robbing the place with him. So we're sitting there having dinner. We have steak. I only ever ate steak in Vegas, cos it was cheap. And I've got quite a taste for steak.

Leans in closer again.

"I'm gonna go over the road. You can't come with me."

"How come?"

"Oh, you know, it'll be a bit complicated. But honestly I'll go over there and sort it out. Have you got that money?"

"Why can't I come with you? I'd rather come with you."

"Seriously. Honestly. It's best if I go and sort it out."

"Well, if you go and sort it out, I'll give you the money after."

"No, it won't work like that. Seriously. Honestly. It won't work like that. If you give me the money I'll go and sort it out."

"Well, how much is it gonna be?"

"Hang on a second."

And he disappears.

I see him go into this place over the road. Then he comes back out. I'm sitting at the bar drinking but I can see him out the window. He comes back.

"Right, it's all sorted. I need two hundred dollars."

"Why can't I come in?"

"Seriously, man. You know, I'm trying to do you a favour. Do you want this room or not?"

"Yeah, I do, I do. I'm sorry. OK." Cos, you know, where else am I gonna go now? I take two hundred dollars out and give it to him.

Off he goes.

I see him go in.

I'm sitting there. Drinking. Drinking.

Five minutes has passed. Drinking. Drinking.

Ten minutes has passed. You can see where this is going. Drinking. Drinking.

237

Fifteen minutes later. Fucker. What an absolute fucker. This fucker ain't coming back. This fucker ain't coming back.

He didn't.

That was my introduction to Vegas. A harsh learning curve. Cos as I said until that point everyone, and I mean everyone, had been nice to me. I'd taken risks, I'd stayed round people's houses, you know, and no one had screwed me over. Maybe I'd just been lucky. But if there was one place I shouldof put my guard back up, it was Vegas. It was an apt but needed, possibly, slap in the face. You know, even if you want to, you can't fucking trust everyone. Count yourself lucky you're not shot or dead or involved in some kind of drug deal. Or that it weren't a thousand dollars. A hundred quid's a lotta money, but…

I felt gutted, though, and I didn't tell anybody about it for ages. Even when I got back to the UK I didn't tell people about it, cos I knew they'd just say, you fucking idiot, know what I mean? It's embarrassing. Nobody likes being hustled. No one likes to be scammed. But that's what it was. The guy built up a certain rapport with me. He was a little bit intimidating at times. You know, maybe I shouldof said to him, no. But it is difficult. Things are in your mind, like why would he take me round his sister's house if he was gonna screw me over? Calm, stay calm. You know, take the guy at his word. But unfortunately some people will take advantage of that and go and fuck you over. Which is what he did.

So I'm a little bit pissed off. I have a few more drinks. I think, crap, that's two hundred dollars down the fucking drain and I still haven't got anywhere to stay. However, I'm glad I took my bag with me, cos I'd've never ever been able to find my way back to his sister's apartment.

I say to the barman I need a place to stay.

"Well, there's a place over the street."

I ain't gonna fucking stay over there. This casino is rough, full of old ladies all looking like they've been awake for forty-eight hours, stinky, sticky carpet; this is not a nice casino, yeah? We're way off the Strip now.

I go outside and flag down a cab.

"I wanna nice hotel. I wanna be on the Strip."

"Any in particular?"

"Can you just drop me off at the end and I'll walk down?"

"Climb in, buddy."

Cab driver drops me off.

I go in everywhere. We're talking one thousand two hundred dollars for three nights. Can't afford it. That's six or seven hundred quid. Never gonna touch it. Go into another one, we're talking nine hundred dollars, better, still can't afford it. Go into another one, no room, sorry. Next one, no room, sorry. Can't find anywhere.

I'm getting stressed now. I've lost two hundred dollars. It's getting late. I'm tired. You know, I wanna sort this out, but it looks like I'm never gonna find anywhere to stay. And hostels are not something that exist in Vegas. New York, Chicago, your big cities, yeah; but Vegas is not a hostel town. You don't go to Vegas if you haven't got any money, do you know what I mean? So I'm getting a bit panicked and I go into the next place, even though it's full up, and walk up to the lady at the reception.

"Miss, look, I'm really getting worried," and I think she could see I was getting stressed, "I know you can't fit me in, but where could you recommend?"

"The only thing I can think of is if you go off the Strip."

I'm like, I really don't wanna go anywhere that's dodgy.

"Well, there's the Hilton."

And I'm thinking, fucking hell, Hilton's gonna cost me a fortune!

"They're off the Strip. I'll give them a call."

That was nice of her. Calls up. Yeah, they've gotta room. Seven hundred and fifty dollars for three nights. It's a lotta money.

At this moment in time I've never spent anywhere near seven hundred and fifty dollars on my whole trip. I've either been sleeping on people's sofas, staying in hostels or twenty to thirty-dollar a night crummy sheet-stained places like the Chicago flophouse, not seven hundred and fifty dollars for three nights. But I'm like,

239

fuckit. I want somewhere to go to sleep. Somewhere reasonably nice. Hilton's well renowned; I'll stay there.

Nice receptionist lady calls me a cab. I get in the cab and arrive at the Hilton.

This place is pimp. I later found out that the Hilton is a venue for all sorts of major conferences in Las Vegas; we're talking electronics conferences, gaming conferences, the sort of place where Microsoft hold their big releases, you know, 'at the Hilton, Las Vegas!' It is a really nice place. And they've actually got a permanently stationed exhibit of *Star Trek Deep Space Nine* built within the ground floor, so you can eat within the cantina of Deep Space Nine. It's gimmicky, it's like whatever, but that's Vegas. The Hilton's off the Strip and the room I had was the nicest room I've stayed in ever. Basically what they'd done is, they couldn't fill all the rooms, so they'd given me a deal for seven hundred and fifty dollars for three nights, and I had two double beds. They just needed someone in the room, you know, better than having no one in there. So one night I slept in one bed and the next night I slept in the other bed, and that bed got made the night I slept in this one, and then I went back into that one. That was quite cool.

I have a wash, go downstairs and get something to eat.

I'm a bit pissed off that I'm not on the Strip and can't just walk there. But I have something to eat in a diner thing which is reasonably cheap, and that makes me feel a bit better, cos everything in Vegas is expensive. Go back, watch some crappy TV and fall asleep.

Chapter Eighteen

Windows 98 Pre-Installed

What's happened to happy?

"An Italian goes to a restaurant. It's an Italian restaurant. The waiter comes to the table, trips and spills the spaghetti he is carrying all over the Italian. The Italian starts shouting, *imbecille!* Same restaurant. An Englishman at the table. Same thing happens. The Englishman says, if you've got a towel and a mop we can clear this mess up. You see the difference? The Italian is emotion-focused coping and the Englishman is problem-solving-focused coping."

"Which one's better?"

"They need to be in balance. If we have a trauma, as you have, we become more emotion-focused coping than problem-solving-focused coping. With treatment the balance can be restored. You're ignoring your emotions because you're problem-solving everything. You mustn't be like the Italian; but you mustn't be like the Englishman either, because the Brit will solve all the problems, but there'll be no reactions. And it's human to have a reaction. What you need to try to do is marry the fact and the feelings. The way your mind has coped, quite rightly, is to split off the fact, problem-solving, from the feeling. It's kind of gone down a 'why?' road. And the reason you've split them off is that to have them together is too frightening. Right?"

"OK."

"It's important to have feelings, real feelings, and I mean good feelings, positive, bad feelings, negative; but what you've had is them all mixed up together in one lump. You've had anger. Or irritability. Or suddenly feelings that you need to do something really quickly and explode, that kind of stuff."

NOD.

"What's happened to happy? Feeling happy? Have you felt happy in the last five years?"

"I can't even remember the last time I felt happy."

"What should happy be? What does it look like? What's happy?"

"I don't know. I don't even know how you get to it."

"Before Dad was injured, do you remember feeling happy?"

"Yeah."

"What made you happy?"

"Small things. Now, I can't do anything without thinking, am I wasting time?"

"Wasting time for what?"

"I don't know. Feel under pressure a lot. Me putting it on myself."

"That's the ultimate problem-solver, isn't it? Someone who needs to be occupied all the time."

"I'm trying to achieve something in my own mind. But I'm never happy with what I've done; therefore there's never a limit to how far I push it, and I never know where to stop, which in the end is often my downfall."

"We don't know how to relax, do we?"

"Never ever."

"We're over that curve on the graph and going down the breakdown zone."

"Everything. Ah. Just does my nut in."

TEARS.

"It's OK to have a good cry, you know. Don't feel ashamed about that."

"I do."

"Well, don't. Ninety-nine point nine per cent of people come and have a cry here. OK? So don't worry."

"Feel like an idiot."

"You're not an idiot. You have a lot of pent-up feelings that you have never expressed and it's really hard to express them."

SNIFFLE.

"Feel weak."

"It's not weak to cry. You're feeling feelings for the first time in ages. Before, you've been thinking about doing stuff and finding ways to distract your mind away from feelings."

"I don't like them."

"Feelings are really important because that's what makes us tick. We'd be all British if we didn't have feelings. There'd be no Italian in us; and what's funny and makes us laugh and what makes us human is to have some Italian in us. It's very important to have feelings and to get in touch with them. And it's also important not to intellectualise everything and not to problem-solve it."

TISSUES.

"There's nothing wrong with crying. It is a catharsis. A catharsis means that we let go and cry. It's actually therapeutic and will do you a lot of good."

GULP.

"Somewhere along the line I expected this to happen."

NOSEBLOW.

"Let's take a look at the three basic assumptions we're all born with. One, we believe we are invulnerable or Dad's invulnerable; two, we believe that the world has a meaning, things happen for a reason; three, we believe that we are positive. And that's all smashed to bits when there's a catastrophe and somehow our mind has to incorporate these three assumptions and work them out again. So it might be that people aren't invulnerable, and they should try and stay out of situations that might cause accidents; so I won't ski any more or bungee jump. Or the world has a meaning, and Dad's in such a state, so God wants us to pray; some people work it out like that."

243

"Is that a good thing? To give meaning to it?"

"I think it's a good thing."

"But aren't they fooling themselves?"

"Well, to a certain degree, but it is helpful. And you need to give it meaning even if just for yourself. Perception of oneself as positive; if somebody hurts me, I think, that wasn't my fault, or my dad, it wasn't his fault. What's happened? I must be second-rate. And you need to work out how to deal with that one, because it's big time negative. Special parts of the brain are affected by trauma, especially the emotional centres, the limbic system."

"OK."

"So we're programmed with these three basic assumptions; this is how we come out of the computer shop when we're born. It's the default setting for everybody."

"But I feel I've been suckered."

"What does a seventy-year-old man think about life?"

"I know what my granddad thinks. And he's seventy. He just accepts day to day and he knows he's gonna die so he tries to enjoy himself as much as he can. He's not an idiot, though. He doesn't put himself into any danger; but at the same time he understands he's got to go outside and do things, take risks. But lately he's been depressed cos he's got arthritis. So he can't feel invulnerable."

"And that's how you're supposed to feel at seventy. You feel vulnerable, the meaning of life has been explained to you."

"But then my other granddad, he was bitter to the end. When he died he hated everybody."

"Maybe it's genetic then. No, I'm only joking. But when you're old, you've sussed the three basic assumptions, however you decide to live."

"But you're too old to do anything. That's pants! I should have what they're thinking now while I can still get up and do stuff."

"But you're learning what you're thinking now only because you've prematurely been faced with the ultimate kind of tragedy."

"And I don't like it."

"It's not come at the right time for you. You're a teenager-cum-young adult and you should be feeling positive about life: life has meaning, I'm invulnerable and I want to go skiing. I don't care, don't want to worry about things."

"And that's how everybody else is."

"And that's why you can't communicate with them. So this part of you is accelerated in terms of maturity, age, call it what you like; you have insight that doesn't really belong to you. And it's one thing to stay stuck with this, and it's another thing to use this wisely."

MORE TEARS. THIRTY SECONDS OF.

"It's OK to be upset. It is a terrible burden to have. You've been let into this big secret in relation to what life can do; how unfair life can be. It's not age-correct. This isn't the kind of stuff you bring kids up on. Look at all the children in Palestine. Look at the ones in Israel. Look at what they've gone through and are having to put up with. This is really horrible stuff, and we're not designed for it. We're designed to think life is good. And when we can't, and we see life is full of bad things, we think, well, it must be my fault, or why is it me?, or woe is me, all these kinds of things."

BIG NOSEBLOW.

"The way you've had to handle it is in such a way that you can't move on. Problem-solving leaves the emotions behind. This trauma thing is something we're not really designed for. We're not designed to travel in cars. We're designed to walk in a nice garden and have nice people tell us nice things. That's all we're designed for. That's how we come out of the computer shop. And over the years these beliefs are eroded; and the older you are the more wise you are in relation to how eroded these beliefs are. The point is you need to think about these dual functions: problem-solving-focused coping and emotion-focused coping. They need to be in balance because, if they're not, someone who hasn't cried for years, hasn't been upset, and has a lot of funny behaviours that are jinxed, or else who works, works, works and can't feel anything: blank. And when we start to attack it, it's open floodgates. But that's fine. It's pent-up emotion that's been held on to for quite a long time."

245

"I feel angry."

"Do you know what you feel angry about?"

"The situation. The sheer fact that it could happen. Almost the fact that I was lied to. You know, the myth that life is meant to be all roses."

"The meaning of life?"

"I never had a meaning of life. But when you're a little kid you think good things happen to good people and bad things happen to bad."

"That's what we're born with. The software loaded into us in the computer shop: we are invulnerable, the world has meaning and we are positive. And when all this is shattered by a near-death experience either for ourselves or somebody we love, all those beliefs go out the window and have to be rejigged. And we have to come to terms with that."

"But these aren't really intelligent beliefs."

"They're not."

"Cos we're not invulnerable."

"We're not."

"And we're not actually sure if there is a meaning."

"But they come with us from the computer shop."

"Like Windows 98 pre-installed. And now we need the upgrade."

"We need a big upgrade. In fact we need to reset our computer and bear in mind that we're not invulnerable, the world is not positive, there is no longer meaning; these are things that men only realise after they've lived their lives."

"It's ironic that they only realise it when they're close to death."

"Well, maybe not close to death, but certainly middle age, maturity."

"I suppose that's why a lot of men go off on some weird journey in middle age, you know, like walking the Appalachian Trail."

"Let's say some women as well."

"But you never really hear about women having a mid-life crisis, do you? It's more of a man thing."

246

"It's more of a man thing, yes; we're more, kind of, stupid. We really believe we're strong and invulnerable, macho, gung-ho, let's go and have a drink with the boys and everything'll be fine."

"OK."

"Part of it's that. But even as kids all of us, men and women, have these three basic assumptions, this belief system, because that's what we start off with. And it's really hard now to reset our clock, especially if we've held onto these beliefs with a lot of rubbish going on around us. And you've had a lot of rubbish going on around you for years. You've functioned in the only way you've managed to, and held it together, and that's really been the only way you've managed to cope, using the rituals, bottling all the feelings, being a nice guy; and then suddenly I come along and take the lid off and say, hey, take a look now! And things come volcanoing out, which is fine. But what we don't want is for you to have an epileptic fit on the alcohol and the medication and for you to get into trouble. Alcohol will make you feel depressed and disinhibited, so you have trouble with the police or trouble with somebody, because it's the Wild West out there, so be careful."

ANOTHER BOX OF TISSUES.

"Let's try some basic psychology. A monkey is in a cage and he's got a puzzle. He presses a button and a banana comes out. Every time he presses the button the banana comes out. OK? So he's certain of the result."

"He knows that button gives him a banana."

"He knows if he wants four bananas a day he presses it four times. OK. Different monkey, different cage, different puzzle. This monkey presses a button and sometimes he gets good music and sometimes a banana comes out."

"So he gets good music or a banana?"

"That's it."

"Does he like this music?"

"He likes the music. But he likes the banana more."

"Right."

"How many times is he going to press that button?"

"Until he gets a banana."

"So it's more than four times."

"Probably."

"So what about the second monkey? How in control of his banana is he?"

"He's not really in control at all. Because he doesn't know for certain whether, you know... Is it like music-banana-music-banana-music-banana? Cos then he could work it out."

"No, it's random."

"Then he never knows whether he's gonna get a banana or music."

"What about the first one?"

"He's guaranteed."

"He can do everything. He can work, play, do anything until he feels like having a banana."

"He's sorted."

"Which monkey are you?"

"Well, I'm definitely not the first one, am I? So I must be the second one, cos I can't guarantee that what I want to happen's gonna happen when I press that button, can I?"

"No. But usually does anything disastrous happen when you push that button?"

"No."

"When you shower for ten minutes rather than thirty it's usually OK."

"Usually OK."

"When you eat a sandwich prepared by hands not wearing latex gloves, it's usually OK."

"Usually OK."

"When you, I don't know, take a risk with a girlfriend?"

"Usually OK."

"Why then are you obsessed by the time once when it's not been OK?"

"Cos that once was so bad, it changed my life forever. And I don't want that once to happen again."

"What could you have done at that time to prevent it happening?"

"Nothing."

"OK. Third monkey. Sometimes when he presses the button he gets a banana, but sometimes he gets an electric shock. He dares not press the button."

"Cos it hurts."

"But he wants the banana. He's starving. He's going to try. But you're not trying to press that button. You've been scared off. Sod this, I'm not pressing that, I'll go and sit in a corner and starve. But life is about pressing the button."

"OK."

"Your life globally has been taken over by this over-pessimistic, obsessional, careful, safety-conscious attitude."

"But part of me thinks, that's just the way I am. I'm just a pessimist."

"Do you want to be like that?"

"I don't particularly like it. But I don't wanna be no schmuck."

"If you don't take a chance you'll enjoy nothing. You'll be miserable."

"So it's better to push the button and get a disaster than not push it at all."

"It's better to push the button and get a disaster, because life is about pushing the button. Because if we didn't push the button, we'd just stay in the corner and do nothing. Which is what you've been doing."

"Living in a bubble."

"But the bubble's burst."

"Big time."

"What you need to come to terms with is that, unfortunately, your dad's accident, given today's society, and the way society has gone, with cars and drugs and that sort of thing, it's not kind of expected, but it's not out of the realm of what one would statistically expect to happen. So if I got on an airplane and it crashed, it would be one in a million. I'm unlucky; but it's a risk

249

and how could I protect myself against that? It depends on how optimistic you're allowing yourself to be."

"But is optimism just a trick?"

"You have to judge that. But this is an important point. I can't make you an optimist and I can't say be a pessimist; but you've acted the pessimist for the last x years, and they've been very unpleasant for you."

"But being an optimist all the time isn't really realistic is it?"

"No, but let's say when I take a holiday, I optimistically get on an airplane."

"Cos those odds are pretty good."

"Thinking nine hundred and ninety-nine point whatever times, it's not gonna happen to me. What you can't see is that the chances of something similar happening to any member of your family or yourself again, like what happened to your dad, are similar odds to my getting on an airplane. You can't see that because you've been the monkey that gets the surprise. But life is about pressing the button."

"OK, I get the drift."

"How are the rituals coming along?"

"Better. Handwashing on a scale of one to ten down to around five. So down by a half. But the rituals are still around seven or eight."

"Ritual includes handwashing in my book. Remind me of the others."

"Two steps then jig through doorways; checking front door locked three times; standing on edge of carpet; light switches; plugs; anything I see as a potential danger to me and the family as a whole, like gas, kettle."

"So you're like the Guardian Angel of the family?"

"Sort of. But I'd say I'm more selfish than that. It's more to do with me not wanting to die than looking after everybody else, but I suppose that is obviously like a worry of mine, in that I don't want any of the others to get hurt. And also I'm, like, obsessive about my little brother's safety. You know, he's always

250

saying, I don't wanna hold your hand, but I'm, like, you've got to hold my hand when we cross the road. And even though I could just drop him off at the bottom of the hill for school and he could just walk the last twenty yards, doesn't matter if I'm half an hour late for where I've gotta be, I get out and walk up the hill with him for that last twenty yards. I mean, he hates it, you know, don't do this in front of my friends. And it's true he is with friends; it's not like he's going on his own. And I used to walk up that hill on my own. But I can't handle it; I have to make sure he gets there."

"You could just stop and watch him go up the hill. Just let him go."

"Yeah, I suppose. But I don't know how I'd feel about that."

"I understand. This is hypervigilance. Why is it all about safety, do you think?"

"Cos I don't want another accident to happen. It's pretty basic."

"Right. That's the link with this post-traumatic stress disorder. That's the link with the accident."

"I don't want anything to happen that's bad."

"This is important. You have concluded that it's all about safety: so it's logical; it's not illogical. You were at first terrified out of your wits and you established these barriers to protect against the Russians that were about to infect us. So you're hypervigilant. This is part of the hyper-arousal symptoms of post-traumatic stress. So whereas someone on the outside would say, 'he's got obsessive compulsive disorder', I would say, I agree, but it's a manifestation of his hyper-arousal, hypervigilance, as part of his post-traumatic stress disorder, and we can understand where it comes from. Does that make you feel any better?"

"It makes sense."

"Are you a freak, then?"

"I wouldn't say I am a freak. I could be working as a bodyguard for the Queen and you wouldn't call me a freak then. You'd just say I was professional."

"So why have you taken the job of the bodyguard of the family?"

"Cos I don't wanna go through the pain and suffering of having another member of the family go downhill."

"Aren't we in this world to suffer pain and suffering and stuff like that?"

"I wouldn't have thought so."

"Well, you've concluded that."

"What I mean is, bad stuff, I've realised, does happen. It happens to good people; it happens to bad people. But I wanna limit the chances of this happening."

"But can you realistically limit it?"

"Obviously you can to a certain degree, otherwise people wouldn't be employed to do that would they, like be bodyguards?"

"To some degree. But it doesn't have to be your job. You need to do your job, which is being a civilian. How's your skin on your hands doing?"

"Getting better. In comparison to yours you can still see a definition between where I'm washing and not washing."

"Let's have a look. Blimey."

"But in comparison to what it was before it's a lot better."

"You know what you're like? You're like an institutionalised patient scrubbed by nurses. You've got powder at the ends of your fingers."

"Yeah, if I go like that my skin cracks."

"Dermatitis as well."

"But while they're still sore the bleeding's stopped. But you can see I wash them more than the average person."

"The way we think about dirt needs to kind of change a little. In fact you're more likely to damage yourself and allow an infection to come into your hands by repeated washing; cos you get dermatitis, the skin cracks and skin's the best barrier to reduce infection coming into the body. So challenge these thoughts a little. I'm not saying all the time, don't get obsessed by it. You know, as you walk up the hill with your brother, think to yourself, there's the last twenty yards, let's try, bye, Stevie. What'd he say?"

252

"What's happened to you? What's wrong today?"

"He's not stupid enough just to run across the road, is he? He's not thick. You trust him?"

"It's not that I don't trust him but you keep reading about, you know, 'Boy Kidnapped!', and that kind of thing."

"You can still watch him. I mean, we can diminish the problem. Cos I know, it is scary. I don't let my kids walk twenty yards without seeing them. But at least I don't have to hold their hand any more. You need to be a bit more logical. If you're on guard all the time, if you worry about all the things you can worry about, you will make yourself sick."

"So if we were to create the perfect state of mind for everyday living, what would it be?"

"A level of arousal and anxiety that allows us to perform. Enough arousal and stress to allow us to perform at a plateau; the more arousal and stress we have beyond that, the more likely we'll then break down and fall off the edge. So if we have ten things to worry about and we're falling off the edge, we need to reduce them to nine to stay on the plateau."

"But society doesn't allow us the freedom to choose."

"Then society has to change."

Chapter Nineteen

Vegas Part Two

A glimpse of Mag Mell

I get up late, cos I'm knackered. Need to build my spirits back up after losing all that money, so I think, nah, shit happens, couldof been worse, let's explore. I pass a massive gold statue of Elvis in the hotel lobby and that makes me laugh cos it reminds me of Keith. As my head doctor told me, the key to everything is switching thoughts. I'm starting to feel better already, getting excited again.

I walk around the streets, visit different sights. Vegas is the ultimate post-modern city. I mean, where else are you gonna find within a square mile the Statue of Liberty, the Arc de Triomphe, the Bridge of Sighs and the Great Pyramid of Giza? I went to all the typical stuff, like the big volcano that erupts on the hour every hour, and the hotel with the roller coaster on the roof. It was expensive, twelve dollars fifty for one go, but scary as hell. There's a bit that shoots out off the roof so you're looking down and you're well high; that was good.

If you stay on the Strip everyone's walking up and down, and as it's so hot they've got this cool jet thing that shoots up from the sidewalk and sprays you WHFFFHHH with this really fine mist of water. Hits your face, goes SCHNLKGHHH and instantly evaporates. I mean, it really is hot in Vegas. A dry heat. And you're not even sweating, cos as soon as you produce a bead of perspiration, it goes SSZZZZZ and instantly dries. And because it never fucking rains they've built escalators outside, I mean how lazy is this, so that when you need to walk over a bridge, an escalator takes you up and an escalator brings you down the other side, cutting down on the legwork.

Off the Strip nobody walks in Vegas. It's like car park city. I found myself in a concrete desert and nearly got run over four or five times. I was wandering from the beaten track and how I fell for this, I don't know, again a stupid move, this attractive woman, very attractive, comes up and says to me, "Have you got any change?"

She was like a typical hot woman, sexy but not a hooker or anything, early twenties probably, just a little older and taller than me, blondish shoulder-length hair, faded denim hot pants, red shirt tied at the navel with a silver brooch, reasonable-sized breasts; you know, she was fit, typical attractive American as you would imagine.

"I'm not sure." I take out my wallet and have a look.

It's dry and it's hot. No wind. Nothing. Street is deserted and shadowless; flat, white, parched and airtight like a de Chirico picture.

"Come in out of the wind."

You know, you don't think. You don't run the reality test.

"Oh, OK."

There's a doorway, like an alcove, in some building. She motions. I step in.

Another woman there. I'm like, uh? Same age, dark hair, wearing shades. Again attractive, fit. Only she's got a knife.

Everyone always says to me, how big was it? I don't care how fucking big it was; you know, you just don't wanna get stabbed with it. If it's an inch long you still don't wanna get stabbed with it. But people just say, oh, you wimp. OK, it might've been tiny; but if you get stabbed in the eye, it's still gonna hurt, you know? Ask that guy in *Eastern Promises.*

I don't take any of this in at first.

"How much change do you want?"

255

"All of it."

"All of it?"

Still not taking it in.

Then I see something in her expression and think, oh fuck I'm being mugged. I suppose it's because these two hot women just did not match the photofit of a mugger. If they'd been two rough, burly men, I'd've worked it out a lot sooner. I suppose that was part of their gimmick. Why it worked.

"There you go." I just give her the money. It wasn't a lot. Eighty dollars.

"Have you got any more?"

"No, I haven't."

They melt away into wherever they came from. As quick as it started it was over.

I'm now feeling crap again. And I'm beginning to hate Vegas. This ain't a very nice place and it's starting to do my head in, you know? This place is fake, phoney, all about money. Horrible people that'll tell you anything. Just lie upon lie upon lie, just to squeeze you out of money. You got money, they wannit. And they aren't even ashamed about it. They're open three hundred and sixty-five days of the year and proud of it. Vegas never sleeps. New York? They go to bed sometime. London, a lot earlier. Vegas is hardcore non-stop twenty-four-seven-fifty-two. You can go to a strip club on Christmas Day. They don't care. It's all about the money, all about the money.

It was harsh. The harshest place I've ever been. And yet I couldn't help finding something attractive about it as well. You feel like, this is on the edge. This is different. Anything goes. You can do anything. If you've got the money, you can buy it. Definitely. It was a city where everyone was living to the utmost; maybe not the residents, but you didn't see them. And that was one of the scariest things about Vegas; where are the normal people? There weren't any normal people. Only ones I saw in my five days were cab drivers, and they're not particularly normal. I wonder whether the women that mugged me were strippers, cos they were hot. Only in Vegas could you get mugged by two attractive women. Like a Quentin Tarantino film. It's crazy. Go. Just so you can see it. It's like nothing you've ever seen.

So getting ripped off and mugged didn't stop me becoming seriously addicted to Vegas, everything about it, the city. It was a harsh, cruel, exploitative, debauched, hot-as-hell infernal setup; but you could get anything at any time. Everything, all the time. I could get up two, three, four, five, any time of day, and have anything I wanted. I wanna beer, I can get one. I wanna burger, I can get one. I wanna steak, I can get one. I wanna watch TV, I can watch it. What I mean is, it didn't matter any more. You can do anything you want at any time. Where else can you go and think, you know, I fancy a lobster and it didn't matter, whatever it was, it was there, there it is. There's a mall where you can go buy a shirt at 3am. A lot of these places are built into the hotels and the hotels never shut. I don't know about the roller coaster, maybe that wasn't open twenty-four-seven; but it was open fucking late if it wasn't. But honestly I could go and buy a pair of shoes any time. It is scary, it is freaky, and it is totally disorientating.

And I knew before, but didn't believe it till I saw it, there are no windows in the casinos. And no clocks. Nothing. You can walk around a casino all day and you'll never find a wall clock. Cos they don't want you to know what time it is, and they don't want you to see what time it is outside. They want you to be disorientated. They want you to lose track. That's why it's so easy to get addicted to Vegas. Maybe it's just my personality, I don't know. But it's like an adult crazy playground really. One strip club had this thing called Legs and Eggs. That was their gimmick. You could go there and get your breakfast, eggs, you know, eggs and bacon, eggs on toast, and see strippers while you're eating. You gotta give it to them. If they want your money, they'll come up with something. Where else in the world can you go and have eggs and legs?

Unlike my dad and granddad, I'm not that great a gambler, to tell the truth, never had much of an interest in it, so I didn't spend much time in the casinos. Played blackjack once or twice, won my money back, that was about it. Didn't bother with the slots. However, there was something else. There is always something else in Vegas; something else to draw you in, like a siren's call, and lure you to the rocks.

Second night I go downstairs. I've got about five hundred dollars in my wallet. It's about eleven o'clock. I've had a few drinks. I'm on my own. My only options are: go and see a show, and it's gonna be something like Penn and Teller, OK they're quite good magicians, but it kind of felt weird going on my own; go to a nightclub, but again, I didn't wanna go to a classic nightclub on my own, and I didn't have any clothes, just one pair of jeans and a shirt. Couldn't get dressed up or anything. So I get in a cab.

"Where do you wanna go?"

"I dunno. Where do you recommend?"

"Titty bar?" That's the first thing he says.

"Yeah, alright." Instant. I didn't give it much thought.

"I've got these tickets. These'll get you in. Normally it'll cost you twenty dollars to get in. With these tickets it'll cost you ten dollars. I'll let you have them off of me for five." All very quick; that's the way they do it.

"Nah, I dunno."

"I'm saving you money, buddy. I'm saving you money."

"Nnnooo, I don't think so."

"Which one do you wanna go to?"

"I don't know. Which is a good one?"

He knew them all.

"I take you."

"I wanna go to a good one. Wanna go to a nice one."

He laughs at 'nice'.

"You know what I mean."

Laughs again. "You want good-looking broads."

"Yeah. OK."

"This place has got the nicest bitches."

We get to this place and I pay him. Next thing I know I've got these tickets. He's just whacked them into the price of my cab fare.

258

"I'm doing you a favour, buddy."

Drives off.

Later I discover you get these fucking tickets for free. It was a scam. Another fucking hustler. Everywhere I went in Vegas I got screwed over.

I'm now standing outside Club Paradise. Looks classy. In front of me is this massive behemoth, largest bouncer I've ever seen, with another man-mountain beside him, both in suits. I feel like a little boy lost in the woods. And I'm only in jeans and a black shirt plus a leather jacket from Slovenia I go everywhere in.

"C'n ah help ya." More of a statement than a question.

I'm thinking I'm gonna get kicked out and I haven't even got in yet. The guy's huge. I mean, I don't know where they get these people, but I'd be straining just to punch his shins.

"This way." The other man-mountain. I follow.

We come to a door and they ask for my ID. I show them my passport; and as soon as they see that crown on the cover, they don't even bother to look inside, you know, done. They don't care. Seems the Queen counts for something in Vegas. I give the lady at the door the ticket, which I now realise you get for fucking free, and as soon as I walk in, I'm like, I don't know where to look.

Boobs everywhere. And these women, some of them are stunning, like catwalk, fine-looking women. Others marginally less so, but still attractive, you know, not trashy. It's dark everywhere other than on the main stage, where there's this incredibly energetic acrobatic show being performed. In the seats people are having lap dances, businessmen, older men. Even fitter women are walking around in hot-pant things serving the drinks. They're not strippers, just barmaid women; but they are fantastic-looking.

Other than the strippers I'm the youngest person in the club and I feel out of my depth instantly. Everyone else is smartly dressed in suits or whatever. I don't know anyone, cos I'm on my own, so I go straight to the bar and order a drink. Twelve dollars fifty. First shock of the evening. It would normally cost me three or four. I'm thinking, fucking hell, this is gonna cost me a fortune. Stay cool,

Matt, stay cool, this is all an experience, this is something you'll wanna remember. So I have a few drinks. Then I think, I'll go and find myself a seat. I find myself a big armchair thing, slump down in it and try and hide a bit, cos I'm still trying to take it all in. Next thing I know this girl comes and sits on my lap.

"How're you doing?" She's American. Puts her arm round me.

I'm like uuuuhhhhh. She's wearing just a bra and knickers, but really nice material and design, you know, not some crappy white support bra or anything, nice stuff. She's not beautiful in the sense that you wanna make an oil painting of her, or craft her in a sculpture, but in terms of Hollywood beautiful, in terms of put her in a movie, or take pictures of her for a swimsuit catalogue or have her as a lingerie model, that was the standard she was. You know, you're not gonna be writing poetry about this girl, she's not unique; but she's good-looking, very, you know, that's why she's in here; that's why they get paid a lot of money. These are very attractive women. I mean, ridiculously attractive women. Americans, Italians, Eastern Europeans; the fittest women in the world of that type fly into Vegas.

So I'm sitting there and I'm totally out of my depth. I'm not drunk, so I haven't even got that to fall back on; I'm just tongue-tied, you know, can't think of anything to say to her. I mean, she's on my lap, this close, arm around my neck, boob pressing against me, and I'm twenty-one and kind of like, holy shit, I'm nervous and really don't know what to do; I don't normally have attractive semi-naked women sitting on my lap, know what I mean?

"You OK?" She's totally at ease with the situation, as she would be, cos she's done this about a million times before.

"Yeah, I'm OK."

"Where you from?"

That starts off a conversation, and I start to relax a bit.

I'm sitting there talking to her. I'm nervous as hell and I think she can tell.

"Do you want a dance?"

I don't even know what that is at this moment in time.

"No, I'm OK."

She doesn't get angry or anything, just says my name's, you know, something typical, like Candy, or something fake, can't remember, and if I see her around later, just give her a nod and she'll come over and show me a good time. I'm like, OK, I mean, I don't know what the hell all this is about. Sit there. Have a few more drinks. Even hotter waitress comes over.

"Can I get you a drink?"

As I said, one of the weird things is that the waitresses are even hotter than the strippers. Maybe that's why they can be waitresses, because they don't have to resort to being strippers, I don't know.

"Can I have a Jack Daniels and Coke, please?" I was going through a Jack Daniels and Coke phase at this point, cos it didn't bloat me out as much as beer. She brings me over the drink. I take it. Tip her. You're always tipping, always tipping. You need to have money, right?

So I'm now sitting there and drinking away and getting more and more wasted, just taking it in, cos this is like nothing I've ever seen. I'm truly blown away. I mean, this was not your stereotypical, sawdust on the floor, pass the pint glass around and put a pound in the jar strip joint. I realise that there is a certain level of sleaze that's always gonna run through these places; but this is as high-class as a strip club is ever gonna get. The collective wealth of the people in here is probably some minor African country's GNP. I'm seeing people that look minted; wads of cash are coming out. I don't know how these people are making their money, but I'm definitely out of my depth. Everyone's polite, the glasses are nice, you know, we're not talking pptttt there ya go, boy. The stage show has guys in leotards with six-packs flipping each other, stacking up into a pyramid, with all these fit semi-clad women dancing around them. It was a spectacle, cheesy as it is. I'm like, whooa! I have a few more drinks.

Another girl comes over.

"Do you want a dance?"

I think, well, may as well, not understanding how much that is gonna cost me or what that even involves. She tells me she'll just

261

wait for the next song. There's constant music in the background, pop, upbeat stuff that women can gyrate to. She sits down on my lap and starts talking to me, telling me she likes my leather jacket.

"Thanks."

"Where you from?"

I tell her. She's like, oh right, I've got friends over there; you know, nice enough. Next song starts and she gets up and starts dancing in front of me. The chairs are built purposely for this. She gyrates a few inches in front of me, the fittest woman I've ever seen, and slowly starts to get undressed. I'm kind of a bit uncomfortable and don't really know what to do. She's slowly undressing. I mean, slowly, very slowly. Standing up dancing and undressing, there in front of you. This woman's a professional. Your average woman isn't gonna know how to do this. I look across and see other people having the same thing, other people just talking, over there the stage show is going on. It's all going on. You're in the zone now. This woman is here. These women have blocked you in. I'm there and trying to take all this in. I mean, it's like art to a certain degree. I don't know what you'd call it. This woman knows what she's doing. You're slightly intoxicated, the music's pumping, your adrenalin's pumping, cos you've never seen this before, and she does it slowly, she doesn't just go whhssh, whhssh, you know, very slowly, and you're not allowed to touch, you know, cos you know you're gonna get your arms broken if you touch them, but she'll like rub past you, you know, these women know exactly what they're doing.

So I'm sitting there and all this is going on. I know of the bouncers, know they're in the vicinity, saw them when they came in, and there are other man-mountains around, people that would probably take you outside and shoot you, but they're dressed in the best Armani suits, you know, they'll kill ya, but they dress well, so I know that I'm not allowed to touch and there will be consequences if I even think of trying it. But I've got my drink anyway, and that gives me enough tactile stimulation. But then she takes my drink and puts it on the side and the next thing

I know she's turned round and leant over and her butt is right there inches away. I can't touch, but she starts rubbing. She's still in knickers but topless and starts moving her butt around, gently rubbing it in my crotch. Lap dancing. And that's why they wait for the new song to start, cos that's how they know how long to give you. Some songs last two or three minutes, some only one minute twenty, depends how lucky you are.

My cousin Gary has been to many strip clubs, and he says he has never been to anywhere like Vegas. London, Paris, Prague, you name it; there's always a barrier, always a distance. But not in Vegas. In Vegas they rub big time. You get a lotta friction. You're not allowed to touch them, but they rub in. Which is what she's doing a lot of now. She then turns round and slowly takes her knickers off. All this is going on. She's now completely naked. Her breasts are in my face. I feel her nipple brush past me. It's crazy. I've never seen anything like it. Never felt anything like it. Then it ends.

She gets re-dressed; but, again, with incredible grace. There's beauty and art in how she gets re-dressed. You've gotta give credit where credit's due. Don't get me wrong, these are hustlers, these women know what they're doing, they're in it for the money, there's no love there, obviously. They're cold in that respect. But nonetheless there's a certain skill in what they're doing. She then sits down, all very pleasant and businesslike. Not like, where's my money or anything. Talks to me a bit more.

"Do you want to buy me a drink?"

Again, I'm not stupid; I know she's fucking hustling me. I know it's a con. I know the price of drinks round here. But nonetheless I quite like her. She's talkative. I'm slightly pissed. She orders a drink. Probably the most expensive in the bar. We talk. I haven't paid for this dance yet, but there seems to be no urgency for it. You can guess why. We have a drink, we're talking, she's asking me about England, where I'm staying, I tell her about my getting mugged, she says she's really sorry to hear that and asks if I want another dance.

263

"Not right now, but maybe again later." I'm getting a bit more confident now. And I've still no idea how much any of this is gonna cost. I'm slightly drunk, I've bought her a drink, and I don't wanna get my arms broken, so I'd rather upset her but be able to pay her, than not be able to pay her and get taken outside and shot in the head.

"OK, that'll be twenty dollars."

I give her twenty dollars. I only ever gave strippers what they asked for. My cousin Gary told me I'm lucky I didn't get killed. When he went to Vegas on my recommendation, he tipped every single time. They mustof all loved him and hated me, cos I only ever gave them what they asked for. But they never ever seemed pissed off or upset.

"OK, thank you very much."

Off she goes.

That was my introduction. My seduction. My ensnarement. To a vice I didn't even know I had. And it was instantly like a drug. Like heroin. In that two minutes thirty or whatever I didn't worry about home, didn't worry about money, didn't worry about what I'm gonna do with my life, didn't worry about OCD, didn't worry about S., didn't worry about anything. With that woman everything vanished. You've got alcohol running through your body, you feel relaxed, you feel like money can buy you anything; OK, I know a lot of this is flawed, obviously, as I found out three days later, when I felt a certain emptiness, a certain this isn't reality, I need to get the fuck out of here. But for those nights I lived in a different world. And I know you might say, but you couldn't touch this woman, surely that cannot have been enjoyable. But it's not about that. I didn't wanna have sex with her. And not only that, I wouldof been too worried about diseases to have done that anyway. But this woman gave me a certain peace in that moment. There was no catch. I knew what I was getting. There was a certain attractiveness about that situation.

Obviously I knew it couldn't be sustained and eventually I had to get out of Vegas cos it was doing my head in, I was spending way too much money and I needed to get back to reality and normal life. But for those few evenings it was different. I felt like just for a moment time had ceased and I had passed through a portal into an otherworld, like the Mag Mell of the Celts, a parallel universe Mona's dad once told me about, grazing alongside ours, and which you might slip into by accident, or when spellbound, through some glitch in the fabric of time and space, and where a second lasts a thousand years; a fairyland without mourning, grief or pain, only eternal youth, an enchanted world too beautiful for the mortal eye to take in and the poet to capture, flowing away through the gaps and holes of words like water through a net. The only world, my head doctor would say, designed for our living.

I never got back to how good that first night felt. I was always chasing it after that. Just like a drug. I chased that feeling for the next two nights and never ever found it. Don't get me wrong, they were good, but that first encounter, like anything, was special.

Chapter Twenty

The Angel of Freetown

*The most striking features displayed by the
more disagreeable sections of the English lower
class include a lack of personal ambition,
indifference to the demands of community and
nation, and interests that stop with sport and
frivolity, the sensations of city life. In some cases
one is dealing here with the residue of an urban
social group that has already been making
its presence felt for over a hundred years and
whose numbers already make up an alarming
proportion of the population as a whole.*
(Military High Command, Berlin, *German Invasion Plans
for the British Isles 1940*)

*…the haddalada-babra of babbling world
tongues coming in thru my window at
midnight no matter where I live or what I'm
doing … the sounds of people yakking and of
myself yakking among, ending finally in great
intuitions of the sounds of tongues throughout
the entire universe in all directions in and out
forever … God in his Infinity wouldn't have
had a world otherwise — Amen*
(Jack Kerouac on 'Old Angel Midnight')

266

Saturday night in Freetown and all is well unwell. Club Purple near the barracks looking like Bosnia-Herzegovina, dingily lit, no streetlighting, cold post-nuclear orange glowing Eastern European air of dreary dickensworld and always, always wet. Not the prairie of the Wild West, more Sniper Alley, Sarajevo; you know, keep moving, get outta sight, outta sight, outta the line of fire, neverknowing when something's gonna kick off. Now broken off from the pack you've gotta get home to safety through jungleland streets prowled by nutters; a little lost cub and the coyotes and hyenas are out and ready to pounce. They're drunk or frustrated, maybe someone's had an argument with their girlfriend, maybe they didn't pull and they're angry that someone else gets; loads of different reasons. But it's always over something stupid.

"Wha' the fu' are yu lookin' a'?"

"Nothing."

"Well, don't fu'in' look at me like tha', yu cun'."

"Huh?"

"Leo Sayer, motherfucker."

When my hair's longer it gets a bit wild and curly, so this guy, strangely not old enough to remember, is comparing me with some 1970s pop singer. I mean, I had to google him when I got home, cos I've got no idea what Leo Sayer looks like. 'Course I don't look anything like him; Leo Sayer's got a perm which I've never had. But you know.

It's always a nightmare wildside walk. The squaddies are coming home in one direction and you're trying to get home in the other, so it's keep your head down, just get out of there. Fast extraction. Go, go, go. You're not gonna engage; you've not got the manpower. Whenever I was with Joe we'd be outnumbered ten to two, so it's quick extraction to some checkpoint, like a wall you need to get beyond, out of their line of sight. But Joe, who's a mouthy fucker and wants to talk to everyone, especially when he's drunk, would always stop at border control to have some kind of Freetown banter while I'm just like keep on moving, keep on moving, you know, this is my assessment of the situation, cos I know if I engage I'm gonna get punched in the head, and sure enough next thing I know Joe's down and I've now got to go back and pull out the walking wounded.

I'd never seen a prostitute until I started drinking in Freetown with Joe, and they're, like, everywhere, every corner, especially around the station, loitering and there-standing, aged anywhere between twelve and seventy, and skanky. I don't mean to be horrible, cos I don't think they picked their profession, probably heroin addiction or whatever, cos these aren't willing prostitutes; but they're definitely not what you'd call beauties. They wouldn't arouse me or you, you know; we're talking white stilettos, white miniskirts, latex tights, all hanging out. Not subtle at all.

Down the road sodium lamps and neon signs light up burger vans and kebab houses, soaking brick and cobbled pee-smelling streets and miry puddles, gaudy reflections cast on everything, distorted shards of Caligaritown, non-stop open-all-hours corner newsagents where crisps and cigarettes cross counters to Bangla music and barfing outside, bringing wonderment to Asian eyes and ears, massive queues and fights kicking off over pushers in, laughing and joking, not hohoho but ravensquawking, overly drunk, short-skirted women being way too loud, arguments between men and women, women and men, boyfriends and girlfriends, *soi-disants*, disputing with each other.

"Ah, u cun' I can' beeleeve u go' off wiv 'er righ' in fron' ov me. I can' beleeve u'd do tha', u basturd."

"Oh fu' off."

Demoiselle departs.

"Oh, cummm baaack! Cummm baaack!"

This is all happening.

Grinning faces and hamster cheeks puffed with pitta and doner kebab and salad and big pickled pepper chilli things, horrible, Joe loves a kebab, but I've never liked them; dead and defunct roads cos everyone's drunk, so huge two-hour queues for taxis, massive, just standing there, mostly one person per cab.

"You're takin' the fuckin' piss!"

268

"Loo' at theeze sad fu'in' pricks. They couldn' pull so they're takin' up a taxi one ta themselves!"

OMG.

Bill Hicks once said that he goes to a nightclub once a year to stock up on all the hatred that he needs, and then he's fine. His hatred battery of dance clubs, as he calls them, nightclubs to us, would slowly wear down over the whole year, and he'd get to the three hundred and sixty-fourth day and think, maybe it won't be so bad, maybe I was mistaken, and he'd go and have one night of hell, replenish the rage, like AARRGGHHHH, never go again, and then halfway through the year, it weren't really that bad, but it was bad; and then, come that three hundred and sixty-fourth day, he's changed his mind, maybe I was mistaken, maybe it would be alright.

Gary's the total opposite to Bill Hicks. Gary's a good drunk in the respect that he can get pissed, not kick off, not have a fight, not get overly emotional, go home, eat a kebab, sleep, goodnight. As he's said to me many times, he enjoys getting drunk. He likes it. To him it's an enjoyable thing. And why not? Cos other than the hangover, there's no downside for Gary, cos he can do it without any emotional turmoil or epic kick off. Of course some people (yours truly) aren't so great. But Gary can go and get drunk on a Friday or a Saturday, come home drunk, not a bad night, go to sleep, wake up, oh, got a bit of a hangover, par for the course, watch some Formula One, have some dinner, ready for work Monday. It's what he does. And he likes it. You know, 'I go out cos I wanna meet girls,' fair enough. Me and you could talk all day about why this is not the ideal way to meet girls, i.e. in an inebriated state; but nonetheless where else is he gonna meet women? And, as I say, he enjoys it. That is his weekend. Going down the pub at three in the afternoon, starting off in one pub where there's a barmaid he likes, chatting with her, having a few pints, which he'll be drinking slowly, like a casual, gentle drinker; totally different rulebook to that of me and Joe, who are military style in and out, so we don't go out till eleven. And we have to have preparation. But Gary's style's also different cos he's got a good job, whereas me and Joe never have any money, so we need to go to Asda's and buy that cheap bottle of vodka to get fucked up on before we go out; and the whole point of our going out is to get fucked up. Whereas Gary's more about the whole experience thing, perving, as he calls it, on girls, you know, Joe just wants to get in there, but Gary's quite happy to stand back, sip beers, watch pretty girls go by, meet friends and chat.

But Gary hates the nightclubs, cos he'll always end up at places like Pineapple Paradise which is chav heaven; shit music, shit women, shit booze. Gary's never gonna go down the chav route; but he's not gonna go and get a crapload of piercings either. He's always in the middle. So when he goes to Pineapple Paradise he's amongst women who are not the sort of women that are gonna watch Michael Haneke films, you know, not gonna wanna read books or listen to his kind of music; they wanna go and see the latest *Step Up* movie, which he tells them is shit, so even though he dresses OK they now think he's weird. But while the goths and indies can respect someone who watches *Benny's Video*, they can also see that Gary hasn't got a cool haircut; so he loses both ways, which is why he hates nightclubs impressively and calls them cattle markets.

Obviously there are nice and attractive women in Freetown; but the ones that have got boyfriends and the ones that are nice, they've gone home already, or their boyfriends are driving them home or leading them away. The ones that are outside a kebab shop going, 'Eeyrr ya fu'in' basturd,' you know; just watch Sky Three or any of those *UK After Ten* sort of documentary style life-on-the-street things, that's Freetown, these kinds of women.

And these kinds of guys. Chino-dressed with ironed shirts, usually chequered for some reason, you know, smart, I'd never go out like that, not my style, but aggressive, dragging the girls about, or shouting oioioi across at them.

"Aoowrr yu fu'in' wish!" Wafts the reply. "Een yoar dreems!"

And then there's fighting, of course. Stupid stuff.

"U fuckin' lookin' at my woman?"

"I never looked at your woman."

"Why no'? Djoo no' think shez pri'ee?"

You can't win. They're looking for a fight. Say something clever, you're gonna get punched in the head. Say something dumb, you're gonna get punched in the head. Say nothing at all, probably gonna get punched in the head. Like the Leo Sayer thing. You don't ask for it; it just turns up. So, you know, you may as well just say, she's a skank. PPPSSHHH!!

Inside their heads, they just wanna forget the week. They've taken shit for the last five days and they wanna let off a bit of steam, heave a sigh of relief, you know, swear, do things they're not allowed to during the working week, so there's a lot of puke and urine around, and you're always stepping with care cos the pavement slopes down into the drains in the middle of the high street and a criss-cross pattern of pee-trails links shop to shop, nooks, alcoves, side streets, anywhere you can tuck in, cos the queues in the pubs are so bad people just go against the walls outside and then come back in; they're not doing it right now, but you could do a time study on a trail, you know, like animal tracking or forensics, and work out that for that to have got from there to here, they must have done this five minutes ago.

And the pairs of police in high-vis vests, his and hers, she with tied-back hair, regulation coiffure, not stopping anything, or arresting anyone for, like, peeing in the street, cos there are too many, it's de facto everywhere, so just keep an eye on things. People talking and chatting, sitting on benches and eating kebabs, throwing chips at each other. It's a mess. Snapshot of twenty-four-hour binge drinking Britain: vomit, pee trails, kebab contents thrown all over the ground, chip wrappers catching the wind like tumbleweed, denizens staggering home in the gloaming. And then the street cleaners come out at four thirty in the morning in HHNNNNN HHNNNN SSHHHHHH machines, slow-moving, busy like dung beetles ingesting mephitic, rotting, nocturnal excretions, scraping, sucking, churning, breaking down, assimilating, converting and recycling, against all odds, returning night to day. The modern urban ecosystem circle of life.

I'm painting a bleak picture. And it's definitely not nice; not tranquil. But it's not hell. The fact that you're quite drunk and you're with your friends makes it surprisingly tolerable, even OK. And although some people wanna start fights with you, sometimes you'll have the craziest talks with people you'd never normally ever talk to. It'd be like a bridge separating those in tight corduroy trousers and leather jackets on one side, and chavdom on the other, and somehow you'd find yourself talking during some lull in the crossfire. I mean, you're not gonna be friends or ever talk to these people again; but for a small moment in time differences are put aside. You could walk two paces further down the road and some other chav'll punch you in the head; but for some bizarre reason here and now we're talking, maybe not that eloquently or intelligently, and without anything in common except this Saturday night, and perhaps all we've got to say to each other is, you know, cool jacket. But that in itself is slightly redeeming. So maybe it's more like Purgatory, cos there's still a sense of community, the camaraderie of the downbeat, the huddled togetherness of the damned, the unfit and the outcast, where everyone still has a somewhere in their heads where one day they can get it together beyond all this.

Saturday night's for superficial people having superficial pleasure in superficial places, doing what they wanna do, rather than what they're supposed to do, feeling slightly liberated; but it takes an English person to get wasted before they can feel unrepressed. It's not pretty; but it's honest. Maybe it's animalistic at times, you know, not an attractive thing. But the English are a nation of extremes, you can't edge them in gently; it's all or fucking nothing, you know, it's you can't do that, don't do that, don't show that level of emotion, uncool to do this, don't show any kind of real creativity, whatever; then you give them a little bit of a leash and they go mad. But I wouldn't say they're always aggressive; normally just loud. Like my Italian co-runner at the Beeb once said: English girls get drunk; but they would talk to him where Italian girls wouldn't.

But once they're off the leash, it's all about oblivion and adventure, you know, what's gonna happen?, what's gonna happen?, is this gonna be the best night ever?, is this gonna be the shittest night ever?, are we gonna see something crazy?, is there gonna be a good band on?, are we gonna meet women? That whole thing. And you get more and more excitable, you're talking to people, they're getting excited, on a good night the whole place is like you feel you're really alive now, cos everyday life is boring and dull, you know, get up, go to work, come home, have your dinner, go to bed, get up, bam, bam; and if you don't you're not gonna survive. So come Friday night/Saturday it's *my* time; you know, I've got forty-eight hours, I wanna push it. I wanna live for fucking once. I've been told all week do this do that, I haven't been able to swear, I haven't been able to be myself, I've had to take shit from the man each and every hour of the day; now I've got forty-eight hours and I'm gonna make it worthwhile. I'm gonna sink into oblivion and forget about all the bullshit, forget about the fact that I may not have a job next week, forget about the cost of living, forget about the fact that I'm stressed. Just forget. You know, we work some of the longest hours in Europe, but there's no real job security, so everyone is mega-stressed, and it's the only way of unwinding and letting your hair down, and you've gotta do it quick: two days is not long, and you've gotta recover. So you live for Saturday night.

And I'm just the same. You know, I've been working fucking hard all week, on the lorry, watching CCTV, whatever; I need to be doing something. I may be knackered, but let's go out, cos I need to be out, I need to hear people talking, I need to be whatever. I've had to concentrate non-stop and now I just wanna be numbed out. And this was always my state of mind whenever I went out drinking with Joe in Freetown. But as I say, first there were preparations.

"You have to have a good base. Good base means anything can fall on it. And I mean anything." Joe is cooking up baked beans and layering them thickly with a spoon onto slices of toast like some leftfield wired Michelin Star chef. "Used to have a pint of milk as well, just to give it an extra lining; but drink on drink is very bad method. That's for schmucks. Now we need to kick in the special ingredient, where is it now?... Aha, we're in luck... aspirin ... four... NB not paracetamol."

"Why's that?"

"You can OD on paracetamol. And ibuprofen. But not aspirin."

"Right."

"Top it off with a swig of water... thus... and ready to serve. Learnt this technique from some Chatham pissheads, who've got it down to a science. Basically, the bread soaks everything up while the aspirin thins the blood, so the alcohol travels faster round your system. Net result, you get to double the quantity of alcohol you can intake."

"And the beans?"

"They sort you out in the morning."

We're outside Asda now. I'm wearing my other black leather jacket which I got from Camden Market for forty quid and I'm looking cool; this jacket's the best. You know when a jacket fits perfect, goes in at the right places, feels good when you've got it on? That's how this jacket was. Wasn't too big, wasn't too small, didn't weigh too much. It was like a fitted suit jacket, but leather. It was as if someone had made it for me. And because it wasn't brand new it had character. It had had lives before me. There was history in this jacket. You know, when I got it I found loads of sesame seeds in the pockets. No idea what for. There were bits that looked really worn in, bits that looked like they were on their way out, but like I say it fitted perfectly. I loved that jacket. And I miss that jacket, though it wouldn't fit me now cos I've got bigger, especially across the shoulders. You know, I had a skinnier frame then. Anyway, me and Joe take a tenner each from the cash machine, never more than a tenner, cos we don't have much money, and for Joe it's important to stick to the rules of the game. Asda got these rotating doors, and Joe always says the doors are the gateway, the portals, separating the workaday week from Saturday night, so once we're

274

through those doors we cross the threshold into our time and go straight up to the alcohol counter to check out the buy-one-get-one-free bargains, usually vodka, sometimes tequila, spend our twenty quid, if there's any change get some more aspirin or some Pro Plus, and then proceed to get wasted. I mean, I've seen Joe down a whole bottle of vodka neat in one gulp, YEAGHHH! Joe can do this and he's proud of it. But he would always say it's only cos of the preparation. Without that it'd probably kill you.

"I can feel my blood thinning. I can feel my blood thinning," he'd say and then down his bottle. "Mmm, beginning to feel it," and now Joe's pretty away.

I'm not even gonna try to keep up with him, cos no one can keep up with Joe, so I'm just sipping away, a stage behind and always a lot more serious, which invariably pisses Joe off.

"You're always in the wrong mindset before we go out. You've gotta psych yourself up! This is gonna be good, I'm gonna get a girl, I'm happy; it's fucking all good."

But I'd be like, "Fuck it, I hate the world. It's really bad. Nothing good's gonna happen. We're gonna get beat up. It's gonna cost us money. It's gonna be cold. It's gonna be raining."

"NO, it's gonna be GREAT, it's gonna be AMAZING," not hyper, you know, just mellow high. Joe was always like that. You could shoot him and he'd still be like that, cos even though Joe's a bit of a depressive, he'll always give himself an excuse to be happy when he's drunk. I mean, Saturday night is a big thing for Joe, you know, and that's why he goes home with some of the dogs he goes home with, cos he can't be going home with nobody, it's Saturday night and he's gotta go home with someone; even if it's this girl, Sharon, with the smelly crotch and bad teeth and bad hair, Joe will go home with this girl.

We're now at the Archangel bar. I've finished my bottle of vodka and am still savouring the throat burn. You can now see why Joe's method is what it is, cos ten pounds each at the Archangel bar would nowhere near get us as wasted as me and Joe are now wasted. Pass the bouncers, no-neck, wide as tall, indulge in the usual pointless banter.

"Sorry, fellas, lesbian night tonight."

"Ha ha."

One of them has a lollipop. It's a bouncer thing, you know, symbol of hardness to be standing at the door and sucking a lollipop, sort of daring you to comment; but no one's gonna be that stupid. Once we're inside there's a wide stairwell to the basement and it's like you're going down to the catacombs. It's dark, a few lights on and a smoke machine going. The floor's always sticky and you never wanna see it when the lights are fully on. At the bottom of the steps there's a dancefloor and further down tables and benches that look like they've come straight out of a church, and where strangers are getting off with each other sometimes so explicitly you have to turn away. There's a corner where the most wasted people sit, often passed out but still smoking. Directly in front is the bar and to the right some arcade machines where you can play racing games. A little further back is a small recess where everyone gets off. The dancefloor is packed with moshers leaping and slamming into each other to high-tempo aggressive music with bouncers occasionally jumping in and grabbing someone by the scruff of the neck when things go too far. If they really don't like you, they'll twist your arm behind your back, force it between your shoulder blades ignoring all agonised cries and march you out. I've also seen couples dancing where the girl's trousers are unbuttoned and the guy's hand is moving around inside her pants, and vice versa, right bang in the middle of the floor, with everyone dancing and puking around. When I went there with Gary one time I saw a guy get his thing out and piss on the dancefloor. He was very drunk.

WHOOSH me and Joe warp *Matrix* style straight to the bar. I order six Jack Daniels and a splash of Coke in a pint glass, cos I'm going through my Dennis Hopper phase, and Joe's instantly hitting on the barmaid. He's been trying to get off with this girl for ages but never got anywhere.

"Go on, try one."

"I don't like them."

"It's OK, they're not Es. Just purple sweets. But special. Try one."

"Why special?"

"The taste, you know."

"No, I don't know."

"They're… sweet. Like violets."

"Violets are blue flowers, not sweets."

"Not real violets. Just violet-scented. Like you used to have as a kid. Look, I can't explain. Just try one, will ya?"

The bargirl eventually relents and takes one from the packet, examining it closely before placing it carefully in her mouth.

"That wasn't so hard, was it? Bet no one else's ever offered you one of those before."

Bargirls sucks slowly and thoughtfully.

"Tastes like soap."

"I know, but it's unusual, wouldn't you say? Different? Memorable? 'Course, it's an aphrodisiac."

"Does nothing for me."

Then using just her lips and the edge of her tongue, the bargirl removes the sweet from her mouth, really sensuously, and drops it in her hand. There's a tiny gossamer filament of spittle trickle that trails down as the sweet passes from mouth to hand, but visually this looks good, and it does look sexy. It's spittle; but, you know, the spittle of a beautiful girl.

"And neither do you."

Joe holds out his hand and the bargirl empties the contents of her palm into his, but again really gracefully. Then Joe pops the thoroughly salivated sweet straight into his mouth and NNGCCK starts eating it, freaking both of us out, even though I know that Joe's an oral guy. I down my glass of JDs and Coke in one, savour the afterburn, less extreme than with the vodka, and suddenly realise I need to go to the toilet.

The toilets at the Archangel are mank and nasty. Someone's either just had a crap or the bowls are blocked cos of toilet roll, puke or shit. There are poo marks on the wall, I don't wanna know how, and graffiti everywhere. When you go in the first thing you've

277

got to decide is whether to use the urinal or one of the ramshackle booths, cos you ain't never ever gonna do a shit in the Archangel bar, unless you're very, very desperate. I mean, only a madman is gonna do that. Joe will go for a shit anywhere. He don't care. He'll go for a crap anywhere. 'If I've got to go, I'll go. I'm not gonna hold it. I don't care if I've got to hover,' cos Joe's got the hovering technique down and he knows how to strategically place three bits of toilet paper and cover the whole toilet seat, so if he ever does, like, do an accidental landing, his arse is protected. So your first decision is always whether you want to pee in private, cos sometimes there are guys in there that just seem to be standing, and you can't go if someone's standing like that. I don't know if they can't go or whatever, but it feels uncomfortable and you can't go for a piss in front of someone who's not going for a piss. So generally I go the booth route, depending on how drunk I am.

As soon as you walk into the toilets you can hear ZSSHHH, ZSSHHH and you can feel it under your feet; the piss is that high on the floor. Someone's generally blocked up the sinks and they're overflowing, or some guy's puked and it's blocked up the U-bend or whatever, and generally when you go into one of the booths there's some guy in the other one straining and going, UHHHHHMMMMMMMM! like that, or someone going BLLUURRRGGHH, BLLUURRRGGHH. But they're never in there on their own, you know; "That's alright, Pete, you get it all up, you get it all up."

"BLLUURRRRRRGGHHHH."

"Yep, yep, that's it, that's it."

And there's always a round of applause once he's finished. I mean, I've had a round of applause when I've puked in there, you know, you walk out and everyone's like, heeyyyy, recognising that you've been to that level.

So you go into a booth, but the door lock doesn't work. And this is an art in itself, especially when you're drunk, but I've got it down. You go in, shut the door. Toilet's there, right. Now, what happens is, and I've learnt this, if you're going for a piss, you know,

278

like this, the door will go BBSSHH and you'll go ARGHHHH! lose balance, piss goes everywhere and generally your hand lands somewhere you don't wannit to land. So what you need to do, for future reference, is get your leg locked so that your back foot is wedged against the door, so no one's gonna come through that door unless they really force it, and you've now got both hands free which is what you need. Only problem is you've got a long way to reach; it's OK at the beginning, cos you've got a lot of oomph and it goes straight into the bowl, after you've made whatever necessary adjustments to get the arc just right. However, the stream soon wanes and some of it, and then quite a lot of it, will go on the floor; but you just have to live with that. Then afterwards you get your little finger or, if you're not too wasted, your foot, cos you don't wanna be touching the locks, and push or hook and flick under the door so it swings open on its hinges and you're out. It's a true art form. And the next trick is to walk right behind someone so that when they open the main door to get out of the toilets you can WHOO HOO slip in behind them without touching anything, cos you don't ever want to wash your hands in the Archangel toilet, because you just get more dirty. I mean, those sinks are full of puke stains and horrible stuff that is absolutely non-biodegradable. However, when you are wasted you sometimes can't help touching something, like when I puked and put one hand on each of the walls. After everyone had gone heeyyy I went straight back to the bar and got another drink, cos you need to wash the taste out.

Apparently the girls' toilets are not much better. There's a bigger wall area on account of there being no urinals, so there's a lot more graffiti, usually scrawled death threats towards some member of their group, you know, 'Lucy will die, that caa,' written by Lucy's best friend, naturally. Anyway, one night out of this graffiti-walled underground lady's lair a very wasted but very pretty young girl emerges carrying a wand and waving it around, casting spells everywhere like Hermione in *Harry Potter*. She's wearing baggy grungy stuff, you know, jeans and hoodie, and I'd seen her earlier jumping around highly energetically on the dancefloor and recognised her from college. I remember thinking, hmmm, this girl's cool. You know how someone just makes an instant impression on you and you get a kick inside? When I first saw her at college I thought, that girl's pretty fit. Then I sort of went off her and thought, no she's not. You know, one of those. But now I'm seeing her much closer up and I'm thinking this girl's really fit and really cool. Petite with pale skin, dark hair and strikingly large brown eyes. Had a doll-like quality about her, but not fragile; you knew she could look after herself. Sort of Japanese skinny-girl look, and I've always liked Jap ever since my Anime days; and I guess I've also always been a little into, you know, heroin chic. Anyway, she walks right up to me, smiles, waves her wand over my head and then collapses in my arms. Her name is Sandy.

Joe's now completely disappeared. I discover later what happened. The barmaid thing has not done Joe's confidence any good; he's been knocked back and has totally failed to pull tonight. He's tried everything, every technique, every line, possible body movement, stance, standing in a corner, nothing is working; he's hit a brick wall and he's drowning and has been reduced to slobbering out drunken I-really-fancy-yous, and that's as bad as it can get. He's on the dancefloor, grabs a girl by the arm, but, you know, gently.

"Letz dance." He's spitting all over her, a very pissed version of himself, so she's having to wipe her brow. Turns out Joe's picked the wrong girl.

"She's with me." Polite.

"I'm only tryin'ta talk ta her."

"Leave her alone."

"She wanz ta talk ta me."

The girl's now like, "I don't care, I don't care," you know, she's just trying to stop her boyfriend going nuts.

"See?"

Guy goes, "Fuck off," and pushes Joe away. Instantly Joe goes NNNAAARRRGGH, leaps on the guy and bashes him up against one of the walls, holding him there, shouting, fuck off, fuck off, and the guy is like, OK, OK, and then the bouncers have gone WAPPPSSHHH and jumped in, BSSHH BSSHH GRAB, Joe's arms are now pinned behind his back, and this is all happening quick, no more than a couple of seconds, GET OFF! GET OFF! and the bouncers carry him up the stairs and throw him down on to the pavement outside.

"Now fuck off, you cunt. And don't come back."

But the weird thing is, after all this, that girl goes home with Joe.

Meanwhile, I've managed to carry Sandy outside so she can sober up and we're sitting on the pavement together. When I'm wasted I think even more intensely. I know it sounds crazy, but I'm constantly saying to myself, 'Don't make a mistake now, Matt, you're out of your head, so be even more vigilant than usual.' And this is why I'm always looking so intense when I'm wasted, although it comes across as pissed-off. Girls keep asking me, why are you looking so worried, why are you looking so worried?

"You don't wanna know."

"Oh, I do."

"You don't wanna know."

"I do."

So I told one once; she never talked to me again.

But it has its uses, cos I've now quickly snapped into problem-solving-focused coping mode, as my shrink would call it; specifically, how do I get this drunk and semi-conscious girl, who keeps telling me she isn't drunk, but who's unable to take a step without falling over, back to her home, which she's telling me, with intermittent coherence, is three and a half miles away, at one thirty in the morning, with Joe gone, her friends gone, everyone gone, and neither of us having any money. But in my now zeroed-in state, I come to a rapid assessment of the situation, pick her up and hoist her onto my back, cos she doesn't weigh a thing and, you know, I've been lifting furniture all week, and we piggyback off on a yomp across the narrow, wet and winding cobbled streets of a class A area of deprivation in the wee small hours of a Sunday morning.

According to Galileo everything weighs as light as a feather in a vacuum. But the streets of Freetown are no vacuum, and after about two miles this lissom, waiflike, kokeshi girl is weighing like a twenty-stone mama. I mean, this journey's killing; I'm sweating and breathing heavily, wheezing a bit, my heart's going boomboomboom, my mental faculties are intact, but the alcohol's obviously taking its toll on my physical performance to the extent that the whole operation is suddenly looking very shaky.

"I need the toilet."

Probably the first complete sentence she's said to me.

"Caantchewwaaaait?"

"Nooo!"

Even though I need a rest, this is definitely not the place to be taking it. Dodgy as hell. Broken bottle shards everywhere. But what else is there to do?, cos I'm not offering myself as a human chamber pot, so I head down this narrow alley into a dimly lit backstreet car park, let her off my back and prop her up against a ticket machine. Man, I wish I'd had my camera at the time, cos this was a classic picture that wouldof won the Turner Prize.

"OK?"

"Can't get my things down."

"What do you mean?"

"Can't get them down."

"Oh man."

"You've got to."

"What?"

"Pull them down."

"Jesus! This is gonna look so dodgy."

I'm now trying to take her trousers and knickers down while looking out for security CCTV, cos, you know, it looks like I'm doing something very bad.

"That OK?"

"OK."

"I'll leave you to the rest."

"Yeah, alright."

282

Come back a minute later. It's not nice. Sandy's slumped against the machine, legs partly spread, trousers and knickers wrapped round her ankles, knee-length stripy socks soaking wet with pee patches, head bowed forward and gently bobbing on her chest. There's piss going this way and that way. But it's the way the piss went in equal trails, you know, bifurcating in perfect symmetry, like in James Joyce's *Ulysses*, which wouldof had it hanging in the Tate Modern.

"Come on, you need to get up. Come on you need to get up."

I'm now getting piss all over me, but I eventually manage to pull everything up, sling her on my back and carry her home.

Get to her house. It's an old terraced house with the first floor about twelve feet underground, so there's this concrete crevice, where there's space for a small garden and a dustbin, and some tricky slanted steps, you know, perfectly designed health and safety hazard, which you have to successfully negotiate in order to get to the front door. We sway a little but manage to get there, she finds her key, we shuffle inside. I carry her into the lounge, put her on the sofa, trying to make the least noise possible, though she tells me it doesn't matter cos her mum takes heavy-duty sleeping pills which render her comatose, which sounds highly dangerous to me, cos what happens in an emergency?, but I'm not going there. Instead, cos I'm feeling a bit hungry now, I make sure she's comfortable on the sofa and then go into the kitchen and take a look in the fridge.

"I'm gonna be sick. I'm gonna be sick."

Grab the bowl from the kitchen and just manage to get it under her in time. She's now puking into this bowl, saying sorry, I'm really sorry, and I'm quite touched and say, that's alright, you get it all up, that kind of thing. I then say I'm gonna get something to eat, go back into the kitchen, find a Pot Noodle, make it, go back into the lounge, sit down and eat this Pot Noodle while she's puking into the bowl, cos I've now got to the stage where my stomach can handle it. I'm just eating and trying to stay awake to make sure she doesn't choke on her own vomit, watching her puke while I eat and, you know, feeling quite proud of myself for dealing with all this. Finish the Pot Noodle. Chicken and mushroom. Tops.

"Can you take me upstairs, please?"

"You gonna puke any more?"

"No."

"OK."

I take the bowl from her and put it down beside the sofa while I go to open the door. Mistake.

While my back is turned, she decides to try to get up and kicks the bowl. Puke goes flying everywhere. All over the walls. Everywhere. It's bad. Disgusting. And now I'm like, that's it. After all I've been through tonight, I just can't do any more. Can't be bothered with it. Take the bowl back to the kitchen, pull on the thickest pair of Marigolds I can find, give the walls and carpet the skimpiest of cleanovers and then carry her upstairs to her bedroom.

CHCHCHCHCHCH CHCHCHCHCH. What the fuck's that?

"Raymond."

At the end of her bed is this big wire cage. Inside a white rat is flying around on a rotating treadwheel.

"Raymond?"

"Carver. Working on his latest novel."

And I had to admit that the sound Raymond the Rat was making was just like someone banging on typewriter keys at express speed. And it was right then that I realised that me and Sandy were alike in lots of ways. Both poor, both creative, both been through stuff, both with a weird take on things, both bright with active imaginations but educational low-graders, both romantics; both vulnerable people.

"Please stay here with me tonight."

"OK."

"In the bed."

"OK."

"You'll have to be downstairs before Mum gets up, though. So it looks like you've spent the night on the sofa."

"OK."

"And you'll have to take these clothes off me."

"You sure?"

"It's OK."

So I help take Sandy's clothes off and, even though they are a bit, you know, soiled in places, fold them neatly on the chair and get her into a clean nightdress. She's now totally exhausted, and once we're both in bed she falls asleep instantly while I lie beside her with all my clothes on, including my leather jacket. It doesn't feel strange; in fact it feels the complete opposite. I mean, the whole night's been nuts and I'm tired and head-done. I know I need to make sure I time my exit before her mum wakes up, but that's doable, since I'm not gonna be getting any sleep anyway, what with Raymond's blockbuster and my own thoughts churning away.

And then a weird thing happens. I suddenly stop worrying. About everything. Everything. I don't even care about the puke on my jacket. Because the whole thing's just one fucking mess. I mean, so much has happened, so much has been thrown at me that there's no more I can possibly worry about. And I just know, as I lie there, next to this slightly odd, but very alluring, if a little tangy, girl, whom I have known for all of five hours, even as I lie there fully clothed on her duvet, I know I am happier than I've ever been in my whole life. And at that moment I fall asleep.

Next morning when it's time for me to get up, my cheek is stuck fast to hers, so when I move my head it's like peeling off a sticking plaster. SLLRRRRPP.

285

Chapter Twenty-One

In the Shape of a Heart

*The secret of happiness lies in maintaining
positive illusions in the face of negative
information.*
(Shelley Taylor et al., *Journal of Clinical and Social
Psychology 8*)

The New Girl drinks, swears, fucks, does drugs, sports tattoos, is gender-relative, in your face and scary. However, Sandy didn't swear, which was a bit of a problem for me, cos, as you know, swearing's an important part of my expressive vocabulary, and I had to tone it down when I was with her. A lot of my friends said she spoke quite posh; but anyone who makes an effort sounds posh in Freetown. I think it was cos she was well spoken and came across as intelligent, which she was. Read lots of books and was good at English, though she never got high grades. Had this low, husky voice as if she'd been smoking for years, even though she was a non-smoker, and was very shy until you got to know her. Bit like me, really. Shy until you get to know them, and as soon as you get to know them, can't fucking shut them up. I have improved slightly, but I just come across as bitter when I'm shy. Anyway. Sandy always walked like she was hiding, and she could do this amazing thing with her legs where she would fit her whole body into a chair. Never seen anybody be able to do that. We began spending time together without ever defining the exact nature of our relationship. She told me straight out that she didn't want a boyfriend.

"You don't wanna get mixed up with me, anyway."

But of course, in true *film noir* schmuck fashion, I did.

As I say, Sandy was quite like me in terms of personality; but I was amazed at how reserved she was in any public space she'd never been to before. I mean, I'd seen her jumping around in the Archangel, and once you got her talking she was all confidence, cos she liked talking. But when you took her to a new environment she was very reserved, more so than your average person, almost withdrawn. She told me she had to study at home before coming to college because her dad had left her. That sort of hit me. I mean, you're not expecting to hear this kind of thing in casual conversation. Not age-correct as my head doctor would say. So I'm thinking, this girl's different; not your average girl. She obviously had issues; but then I liked that, even though it did my head in. And she looked so young, so incredibly young.

Her daily wear was grunge, black T-shirt, hoodie and baggy jeans, not particularly feminine. But when she went out on a Friday or Saturday she definitely dressed to look attractive. My grandma gave us a couple of tickets once for the opera and Sandy wore a tartan, pleated miniskirt. She looked fantastic: micro kilt, tank top, dark eye make-up and red lipstick, not freaky red, just dark red, and knee-high pull-up stripey black and white socks. She looked good, no two ways about it. Different but still sexy. Right from the start I was attracted to her physically, as with whenever you meet anyone; but when I got to know her there was definitely a mysterious I-can't-fathom-this-girl-at-all quality to her which drew me in even more. But I also discovered that if you were in it to win it, you needed to be the sort of person who was like, neh, I ain't even thinking about it. That's how you survived. And unfortunately I fell into the other category, where you try to fathom everything she ever did, and you're on to a loser, you know, you're a dead man before you've even walked into the room. Because she was so complex. There was no rhyme or

287

reason to anything. I mean, obviously there was some reason; but if you tried to fathom every part of it you'd go mad. I think she enjoyed the fact that people didn't understand her. And she liked to shock. The most fucked-up, messed-up thing you could think of, she would say. I remember her once during some conversation about world hunger saying that if you got all the aborted foetuses and, like, fried them up you could probably feed half of the Third World. Yeah. Stuff like that she'd come out with.

Our biggest bone of contention was the Archangel. Sandy was always wanting to go there, whereas I hated it. For me it was just a place to get drunk till one thirty in the morning, but for Sandy it was a major part of her life. All her friends went down there. It was like a social meeting place for them to talk and gather, give meaning to their lives and share their misery. They'd sit in this corner, part of some exclusive moody club, whilst I, not wanting to be a member, would be at the bar getting wasted. As I say, I was going through my Dennis Hopper phase at this time, lining up as many shorts as I could afford and getting through them in less than twenty seconds. You know, I'd just be getting loaded and wasted and watching her getting off with guys, everybody, including really bad people, which was such a head fuck, cos I'd built myself up that this girl wanted me big time, and she did, from every way you looked at it; but I thought she wanted me big time in terms of something more than what she actually wanted me as. So I came to hate being there, but I had to go cos she wanted to go, and so I just got pissed up to handle it.

And it was in the Archangel, when she was wasted, that she would tell me about all the bad things that had happened in her life. It began on our first date. We were driving from hers in my car and she asked me about my family. I say I've got a brother, she says, oh right, I've only got my mum, oh right, and I'm thinking, fuck, this could be dangerous to handle, and I then say something probably totally inappropriate, and she says, yeah, my dad walked out. There was no beating around the bush. Obviously didn't want it to linger and didn't want me ever asking, you know, why isn't he

288

around? It was just, fuck it, I'll get it over with. I then said, oh, my dad was in an accident, and instantly there was this bizarre thing we had in common; both our dads were kind of absent. Somehow it worked for us and created this bond, even though it was hardly what you'd call normal. But then I don't think it ever will be with the women I meet. There will always be something odd; and if there isn't I'll probably get bored.

The best conversations I had with Sandy were about nothing of any serious nature, cos that suited both of us. What I mean is, the more ludicrous the nonsensical bullshit, the more comfortable we were with each other. Not chatting, cos chatting can be about your life, even if it's only superficial stuff. Our talk wasn't even that. I'd say something that would make her laugh, and she'd add to it, and in the end we'd have this sort of fantasy scene scenario where it was all made-up and nonsensical, like a children's game, or an improv comedy routine, and I kind of liked that, you know, hit 'em quick, get the first laugh, then keep 'em going, keep 'em going. It would be like at first she wouldn't wanna talk, then she'd laugh at what I'd just said and think, hang on a minute, and add an idea to the funny scene, and then I'd go bang and she'd laugh again, and then she'd forget why she didn't wanna talk to me, or everything that had gone before, and now we were in this whole other place. I can't remember any of the conversations because they were so meaningless, and I don't think any of the jokes were ever actually funny. They were built around circumstantial stuff, like I'd be in a phone box and the window might be smashed next to me, and I'd say, the window's fucking smashed next to me, and she'd be into this and go, how did that happen?, and we'd build on that, introducing characters, until the whole window-getting-smashed-thing would turn into a comic sketch of how we imagined a history of actions leading to this end result and the reactions of people around it. It sounds gay and stupid but at the time it worked; you know, it was fun, enjoyable and cool. It was the best time. Cos whenever our conversation got serious it became too heavy. But the darker stuff always came out when she got wasted at the Archangel.

I never knew the nitty-gritty, mainly because I never wanted to know. I had enough trouble at my age fathoming what it all meant anyway. But as far as I can tell her father left when she was four years old. A couple of years later her mother meets someone. They have a relationship for a few years and eventually he moves in. Mother thinks, as you would, that this man's just interested in her. And as the mother begins to trust him, he begins to spend more time at home alone with Sandy, who's now between twelve and thirteen. And this is when things began to take place. I don't know the details, but he would wait for Sandy's mum to go out and then take Sandy upstairs and stuff would occur. She would never tell me what and, like I say, I didn't really wanna know. But he would manipulate her as, apparently, a lot of these people do, you know, your mum would be very upset if you told her about any of this, using her naivety, and her not wanting to distress her mum, to his advantage.

Sandy began self-harming, cutting herself on the arms, during the latter years of this, just before her mum kicked him out. One of the weirdest scars she had was on her inner thigh. Mustof been deep cos it was permanent. Never explained why she did it. I tried to persuade her not to, naturally. Said I didn't understand why she was doing it. The only reason she gave me was that it's like when you get drunk, or something like that; it takes your mind off whatever. Like that joke: guy goes up to a soldier, soldier says my leg's been blown off, guy says hold out your hand and breaks the soldier's little finger. You know, you cause another level of pain to take your mind off the other pain. That was the best description she ever gave me. She cut her arm once when I was taking her out and when I tried to point out that this was really not a good thing to be doing she just said, well, it's my arm and it's over now. She could be very stubborn and would never listen to anything I had to say on this subject.

Sandy was major unstable. Mega. A loose cannon. Mood swings like crazy. One minute hyper, one minute major I wanna do everything, wanna have everything, wanna see everything; next minute I don't wanna get outta bed. Hyper manic-depressive. But she was different, exciting, interesting, intelligent, totally unlike other girls I'd ever seen. This was a girl who was into films, into music and had a sense of humour and an outlook on life different from any girl I'd ever met. Normal girls I'd met were, you know, let's go and see the latest romantic comedy. They didn't wanna watch *Taxi Driver* four times a week. I mean, at one point Sandy watched *Taxi Driver* every day she came home from school. That tells you something about her mental state. There were two opposing films that she absolutely loved: *Taxi Driver* and *The Rocky Horror Picture Show*. Every night she would watch one of those two movies obsessively. She loved *Taxi Driver*. Identified with Travis Bickle, which is unusual for a girl, and could see where he was coming from, which shouldof been a warning sign. With *Rocky Horror* she loved the outfits, the campness, the unreality, the sexual element, the whole hyper whatever make-believe of it all, and she said she would wanna be one of the characters in that castle. Knew all the words and all the dance moves. It's a weird film; don't know if you've ever seen it? Personally I've never really been into it, but it epitomised Sandy, you know, the vamp look with corsets and suspenders, which was kind of the way she saw herself and wanted to dress, and the outlook on relationships. She was moving into the goth look and eventually had a piercing on her lip which I thought looked cool, and it felt nice when I kissed her. And it suited her. You see it on some people and it doesn't; hers did.

You never knew where you were with Sandy and what she was gonna do. And she was hard work. If you cared about her you were in trouble, because you would want to keep her safe; but she didn't wanna be kept safe. She'd go off with people, you know. I don't think she ever really wanted a relationship. Yet I wasn't put off and we ended up going out loads. But I made the decision early on that as far as possible whenever I took her somewhere it had to be, like, a major thing. This was part of my strategy of weaning her off the Archangel. And also I wanted to do something more exciting than just the average day. So it was always London, Hastings, Brighton; those kinds of places.

The first time I took Sandy somewhere special, I decided I wanted to buy some tickets to an event without asking her whether she wanted to go, cos I wanted to be able to say, I've got these tickets, do you wanna come? That was how I wanted to play it. So I'm thinking hard about what music she likes and I end up buying a couple of tickets from three dodgy-looking guys at college for a Marilyn Manson concert in Docklands. I mean, the concert was sold out and the tickets cost me sixty-five quid each. I was told I would be getting them for forty and only had ninety quid in total on me at the time, but these guys wouldn't bargain and insisted on driving me out to a cash machine for the rest. They were scary but I had to go with them despite my paranoia cos I needed the tickets. I got seriously ripped off, but it had to be done. And you shouldof seen her face light up when I told her I had the tickets. Like an angel. I mean, generally there's a level of persuasion I have to undertake, but here it was just, I've got tickets, do you wanna come? It was the best. I was in.

"Come and meet my mum," says Sandy when I arrive like two hours early to pick her up. I'm thinking, I don't wanna meet your mum, not realising this is a key issue. However, avoiding the mum was never gonna be an option, and in fairness Sandy's mum was really nice, tall and slim and young-looking with green eyes and a warm smile.

"Hello, Matt. Would you like a cup of tea?"

My instinct is to say no, but I don't wanna be impolite.

"Nnnyeessss please."

Mum disappears into the kitchen and Sandy and I are left alone, sitting at the opposite ends of a large sofa, in order to, you know, reassure parental eyes with spatial confirmation that nothing physical has been going on between us. Which up to this point it hadn't anyway. We're watching the TV which is small screen and far back, and I remember finding this strangely disappointing, you know, like a sign of deprivation. But pretty soon I start mocking some programme, bang, bang, bang I'm laughing, Sandy's laughing, I'm laughing, Sandy's laughing, cos in that situation I am quite good at making people laugh and stuff, and suddenly the atmosphere is light and the whole thing's going well. And so when Sandy's mum comes back in, instantly she's impressed, cos normally all a parent gets to hear is an air of silence. Mum sees that I'm not quiet or shy, that I'm comfortable in this environment, polite over the cup of tea, everything. I mean, I played it excellent. I've never done it so well in my life. I'm proud of that moment in time. Sandy's mum liked me cos I wasn't like other guys, trying it on. And most importantly I made Sandy laugh. No other boyfriend had apparently ever succeeded in this. And Sandy was like the Princess Who Never Laughed when her mum was around. But I was always making Sandy laugh and her mum liked that. And I made her mum laugh, too. Every other boyfriend that Sandy had round just sat there without saying a word, you know; 'how are you?', 'alright', 'had a good day?', 'yup', see my point? whereas I'd engage in conversation. I mean, her mum would go to a Dali exhibition and discuss it with me. And sometimes it seemed like she had gone to places just so she could discuss them with me later. As time went on, I knew her mum felt comfortable with me taking Sandy out when she stopped phoning Sandy at midnight on her mobile and asking her when she was coming home. That's when I knew then that I was trusted.

Sandy's mum had made us a packed lunch. She always used to do this wherever you were going. I mean, who'd take sandwiches to a Marilyn Manson concert? And we're talking food-aid level of supply, you know, armies that go to war don't carry this many rations. Later on when we went to Stonehenge we couldof got lost for days on her mum's provisions.

"Thank you, Mrs Jackson. Thank you for the sandwiches and the biscuits and the Kit Kats and the oranges and the fruit juice."

"How many bananas do you eat, Matt?"

How many?

"Errr, one?"

We eat what we can on the way but end up feeding most of it to the pigeons in Trafalgar Square. When we arrive at the Docklands Arena we get patted down by the bouncers. Sandy has these trousers on with tiny safety pins all around, you know, the sort they put on babies' nappies, and at first the bouncers tell her she has to take the pins off, but when she shows them how many of them there are they relent and let her through. Had to give up our water bottles though, you know, in case they contained drugs or alcohol.

Inside it's packed and there's, like, six-foot men with black make-up on dressed as women. Every freak and goth has come out this evening, strutting their stuff on some invisible catwalk. Some bald-headed guy is bleeding from the head from moshing and the security guards take him out. It's amazing and Sandy is loving it. She's never been to a concert in her life, let alone in London. Suddenly a big banner drops and reveals some dress on hydraulics which extends and then Marilyn Manson appears above all our heads. This is one impressive stage show. Then everyone spontaneously starts throwing bottles and stuff. Someone throws a shoe which hits Marilyn Manson, who explodes in mock rage, "Whose fucking shoe is this?", and s/he hurls the shoe back into the crowd, and then gets it out and pisses on everyone, which raises a cheer that nearly blows the roof off. Things just get crazier and crazier and Sandy is well into it, like she's finally arrived at her *Rocky Horror* castle. I don't remember anything about the music at all, except that it was incredibly loud. What I do remember is that I had my first proper kiss with Sandy. Probably my first proper kiss ever. It lasted forty-five minutes, and only stopped cos her hair got tangled in my glasses, which made her laugh.

On the train back Sandy rested her legs on me and kept kissing me on the neck and sucking it. She didn't care about doing this in front of everybody, and I wasn't bothered either. We were kissing and laughing and talking in our usual make-believe sort of way and then she took some chewing gum out her mouth, stuck it on my face and sucked it off. Sounds disgusting and weird, but at the same time it felt very affectionate. The whole chemistry thing between us was A-grade. Everything flowed. I didn't have to force anything. She called me manic; but I think she liked that.

When we got back to her house it was well after midnight. She checked her mum was upstairs and then I started getting off with her on the sofa, undressing her almost, while I'm still fully clothed, kissing her, kissing her, kissing her, kissing her, and then suddenly, for reasons I still don't entirely understand, I start thinking, shit, man, do I want to do this or not?, you know, already my mind's kicking in, you can't do this, you can't do this, you can't do this, you haven't got any whatever, but then you gotta, man, you gotta, this is cool, no, can't do it, yeah you can, DZZHH, DZZHH, DZZHH, and I'm turning this girl on, winding her up, winding her up, winding her up, she's getting really, like, horny, yeah, and I remember putting my hand down there and it's all going well, but then she tries to put her hand down here, and I'm like, no, right, and she's like, hmmm, but she doesn't care cos what I'm doing, you know, digital, is going quite well, and I'm kissing her, then suddenly I go, OK bye. Bang. See you later.

And she's like wha? I'm like, I've gotta go. Instantly.

That fucks her up big time. Why? Why don't you wanna do this? I don't wanna do it here. You know, I made some lame excuse. Don't wanna do it here. Haven't got any things. Then she said, I have, upstairs. And that fucked me up big time, cos I'm now like, well, why has she got them? When of course there's no reason why she shouldn't have them. Know what I mean? And then her mobile goes off. It's an old boyfriend, and instantly I'm jealous as fuck. I mean, I still haven't got any closure on whether we're supposed to be going out with each other or not, and she's now virtually naked, looking more stunning than ever, and totally absorbed in a conversation with another guy.

"I'm leaving."

"OK."

And that did my head in as well. The fact that she didn't make any kind of fuss. Didn't even say goodnight. Driving back in the car I thought what a fucking idiot I'd been. We didn't speak for weeks after that. J-J told me not to get mixed up with this girl, said no good could come of it; but, you know, I just couldn't stop myself. The *film noir* fate thing.

But there were times when it was almost perfect between us, like on our trips to Hastings. We didn't do much, just walked around and bought chips, threw some of the chips at things, but it was great, she was really happy. I remember her licking some massive metal buoy on a plaque which freaked me out a bit, cos I'm, like, at the height of my germ problem at this time, but she doesn't know anything about it. At these moments I could tell she liked me a lot. She would even get quite clingy. But then all of a sudden something would happen and it would change. Then she'd start telling me that she couldn't have any relationship with anyone else cos of this old boyfriend who she was still kind of with, but wouldn't give any more details.

Sandy wanted to be a writer. Although she wasn't money-orientated in any way, the image she carried in her mind of herself at thirty or forty was of a wealthy her, not a poor her. Probably a journalist writing for *NME* or something like that, cos she liked to talk about music. She hated pop trash, as she called it, said it had no feeling to it, mass-produced rubbish; but she liked Deftones, because even though you could say that what they were singing about was rubbish as well, at least they meant it, so it felt real. I remember sitting in the car with her and talking for hours. The car was always a special place. She said to me that some of the best times she'd ever had were in my car, cos it was neutral and never stops. And if it does stop, it's because you can stop anywhere at any time. And she loved that. We'd sit for hours in that car just talking, freezing our nuts off, or my nuts, because it was the only place we had that was ours. I never knew that it was possible just sitting with someone for hours on end and never getting bored. There was this constant sexual tension between both of us as well. I would always wind her up, but then always go, nope, we can't do it, and she accepted this for longer than most women would; I mean, most women would go, well, fuck off then, you know, ain't doing that again; but Sandy let me do it over and over and over again. Hastings days were always good and there was almost like a soundtrack to that time cos we always had music on, particularly *White Pony* by Deftones.

She liked being on the move, like me. Enjoyed going to places. Anywhere. I mean, we'd go on fucking trips to twenty-four-hour Asda just as long as we were going somewhere. Going to supermarkets was exciting for her because it would be midnight and we could again make up scenarios and the trip would be to see what obscure shit you could get and eat. Stuff you wouldn't eat every day, like a very powerful chilli sauce, or Hula Hoops. I once bought a hundred packets of Hula Hoops which were past their sell-by date. Sandy liked stupid food, like candyfloss, penny sweets, ten-pence chews, childish food; loved all that crap. She lit up when she saw it and ate loads of it. She didn't go for chocolate, just obscure chews like Fruit Salads and Black Jacks. You get the picture. Many a time we had to go for a drive to get this stuff.

Moving somewhere in the car, didn't matter what bullshit place you were going to as long as you were going somewhere. She hated sitting still, just like me. And because she liked being on the move we'd go places without even wanting to go there. We'd make up excuses to go long distances, like setting off to find some rare delicacy, you know, Fruit Twisters, which were, like, fruit turned into jelly and then rolled, like hard jam, and wrapped in paper, so you could peel it off, layer by layer, and which no shop in Freetown ever had, so we'd have to go miles in search of one that did. Neither of us liked this snack particularly and sometimes when we got there we wouldn't even bother getting out the car, you know, we'd just park up in front of the shop and talk and listen to music. We made each other laugh all the time, cos, like I say, you could never be too serious with Sandy. I mean, she could talk politics and stuff; but you couldn't talk anything personally serious with her, cos that was the last thing she ever wanted. The more stupid your conversation could be, that was so much for the better, you know, she loved that. And we could make a joke out of anything we saw or did or whatever.

But she could be weird sometimes. One day she suddenly found this watch she hadn't seen for years. It was a kids' watch, really old, plastic, with some Disney character on it, Minnie Mouse. She was looking for some buttons to sew onto her bag and her mum gave her this button tin, and as she was sifting through it she found the watch. She didn't ever wear this watch but she wanted batteries to see if it would go again. But it was really late. Eleven o'clock. We drove everywhere to try and find these batteries, which weren't standard size. We tried every Tesco and Asda. Even woke up my granddad to see if he knew where to get them. I mean, she was never, ever gonna wear this watch. But it meant a lot to her. And she told me why.

She never knew why her dad had walked out until the day when she overheard her mum talking about it. And she was wearing this watch at the time. Mustof been about seven years old. She gave up wearing this watch from that moment. So I suppose this watch was when she was at her happiest, if you can call it that; when she thought her dad might still come home. Before she knew he never would; before the bad stuff with the mum's boyfriend; before she started cutting herself. You know, she's happy living with her mum; maybe happy's not the right word, but she's comfortable in her own head that her father isn't around. Obviously that's still gonna hurt you; but at the same time inside your mind it's written in black and white that he can't be here at the moment, and, you know, you haven't got all these questions, like, why did my dad leave, without saying a word? Knowing he had a young daughter? You know, was I that bad? Did he not love me enough? So I suppose the watch represented the time when she was most together. She wasn't gonna wear it, but wanted to know if it would go again. We tried every possible place. And she was getting more and more upset and I was feeling more and more like I was failing her, you know, why aren't you helping me out?, I need this. But we never did find those batteries.

298

She was so confusing. There's a song by some depressive which J-J used to play on the guitar called 'In the Shape of a Heart'. Jackson Browne, that's the guy. He also wrote a song that's used in *Taxi Driver*, when Travis Bickle is pointing a gun at the TV. I've always liked that scene. Anyhow, the point of 'In the Shape of a Heart', as J-J explained to me, is that there are so many shapes and sizes, no matter that they tell you there is only one. I personally don't find Jackson Browne and his song depressive at all, just very truthful. But the fact is that the truth is usually depressing. It's just how you deal with that fact which matters and makes you who you are. You know, you have to get beyond it and find a way into joy and wonder, maintaining what positive illusions you can in the face of negative information. And as Sandy once told me, love and hate are really close together; they can switch, which means the more you love someone the more you can hate them if things go badly. There's no grey. No middle ground.

Chapter Twenty-Two

Women

Ferdinand: Why do you look unhappy?
Marianne: Because you talk to me with words
and I look at you with feelings.
(Jean-Luc Godard, *Pierrot le Fou*)

"Oh man, I'm having real trouble with women at the moment."

"What's the problem?"

"I don't know. I can't understand them at all."

"Who does?"

"I mean, I've tried to stay friends with Sandy, you know, not being boyfriend and girlfriend, cos she doesn't want any of that; but she still complains at me all the time. She either says I'm too clingy, or too faraway. Total opposite extremes. And I'm like, but I'm not either of these things! And it's just annoying. And you're always getting criticised for doing stuff you never even thought you were doing. And then when you do what they want you to do, they moan at you for the fact that you're not doing the right thing. So it's like you can't do anything right."

"That's OK. That's normal."

"Yeah but I don't like it."

"Yeah well."

"I don't know whether it's just that I find complicated women, or all women are complicated."

"They're all complicated. Especially at this age."

"And, you know, they say they want one thing, but to be honest with you they seem to want another. They'll say they want a guy that won't call them and acts like, you know, treat them mean keep them keen; but then when you DO that, they complain that you are horrible. So I don't understand. It's like when Sandy asks for me to call on a Wednesday, I'll call on a Wednesday, because that's what she's asked me to do; but then she says she prefers it if I call on a Saturday. Does my head in. But I'm definitely feeling better. I don't think so much. Perhaps my handwashing and obsessional behaviour isn't so great, but in terms of how I feel in myself I am actually feeling better and getting on and doing more."

"How often are you washing your hands?"

"Say if I'm gonna prepare some food, I'll always wash my hands."

"OK."

"But I'll do it if I'm making a sandwich, and people ask why, I just say it's food handling, you know, it's the way I was brought up. But I know it's not that normal to wash your hands for something like that. Other times it depends on my mood and how busy I am in my brain doing something else. You know, I might say to myself, I'm too busy, can't be bothered to wash my hands. I think I've probably developed a better understanding of how my brain works now."

"So it's not just because you're busy; you're operating at a higher level?"

"Maybe."

"Well, that's a good sign. Tell me some more about your feelings towards Sandy."

"She's sort of incredibly like, don't know what the word is, almost, I don't know, she just makes me feel totally at ease and happy and I don't worry about anything when I'm with her."

"You feel irresponsible?"

"I don't know. Before I was worrying about everything and ultra-tense. She makes me do stupid things, but doesn't ask me to do them. I just do them. I seem to feel liberated when I'm with

301

her. It's like everything that wouldof held me back before, when I'm with her, she unleashes it all. So it's almost as if I see her as some kind of ultra cure. But unfortunately when I wake up the next day, cos of the way she is, she's like, you'll speak to her, she won't call you again, you'll speak to her, and she'll be like, oh, it didn't happen, you know, I can't remember, and that leaves you feeling like, man, that was harsh, but then at the same time you're like this is just temporary. But I know for a fact that if I went and saw her again it would happen again; I'd feel like whooah again, but the next day I'd be head done."

"Has she got problems with relationships? You said last time that she was all screwed up."

"She's got problems with everything. Relationships; everything. She's with this boy at the moment. Been with him for about a year. The only reason I think she's with him still is that he doesn't really care. He won't call her for three weeks and then he'll turn up again. He's very easy-going, so he's no pressure on her; whereas I worry about her all the time. Cos she explained a lot of things that had happened to her in her life, and some of those things are ten thousand times worse than what's happened to me. She's tried to kill herself a few times. And she cuts herself as well. I don't know. She never wants to approach the subject. She'll never wanna talk about it, never wanna resolve any of it. And whenever we talk we go into some kindof fantasy world. If you were to record our conversations you would say they were nothing but rubbish; but her imagination and my imagination are very good, so when we actually get together something sparks between us and this whole world gets created. You know, I'll say something then she'll say something then I'll say something then she'll say something CHHT, CHHT, CHHT, CHHT. When we sit down we can talk to each other for hours; but if you were to ask afterwards what the hell we talked about, it would all have been made up, and all of it a joke."

"People who have been through very traumatic experiences tend to try to avoid reality."

302

"Which is what I do, too."

"Because you want to avoid real life."

"That is what I mean by the ultra cure. When I sit down with Sandy, it's like I'm taken out of all that. But as soon as I wake up the next day I'm ten thousand times more depressed."

"That's because it's false, you see. It's a false thing. Not real."

"But I keep coming up with like mad theories of what to do, like calling Sandy up and running off to Cuba with her. All I want to do is stay forever in that fantasy world. But I'm intelligent enough to realise that the only reason it's a fantasy world when I'm with her is because she supplies that to me. And also I'm usually wasted and as soon as the alcohol wears off and it becomes morning again everything disappears and she's back to reality, feeling guilty about all the stuff that she's done the night before, having all that bad stuff back hanging over her head. You just can't sustain our kind of fantasy world for any long period of time; it would be like someone on heroin or whatever. You'd say to someone, OK take heroin and you'll get a hit off of it for so many hours; but next day you're probably gonna be on the biggest downer ever."

Chapter Twenty-Three

Coming Apart

Things fall apart; the centre cannot hold
(W. B. Yeats)

One of the best days of my life was a Saturday when Sandy and I didn't go anywhere at all. We'd been down to the Archangel the previous Friday night, left at a reasonable time, nothing bad happened, I wanted her, she wanted me; everything's cool, we're listening to good music, totally in tune with each other, everyone's happy. We just stayed in my room all day; it was brilliant. I kept turning her on, leading her, getting off with her, doing more than that; but never going all the way. She really wanted to, you know, she was naked but I was still dressed, as always. She wasn't questioning why I wasn't having sex with her. But it drove her mad, made her more passionate about wanting to do it, you know? She's thinking, most guys only have to do this to have sex with me, but this guy is doing all of this, and it feels good and he doesn't; you know, to a certain degree, it worked in my favour. If I'd've thought about it and played it that way, I'd have been a master. But it wasn't that I was playing it any way; it was just that I couldn't do it, could I?

But another Saturday she was sitting in my room crying, partly cos of the come-down from the night before, when she'd been taking loads of pills and stuff, Es and all the rest. It was pretty bad. My mum was even having a go at me, you know, how've you made her cry? I haven't made her cry, just leave me alone. And I'm a nervous wreck at this time, can't do anything right, nothing, everything I do upsets her. In the end I just hold her but she doesn't even want that. So I say, OK, let's go to the Archangel. Even though this was against all my principles, I felt like I owed it to her in view of the pain she was going through.

So we get to the Archangel and in no time she sets about getting wasted, more wasted than anybody. I'm at the bar and I order eight shots of JD and four shots of tequila in one glass. A twelve-shot drink. Neat. It would kill a man that hadn't been training himself like I had. I managed to swallow the whole glass in one go. It was caning. EEEUUURRRRGHHHHHHHHWHOOOAHHH. I think I even made some bizarre noise like that. Everybody's like, whooa! And then I followed up with two bottles of Becks. I mean, I was a man on a mission, cos Sandy was over in the corner talking to her friends, getting wasted and getting off with guys and I didn't wanna communicate with anyone there except her. Didn't wanna be in this place at all. Couldn't see why we had to be here in this shithole, you know what I mean?

So I'm now wasted, but credit to me, I'm handling it; I'm not angry, I'm not bitter, I'm walking straight. Everybody's coming up to me and saying, did you really have that twelve-shot drink? Yeah. I mean, the word spread. Yeah, here, get yourself a tequila, I don't like drinking on my own. I'm now buying drinks for everyone; but I'm not trying to act big or be clever, I just fucking hate being at this place and this is the only way to get through it and, you know, everybody's coming wimme, even if I have to pay. That night cost me over a hundred quid. But oh, man, that drink made me a legend. And I didn't even puke.

Sandy's by now completely wasted. I'm drinking more tequilas, sucking on a lime, drinking tequila, sucking lime, over and over, seeing just how far I can go. Evening ends. Sandy's pissed off. I'm out of it.

"Come on, Sandy, it's time to go."

"I don't wanna go."

"Come on."

"I don't wanna go!"

"OK, fuck off then." I now push her away.

"No, come back."

"No, fuck off."

You know, classic Freetown dialogue.

"Please come back. I wanna kebab."

"But you don't eat meat."

"I wanna kebab."

"You don't eat meat!"

I'm pretty sober now, after everything that's happened. And she's straightened up as well, but still very wobbly.

"I'm sorry. I really love you. I can't imagine going with anyone else."

"Don't tell me this shit, just shut up."

"Why don't you wanna hear it?"

"Cos you're always doing this and it does my head in. Just tell me you hate me or you like me. Don't fucking do this every time."

"I'm so sorry." And now she's holding onto me and stuff and I have to prop her up against a wall. It looks so dodgy. People are walking past and thinking I'm gonna rape her.

"She's just drunk."

"I need the toilet."

And this was when she started saying, you remind me of my mum's boyfriend. Now that's gonna screw you up. You know, what the fuck am I meant to do about it? One minute she wants me, the next minute she doesn't. I do things for her, then she tells me to get lost. Now she's telling me I remind her of bad things and my name's being mentioned in the same sentence as the most hateful person she's known.

"Your hair's the same."

"I'll get it cut."

"It won't matter. And he wore glasses."

"I'll wear contacts." You know, I'll change, I'll do anything.

"It's the jacket as well."

306

"Fuck it."

We're walking over Freetown Bridge at the time. I rip off my jacket and sling it over the side into the water below. You know what I'm like sometimes. My jacket floats a few feet then sinks and disappears altogether as the current grips it. Then gone. No more than five seconds. I mean, I loved that jacket. But I loved her more.

Yet even though I loved her and was physically attracted to her, I was still having difficulty consummating whatever relationship it was that we had. We were at my house once. My parents were on holiday in Tenerife and my brother was sleeping over at a friend's. Everything is set up beautifully. We're in my bedroom watching TV and then she turns to me and asks me if I would please go downstairs and make her a cup of tea.

"And when you come back up I'm going to be naked."

And sure enough, when I return with cups of tea, there is this beautiful naked girl in my bed. I've now kind of got no choice but to take off my clothes as well. So Sandy's naked, I'm naked. This is a first.

We kiss and initiate foreplay which, as I've said, I've become something of a master at by default. I'm using my hand, getting off with her and doing all this stuff; my hand is now really goopy and that's starting to worry me. I can't handle it and keep making excuses like, I've just gotta get something, or, I thought I heard someone, and every five minutes I'll be doing something, then, sorry, back in a sec, go and wash my hands, back, need to go again, and sometimes I'd just be standing outside on the landing, thinking, what are you doing?, what are you doing? You're an idiot. Then I'd come back in. I mean, I mustof left a dozen times and the last time lasted forever. "I'll be back in a minute," and didn't come back for twenty.

What was going on? I was washing my hands intensely in the bathroom. I was stressed, omigod, omigod, omigod, you're out here, you need to be in there, I was mucking things up and not playing by any of the rules that I'd set up for myself. Wash my hands, dry my hands with a towel, that ain't a clean towel, use another one, not good enough, I didn't do that thing with the soap, shit, OK, do it again, and because I was rushing it I was never pleasing myself with what I was doing, you know, oh man, my fingernails WHOOSH, DJUH DJUH DJUH, cut my fingernails, shit man, gotta wash them again, etc. you know, that's why it took twenty minutes. And when I finally came back in, twisting the handle to my bedroom door with my foot, which is something I've got really skilled at, Sandy was fully dressed and was wearing a look of pure pissed-offness.

"What's wrong?"

"What have you been doing?"

You know, we're in complete role reversal: I'm now naked and she's fully clothed. And I can't find any words to cover myself with.

I'd discussed such a scenario with J-J the week before, because I knew it might come to this. He'd said that I just had to give it my best shot. So I'd psyched myself up, you know, you've done this before, so it ain't that. But I think it was just the sheer fact that this girl wasn't normal. The girls I'd known before had always been like country girls, quiet, didn't drink, didn't go to the Archangel, didn't get off with eight guys in one night, so in my mind these girls were sound. You know, not exactly logical, but nevertheless these kind of thoughts were playing in the back of my head. Whereas Sandy was, like, the exact opposite. She didn't look unkosher; she was beautiful. But at the same time I'd seen her do things that I didn't want her to be doing. And that was the real issue. I mean, she's told me lots of stuff, like what the boyfriend of the mother used to do, and although I don't know how far it ever went, this was wrecking me. I mean, it wasn't good stuff, not the sort of thing your mother's boyfriend should be doing with a fourteen/fifteen-year-old girl. You know, I'm almost allergic to those numbers now, I mean in weird ways. I won't put the stereo up to fifteen. If the date's the fifteenth, I won't write it down. I'll put the sixteenth or thirteenth. Really bizarre. Worrying. So in the end all I could do was look at her and say, "I can't do it."

BANG.

"No. Never again! Not doing this any more."

I've really upset her now; and fair enough you're gonna get pissed off, you know, led down this track every time, every time, only for someone to go, no, I don't like doing this. So she's angry and hurt. And I know I now have no choice but to tell her. Either it's the end of us and we never do this again, and I didn't want that, I wanted to have sex with this girl, I just needed to get over what I was getting over; or I tell her the truth. So I told her the truth. And that didn't do too good either.

Naturally I didn't spell it out; but she put two and two together. I mean, it doesn't take a brain surgeon, does it?

"What, you think I'm dirty?"

"No, not at all."

"You obviously do."

"No, it doesn't matter who you are," which wasn't true, "doesn't matter, you know, you could be a nun, and I'd still have this problem."

She calmed down a bit after that, and I kind of managed just about to extricate myself by the skin of my teeth, though I don't think she fully believed me.

From that day on, I could still get off with Sandy, but I wasn't allowed to do anything to her unless she did something to me, know what I mean? I'd be getting off with her and she'd start doing something rather than me doing something. And once she'd done that to me, then I was allowed to do something again. And that was how it developed until finally I said, OK, we'll do it. I didn't put it quite that bluntly, can't remember the exact dialogue, but I said, we'll do it, and she said, OK. Then off the top of her head, almost joking: "We'll do it Monday at six."

Monday comes. I'm panicking, driving around in circles, thinking gotta do this, can't do this, can't do it, what'm I gonna do? Pressure, pressure, pressure. I'm shitting myself and I've gone out and bought some protection, even though I know she will have protection, cos she's said she'll sort all that out; but I want

309

to be sure in my own mind. Normally I would get it at Asda but I buy it at Tesco and it doesn't scan. BEEP. BEEP. BEEP. BEEP. Lady behind the counter's trying, you know, but it's as if the BEEP is getting louder and louder, you know BBOOORR BBOOORRR in response to the futility of her efforts. Finally she puts it through the machine but she's like, can't... read... the... numbers... on... the... back, and so she's holding the packet up to the light, twiddling it in her fingers to cut out the reflection while she's pressing one or two at a time of the seventeen digits, makes a mistake and has to start over, and all the while everyone's looking at me and I'm thinking yes, OK, yes, and getting redder and redder. Didn't go to that Tesco for weeks afterwards.

I turn up to Sandy's house. Her mum's on some course in Scotland and won't be back till Tuesday lunchtime. I'm sweating. I mean, this should be an enjoyable experience, and I should be excited by the prospect of it, but I'm not. It's almost as if I'm being sentenced. And that makes me feel even more guilty, cos she's clearly looking forward to it, as you would be, while it's blatant that I'm not. I can barely move. She keeps trying to turn me on, but it just isn't working. I mean, I haven't got a problem in that way normally, but at this moment in time, with the stress and pressure, I can't do it. I mean, it did eventually happen, but it was probably the most unenjoyable experience either of us had ever had; and that's not good. Cos I was doing it for the sake of doing it, and I didn't wanna do it. So it ended quickly, cos even though I couldn't get turned on, I wanted to get it over with. I mean, normally you've like got some kind of game plan, but mine was just to get in there and get it done. You know what I mean? And I felt so bad. One, because I had performed really badly, two, I knew I could do better, and three, I just felt like shit. I didn't wanna worry about what I'd just done, but I couldn't help but worry about it. And now I'd done it, and done it so badly, I wanted to do it again to prove to her that I could do it better. So I was going through some very bizarre emotions. Part of me was like, fuck that shit, that was crap, I can do ten thousand times better than that on

310

one leg or whatever; but the other part was like, no, you've done it once, you're doomed. Never do it again. So I'm fucked and I'm like, what have I done? And how fucked-up must I have made her feel? But she was incredibly understanding, you know, it's alright, we'll do it again, another time, don't worry. I mean, it wasn't hard to see that this was the poorest performance you've ever seen in your life, cos basically I didn't wanna do it at all. Like sending someone in the ring who's just holding on so that they can get hit. You know, hit me, knock me out, quick. That's what I was like.

It got better. But that was only when I started to give up on everything. I was like, what's the point?, might as well do it anyway. And I came round to seeing that the worrying was nothing in comparison to the gains. And, you know, I'd done it once and didn't catch anything; so having gone past the point of no return I was like, well, you've done it once, might as well do it a thousand times or ten thousand times. So I just went into freefall and it was ten thousand times better. But the fact that the physical became more possible didn't change any of the underlying issues we had with each other, and we started to see ourselves as not being together any more, or at least not as much as we had been. Which meant that I accepted we were not in a relationship, and probably couldn't be, even though I still had strong feelings for her, and I think she had the same for me.

On the anniversary of our coming together at the Archangel I decide to take Sandy to Stonehenge and take Marcus along with us, to reassure her that I won't be freaky or anything. Marcus is at art college and wants to be a painter but seems to love music almost as much as he loves art. I knew Marcus would be cool to take, because he sees himself as a car DJ and always brings along a bag of CDs. He's got eclectic taste and mixes up weird combinations, like Jeff Buckley followed by Black Sabbath followed by 'Me and You and a Dog Named Boo'. But the really cool thing about Marcus' DJing is that he always knows the history behind every band and every song. He'll tell you about a certain track by the Beach Boys and how it was only recorded in mono, and you get to learn a

311

lot of stuff, not geeky stuff, just stuff you wanna hear, like after recording this song the singer went mad, you know, that sort of thing. And I knew Sandy would love all that.

We picked Sandy up on Sunday night around half nine so we could get there before sun-up. Her mum had prepared a humungous packed lunch; a massive hiking rucksack containing marmite, jam, ham and cheese and pickle sandwiches, homemade bread, two packs of Kit Kats, four sealed Mars bars and four sealed Snickers, fruit to balance out the chocolate, oranges, pears, two bunches of bananas, litres of orange cartons and cups that sprang up when you flipped them. When she put this rucksack on the floor it went THMMMP.

The weird thing about our whole journey to Stonehenge is that Sandy fell asleep about half an hour into it. Didn't wake up when we got there; didn't wake up until an hour before we got home. All she did was sleep. Didn't get to see Stonehenge. But then none of us did, because foot and mouth had broken out. So we drove all the way there only for four council guys in orange reflective clothing to turn us away. In truth we kind of knew this might happen, as we'd heard something about it on the radio; but we were just wanting to go on a big drive somewhere, whatever. I remember it being almost pitch-black all the way with nobody on the roads but us. Sandy was asleep in the back but it felt good that she was with us. Marcus and I just talked in the front about life, music, where we were going. Marcus told me about what he wanted to do when he left art college: live in Whitstable and paint seashores. I talked through my situation with Sandy. It was a fantastic trip; one of the best trips ever. People don't understand that. They say, but you didn't see Stonehenge! It wasn't the point. Just like in *On the Road* it's not about getting anywhere; it's about relating.

After we'd been turned away we parked up down some Wiltshire country lane. The land was flat and the wind was strong. Marcus and I left Sandy sleeping in the car and we went for a walk and ended up sitting by the roadside throwing stones. Suddenly we heard this

NNAAAAA and looked at each other, like, what the hell was that?, and this sheep suddenly appeared. It was the coolest thing ever. Like a David Lynch film. We wondered about the foot and mouth, but figured we'd be OK and so would the sheep if we kept quiet about it. Marcus gave the sheep a sandwich, which surprised me, cos he really loved the bread that Sandy's mum had baked and kept wanting more and more of it. The sheep just goes BAAAA, licks the sandwich, pushes it around a little and then walks off. Marcus picks up the sheep-nibbled sandwich and then finishes it off himself.

"Good bread don't go to waste."

"Man, what about the foot and mouth?" I mean, I'm horrified and won't even touch it.

"I'll be alright."

We had the car lights streaked along the road. It was just a magical moment, like in *Badlands* or Van Morrison's 'Madame George'.

On the way back Sandy woke up. I had my silver Toyota Corolla at the time and she fitted perfect in the back. I mean, I couldn't sleep like that, nor could Marcus. We'd be folded up every which way. But she took up those two back seats perfect. And with the music and everything, she said it was the best sleeping she'd ever done. When we were on the M25 all she could hear was the noise of the road, which she couldn't see at all, WHHISSHHING by; and the lights going past the window was also cool. By this time I'm almost falling asleep at the wheel so we put on Radio 1, and at four in the morning on a Monday Radio 1 is not good, you know, it's DVVV, DVVV, DVVV, DVVV, DVVV, DVVV, DOODOOODOOO, DVVVV, DVVV, DVVV, DVVV.

"Goddamn! What is this music?" shouts Marcus.

"Just trying to keep myself awake, man." I turn it up.

Marcus then winds down the electric window, and cos there's rain on it it goes WUUUUDIJJJUGGA, WUUUUDIJJJUGGA, WUUUUDIJJJUGGA, WUUUUDIJJJUGGA. And every time I switch on the window wipers, cos I'm wiping too much, it would go EEE, EEE, EEE, EEE. So this music's going DVVV, DVVV,

DVVV, DVVV, WUUUUDIJJJUGGA, WUUUUDIJJJUGGA, EEE, EEE, EEE, EEE, DVVV, DVVV, DVVV, DVVV, WUUUUDIJJJUGGA, WUUUUDIJJJUGGA, EEE, EEE, EEE, EEE, WUUUUDIJJJUGGA, WUUUUDIJJJUGGA, EEE, EEE, EEE, EEE.

And Sandy's now like, what are you two doing? And we're like, yeah, it's working; we're making music!

I dropped Marcus off and drove back to Sandy's house. She said, let's go to bed, and we did and slept till twelve. Sandy slept all night. And for the first time ever of us waking up together Sandy was happier than I think I'd ever seen her. I mean, at this point I've given up on the relationship and we're not going out with each other any more; but she was more loving and showed more warmth that day than on any other morning after, ever. She was like, let's go and have breakfast. First time we'd ever had breakfast together. She cooked this breakfast and I'm thinking, don't do this, you're not with this girl; but when it's being pushed against you, you want it even more. I didn't say anything. I knew if I did I would muck things up, so I kept quiet and went along for the ride. I didn't say, does this mean we're together?, or, why are we breaking up if it's this good?, or anything like that. I didn't ask, didn't argue; just let it pan.

We managed to keep it going for a few more weeks doing that thing where we were trying to stay friends, even though we'd split up. But it wasn't satisfactory for either of us really.

"This isn't gonna work, is it?"

I think she wanted me to say, 'no it's not', so she could then say, 'OK then'. But I didn't.

"Well, it could do." I replied.

That killed her.

"But I don't think you want it to."

Which was sort of true.

She started crying. Don't know if she was doing it to make me feel better, but the tears were genuine. But I had come to the point where I just wanted to see it all burn, so I could start feeling upset.

314

However, getting over Sandy was never going to be as cut and shut as I wanted it to be; so we propped each other up, bandaged our emotions and hobbled on for a couple more weeks.

Then one night I was driving her home from mine and we got into an argument and I just lost it. I mean, this had been building and building and finally I'd just had enough of this yes-no, on-off, love-hate, push-pull ambiguity of everything. Enough of the way she was and the way I was trying to sort it. I mean, she did so many stupid things and I was, like, just trying to protect her, you know. It makes me sound like an idiot, or like Travis Bickle and Iris, misguidedly intervening to help someone who never wanted help in the first place. But I would be out with her on a Friday or Saturday night and she'd be taking all these drugs, ecstasy, cannabis, whatever, hanging around with all these different boys, getting off with everyone. And people just saw her as this fun, outgoing, crazy, you know, the hyper side; but I saw the depressive side and I could see the link between the two and I'm thinking, well, if we sort out this bit in the middle, maybe you won't be so depressed. But she didn't want this, which led to me in my late-teen mind not really knowing what the fuck to do; you know, I'd been told all this information, about her present and her past, most of it I couldn't handle, and I didn't know what to do, and it led to a major argument and I drove too fast down a country lane and nearly killed us. But I didn't.

I'm not proud that I got ourselves into that situation; but I am proud of how I got us out of it. Because that car was going sideways, and I mean, phheew, I don't know how I recovered it. Mustof been my dad's genes or something. I'm telling you, Stig Blomqvist wouldof been impressed, cos we're heading towards Tesco and going plenty quick, you know, I'm animated and talking fast and by mental–physical association I'm driving that way, too, doing sixty easy in a thirty zone, and then suddenly I feel the back end twitch and we're going sideways. Thank God nothing was coming in the other direction, cos I was taking up all two lanes. And this happened twice. I mean, I recovered it once, got into an

315

even bigger rage, hit another corner too fast and ended up going in the opposite direction sideways. And both times I sorted it out. It was pure instinct. But I have to admit there was a thrill to it as well. I mean, I'm shitting my pants, but it was like body and mind suddenly becoming one. And for a brief moment I'm an integral part of the car and it's an integral part of me. I'm not trying to be big-headed or glamourise what I did in any way, but it's like what a lot of boxers say when they step into the ring, you know, there is no contemplation, there is no working a plan out, you're in it and you've gotta get out of it. And I remember just knowing what to do. I remember not braking and accelerating out of it and turning the right way and doing everything to get us out of it. I just felt my way through it. And then I did it again. It was the flukiest thing, and I don't know whether I would ever be able to repeat it, but I pulled that car back from the brink.

Sandy stayed silent throughout. I could tell she was in a really fucking bad mood about it. When we got to her house she jumped out the car and ran off indoors. I didn't know what to do. I drove off, stopped at a garage and tried to give her a call. I'm in the car, distraught and crying, and just don't know any more what to do. Her mum picks up the phone and tells me not to call, because Sandy's really upset. Then she tells me never to call again. Ever.

I'm in tears and drive home slowly. When I get back I lock myself in my bedroom and give J-J a call. I called J-J a lot back then when I needed help.

Chapter Twenty-Four

Dirt

Normal normal

"I feel bad about the way it ended. I've had girlfriends before but nothing serious, no one that I've ever really cared about. That sounds harsh. But what I mean is, I've always been like Mr Non-Emotion, you know, like, OK, this ain't gonna pan out. But with Sandy it was different."

"There's always one, you know."

"I still think about her all the time."

"Were you in love?"

"I was. You know I HATE that word, cos it sounds so pants. People throw it around all the time. But, yes, that girl I did love. But it was getting too weird. It was the only time I actually felt mad. I mean, in that situation, it was like crazy, irrational. It was like a short circuit and I was like uhuhuhuhuhuhuhuhuh. She was the total opposite of me. Didn't care about her hands. Didn't care about cleanliness. If you could imagine someone at the other end of my spectrum that was what she was. But she wasn't totally all right in the mental region either. The things that had happened to her in her past mucked up her thinking to a certain degree. I don't think I even know how to talk to her any more. I thought about writing her a letter, but I don't even know what to say."

"What do you want to say?"

"I don't know. When I was with her, it was not like I was seeking this out, but I was getting close to getting away from my obsessional behaviour, and that frightened me, so I think I purposely bagged it. We both kind of scared each other off."

"It doesn't mean you can't still have a relationship. History doesn't necessarily need to repeat itself. People with your problems can get better if properly treated."

"I told her once that half of it was that I was drinking on anti-depressants. She asked me which ones I was on, I told her Seroxat, she said, oh, I'm on such and such, bet mine are stronger than yours, I say, bet mine are stronger, we go back and forth, then I ask how many milligrams a day she's on, she says forty, I say, man, I'm on fifty, she says, man, that's nothing, I'm a smaller weight so therefore I'm on more than you, you know, we just laughed and made a joke out of her twitching and my twitching; this is how we always talked. Unreal. When I'm with Alice it's like reality. We talk about real things, you know, what we're gonna do in a week's time and what we've done two weeks back. But me and Sandy were always escaping into fantasyland. Never talking about the here and now and real issues. Just imaginative bullshit."

"You had to talk about superficial, funny things, because the last thing she wanted was a serious conversation."

"And whenever you did have a serious conversation with her, you know."

"She went downhill."

"Big time. She'd cry. And she was drinking a lot and taking other things. It's weird because she was the least likely girl for me ever to find attractive. She'd do things I'd never ever do, like lick lamp posts. What the hell is that all about? She's pretty fucked up."

"She's not well."

"And even though Alice is also pretty weird in her own way, she's level-headed in comparison to Sandy. And less 'germified'. I mean, I know this sounds horrible; sounds evil. But I knew Sandy had slept with this guy, kissed that man, licked lamp posts and all the rest. So she was always kind of 'unclean' to my way of thinking."

318

"You mean she was quite dirty."

"Don't say that! That's a horrible word to say."

"Contaminated."

"Contaminated I prefer. Like Bill Hicks with his girlfriend. You know, I'd kiss Sandy and then I'd go and brush my teeth or wash my mouth out. But unlike Hicks I'd still be wanting to kiss her more and more. Cos when I kissed her it was dangerous in my own mind, and I got off on that."

"We need to understand this cleanliness thing more. Let's say we're in the desert and we need to disinfect something. There's a wound that's infected and we need some sterile liquid. What is the sterile liquid that's around in the desert?"

"Well, there ain't much water, so I'm guessing it's pee."

"Right. Urine. As long as you don't have a kidney or a bladder infection you're going to be alright. It's sterile. It's got to be. For you to be healthy, it's sterile."

"You're not winding me up?"

"It's the honest truth. The cleanest produce that we can ever produce that is sterile is not saliva, not tears, not sweat, not any other liquid, other than urine."

"That makes sense, because it's gone through all those processes."

"We've filtered out all the impurities."

"Right."

"The dirtiest thing we produce is excrement."

"And we aren't gonna start smearing that over wounds."

"No. But if it's well rotted you probably can. It's actually not bad for you. Some desert Arabs will use camel dung as a dressing for wounds. Well rotted, well dried. So the way we need to think about dirt needs to change a little. In fact you're more likely to damage yourself and allow an infection to come into your hands by repeated washing; because you have dermatitis, the skin cracks, and skin is the best barrier to reduce infection coming into the body. So just try and challenge these thoughts a little. I'm not saying all the time, you know; don't get obsessed by it."

"I have on and off days, actually. Like I'll wash my hands more one day than another. It depends. Some days I won't wanna wash them at all. Other days it's like thirty or forty times."

"How about the showers?"

"I haven't had a shower today to be honest. Mainly because I got up late."

"And you didn't care."

"No I just threw some clothes on."

"Excellent."

"And another difference is, I would never have made myself a sandwich before, and now I do. Perhaps I make it a little bit more slowly and more carefully than other people. I mean, I don't think I could ever be a chef, for the simple fact that I'd be too slow and paranoid about poisoning people. But in terms of beginning to feed myself and look after myself, I reckon I could handle that now, whereas before I couldn't. Before I wouldof been like, oh, I won't eat, and I wouldof ended up skinny and miserable. Now I can do it, it just takes me a little bit longer. Mum, understandably, would like me to be a bit more normal normal. But I say to her, I'm never gonna be normal normal."

"The thing is you're coming out of a situation where everything has been contaminated."

"But I worry that whenever I do meet a girl it'll always be just another Sandy or another Mona or another Alice, who will always end up doing my head in."

"Everyone's different. And girls are not thinking straight at nineteen. They don't know what they're thinking. They're not all going to do your head in."

"But they do in the end, don't they?"

"Unless they're the right one that you're gonna marry, they all kind of cause grief, yes. But that is normal."

"And I don't really understand sex. Not in the way you think. I mean, I understand the technicalities of it. Know how it works. But in terms of what's it all about, man? At one level I can see it is kind of a horrible, like, animalistic thing that can be used as a

320

weapon, but then on another level I'm kindof guessing it's like a good thing. But what I can't work out is how something can be two different extremes."

"It's all about context. But let's get back to your present situation. How are you at the moment? Are you feeling better?"

"Better in one way and worse in another. Better in that, as I said, I can make my own sandwiches and I'm not in the shower for hours."

"Which ways are you worse in?"

"Social behaviour and aggression."

"We know where this is coming from and we need to do work with this. You're still a bit fragmented; this is a long process."

"And how many together twenty-year-olds are there?"

"Not many. Many feel aggressive, angry and get involved in fights. A lot of them are worse than you, with boozing and drugs. You're pretty together in one way; in other ways you still have some growing up to do."

"It seems like everyone I meet has got some kind of problem, like drugs, disturbing sexual history, violent tendencies; you know, the picture of the world I've got in my head is one of misery, anger and pain."

"And a lot of it is misery, anger and pain; but it's not all like that. There are some very happy stories that I hear as well. Some very good people. People who do a lot of charity work, in the church, not in the church, people who are kind to each other, people who look after each other."

"I still don't understand how all the bad stuff can be allowed to go on. If I see anything like a man hitting a woman on TV, or a guy abusing his wife or whatever, my anger levels just shoot up."

"But look, Matt, you're becoming like them. You can't go throwing glasses of beer at people; you'll kill someone."

"I know. It scares me."

"Your anger needs to be bridled. At the moment it is going nowhere, it's got no direction, it's free-floating; and that's not good. It's dangerous for you. You need to be more constructive instead of isolating yourself more and more, churning these thoughts over like someone in solitary confinement. There's a lot of theory about isolation and solitary confinement, but one of the first things that happens when people are solitarily confined is that they start thinking about their life, the past, all the positive things; but then all the negative things start up, all the worries and what do we do next?, you know, it's not good for you."

"Yeah. A bit like Travis Bickle, I suppose. But at the same time isn't it a weakness of character to need others? What I mean is, surely me and you should be able to sit on our own and think without going insane?"

"We're not designed to sit for ten hours at a time by ourselves."

"What about Shaolin monks? They sit on rocks for fourteen hours a day."

"They're trained. If you look at Antarctic expeditions, they all receive special training in order to be able to go out in small groups and get on, or else be solitary, like the ones that go up to the North Pole on their own."

"But what about those guys that used to fire-watch up in those towers in Big Sur? They were on their own for, like, six months."

"A lot of them jumped off."

"No they didn't!"

"It's not a sane, healthy thing to do."

"But why isn't it?"

"Because we're not designed for it."

"Are you sure?"

"Well, my special expertise in the military was solitary confinement, torture and interrogation."

"But some people live on their own for years and years and they're fine."

"They're not quite fine. There are always a couple of loose screws somewhere."

"Are you sure?"

"Yes. There's always cause and effect."

"But what about guys that go and live up a mountain for, like, twelve years on their own?"

"It's not a good idea. I mean, people with PTSD, like the Vietnam vets, go and live in the Appalachian Mountains."

"Which is what I'd like to do."

"Only because of the anger and the frustration that has built up over years and years, not knowing why, seeing your dad suffer, seeing everyone else's dad as OK. This anger and frustration has brewed and brewed. It's like a cake that's been in the oven for ages. We need to channel it and make it constructive. So if you are going to be really concerned about injustice in the world, join an injustice movement, so that when you feel life is unjust, at least you can say, I'm doing my bit."

"I see what you're saying."

"At the moment, you're Mr Angry, and with good reason; but it's going to lead to trouble. And we know that alcohol disinhibits you even more and makes it ten times worse. So rather than isolate yourself, and brew more worry and anger, you need to find a balance. And the other thing is not to watch the kind of things on TV which fuel that anger."

"I keep worrying about her."

"You can't worry about her. People have to be responsible for themselves. If I worried about each patient I couldn't function. So I don't worry about patients. They have to take responsibility. Sandy has to take responsibility."

NOD

"And you need to take responsibility for yourself."

323

Chapter Twenty-Five
Vegas #3

Alles vergängliche ist nur ein Gleichnis
All that is transitory is but an image
(J.W. von Goethe, *Faust*)

Vegas is hyperreality; capitalist hyperreality, naturally. In *On the Road* Dean Moriarty is always saying, 'We know time, we know TIME', and I never really understood what he meant by that until I was in Vegas, where everyone knows that time is money and money is time. I'm not sure if that's what Dean was meaning; he probably had something more intelligent in mind. But Vegas is a low-IQ city. A modern-postmodern city. Vegas works on the vagus; mainlining into the stomach, whetting the appetite, feeding the hunger, sating the need, bloating you out, and disconnecting rational speech and thought at no extra charge, so you can pretty much sleepwalk through it all. Somnambulist city. As for your soul, in place of salvation Vegas offers salivation. Sin city. Insomniac city. Diurnally challenged and shot day for night. A city of emotional unintelligence; amygdala hijack city. Gambler's city. Hustler's city. A city not built on winners, which wise heads tell you, but your memory lapses. Amnesiac city. But Vegas is designed to be a city where you can forget easily. Until you wake up. Or until you go broke.

I got through three hundred and fifty dollars' worth of dances on my first night. A hundred and seventy quid. Ridiculous. But you get into it. And you get more and more picky. At first all the girls are stunning; then it's like, hmmm, move on. Sounds horrible, but that's just the way it was. A really fit girl would walk past and you'd go, hmmm, maybe; you know, you get more confident because you're starting to know the system now, how it works, which is basically through eye contact. A girl's over there, you watch her, watch her, watch her, wait, wait, wait, then she catches eyes with you, you catch eyes with her, and you hold it, hold it, you could look away and they'd be like oh, alright, you know, like if you see someone anyway; but you hold it, they see, they smile at you, you smile at them, they come over, they sit down, you have a chat with them, some of them chat longer than others, some of them are pushier than others.

There were times, however, when I felt I was getting out of my depth. Like with this scary Eastern European girl.

"Ah, you're a young boy. You're a virgin."

Obviously I wasn't, as we know, but I remembered something my video teacher once told me. He'd been in the navy for a few years, travelled round the world a couple of times, slept with many a girl in many a port, you know, Rio or wherever, and he said, always tell them that you are, cos they like that and you'll get it cheaper. He was talking prostitutes rather than strippers, but I'm thinking it may work and she seems happy with the idea.

"Mmmm."

"Ah, I show you a really good time. Take you to the private room."

"Alright." But suddenly I'm thinking this is getting a bit heavy and now I'm not sure I want this. "No, it's OK."

"Oh, I'll show you a REALLY good time."

"No, no, really. I'm OK."

"Go on, go on." This girl is pushy and I'm feeling a little uncomfortable.

"No, seriously, I haven't got enough money." That'll get rid of her.

"Have you got a credit card?" I mean, this woman is a serious hustler.

"No I haven't got a credit card."

"You must have a credit card. How are you here without a credit card?"

"Honestly, I haven't got a credit card."

"Let me see, let me see," and she dives into my pockets and I'm thinking, fucking hell.

"What's this? What's this? You lied! You lied!" In a playful sort of way, but nonetheless an Eastern scary fucking Russian sort of way.

"Oh, that's a Switch card. It's not a credit card."

"A Switch card?" She doesn't understand. "Go on, go on, go on."

There's only one way to get rid of her so I say, alright then, and she calls over the bouncer, who arrives with a swipe machine, swipes my card; I'm thinking, this better not fucking work, this better not fucking work.

"Sorry, it's not gonna work."

"Oh, what a shame." She pecks me on the cheek and then leaves. The scariest girl I ever met.

After that first night I got back to the Hilton at seven in the morning, felt like crap, went to bed and woke up at four in the afternoon. Still felt rough. Washed. Went downstairs. Had something to eat. Wandered around. Went back onto the Strip. Looked at more stuff like the volcano, and a fountain where the water jets are synchronised to music. Cool. Nighttime came around. Caught a cab. Driver took me to another strip club. Jaguars. Massive. Two hundred to three hundred different women in there. It just became more and more normal.

When I first went into a strip club, I didn't know anything, wasn't sure how to handle it; it was new. By the third night I'm a veteran. It became too normal, and I realised I needed to leave. I was drinking way too much, feeling like shit in the morning and becoming a vampire, and that feels weird, you know, it messes up your system when you're going to bed at seven and getting up at four. And as I say, it was just getting more and more normal.

326

And it isn't normal. And I knew this. Somewhere within me was the feeling that, no matter how exciting this is, there is something ultimately unfulfilling about it. Do you know what I mean? I was becoming a junkie, like Elvis; junk sex rather than junk food, but equally bad for you. I mustof spent three thousand dollars on lap dances over three nights, an average of a thousand dollars a night. How many lap dances is that? You do the math. But in Vegas an expensive habit is the norm. In fact norm is abnorm.

So I began to get into this horrible rhythm of staying up all night and waking up late afternoon. I'd been there four days now but it felt like months. A mood started to come over me. A dark mood. I don't wanna sound like a pervert, but it was, you know, normally you're like, oh that girl's not gonna be into me, I don't know if I can talk to that girl, whatever; you didn't have any of that in strip clubs, cos you knew the score. If you stepped over the line, they took you out and broke your arms. If you played it by the rules, were polite, paid the money, everybody was happy. And you didn't feel like you were in a seedy place. Maybe if I'd been in some sawdust-floored shithole, it wouldof felt horrible. But because everyone was wealthy and, you know, clean, it felt OK.

I never went up another level though. Never progressed from lap dances to anything else. I swear. I'd've had too many issues. There was a deal a girl put to me, sort of buy one get one free. Say you're sitting next to me and we're both having a lap dance; it's not particularly private, is it?

"OK, for three hundred dollars I take you up to the private room."

You've got the open room, the private room and some private private room.

"What's that involve?"

"You get four dances and a drink, and it's much more private."

I agree to it, cos I think why not?

We go up. The room is empty. Just me and her basically. We talk. She dances. It's the same as usual but a bit more. Maybe cos I'm a bit drunk I hold her breasts and kiss her on the neck. But

327

that wasn't why it was three hundred dollars. It just evolved out of what we were doing, that's all. And I only did it cos I couldn't really see the point of paying three hundred dollars otherwise.

After my fourth night I was again back in my hotel at seven in the morning and again I felt like shit. I'd not been eating anything cos I'd been spending all my money on the women. There was a cap on how much I could take out from the ATM, and because I wanted to spend it all on the evenings, I couldn't afford to spend any on food during the day. So I'd take it all out at midnight, spend it all by seven in the morning, but then I couldn't get any more out until midnight again, so I'd sleep from seven in the morning and get up at four, but I couldn't buy any food, cos I didn't have any money left, so I had to wait until midnight again, take the midnight money out, and get very little to eat so I could spend it on going out, etc. That was the cycle. And you can imagine the result of the combination of very little, usually crappy, food and drinking a lot. After my fourth night I took off my shirt and looked in the mirror; and what I saw was a sweaty, bloated mess. I looked like shit. I was in this vest that had a rip in it, and it looked like I'd aged twenty years. I felt knackered, worn. I knew it was time to go.

It sounds cheesy, but I vividly remember looking in that mirror, you know when you just surprise yourself and think, oh God, is that me? Jesus Christ. What a mess. I was just so sweaty, you know, when you've been drinking too much beer you just sweat and you're bloated and you look tired and your eyes are all red. I was just like, bloody hell. I looked like I'd been on a bender for months. I looked jaded, pasty-faced. I mean, I'd been getting drunk every night, and that's not good for you, especially when you're not eating or getting much sleep. Didn't look well. And I was spending all my money. It was becoming an obsession. That's what this sweaty, bloated, unwell stranger of low financial status staring back at me was telling me. And I just thought, man, I gotta get out of here. You know, I'm starting to dislocate. I'd set out looking for Jack Kerouac and ended up finding fucking Hunter

S. Thompson. I went to sleep and later that night actually bought something to eat. The following day I got the hell out of Vegas.

But I'm not gonna lie to you. There was a part of me that wanted to go on, you know, one more night, one more night. But the other part was going no, no, gotta get out, gotta get out, gotta go, gotta go. But even right up to the point of getting on the bus I was wondering whether I could just go in there again for one last time, you know, before boarding. But I didn't. I got on the bus. And when that bus drove off, and I was trapped in there and knew I was being taken away, I felt a real sense of relief. Cos I knew that the thing that had brought me so many moments of happiness was also the thing that was gonna bring me down right to the bottom.

Ultimately it was the lifestyle that got to me. And also, I don't care what anyone says – after that, no matter how much joy, joy's the wrong word, no matter how much whatever, that moment of nothingness, that feeling of serenity, that blissful glimpse of Nirvana, you wake up from that. And when you wake up from it, you realise how futile it is chasing that, cos it's not real. You know, that very thing that you get into chasing, you can't sustain it; it's not a long-term achievable, desirable goal. You gotta get it another way. That's a short cut. It's not gonna get you there.

And no matter what I say, there was also an element of me that felt this is maybe not the right thing to do. I knew I wasn't doing anything wrong, wasn't breaking any laws. But, and again this sounds really cheesy, I felt it wasn't necessarily good for my soul. It's not that I thought this is not the right thing to be doing; I just knew that happiness was not going to be found this way. Do you know what I mean? I'm sure those strippers' mothers didn't want them being strippers. No matter that they were earning shitloads of money, and I weren't making them do anything they didn't wanna do; I'm sure there was an element inside of them that didn't necessarily wanna be a stripper. It's a bit like JK looking at the Mexicans picking cotton and thinking how beautiful and poetic and wonderful it all is, without considering how their world might appear through their eyes.

There was a Mexican girl in Jaguars, early twenties/twenty-one, my age to be honest at the time. I got talking to her and actually felt, I really wanna go for a coffee with her, you know, get to know her. Not have sex with her. Nothing like that. Didn't wanna go out with her; sounds really cheesy, but I wanted to be friends with her. You know, I felt like this is a nice girl. And even she was like, oh you know, my mum and dad aren't very happy about me doing this, but I'm only doing this for the short term, you know, the typical stripper story. I'm sure every single one of them started off like that, do you know what I mean? Of course I couldn't go for a drink with her, cos she was a stripper, and I didn't even ask because I thought that would be ridiculous, you know, she'd probably laugh at me; well, not laugh at me, but she'd be like, you know. But I didn't even have a lap dance with her, cos I didn't wanna lap dance with her because of that. I felt weird, do you know what I mean? She sat down for a dance and we got talking, and we talked to such a degree that I actually felt she'd forgotten that she was a stripper, you know, that we were just talking. With the others it was all part of a hustle. All of them. You know, I'll talk to him for a little bit, get him to buy me a drink, dance for him, take his money, job done. Maybe I'm wrong, maybe I'm just a schmuck, but I genuinely felt I was actually talking to this Mexican girl rather than just going through the motions before she dances. And she even seemed almost relieved when I didn't wanna dance, you know, when I said, "Do you mind, but I think I'd rather just sit here for a little bit?" She seemed happy with that. "Oh, that's fine," you know, as if this was perfectly normal. She didn't get up and go, and we talked a little bit more. It was like she was having a break, do you know what I mean? She even had a cigarette and got told off by one of the bouncers.

"They're worried cos I'm having a cigarette."

"Oh, that's OK, I don't mind."

"They're worried in case I burn you."

"Oh, don't worry about it. You won't."

330

So we just sat there and talked some more. It was like we weren't in that surrounding any longer. I'd forgotten I was in a strip club and had a semi-naked woman sitting on my lap. And she seemed in no rush to get off. The other girls were always like, do a talk, do a talk, and you felt like, they're talking to me, that's nice, but ladaladalada, dance, OK, very nice, how about, no, gotta go, money, money, money, money.

But this Mexican girl is smoking a cigarette, taking her time. She's already asked me if I wanna dance, and I've said no; you know, money's already been nullified, but she's still here. We've stepped outside of the cash nexus for a brief moment. Slipped through a glitch into Mag Mell, where time has stopped because money has stopped. Can't remember for how long; but in a timeless otherworld you never do. Maybe that's what Dean Moriarty meant; making that step from time without being, to being without time, suspended everlastingly in an ecstatic unreckoned moment stretched out to infinity.

Chapter Twenty-Six

Going Down

The more you know, the more
you know you don't know
(Aristotle, *Metaphysics*)

A year goes by. I've been going out with Mona and Alice, but all that's now tailed off. One afternoon Sandy and I run into each other at college, where thanks to J-J's influence I've been hired to make a wacky student induction video (which I never complete). We've purposely been avoiding each other, but it happens. Was it planned? I dunno. I come up for air from a mega editing session and there she is sitting on one of the wooden trestle benches outside, drinking a Diet Coke. It's a sunny day and she's in a pink top and faded jean cut-offs with this cool straw hat with a ribbon round to finish it off. She looks fantastic, and I'm suddenly very nervous. I've been cut up badly over the twelve months; but I can't pretend I'm not me and she's not she, and we're not here and now in this moment together.

"You talking to me?"

The *Taxi Driver* reference slips out.

"Yeah, I'm talking to you. Why not?"

Typical. All's forgotten. All smiles. Flirting back and forth. She's laughing, I'm laughing. Gives me her new phone number. I think about it. A week or two goes by. The Alice thing has died. It's all sorted. I call Sandy up and ask her what she's doing. I'm bored.

A lot of trouble starts when you're bored.

We go down to the Archangel. I don't know how, but I have a lot of money on me as a result of this induction video gig, for which I've been paid in advance, and we set about getting wasted. I'm on a buzz. You gotta understand, I felt it was all my fault that it had broken up last time, and now here was my second chance. I'd been granted this wish. I was on a high.

We get very drunk, leave the Archangel and go on to the Saxon Warrior. I'm being a prick and showing off and go up to the bar and say, "I wanna shot of everything you've got." I mean, they've got a serious optics rack in the Saxon Warrior.

"That is going to cost you a lotta money, sir." Bargirl's nice and polite; not a goth like you might expect.

"I don't care, I'll have a shot of everything."

Cos I'm still in my Dennis Hopper phase.

"I'm not sure we can do that, sir."

You know, it's almost like we're in America and they're worried about vicarious liability. Luckily the other bargirl, Leanne, knows me and kind of likes me, and most of all is the sort of girl who's like, hey, I've gotta see this; so she says to the other one, "Oh, he's alright, he's alright." It takes about three trays to bring all of these shots out. But Sandy and me get through them between us.

When you drink that amount of alcohol at that strength that quickly, you don't feel any gradual slide into inebriation, you know, along a progressive scale from slight onset of merriness through vague euphoria and an exaggerated sense of goodwill, to stupidity, a definite numbing of the senses, and the impression that motor co-ordination might not be as efficient as it should be, whatever; instead all of a sudden it's like POWWW being hit by a truck. I remember being like fuuuuuucckkk, you know, like, gone. But I did manage to buy a box of Quavers.

"What do you mean a *box* of Quavers?"

"I don't want just one. Gimme a whole box."

So they had to pull out a box from behind the bar. Cost me about forty quid. And I start sharing them out with people in the pub. Every person in the pub I'm giving Quavers to; "Have a Quaver, give him a Quaver, go on, have a Quaver." I even ended up having an arm wrestle with someone who knew my dad, which I won.

Eventually we leave the Saxon Warrior and stumble into a taxi with the box of Quavers, cos there's still some left. My adrenalin's now racing. I mean, I haven't seen this girl in a year and as far as I'm concerned at this moment in time this is the absolute love of my life, and here I am being given a second chance. Sandy leans over and starts kissing me. I start kissing her. She's got a lip ring now. Never experienced this before; it feels good. I'm thinking, fantastic.

We get back to my house and come in way too loud. I ask my mum to wake me up early because Sandy's got to see her therapist in the morning. This is not the sort of thing you wanna be telling your mum at three o'clock in the morning, especially when she saw you go through so much trauma the last time you broke up.

"I don't want her here. What the fuck is she doing here? Why is she going to a therapist? Take her home."

"OK."

Get another taxi. This night is easily costing me a couple of hundred quid. Drop Sandy off. Her mum, not having yet taken her pills, is in a seriously, seriously bad mood with me.

"What have you done with my daughter? She's not well. You can't stay here."

I mean, the last time I had any contact with Sandy's mum she wasn't particularly happy with me then either, so I'm not making a good second impression.

"OK."

I leave, walk a few yards and fall asleep on the pavement. I remember physically lying down on the ground in a foetal position asleep on the pavement outside Sandy's house. You know, like River Phoenix in *My Own Private Idaho*. I just couldn't stop myself. And, you know, I didn't care. A milkman woke me up at four thirty. I managed to sober up a bit and catch a taxi home. It took me two days to recover. But Sandy and I were back in contact.

We saw each other for another nine months. Quite a long time, really. Longer than the first time. And we got to know each other a lot better than we had previously. But the boyfriend was now more of an issue, she was clearly with someone else, so we were never officially an item this time around. Sandy's relationship with her boyfriend was distant, and yet it endured because he was there when she needed him, which was sometimes. But he was what she wanted in the respect that when she wanted a boyfriend he was there, but when she didn't want one he could disappear for a couple of weeks or months and would be quite happy to do so. So he fitted the bill.

And yet I saw her every day. And you're gonna get to know someone if you see them five days a week. Everyone thought we were going out because we were so close, and they only ever used to see us together. You know, we were, like, joined at the hip. And I felt much more comfortable with Sandy the second time around. Our relationship wasn't really physical. Or it was, but it was weird. She would want me to do things for her, but from this point on she would never do anything for me in return. We never had what you would call proper full, you know, seems a strange way of putting it, but 'penetrative' sex. The only thing that we ever did at her request was me going down on her; and that was it. She never returned the favour. Never. But you have to remember that I was so into this girl, wanted to make her happy, that I was willing to settle for that, because I knew it was a case of that or nothing. We did it once or twice a week. I don't know if it helped improve our rapport, but it made me feel slightly closer to her. But she always made it clear to me that we were never ever gonna be in a relationship.

But it was like being told one thing but then acting a different way; that was what was so confusing. I mean, you're told nothing's ever gonna happen between her and you; but then what I've previously told you happens. And I've had hardly any experience of women at this time, so my mind's in a mess, you know, things

335

can't be physical but they are, I'm seeing more of her than her boyfriend does, and I know that I know her emotionally better than he does; and yet it's never gonna happen. It didn't make any sense. It was like having a voice in your left ear and another in your right giving conflicting instructions. And at that age, or at any age, you just don't know what the hell to do.

Then something happened that even now I struggle to talk about. It was a normal day. We'd been watching movies in my bedroom, as we did regularly. I don't remember which ones, probably cos I'm so focused on what happened later that day that you kind of forget what happened previously. We chill out, go to sleep, wake up, have breakfast. Sandy talks to my mum, talks to my dad, everyone's happy. We go outside and clean my car cos I'm gonna sell it. At this point I have a Nissan 200 SX, Ayrton Senna's favourite road car. Best car I've ever had, but I can't afford the running costs any more so we polish it up. Sandy's fine, enjoying the activity, really getting down and into waxing the bodywork. Comes to late afternoon. I've gotta meet the person who's gonna buy my car, so my mum gives Sandy a lift home. Everyone's happy.

Following day I don't hear from Sandy. This is unusual cos I hear from her every day. I call her up from the hall phone.

"Hi, you OK?"

Pause.

"Sandy?"

Pause.

"Are you all right?"

"You tried to rape me."

I remember those exact words. 'You tried to'. It wasn't 'you did'; it was 'tried to'.

"What are you talking about?"

"You know what you did."

"No. Wha?"

And all I can say then is wha?, you know, it's like being hit by a train. I didn't see this coming in any way.

336

That was the end of the conversation.

It was the last conversation we ever had. I tried calling her again but she wouldn't answer any of my calls. I was a mess for days. I just didn't know what the hell was going on. I think I broke down a bit, like in a Jack Kerouackesque way, and like him I went to the one person I always go to when I need help: my mum.

"This is crazy. I was here. We need to sort this out."

Mum's great at cutting through to the essentials, you know, let's get this done; but in a good way. We had a lot of Sandy's stuff in the house; books, clothes, whatever. Mum put them in a black plastic bag and dropped them off and spoke to Sandy face to face. Sandy got upset and mum said, "I'm gonna go now cos I can see you're getting upset. But you know we need to sort this out, because I know that this isn't true."

When Mum came home there was a phone call. It was Sandy's mum. A conversation took place. I don't know the ins and outs of it, because I was downstairs. After it was over my mum came down and told me I was never to talk to Sandy again, but that it was all sorted. And that was the end of that.

I've thought about it a lot over the years, as you might imagine, and I've got two versions of the rationale behind why Sandy did what she did. The paranoid-bitter version, which is that the three-way thing, me, her and the boyfriend, was a head-doer and she wanted a way out. And she wanted a way out quick. And a way from which there was no turning back. And that was it. The other version, which my shrink favours, is that she had some kind of flashback in respect of what she had suffered before and genuinely believed something happened. Apparently that sort of thing can happen. You know, you can have a bad dream and construe it as being reality and connect it with other things that possibly happened in the past. I don't know. I'm not a psychologist. I don't know. We'll never know.

What I do know is that she caused me a great deal of pain and accused me of something that I would never ever do. She did so in a moment's madness maybe; but we don't know whether it was

337

premeditated or not, do we? We don't know; but I'm not gonna put it past her to have come up with something like that. You see, that's another thing you have to remember about Sandy; she was clever. And she was manipulative. These are key words you can use to describe her. She could manipulate people around her big time. Her friends would often say to me, 'You know you're being used, don't you?' I mean, everyone could see that she was playing me, apart from me. You know, there's the carrot, lead me on, hold me back, lead me on. There were several times when I nearly broke free, you know, met someone else, like Alice, nice girl; and then Sandy pulled me back in. Puppet on a string.

I knew I couldn't trust her. And because of my paranoia, which meant I was expecting the police to call at any moment to arrest me, I knew there was only one solution.

I had to get out of the country fast.

Chapter Twenty-Seven
The Next Ten Seconds

Sweet Surrender

I left Vegas at midnight on Monday bound for Los Angeles. Because we're travelling by night there's hardly any traffic on the roads and everyone's mellow; but my barriers are right back up again. I'm sitting next to a black guy who keeps falling asleep and leaning on me. I mean, I've got this whacking great black guy who looks like he should be in a rap video lying on me and looking like he'll cap me if I cause him any grief. I wiggle a tiny bit hoping he'll shift in his sleep, but he wakes up.

"Alright?"

"Alright." You know, in a very thick American accent.

"Where you off to?"

"Los Angeles."

"Right."

A man of few words. He falls back asleep. Good, I think; I haven't insulted him and he hasn't knifed me. I mean, I don't wanna be racially stereotyping, but I admit I was a little bit nervous.

About three in the morning the bus pulls in and stops at a gas station and we all get out to have some food and, you know, use a proper restroom where you can wash your hands rather than use the handwipes. The black guy comes up to me.

"Can you lend me a dollar?"

I mean, Jesus, everyone is on the make.

You mean give you a dollar. I didn't say this, of course; but that's blatantly what it was. So I just say yeah, cos I'm not gonna be saying no, and he's thanks, thanks, thanks. For me, it's like I've paid for my safety. He buys himself this huge drink and he's happy and off he goes. We all get back on the bus and the guy gets off at the next stop.

You never know when the bus is gonna stop; every fifteen minutes, every thirty minutes, every two hours – it all kinda seems a bit random, and of course it's dependent on the length of the journey. Soon the sun starts coming up and I move further down the bus where there's a lady with her daughter eating this humungous packed lunch. The daughter's about sixteen and very black-looking; by that I mean not one of these Beyoncé white-black women, but a black-black girl. Same with the mum, who's in her mid-forties and also black with no white features, you know, not like in the movies where they say, we need a black person, so let's find the whitest looking black person we can, you know; white nose, white lips, but black. These were proper black people; black noses, black lips. You know, I'm not being racist; this is just what they were. Mum's a really nice lady, very bubbly, afro hair but in bunches, you know, I don't know how they do it, I haven't got that sort of hair; but it wasn't like seventies disco or anything like that. The daughter, and again I don't know how it works, but she had afro hair but straightened, so that the curl and the kink had been taken out of it.

As I say they were both incredibly nice and the mother had with her the hugest amount of food I'd ever seen. I mean, I never went prepared foodwise for bus journeys, you know, not like JK who'd make ten salami sandwiches and carefully space them out as he travelled across the country. The mum, however, kept saying, "If you go on a bus trip you've gotta have snacks." This was a favourite phrase of hers. So she had filled this massive coldpack thing, like a cooler, with sandwiches, a bunch of grapes, peanuts, another bunch of grapes, drink, fruit, sweets; everything you could ever imagine. That's how I got talking to them, in fact, cos she noticed I was on my own.

"Do you want some of this? We're not going to eat all of it."

"Are you sure?" I'm, like, starving, but don't wanna impose.

"Oh, where you from?"

The accent, obviously. And that got us into conversation.

They'd been away in Vegas on a short weekend break and had stayed in the hotel with the rollercoaster on top. From the way they were speaking I don't think there was a dad in their lives. Mum ran a cleaning agency and proudly gave me one of her brochures. She was obviously doing alright for herself. This was her venture and she had a couple of other ladies working with her. I mean, they obviously weren't rich people; but they were OK. Daughter was in high school and on her way to Santa Monica Beach. She shouldof been in school that day, but because of the Vegas weekend she missed the Monday and Tuesday and so she was going down to the beach to meet her friends and go surfing and whatever. While they were in Vegas they just went shopping and saw some shows: Céline Dion, who had a two-year residency at one of the hotels, Penn and Teller, Siegfried and Roy, the white tiger guys, before one of them got mauled, the Blue Man group. There's a lot to do in Vegas other than gambling, and at sixteen the daughter wouldof been too young for the casinos anyway. Obviously they didn't go to a strip club.

So the mum's feeding me all this food and her daughter is talking to me and telling me what she studies at school, what her friends get up to, how much she loves surfing and how she's getting a new car soon when she's passed her test. And I'm again amazed by this.

"That ain't how it works in my country. To get a new car you've gotta be rich."

"Everyone here drives a new car."

And it's true; don't know what finance scheme they use, but they pay for it somehow. You have to be damn poor to drive around in a shitter in America.

"What are you doing then?"

"Oh, I'm travelling around."

"Who are you staying with?"

341

"I haven't got anyone to stay with."

"You haven't got anyone to stay with?"

"No, I haven't."

"So where are you staying?"

"Oh, I'll find somewhere. Probably a hostel."

And like most Americans neither of them had any idea what a hostel was, you know, they thought it was a homeless shelter or something.

"Why you wanna stay there?"

"It's cheap."

"Why don't you stay in a hotel?"

"Cos I haven't got enough money."

"I thought you said you were on holiday."

"I am kind of."

They just could not fathom what I was trying to achieve.

"You've got to come with us. We'll sort you out. You've got to come with us."

I didn't say anything to this, cos even though they're really nice, I'm thinking, no way, I'm not going through all that again. Then they ask me why I'm going to LA.

"Just the typical stuff. I wanna see the Hollywood sign. Wanna see the Walk of Fame. Wanna see the Chinese Theatre. Just wanna see all the stuff." I mean, my script might have got lost along the way, but at least one of us is gonna make it there.

"That's cool. But it's dangerous."

She's like a typical mother, you know; it's dangerous, you gotta be careful, don't go into the wrong areas.

"Do you wanna biscuit?"

"Yes please."

I'm like, brilliant, a biscuit! Thinking, Garibaldi or digestive. But this is not what she takes out the box and gives me.

"Oh, thanks." Thinking, like, what the fuck is this? You know, this ain't a biscuit; not gonna dip this in my tea. I mean, it was solid; you couldof killed a man with it. We're talking a rock-hard scone. One of those things in a movie set in the deep south, you

342

know, where you've got the slaves on the plantation, and someone says, 'I want some biscuit and some graavvvee,' you know, 'where are ma grits?' It was a biscuit in those terms.

I'm a bit taken aback and I think she mustof noticed, so I apologise and explain that a biscuit means something slightly different where I come from, whereas obviously in America they have biscuits and thick gravy and grits, so it's clearly another thing entirely; but I'll give it a go, you know, I don't wanna be impolite, especially since they've been so nice, and I've already made some complaints, so I really have to eat it now. So I'm like NNNRRRRRRRR NNNNRRRRR, wondering if my jaw's gonna shatter.

"I'm sorry it's a bit dry. It should be moistened. You're meant to have it with gravy, really."

It was halfway between a scone and a rock-hard dumpling.

"No, it's OK, thanks. This is really nice." And I ate it all cos I was really hungry; but I did think I was gonna break my teeth.

We pull into Los Angeles central bus station at eight o'clock in the morning. As soon as we enter the city I'm getting a bad vibe.

"It's really foggy here."

"That's not fog; it's smog."

I mean, it was nuts. Disgusting. Disturbing.

"This is on a good day. On a bad day you can't see nuttin'. Cloud's just blacked out."

The LA central bus station was one of the roughest places I've ever been to in my life. I mean, I've never come across so many crazy drugged-up nut people. Everywhere topless, saggy dried-up-boobed, weird no-shoes-on blonde-haired crazy people. Proper crackheads, you know. Homeless people ranting. Wouldn't have it in the UK. Or it would be hidden away. But these people were right at the bottom and they were out, and the police weren't touching them, cos there were so many, and I suppose they weren't doing anything; but it was scary all the same. The whole place stank of urine. I was freaked out by it all, but the mother and daughter were clearly used to it.

The city centre was just as bad. I mean, in New York I felt safe, in Chicago I felt safe, and, to a certain degree, in Las Vegas I felt safe; but not in LA. It was like being in a different, rougher, edgier country. New York was tame by comparison. The streets were clean and the air was fresh. And there wasn't that heat, which I think played a major part in it. In LA you had this oppressive smog so you couldn't really see the sun, the streets weren't so clean and the heat made everything feel more tense, you know, everyone's sweating and grumpy and in a rush to get somewhere, and you've got all these crack addicts walking around.

And another reason why it felt like a different country is that half of the posters were in Spanish. I just didn't realise there was such a huge Mexican population. I mean, you know that a population's got big when marketing and advertising is being targeted directly at them. I'm talking big billboard signs, I'm talking bus stop signs; a good fifty per cent of everything was in Spanish. They'd arrived. You know, in my naïvety, I thought America was a predominantly English-speaking country; but central Los Angeles was a real wake-up.

"You've got to come with us. We'll sort you out. You've got to come with us. We're going shopping in Santa Monica. Stick with us."

"No, no, no. You've been too kind already."

"No, stick with us. You gotta be careful here."

And I'm thinking, Jesus, where am I? The locals are telling me I've got to be safe!

"You don't wanna go to the wrong part. You'll get shot."

"Really?"

"Yeah. White guy in the wrong place; you're not gonna last."

"I'll be fine." You know, typical Brit.

"No, no, seriously. This ain't a joke."

And now I'm thinking, Christ, yes, I'm sticking with you. I'd already told them on the bus about being hustled in Vegas.

"You're in Vegas, baby. This is what you've gotta expect." They were quite matter-of-fact about it; like, oh yeah, that will happen.

You shouldn't have done that; idiot. No sympathy. I mean, they were caring in the respect that obviously they didn't want this to happen to me again; but at the same time they weren't like, oh man, that's a poor representation of our country. It was more like, yeah, that's gonna happen in Vegas. So I think this is why they were so worried about me in Santa Monica. They were probably thinking, God, this kid's not streetwise at all.

The lady and her daughter took me to a McDonald's and bought me a McDonald's breakfast meal, which they wouldn't let me pay for, and then we went shopping in Santa Monica. Walked around, went into shoe shops and clothes shops and then they had to go home and do their thing. Mum asked me to take a picture of them, which I did, and then she gave me her address and phone number and asked me to promise to call her once I got back to Boston, cos I told her I was staying with people there.

"You promise me you'll call me. You promise me now you'll call me. I wanna check you're safe. Wanna check you're safe. You promise me you'll call."

"I promise, I promise."

"Be careful now, be careful."

"I will."

We hugged and parted.

Weeks later when I got back to Boston I called her.

"Who's this?"

"It's Matt."

"Who?"

"From the bus."

"Oh, Matt!" And she was well chuffed, you know, over the moon. "I didn't think you'd call. I thought you'd forgotten about us."

"No, I've only just got back to Boston."

"Oh, how are ya doin'?"

And we had like a ten/fifteen minute conversation.

Genuinely nice people. The kind my head doctor said you always have to remember.

345

I really like the idea of going to Canada. Those open spaces. The huge vastness of it all. The freedom. Obviously all this is probably very naïve on my part, but nonetheless I like countries where you can start on one side, drive for three days and still not hit the water, you know; that sense of I can run away and keep on going, do you know what I mean? No border control. No need for a passport. Just Keep On Going. I can see sand, I can see mountains, I can see snow, I can see sunshine; in the one land mass I've got it all. I can piss one person off, drive three hundred miles and be in a different land. You know, that deep-seated thing of, fuck it, I'm nagged at all the time here; but there I won't have to worry about what I'm earning, won't have to worry about what I'm doing with my life, won't have to worry about this, won't have to worry about that: fuck it all, I'm going; I'm going to the woods.

Obviously, as we know, this is possibly not healthy, and my head doctor would certainly confirm that view. But let's face it, in America there ain't that much free land any more. There isn't. Anywhere. Other than possibly the Appalachians. But even then. Whereas in Canada, there's still some wildness there that's untamed. Sure, people go there; but you can still walk and walk and walk, trek and trek and trek and proper be in proper, proper, proper disconnected wilderness. That I like. Somewhere completely out of it. Somewhere where you don't need to calculate the future. Somewhere where you don't need to think beyond the next ten seconds.

I'd build a cabin. Ma cabane au Canada. I mean, I'd need to come back to civilisation every now and again. Everyone would. Well, maybe not everyone, but I would. Bit like Bill Hicks and nightclubs; that's exactly what I would do with civilisation. Once a year come back, realise how crap it all is, think I'm better off, and then go back. Another year'll go by, build up that curiosity again, come back, you know, pick up supplies, realise how crap it is, and then go back to the woods.

I'd learn to hunt and skin. Grow my own crops, to what success I've no idea. Shoot deer, eat deer, smoke it; I'd do all that stuff. I'd love it. Seriously. I'd live on my own. If someone wanted to come visit, I wouldn't stop them. Maybe a woman would happen now and again when I came back to civilisation. I mean, otherwise, let's be honest, it wouldn't work. They'd get bored, I'd worry about them being bored. I think I'd become a little bit monk-like; again, to what success I've no idea. But I'd give it a good shot. Possibly go a little bit mad, you know, like someone in a Werner Herzog film. But it's better than what I'm doing now. And as JK said, you can't become a Buddhist overnight.

I'd be busy all the time, cos there would always be things to do, things to shoot, things to hunt. I'd be non-stop mentally preoccupied. Definitely take a dog with me now. For companionship. Someone that's there with you. That dog would love me. We'd be together all the time. It would die eventually and the relationship would then be lost. But that's no reason not to get one. You know, getting old and dying's part of life so, you know, I'd get another one.

I don't know the chances of survival; but, you know me, I won't go unprepared. If I get eaten by a bear, I get eaten by a bear; but I'll have my rifle with me. You know, I wouldn't be one of those crazy bear people that just let them in; I'd be wary enough. And anyway, you know, step outside of the house; it's dangerous, especially in Freetown. I mean, I bet if you did a statistical study, there's more chance of being hit by a bus in Freetown than being eaten by a bear in Canada. Cos, you know, bears are naturally wary of humans. Unless you've got something they want; and then you have to shoot the fucker. I mean, it wouldn't be like in that film *Grizzly Man*. That guy deserved to get eaten in my view. Don't get me wrong, I really liked him. But he was a sweet, dreamy guy, you know; I'm not gonna hurt them, so they're not gonna hurt me. And they ate him. And unfortunately his girlfriend. Even conservationists say the guy was an idiot. I mean, I respect what he did; I respect that he didn't hurt the bears; I respect the fact that he wanted to get close

347

to them and learn about them. But the fact of the matter is, you play with fire you're gonna get burnt. I mean, he would stroke them, which is why people criticised him, you know; he stopped studying them and started treating them like pets. And a bear is never gonna be a pet.

So I'm maintaining a healthy fear of bears and wouldn't wanna see one unless it was a long way off. If they're there, they're there; not a lot I can do about it. I'm not a bear fan; I'd be quite happy if I didn't see one. But equally I'm not a bear-hater; I respect them and I'd wanna live in harmony with them. But if they try and steal my food, there's gonna be trouble. And they know that. And like I say I'm not gonna go out there with no training or anything. I'm gonna be prepared. And it's gotta be easier living peaceably with bears than with women. More bearable.

I mean, almost every woman I've had a relationship with has been a nutter or borderline nutter. OK, my mum and my head doctor might argue that this is mainly because of the women I hang around with; and maybe this is true. But they've still been genuine up there in terms of irrational. OK, I suppose everyone is up to a point. And I'm certainly not a model of rationality all the time, am I? But it's undeniable that women have quirks and can kick off at any time, which makes them big time unpredictable; more unpredictable than a bear. And whatever anyone says, there is a difference, a definite difference, other than the obvious thing, between the way men and women think. I wouldn't like to try to sum it up, and I certainly couldn't put it into a sentence.

But when you love a woman you go into some kind of special trouble-free space. A peace and serenity. A place of what JK calls 'sweet attention'. I love that phrase. Don't know what it means, but yet I do somehow, like everyone does. That's what JK can do, write words and phrases you don't always understand but yet feel to be true. Touch you to the marrow. But refusing to acknowledge the weird and sometimes fucked-up stuff that plays alongside the romance, sharing the same moment, the same thought, the same passion and the same emotion, is like believing that the heart's truth can be expressed in pop songs. You know, cue a fucking Richard Curtis movie.

This is a fictional story and is not intended to depict real events or persons, living or dead.

The knowledge of Mind is the highest and hardest, just because it is the most 'concrete' of sciences. The significance of that 'absolute' commandment, Know thyself – whether we look at it in itself or under the historical circumstances of its first utterance – is not to promote more self-knowledge in respect of the particular capacities, character, propensities, and foibles of the single self. The knowledge it commands means that of man's genuine reality – of what is essentially and ultimately true and real – of mind as the true and essential being.

(G. W. F. Hegel, *The Phenomenology of Mind*)